TIME OF THE WOLF

Elizabeth Harris was born in Cambridge and brought up in Kent, where she now lives. After graduation, she had a variety of jobs including driving a van, being a lifeguard and working in the Civil Service. She has travelled extensively in Europe and America and lived for some years in the Far East.

Elizabeth Harris was one of the finalists in the 1989 Ian St James Awards. She is also the author of *The Herb Gatherers*, *The Egyptian Years* and *The Sun Worshippers*.

Acclaim for Elizabeth Harris:

The Herb Gatherers:

'Elizabeth Harris writes with sensitivity and skill and a spine-chilling eye for the sinister. I found it enormously enjoyable'

Barbara Erskine

The Sun Worshippers:

'Explorations of fact with fantasy, myth with astrology and love with bitterness are handled with a deftness of touch and insight which threatens to put Harris . . . up among the leaders'

Kent Today

'Harris' heroine is a very vivid creation who commands respect'

Irish Press

ELIZABETH HARRIS

Time of the Wolf

Grafton

This Grafton edition published 1997
by Diamond Books
An imprint of HarperCollins Publishers
77-85 Fulham Palace Rd
Hammersmith, London W6 8JB

First Published in Great Britain by
HarperCollinsPublishers 1994

ISBN 0 261 66984 2

Printed and bound in Great Britain
by Caledonian

For Merric Davidson, with love,
and fond memories of 110 on the A45

*With grateful thanks to Roger Clarke
for his personal memories of Cambridge,
and to Harry for recalling his first time*

Over the seas came the bane from the North,
In secret its dark heart spread forth.
It stole from the wastes of the ice and the snow
And follows where conquerors go.
Crowns of gold keep the evil at bay,
But soon the wolf will hold sway;
Princes and kings will be vanquished in sum
And the time of the wolf will come.

Prelude

The deep silence of the night was broken by a sudden crackle of fire, as a smouldering log burst briefly into flame before falling in fragments into the hearth. The orange light leapt in the air, illuminating the great blackened rafters and, high above, the steeply-pitched roof. There was a smell in the hall, a resinous smell which made the nostrils twitch and which, inhaled too freely, set the head swimming; so that, sitting by the fire while the bard told his tales of heroism, magic, gods and mythical beings, an ordinary man could see visions and think himself one of the Wise.

The man on the leather throne sighed, shifting his position as if to ease an aching back. He lifted a hand and touched the circlet of gold on his head, feeling along its circumference with tentative fingers.

Beside him, on a wooden bench, sat a cloaked and hooded figure. Sensing the movement, he threw back the hood, looking at the king and smiling.

'Does it sit ill, Sire?' he asked.

'Nay.' The king gave him a brief answering smile. 'You have made it well – it is light, and the edges are smooth. I thought only –'

The cloaked man waited for a moment then, when it became obvious the king would not continue, prompted gently, 'What, my lord?'

The light green eyes closed as the king screwed up his face. The man, recognizing the gesture, put his hand to the king's forehead, the fingertips smoothing out the skin.

'Let the pain go,' he murmured softly. And again, four or five times, 'Let it go.'

The echo of his chanted words hung like an incantation, and slowly the king's face cleared.

'I thank you. I was, as I am sure you know, thinking how frail a thing is this crown that you have made, and what a task it has to do.'

'It is gold,' the man said. 'Gold endures.'

'Aye. But against such a foe?' The king shook his head. 'Such a terrible foe,' he repeated, almost to himself.

'There is hope,' the cloaked man said firmly. 'Our hall stands firm, in the main our people thrive, their livestock is healthy and their crops flourish in these wide, flat lands with their abundant water and their fertile soil. Your sons grow wise and strong, your –'

'One of my sons,' the king interrupted. 'One is dead.'

'Aye, and you have had the good sense to admit young Wolfspear to live at court!' the man countered. 'One son lost, another gained.'

'An illegitimate son, who, if what he tells us is true, has been living these many years wild in the forest, running with the wolves!' The king's tone was one of barely-suppressed disgust.

'Think not ill of the boy –' the hypnotic note was back in the voice, ' – rather, admire him that he has survived where other, weaker men would surely have perished.'

'Wolfspear,' the king muttered, not to be mollified. 'Wolfspear, indeed!'

'It is what the people call him,' came the calm response.

'And my Cunning Man also, I note.'

The cloaked man bowed his head in acknowledgement.

They sat awhile in silence, then the king spoke again.

'Will it work?' He fixed the grey eyes of the Cunning Man in a hard stare. 'Is your magic strong enough to keep it at bay?'

For a long time there was no answer. The Cunning Man closed his eyes and sat still, enduring the horrors that he knew must be allowed the run of his mind: these were the people's memories, and he was their custodian. He saw the long ships bravely crossing the cold grey sea, optimism strong in the hearts of men and women. Now here were the new lands, ill protected, the outposts manned by defenceless monks so that the conquerors achieved their purpose with little opposition. And now here came the good times, when it seemed the golden years would roll on for ever and every harvest would be better than the last.

Then, when men were beginning to relax their guard, it struck.

What was it, this evil bane which attacked here as a plague, there as an unprovoked attack, here as a series of unexplained deaths, there as a fearful howl in the night which made even warrior hearts melt with terror?

Nobody knew. None of the wise – no seer, no bard, no Cunning Man – could identify this shifting, secretive enemy that worked from within, taking away the courage, the spirit, the very will of men, leaving them with no choice but to obey its cruel bidding. They knew, though, from whence it came; it came from out of the frozen northlands, and, seeking to flee from it to warmer shores in the west, unwittingly they had brought it with them.

Or, rather, it had made sure that it went with them, for it had a purpose of its own and did not suffer itself to be brought.

The Cunning Man had wrought his magic into the golden crown which the king now wore. Would it be enough? Would the sacrifice of the greater part of his power succeed in holding back the evil?

He sighed. Turning to face the king, he gave the only answer he could.

'Will it work? I hope so, Sire. I hope so.'

For how, he added to himself, can I promise more, when I know not where the bane lies, nor in what form it will strike next?

King and Cunning Man started suddenly as, behind them, a deep voice said softly, 'It is late, my lord. Will you not go to your bed?'

They turned, and out of the shadows emerged a dark figure robed in black. The face was concealed by a low hood and a high collar, but a glimmer of flame from the hearth caught an answering flare in the eyes.

In the firelight, they looked yellow.

PART ONE

Henry

PART ONE

Harry

One

I always thought she was special, right from my first awareness of her. When I was a child, she was the one person with whom I felt really comfortable, the person who understood without me having to explain, whom I could trust to have my best interests at heart and arrange things to work out right for me. Sometimes, listening to her hypnotic voice in the darkness telling me bedtime tales of princes, lost crowns, drowned villages, wolves and wizards, I could make myself believe, with a shudder of delicious fear, that she, too, was more than human.

I never quite lost that belief. As I grew older, through all the ups and downs, the everyday and the abnormal events of my life with her, there remained the ultimate question: what was she?

It is a question I still haven't answered.

When I was nine and a half, I told my parents decisively that I was going to live with my grandmother.

My parents and I lived in Hong Kong. My grandmother lived in the Fens.

'Don't be absurd, Henry.' My mother waved an expensively-manicured hand to detain my father, going in from the balcony of our ninth-floor Repulse Bay flat to make another couple of gin slings. 'Richard –' she had a particular way of saying my father's name, part sigh of resignation, part little-girl petulance all too suggestive of someone who could quite easily scream and scream till she was sick, '– Richard, the boy's not going to let this rest, he's been on about it all afternoon. *You'll* have to cope.'

She got up gracefully from her chaise longue, collected her replenished glass from my father at the drinks bar, and disappeared into the bigger of our two bathrooms.

My father picked up a rattan stool and, putting it down perilously close to my new Dinky Rover, reached out and ruffled my hair.

'What's this all about, old man?' he asked heartily. I hated it when he was hearty – and when he ruffled my hair – since it always seemed to presage being made to do something I didn't want to do. Like play tennis with the officers' sons at Victoria Barracks, which I detested partly because, even though none was much older than me, the boys were even heartier than my father, and partly because I always lost. Or go on a swimming expedition with my mother's friends and their children. Even worse, with the children and their amahs.

I hated all amahs, but my own was the most dreadful of all.

'I'm going home to live with Florence,' I repeated. I had called my paternal grandmother Florence ever since I could speak: 'Grandmother' was too long-winded for a child of two, and she would not tolerate any of the diminutives. Nan, Gran or, horror of horrors, Grannie, was not for her.

'Let Henry call me by my given name,' she said. Not that I can remember – at least, I don't think I

4

can. My parents told me. Or, rather, they told other people in my hearing. They seemed to think it made them something out of the ordinary to have a son who called his grandmother by her Christian name, even though for a long time the best I could manage was 'Flonce'.

My father said, 'Why on earth should you want to go and live in dreary old East Anglia in an isolated barn of a house with only your grandmother for company?' There was an edge to the heartiness: my nine-year-old scowl was enough to daunt stronger men than him. 'Good Lord, Henry, most little boys would give their eyeteeth to live out here in the Jewel of the Orient with their every whim catered for by a posse of servants!'

I was a pedantic child. I counted five things in his speech for the defence with which to argue, and that didn't include being referred to as a little boy or pointing out that even if there were things in the world for which I would give my eyeteeth, whichever they were, living in Hong Kong wasn't one of them.

To begin with, East Anglia wasn't dreary. People who have never been there think it's flat, windswept and featureless, with the Broads the only redeeming feature. Oh, and possibly Cambridge, unless you happen to be an Oxford man. But those people have never met my grandmother. Never been swirled up in her enthusiasm for a muddy hike over Wicken Fen, with the brown peaty water alive with mysterious movement and the wind whispering in the poplars. Never been driven by her in her upright old car round the great bulge of coastline, counting the Roman ruins along the Saxon Shore. Never sat warm at her fireside while January stormed outside, listening, entranced, to her stories of stone-age flint mines and Viking raiders who came on the wings of the storm

5

and forced their way right into the secret heart of the Fens.

And her house wasn't an isolated barn. It had originally been a Fenland farmhouse, converted in the early nineteen hundreds into a slightly shabby but supremely comfortable family home. She lived in it alone now, it was true, but that didn't give my father the right to say, *only* your grandmother for company. She was all the company I – anyone – could ever want. Fountain of all knowledge, patient answerer of a thousand questions that began with, 'But why . . .' and ready next day to answer a thousand more. Affectionate, in a correct, restrained sort of way, but, when the need arose, there with open arms, a welcoming lap and a soft touch of lips on my cheek accompanied by a faint smell of rose-water.

Loving, wise, secure Florence.

And I was countless hundreds of miles away from her, in the Jewel of the Orient. And that was ridiculous, too. Whoever had named it, it hadn't been a nine-and-a-half-year-old child. The glitter of this jewel was reserved entirely for the adult members of its population: for their offspring it was the tedium of an expatriate school staffed by teachers who seemed even more bored with the whole business than their pupils. And, when school was over, before any fun could begin we were all put to bed. Put, at any rate, out of the way. Out of sight, out of mind. Especially me – the more my mother could put me out of her mind, the better she liked it. She was thirty-five when I was born, my father thirty-eight, and very early in my life I realized that they hadn't wanted me.

Yet here I was with them, my every whim catered for by a posse of servants. My father had saved his most inane remark for last. Our posse was Ah Yen, four feet eight inches of malodorous Chinese menace. She was Cantonese. If God had made a less handsome woman than Ah Yen, He had the good sense to keep her hidden. Ah Yen had greasy black hair pulled back into a minuscule bun, and her scalp smelt of rancid meat. Her eyes were so deeply embedded in the puffy yellow lids that they were no more than a dark malevolent glitter. Her nose was porcine, nostrils pointing forwards so that you could see right up them. She wore black pyjamas, and even under the folds of the baggy trousers you could see she was as bandy as a dwarf in a fairy tale.

She had a habit of sniffing, loudly and wetly, swallowing the produce and then hawking it up in her throat with a sound like pebbles being rattled in a handful of slime. Then she'd spit on the ground. *PHLOB!* And when the yellow-green mass landed, I'd want to be sick.

I hated Ah Yen. And Ah Yen hated me.

I said again, more firmly, 'I'm going home. Florence loves me very much, she told me so. She doesn't spit, and she tells me bedtime stories *every night*.' Implying, which is more than I get here because Ah Yen doesn't speak enough English and you and Mummy are always out.

My father floundered about for some more convincing clinchers, but, having used up all his big guns in the opening salvo, was at a loss. He repeated the original arguments, in a different order, to which, quite unfooled, I replied as before. I was going to live with Florence. So he repeated them all over again, and then he lost his temper.

My mother opened the bathroom door and a smell of Chanel No. 5 floated out across the hall. She called in a soft but penetrating voice, 'Richard, we're going to be late.'

My father went 'Hhrumph!', threw me a glare that seemed to bounce against my skull, then, jumping to his feet, stormed off into the marital bedroom and slammed the door.

Ah Yen came slip-slopping in from the kitchen quarters, her face contorted into what presumably was meant to be an ingratiating smile but which, since it didn't reach her cold eyes, came over as a gloat. She said, 'Lice! You have plenty lice, I cook, I make good!', and she made a mime of eating, bowl in one hand, chopsticks in the other, sloshing an imaginary something into the wide frog-like aperture of her mouth.

She did things other than sniffing and spitting which made me equally sick.

I picked up my Dinkies, told her politely that I wasn't hungry, thank you very much, and retired to the far corner of the balcony.

Before we came to Hong Kong, when I was nearly seven, we had lived with Florence on and off throughout my life. My father's job took him abroad so much that he and my mother had never considered it worthwhile to maintain an establishment in England, preferring, for the few weeks out of every year that they were there, to move into the large and otherwise uninhabited west wing of Florence's farmhouse. He was working in Singapore when I was born, and I wasn't taken home to the land of my forefathers till I was eighteen months old. I wish I could remember that first visit to Florence: apparently she and I took to one another on sight, and my mother's elegant nose was put firmly out of joint by my obvious preference, to the mother who'd carried me, borne me, and been my sole nurturer for the year and a half of my life, for a grandmother I'd known a matter of hours.

8

I can't remember the nurturing, either. On my mother's later form, I guess she farmed me out to an Ah Yen equivalent the moment the telephone rang to invite her out to do something more stimulating than looking after a screaming and demanding baby. I know she didn't feed me herself – 'I'd have *loved* to feed Henry, darling,' I overheard her say many years afterwards to a newly-delivered woman friend unwise enough to ask her advice, '– but, oh! *The pain!*'

I looked it up in a baby book at my friend Peter's house. It said a lot about breastfeeding being a good thing because it strengthened the ties between mother and baby. It didn't say anything about it hurting, but then, I worked out, if the book was trying to talk mothers into it, it wouldn't, would it?

We had a month in the Fens, then my father was sent out for a brief spell in Brunei. Back to England when I was two – it was on this visit that Florence and I between us decided on what I should call her – and then a year or so in Tokyo. One of my earliest memories is of my third birthday party, attended by ten children – Japanese, British and American – and how angry I was when the Japanese children kept winning all the games. Although it was my birthday, I was put to bed with a smarting bottom because I'd hit a Japanese girl who was so prissy she made me squirm.

Back to England for my first English autumn and my first English Christmas – Florence gave me a rocking horse, dapple grey with bright red harness, and I remember standing in her huge living room staring up at it in the bay window, nerving myself to get up on it in case she thought I didn't like it and took it away.

My parents gave me a giant teddy bear and a toy

9

piano. I trod on the piano – on purpose, I seem to remember – and managed to leave the teddy behind the next time we went abroad. Tearing myself away from my rocking horse – I called him Garth, because Florence said she used to know a dray horse called Garth who was exactly the same colour – was awful enough to put me off my food for three days. I kept thinking he'd be hungry without me to feed him – silly, when Florence had promised faithfully to look after him – so how could I eat when he wasn't?

When we'd been a week in our new posting – it was Kuala Lumpur – I got a postcard from Florence. On it was a picture of an enormous dapple-grey horse. My father said it was a Shire. He read the card to me; Florence had put, 'Garth is missing you but trying to be brave. I have just given him a rub down and fed him a bran mash. He and I send you our love.'

If Garth was eating, I could too. It was a relief – I was starving.

We were more than two years in Kuala Lumpur, apart from brief home leaves. Too brief – I'd no sooner settle back into my Fen life than it was time to go out to Malaya again. And we wasted quite a lot of one leave in London, my mother complaining that she was *sick* of bloody East Anglia and couldn't my father take her somewhere *interesting* for a change? I'd fully expected them to go off alone and leave Florence and me together. It was a shock when I realized I was going to go with them. Under other circumstances, I suppose I might quite have liked London, what with the buses, the zoo, the parks and Hamleys, but as it was, missing Florence, pining for Garth, the feeling that I was frittering away time that could have been spent in the Fens made me far too resentful to take any of it in.

It was in KL that I started school. Lessons were from eight in the morning till one, when we were all sent home for lunch with our ayahs and a sleep during the hottest hours of the day. Unfortunately, the hottest hours always seemed to coincide with my most active ones, and while my mother, and some- times also my father, lay in their bedroom with the air conditioning humming away, I'd mope around the house looking for something to do. I tried to catch geckos, only they were usually too fast and on the rare occasions I got a hand to them, their tails fell off. Florence had engendered in me a respect for all living things, especially those which couldn't speak up for themselves. I left the geckos alone.

After four terms in the primary school – four terms too many – we went back to England. It was spring in the Fens, and for the first time my unrecognized love for East Anglia came leaping up out of my unconscious and hit me smack between the eyes. Or perhaps it hit me in the heart, for afterwards I was never the same. I was six, old enough to understand the beauty of nature, old enough to be overawed by the wild glory of stormclouds gathering behind the defiant fist of Ely Cathedral's tower. Old enough to understand that, out of all the many people who'd come into my life so far, for longer or shorter times, there was just one who really loved me.

Florence.

Garth still stood in pride of place in the window, and in my affections he had now been joined by another gift from Florence, a golden labrador puppy whom I called Eric (Florence had been telling me a story about Eric the Red). Florence deemed me old enough to be given charge of the hen house, and once a day I dished out their meal of nutty-smelling cereal. I went in to check for eggs and to see if their water-trough needed refilling every time I passed: Florence said the chickens must like all the attention because she'd never known them as productive as when I was around. Whenever I hurried in from the garden, a warm, sticky egg carried carefully in my palms, she'd greet my cry of, 'I've found one! I've found one!' with as much delight as if it had been pure gold.

Florence talked to me as if I were grown up. Until that lovely spring, turning with each new day irrevocably towards summer, I didn't realize how *patronizing* all the other adults in my life were. Florence answered all my questions fully and with all her attention, even the one about where babies came from, sparked off by spending so much time looking for eggs. With her, there was never a suggestion of eyes sliding past me to see if anyone more interesting was within hailing distance. Florence introduced me to her books, inviting me to read to her but willingly taking over when the words got too long or I got too tired. And, every night without fail, she came up to me when I was in bed and told me a story.

There never seemed to be much time for watching television in Florence's house, but even if there had been, the children's programmes of the day would have paled in comparison with Florence's stories. She seemed to know instinctively what would appeal to a boy, and together we plunged into the vivid drama of the past: kings and princes, brave warriors defending the lonely coastline, Viking longboats which ran effortlessly up the shore and disgorged hundreds of screaming, ferocious, yellow-bearded men; the Fen people, invaded and overcome, and a wizard who could see into the future.

Sometimes the storytelling was too real, and I would wake the household by crying out at what I witnessed in my dreams. Florence would come to me and hold my hand, explaining in her calm way that there was nothing to be afraid of. Once one of the dreams sought me out when I was far away – in the early Hong Kong days – and, the vision vivid in my head of a brave hero dying in despair, his dark red blood seeping away into the black earth beneath him, I cried for her and she didn't come. How could she, when half a world separated us?

I didn't want to be separated from her. My understanding was not solely that Florence loved me: it was also that I loved her.

When on Midsummer's Day we left for Hong Kong, I was inconsolable. Leaving Garth had been bad enough, but it was nothing compared to this. As well as the pain of missing her, I was wracked with fear that something awful was going to happen – I was going to die or, even worse, she was, before we had a chance to get back together again. My parents were quite kind at first, expecting, no doubt, that it was just a phase and I'd get over it as soon as the excitement of a new place got to me.

In retrospect, it occurred to me that they hadn't been very observant all those years. Other people's children might have been placated by the thrill of living in Singapore, or Tokyo, or Kuala Lumpur, or Hong Kong, although I doubted it.

But not their son.

I knew what I wanted. I wanted to live with Florence.

For two long years I waited for us to go on home leave; that would be the moment, I thought, to announce my wishes. Florence would back me up, I knew it in my bones, and so I held out for the next time we should be together.

It didn't happen.

My father went home for a couple of weeks on his own, and on another occasion for three weeks accompanied by my mother. I was left with Ah Yen. 'Too unsettling for you, for such a short time,' was all the explanation I got when I demanded why I wasn't going too.

Unsettling. As if I could *be* any more unsettled than I already was.

And so, in the end, I was left with no choice.

Early one evening in Hong Kong, in February 1965 when I was nine and a half, I told my parents decisively that I was going to live with my grandmother.

Two

I was determined to stay up and renew the battle when my parents got home. Ah Yen didn't like that idea at all. Usually when she was left in charge her sole aim was to pack me off as soon as she could – it had been known for me to be in bed at half past six – so as to leave her free to go down to the car park behind the flats and continue the ongoing gossip with her fellow amahs. Their favourite place to sit – to squat – was, most appropriately in my opinion, beside the huge dustbins which stood, stinking gently in the humidity, at the foot of the garbage chute.

'I'm not going to bed,' I told her. She said something in Cantonese, tugging at my sleeve and pulling me towards the bathroom. She clearly had in mind that I should have a quick shower and then make myself scarce.

'Yes! Bed, you go bed!'

'No.'

'Yes! Yes!'

It was typical of her illogical mind that I had to be put to bed before she reckoned it was safe for her to go out. Such things served to increase my contempt – couldn't she see that, for one thing, I was just as much at risk by myself in my bedroom as in any other

15

room in the flat, and, for another, that even though I might be in my room when she went out, there was no guarantee that I was going to stay there?

I said suddenly, 'Okay,' and went to have a bath. Into my pyjamas in record time, and then into my bedroom. I said, very firmly, 'Goodnight, Ah Yen,' and in less than ten minutes – I timed her – she'd let herself quietly out of the door behind the servants' quarters.

I heard the whirr of the servants' elevator and the crump of the door closing as she set off to join the coven.

I got dressed again. I had some notion that it would weaken my standpoint if I argued in my pyjamas, especially as they had Mickey Mouse on the front. I went through into the living room and put the television on, then settled down to wait.

At a quarter to eleven I heard Ah Yen coming in. I turned off the TV and sat in the darkness while she pottered about in the kitchen, then, when I saw the light go out and knew she'd retired for the night, switched on again to catch the end of the John Wayne western I'd been watching.

They got home at half past midnight.

They'd brought home another couple from the Club, and all four of them were what my mother used to describe as 'tiddly-poo'.

In all my previews of the scene, it had never entered my head that they wouldn't be alone. I did some very fast thinking – obviously there was no point at all in confronting them now, when they were half pissed and in one of those silly moods when the husbands made up to each other's wives, putting their arms round them and making remarks which the others would greet with hoots of laughter.

I pretended to be just waking up. Yawning, rubbing

my eyes, I said, 'Mother? What time is it?' I thought about, 'Where am I?', but dismissed it as too much of a cliché.

My mother just stared at me. My father said, 'Gracious me, what are you doing up at this hour, old man?' I noticed that he dropped the hand of the other man's wife with indecent haste.

'I – I must have fallen asleep,' I said. 'I was watching the telly . . .' I frowned in a confused way in the direction of the screen, now showing a theological discussion programme. 'Gosh! It was John Wayne a minute ago!'

'Where's Ah Yen?' my mother asked, looking around as if Ah Yen might be crouching down behind the bureau or standing wrapped up in the curtains.

'She went out.' This was too good a chance to miss. I had a perpetual desire to dump Ah Yen in the cart, and not nearly enough occasions presented themselves. 'I heard her come back, then she must have gone to bed.'

Wriggle your way out of that, Ah Yen!

My father set off purposefully in the direction of the servants' quarters, but my mother, shaken into sobriety, called him back.

'Not now, Richard. I'm not in the mood for scenes. Pour us some drinks and I'll put the child to bed.'

I couldn't remember the last time she'd put me to bed. Probably it had been in the dim, distant past when we were still in the maternity ward and she'd had no choice.

'It's all right,' I said, getting up and mustering a brave smile, 'Please don't leave your guests.' I nodded to them all, then went through to my room. As I closed the door I heard the other man say, 'What a self-possessed little chap!'

'Self-possessed little chap, my arse,' I muttered to myself.

It was at such times that I wished I knew really bad words.

The next day was Saturday, and that combined with all the drink they'd shipped the previous night meant that it was after ten before they put in an appearance.

I observed them closely as they ate their breakfast. They looked cheerful enough. My father even patted my mother's bottom as she got up to fetch some more toast from the kitchen, and although she said somewhat reprovingly, 'Richard!' she seemed to like it.

I took a breath and said, 'I meant what I said yesterday, you know.'

They looked at me, at each other, and back at me. Then my father said, 'What?'

I didn't think he meant, what did you say? After all, I was only across the table from him. I said, 'I'm going to live with Florence.'

My mother said huffily, 'I told you, Richard! I knew he wouldn't let it rest!'

I was quite gratified at that. Before my father could react, I said, 'I don't like it here. I want to live in the Fens with Florence and go to that school in the village. Then on to the grammar school where her gardener's grandson goes.'

'Ely,' my father said vaguely.

'No it's not,' my mother argued, 'it's that other one. Where Florence knows the French teacher.'

'It's Ely,' my father insisted.

They were capable of galloping off down this sort of a tangent for hours. I said firmly, 'Ely is the one I mean. We looked at it from the outside the day Florence took me up the cathedral tower.' What a day that had been. She told me the cathedral was called the Ship of the Fens, which lodged deep in my imagination. She'd shown me Oliver Cromwell's house, too, and said that few people realized he'd lived in Ely.

But thoughts of that happy day constituted going off at a tangent, too. I repeated, for what seemed the hundredth time, 'Anyway, I'm going home to live with Florence.'

My mother said in a sugary voice, 'This is your home, darling. With Daddy and me.'

'I don't like it here.' I wasn't going to be persuaded by her tone into betraying my cause. Not when her sweetness was as artificial as saccharine.

'Don't like it?' my father echoed incredulously. 'But it's a marvellous life for a child! Beach on your doorstep, swimming pools, tennis, fascinating foreign city to study . . .'

I stopped listening. It was his standard Jewel-of-the-Orient and giving-your-eyeteeth speech, and I'd heard it all before. When he stopped speaking I said again, 'I don't like it.'

My mother said wearily, 'So you keep saying, Henry. But what don't you like?'

The heat, the humidity, the crowds of heaving people, the traffic fumes, my school, having to play with army officers' children, being left on my own night after night with rotten telly, being looked after by a spiteful Chinese amah whom I detested. That would have done to begin with. But, inarticulate in the face of so huge an answer, I just said, 'Everything.'

'And what makes you think you'd be any happier with Florence?' my father asked. He gave an abrupt nod, as if he felt he'd scored a point.

I looked at him witheringly. Then said, 'I know I will.'

My mother stood up and tied the sash of her negligée in a determined knot. 'I'm going to have my bath,' she announced.

Leaping up as if he didn't want to be left on his own with me, my father said, 'I'll come with you.'

Was that it? I wondered. Was the answer yes, no, or, we'll think about it? They hadn't given me an answer!

It was the worse tactic to adopt with me. If they'd sat down and reasoned, told me what they were thinking and how they'd reached their decision, I might have been prepared to listen. Even to accept their judgement. But to act as if I'd never even raised the matter, to dismiss my proposition as if I were a tiny child demanding a too-expensive toy, that hurt. And, more significantly, it made me angry.

The phrase 'when the going gets tough, the tough get going' wasn't in popular use in those days. If it had been, it would have been my battle cry.

I began my campaign. A boy doesn't have many weapons, but non-cooperation is one of the few he does have. From that Saturday morning on, I wouldn't do anything. At first, over the weekend, it was just a refusal to go anywhere or do anything with them – it was a busy couple of days socially, with an evening barbecue on the Saturday and a junk trip on the Sunday. I said I wasn't going, and I kept to it. They couldn't go without me because Ah Yen had every other Saturday afternoon and Sunday off to go and see her horrible relations up in the New Territories, and this was an 'other' Saturday.

They didn't believe me at first, I could tell. They got ready for the barbecue as if nothing had happened, and the odd teasing remark floated along to my bedroom from theirs along the lines of, 'Henry won't miss a barbecue with Chinese spare ribs!' or,

'Think of that swimming pool in the floodlights, Henry! You used to call it magic-blue when you were small!'

The confrontation came. My father, dressed in his casual weekend wear and smelling of aftershave, came along to my room.

'Hurry up,' he said, 'get your swimming togs and we'll be off.'

'I'm not going.'

The ensuing argument, flaring very quickly to rage on my father's part and nervous lip-biting on mine, was of the 'yes you are', 'no I'm not' variety, like a sequence in a pantomime. Not something I'm proud to recall. At one point he tried to pick me up and carry me out, but I kicked him on the shin and he hastily put me down. My mother, who had joined us by now, was in tears.

'We'll go on our own and bloody well leave you by yourself!' he raged, hopping on one leg and rubbing the other one.

'No!' my mother protested. For a moment I thought she was on my side. But she added, 'We can't both go! Oh, Richard, please! I do so want to go, the Townsends are going to be there, and it's simply ages since I saw Brenda. Can't you stay with the boy?'

He glared at me, then, taking her arm, ushered her out of my room and banged the door. It was a miracle any of the doors in our flat were still on their hinges. I heard them muttering, then the ping of the telephone, and a little later someone came to the door and I heard my mother gaily call, 'Goodnight!'

She'd got her way, then. As she didn't drive, they must have called friends and asked them to give her a lift. I wondered what my father was doing.

It didn't seem a good idea to find out. Silently I

put my pyjamas on and got into bed. If I put the light out, he might think I'd gone to sleep.

I lay there in the dark for hours, and eventually the first day of my campaign came to an end. I wondered how long I'd be able to hold out.

It was term-time, and since I was at school for so much of the day during the week, my measures of non-cooperation didn't bite very deep. I had to think of something else.

Fate must have been on my side. Or, perhaps, one of the panoply of gods I regularly prayed to – Florence had introduced me to a pantheology stretching from tree-worship to the Mormons – had decided to reward me for my determination. Whatever it was, a golden opportunity fell in my lap, or, more accurately, on my head.

It was sports afternoon – we only had sports afternoons in the spring term, it was too hot for running around after lunch for the rest of the year – and we were playing rounders. I was backstop, and for some reason best known to himself, John Robinson, who was batting, suddenly decided to make a backhand stroke. The heavy wooden bat came swiftly round in a semi-circle and caught me right in the middle of the forehead.

It hurt like hell. I shouted out in pain, and my eyes filled with tears. Blood poured down my face, and one of the girls started screaming. John Robinson was kneeling beside me, saying over and over again, 'I'm sorry! I'm sorry!' till I told him to shut up. Mrs MacKenzie, who took us for games as well as for everything else, kept admirably calm, as if small boys with their heads laid open were an everyday occurrence, and very quickly I was being sent off in an ambulance to the British Military Hospital for stitches and an X-Ray.

They kept me in overnight, but the next morning I felt fine again. They were about to release me into the care of my parents and let me go home when a nurse said, quite off-handedly, 'You may get some headaches. If you do, stay off school for the day and rest in the quiet.'

That same unknown god was still hanging around. I sent up a quiet prayer of thanks.

Whenever my mother got up in time to have breakfast with my father and me, it meant she had a day out planned. She'd sing, and prance around the living room telling us where she was going, who she was going with and what she was going to wear. The next time it happened, I said weakly, 'Oh, golly! My head!', clapped my hand to my forehead with a moan of agony, and crawled back to my room.

There was a suggestion that she might still go, leaving the poor suffering invalid for Ah Yen to see to. But my father, whose faith in Ah Yen had been severely disturbed by the discovery that she regularly went out and left me on my own at night, put his foot down.

'I'm sorry, Amanda, but you'll have to stay with him,' he said in his empire-building, brooking-no-argument voice. 'They did warn us at BMH, after all, and – ' his voice dropped, but not far enough because I could still hear '–think how it'd look if something happened and Ah Yen made a cock-up.'

I heard my mother's angry sobs as she slammed into her bedroom to put her new frock back in the wardrobe.

They knew what I was up to, I'm positive they did. It became a battle of wills, and quite quickly I knew that I was ahead on points. They'd never wanted a child, I was well aware of that, and the rare moments of pleasure which I gave them can't have anywhere near compensated for my nuisance value. Especially now, when I was going out of my way – on the most monumental detour, in fact – to be as obstructive and as relentlessly, obstinately unpleasant as only a nine-and-a-half-year-old can be. A nearly ten-year-old: the months had gone on, Easter was behind us, and summer, accompanied by my birthday, was ahead.

Woken by a tropical storm one night, I wanted a pee. Going quietly along to the bathroom, I heard them talking in the living room. Soft-footed – although over the sound of the wind they wouldn't have heard a troupe of tap-dancers – I crept nearer to listen.

'. . . really don't see why I should put up with it any more.' My mother was weeping. The sight of her, hair all tousled, make-up blotched, lying in my father's arms while he tried to comfort her, made me feel bad. Guilty. 'He won't talk to me, won't go on any of the outings I plan, won't even go to bloody school half the time. What is it, Richard? Oh, what have I done to deserve this?'

She had been a leading light in the amateur dramatic society in Kuala Lumpur. At times like this, you were forcibly reminded of it. My guilt receded.

My father said, 'You know what it is, Amanda. He wants to live with Florence, he doesn't like it here with us.' Her pathetic weeping rose to a crescendo. 'Come on, darling, it's not as bad as all that!'

He bent his head to kiss her. She responded, winding her arms round his neck. They kissed for a long time.

In quite a different voice, she said when they came up for air, 'He could go to that village school, you know. Florence says it has a very good pass rate for the eleven-plus. Much better than bloody Mrs MacKenzie can manage.'

My father had his hand inside her dress. He said, 'Wonder if they'd take him for the second half of term?'

'Do you think Florence would agree?'

He laughed, a low sound in his throat quite unlike anything I'd heard from him before. 'I know she will.'

'You've spoken to her?'

'Yes. Couple of weeks ago.'

'Why didn't you say?' Her voice was a squeak, and she was hitting him playfully on his thighs.

He grabbed her hand. 'A little higher, darling, and not so hard . . . aah!'

'What do you mean, not so hard,' she said in a murmur. 'It feels hard enough to me.'

The wind howled, and I missed the first part of his reply, '. . . fuck you inside out,' he was saying when I could hear again.

They were moving. Getting up, still twined together, heading for their bedroom. I shot into mine, closing the door all but a crack.

As they went past, I heard my father say in that same husky voice, 'When it's just us, we'll get rid of that bloody old baggage out in the back. Then we can do it all over the flat.'

Three

I was to be sent home on an RAF flight bound for some place in Oxfordshire. My parents had talked of holding a farewell party for me, but when they asked whom I'd like to invite I said, 'Nobody,' so that was the end of that. Not that they minded – it was clearly embarrassing for them to be sending a son home in the middle of term-time to take up permanent residence with his grandmother, and I imagine that the less chance they gave people to get inquisitive and start asking awkward questions, the better.

We went out for dinner the evening before my departure. Now that everything was arranged, I could relax, and so, it seemed, could they. We had a great time, and I found that I quite liked them after all. I hope they felt the same about me.

Ah Yen had been given the push the previous week. My mother wrote her a rather grudging reference; like my father, she had neither forgotten nor forgiven the nocturnal wanderings. Covertly, from behind the kitchen door, I watched Ah Yen pack her belongings into five plastic bags. The Chinese never seemed to go anywhere without a few plastic bags crammed to bursting with heaven knows what, getting in everyone's way. I felt a moment's pity, that this poor old woman's entire possessions could quite easily be carried away in one load.

As she was tying up the last bag, she lifted her eyes and glanced round the rooms which had made up her domain. Then, as if giving her final opinion, she hawked and spat on the floor of what had, until that morning, been her bedroom.

I didn't say goodbye to her.

My parents took me to Kai Tak airport and we met up with the RAF man who was in charge of Unaccompanied Juveniles. He gave me a label with my name on it, which my father tied to my collar. (I took it off as soon as they'd gone. *I* knew who I was, and I was quite old enough and sensible enough to tell anyone who asked.) The moment of parting came, and although my mother seemed on the verge of another Kuala Lumpur Am Dram performance, my father told us both a silly joke and she started laughing instead. I wonder, in retrospect, what an observer would have made of us, parents and young son about to be separated by half a world, not sure when they would live together again, not even when they'd meet again, and all three of them giggling as if it were the funniest thing in the world.

'Cheerio, old man,' my father said, wiping the laughter from his eyes and pressing a ten-shilling note into my hand.

'Goodbye, Henry, be good,' my mother added. She gave me a pound, but then perhaps she was twice as pleased to see the back of me as my father was.

I walked away, turning to wave. They were still laughing.

When I turned again, they were walking off, arms

round each other's waists, gazing into each other's eyes like honeymooners, towards the car park. And their wonderfully empty flat.

By the time the first lot of orange squash and curly sandwiches came round – we'd been in the air about a couple of hours – my stomach was tying itself in knots. And it had nothing to do with feeling sick – I did, in fact, but not because of the minor turbulence we'd hit soon after leaving Kai Tak.

For a long time, going home to Florence had been my one and only aim, preoccupying me to the exclusion of all else. Now I'd done it. I'd achieved my goal, and there was a mighty sense of anticlimax. And, if I'm honest, a good deal of fear.

'Don't wish for things too hard,' my mother used to say darkly, 'or your wish might come true.'

It had always seemed a silly saying. Why wish for something unless you *wanted* it to come true? Now, sitting all by myself eight miles above the earth, in transit from one life to another, I understood.

I went through a process of maturation on that long flight. I saw myself as I'd been for the past few months, and I didn't like myself at all. I'd made a decision, perhaps too hastily. 'I'm going to live with Florence.' I heard my voice, and squirmed at the memory. Out of pique because of all the things I didn't like about my life, I'd acted just like all the spoilt boys and girls – and men and women – whom I told myself I despised. I thought of my parents. My mother, crying. My father, hopping about on one leg because I'd crippled the other one.

And what about Florence? I hadn't given one single thought to whether or not an old lady living peacefully by herself would welcome the intrusion of a nine-year-old boy into her household – it might be the last thing she wanted. She *seemed* to enjoy my company for the occasional fortnight once in a while, but having me there all the time was a different matter. And how would it affect *me* if she didn't want me?

I had been a right little sod, all round, and I didn't blame my parents in the least for being glad to see the back of me. And I wouldn't blame Florence, either, if she were less than delighted at my arrival.

Perhaps the knotted stomach was plain remorse. I sat there, unable to eat my singularly unappetizing sandwiches, and after a while a steward came and took them away. A little later he came back up the aisle and, with a sleight of hand better than a magician at a child's party, slipped a bar of Cadbury's Dairy Milk on to my lap.

'Don't shout about it,' he said out of the corner of his mouth, 'or they'll all want one.'

His kind gesture had a strange effect on me. It seemed to tell me, don't worry. People aren't as bad as you think, the world isn't such a big wild place after all. You'll be okay.

My stomach smoothed itself out and I began to feel better.

The next time the sandwiches came round – this time the aim was to rouse us in time for our refuelling stop at Ceylon – I was equal to them.

The next stop was Bahrain. We all got off again, and I was glad I had done, even though I'd been sound asleep, because Bahrain was a great improvement on Ceylon.

Then the last leg. Up, up, ever northwards, to England.

I'd lost track of where we were on the clock – it had gone dark and then got light again, but I wasn't sure if it was still today or had turned into tomorrow. Obligingly the Captain came on the tannoy and told us it was sunny and warm in England, and that we'd be landing at midday, local time.

It seemed too naive a question to ask, midday of *what* day?, so I didn't.

Anyway, by then I had other things to worry about.

My father had said, 'You'll be met the other end, old chap,' and at the time it was too far in the future to be relevant. Of course I'd be met! Now, with England a lovely green and brown pattern beneath us, it was different. *Who* would meet me? Some friend or employee of Florence's – the gardener! I choked with laughter, but it wasn't really funny – or would it be another RAF person, who would see me on to a train with instructions as to what to do when it went no further?

The stomach knots were back. If I hurried, I'd have time to go to the lavatory before we had to fasten our seatbelts for landing.

We were down. The big aeroplane was taxiing towards the row of low buildings that constituted the terminal, and gently we came to a standstill. Out through the door into the fresh English sunshine. Birdsong. A cool, wet-smelling breeze on my cheek. I'd seen pictures of the Pope, kissing the ground when he got off aeroplanes. I knew just how he felt.

There seemed to be an awful lot of people milling around in the arrivals hall, but someone must have been looking out for me. Even though I wasn't wearing my label, a woman in WAAF uniform came up to me and said, 'Henry Woolgar?'

'Yes,' I said.

'Nice flight? Jolly good,' she said cheerfully. 'I've got your bags, you needn't wait behind that lot,' she nodded at the docile file of my fellow passengers waiting patiently for whatever was going to happen next, 'I don't suppose there's much contraband in your luggage!'

I wasn't sure what contraband was, but, wishing to enter into the spirit of things, I said, 'No, no, just a dusky maiden and a few jewels.' It was my father's standard airport joke: 'Goodness, Henry, the bags are taking an age! They must have discovered my dusky maiden and the diamond in her tummy-button.'

The WAAF gave me a funny look.

'Here,' she said, opening a door marked 'VIP Lounge'.

Inside, sitting in a leatherette armchair and calmly drinking a cup of coffee, was Florence.

We looked at each other. I wasn't sure, but it seemed for a second that her eyes held an expression of triumph.

Then it was gone, replaced by a warm, wide smile as she got to her feet and came across to me. She said, 'Henry. Welcome home.' Then she hugged me.

'We shall motor back quite gently,' she said as we went outside. 'Shall you mind if we do not arrive until late?'

I shook my head. 'Not at all.'

'Good. You may sleep, if you need to. Are you tired?'

Was I? I thought I had been, but now I seemed to be buoyed up by the excitement. 'Not at the moment.'

'Are you hungry?'

My empty stomach lurched and rumbled at the thought of food that didn't consist of sandwiches. 'Very.'

She had put my cases in the boot and now, seated beside me in the driver's seat, she started the engine.

She laughed. 'Splendid. So am I. We shall motor for half an hour, then find somewhere suitable for our lunch.'

Exactly thirty minutes later, an attractive-looking roadhouse materialized in front of us and we pulled off into its car park. It came back to me that Florence had always had a way of making predictions which, uncannily, usually came true.

By mid-afternoon I was feeling sleepy. I'd gorged myself at lunch, and now, sitting in the car with the sun on the back of my neck, I found my eyelids drooping. But I didn't want to miss anything. I straightened up and said brightly to Florence, 'Is it much further?'

She glanced across at me. 'Tired?'

I was about to say, no, but then I thought, why lie? 'Well, a bit.'

She smiled. 'And you don't want to yield to fatigue because if you're asleep, you'll no longer be able to study the countryside with such fascinated attention.' She'd noticed, then. 'Look in the glove compartment.' She pointed. 'There's a bag of extra-strong peppermints. I always find they have an unequalled ability to dispel fatigue.'

I did as she said. The peppermints were small, about the size of an aspirin, and when I put one in my mouth it was so hot it seemed to burn my tongue. But she was right – I certainly didn't feel sleepy any more.

'In answer to your question –' she sounded as if she were smiling, and when I looked at her, she was, '– we should be home in another hour and a half. The journey is almost a hundred miles, and we have a little under fifty still to travel.'

It still surprised me that she had come herself to

meet me. I wondered if now was the moment to thank her.

'I – um, it was nice of you to fetch me,' I said awkwardly. 'I mean, I thought I might have been put on a train, or something.'

There was a pause, as if she were thinking about whether or not to speak. Then she said, 'Henry, you will soon come to realize that it is rare for me to do things I do not want to do.' She sounded stern, and I had a moment's fear that she was going to say something awful like, I didn't want to come to meet you and I don't want you living in my house, so this is one of the times I *am* doing something I don't want to. I tensed in anticipation.

Perhaps she saw the small movement. She knew, somehow, what was in my mind. She must have done. She said, very kindly and gently, 'Today is pure pleasure for me. I have been looking forward so much to your homecoming.'

I thought she'd finished. Goodness, it was enough! I could feel the happiness and relief coursing through me. But then she added, almost to herself, 'It is an historic day. The day Henry Woolgar comes home to the place where he belongs.'

I didn't think she meant me to hear. I turned to look out of the window, and resumed my silent joy in green, beautiful England.

Ampthill, Clophill, Shefford. *Biggleswade*. I said the names to myself. We went along the minor roads – Florence had said it was a prettier journey and I wouldn't enjoy sitting in a traffic jam in the middle of Bedford – and the small tidy towns rolled past, one after the other. Halfway along a B road overgrown by summer hedges, we passed a sign that said 'Cambridgeshire'. Florence said, 'Nearly home, Henry.'

We went over a crossroads, and suddenly the road ahead was dead straight for as far as I could see. Florence drew in her breath to speak and, knowing what she was going to say, I got in first. 'This is a Roman road,' I said. 'You can always tell. The Romans built in straight lines because they didn't bother about whose land it was.'

She gave a warble of laughter. 'Well done,' she said. 'You remembered.'

We drove into Cambridge. I recognized things – down to the left, the road along the Backs where we'd walked along by the Cam and watched people punting with long poles. Florence had pointed out a tall and glorious building and said, 'King's College Chapel.' A road branching off north-westwards towards Huntingdon which I knew was still called by its Roman name, the Via Devana. Then the Ely road – our road home.

And, soon, the turning for Willowford Fen.

I kept my eyes open, just, for the first glimpse of the house. I was tired now, so tired that I kept floating off into moments of sleep from which I'd jerk myself back.

We pulled into the drive and the car came gently to a halt. I stared up at the square, solid house. *My* house, now. In echo of my thoughts, Florence said softly, 'We're home.'

Sleep was overtaking me, but not so totally that I could forget one of the most important aspects of my homecoming. I mumbled, 'Is Eric here?'

'No,' she said, and I could tell she was sorry to have to answer like that. 'I've been out all day,' she added. 'It wouldn't have been kind to leave him all by himself, so I took him to one of my friends. You can go and collect him tomorrow.'

Tomorrow. I sighed. But she was right, it wouldn't

have been fair to make him endure a day of loneliness purely in order for me to have the pleasure of him being there to greet me. And I'd been away from him for two years – I could bear another few hours.

With Florence supporting me, I stumbled up the steps and into the cool dark hall. Already half lost in dreams, I thought I heard deep, joyful voices calling my name. Henry! Henry! I mumbled stupidly, 'Hello, everyone.' Florence's arm round my waist tightened in a hug.

We made it up the stairs, and I sat dazedly on my bed while she got my spongebag and pyjamas out of my case. Tactfully she turned her back while I changed – not that I'd have minded, I was too far gone for embarrassment, and anyway she was Florence – and then she turned down the blankets.

'Go and use the bathroom,' she said. She pushed my spongebag at me. 'Clean your teeth.'

I had a pee, and when I pulled the chain, the feel of the porcelain weight in my hand gave me the secure thought, I've done this hundreds of times before. This is where I belong.

I used Florence's tooth-powder, dipping my dampened brush into the little pot as I usually did when she wasn't looking. Then I went back into my room. She had turned off the light, and I could see the friendly Plough through the big window.

She tucked me up and bent to put a kiss on my forehead. It was so lovely being put to bed that I reached out my arms and hugged her. For a moment she held back, then she seemed to soften. She kissed me again, and said, 'Dear Henry. Sleep well.'

I did. For hours, probably. Then, as sometimes happens when your sleep pattern has been disturbed, suddenly I was wide awake and deeply confused. Where was I? What time was it?

35

As I lay in the dark, heart pounding, I heard the ping of the telephone. Was that what had woken me? I got out of bed. Florence, I must find Florence.

She was standing in the hall looking down at the telephone receiver, which was back on its rests. I said, 'Florence?', and, looking up, she saw me and came up the stairs towards me.

'Back to bed, Henry,' she said firmly. 'I did not mean to disturb you.'

'Who was it?' I asked. It must be very late – whoever could have phoned in the middle of the night?

She said, 'I was telephoning your parents, to let them know you have arrived safely.'

'Oh.' Yes. Small hours here would be early morning in Hong Kong. I couldn't think what to say. I got back into bed.

'Were they all right?' I asked, closing my eyes and not really caring.

'They were, I suppose.' She gave a sort of snort, and I opened my eyes again to look at her. She was smiling, in a strange way that made it look as if she wasn't really amused. 'I gather they had been celebrating, last night,' she said tonelessly. 'Your mother made it sound as if it were a great inconvenience to have to wake up and answer the telephone.'

'Mmm.' Not surprised in the least, I curled up under the covers. 'Night, Florence.'

'Goodnight, Henry.' I heard her cross to the door. She said, quite clearly as she closed it, 'I think I can do better than that.'

Four

I woke to the smell of bacon cooking, one of the most appetizing smells in the world. Florence always grilled it, till the fat was crisp and curly. She would accompany it with mushrooms and tomatoes, sometimes a poached egg, and thick slices of new bread. Even in those days, when people fried with gay abandon and didn't bother about saturated fats clogging up their arteries, Florence had no use for the frying pan.

I got out of bed and went to the bathroom. One of the house rules was that nobody went down to breakfast till he or she was dressed, and nobody put on clean clothes till they'd washed. I don't know if the rule applied to adults, nor how Florence would have enforced it if it did. I didn't think about that, then. I only knew the rule applied to me, and that it was no use pretending to have washed when really I hadn't. I'd tried that, and suffered the humiliation of Florence taking me upstairs to feel the towels. 'Quite dry, Henry!' she'd said, turning to me, grey eyes wide with amazement. 'However did you manage to have a bath and get dressed without so much as dampening the corner of one single towel?'

I didn't mind taking a bath in Florence's house. The tub was long and deep, with huge brass taps which I'd been quite unable to master till I was five. The water was kept permanently hot by the range in the kitchen, and Florence never complained about how much you used. She had a theory that it was good for you to lie in water – 'It's where we all began,' she would say enigmatically – and various herbal preparations stood on the edge of the bath in thick glass jars, some to exhilarate, some to calm, some just to make the water nice and bubbly.

I used to play a game with myself in which I'd try to beat the water by not letting it take me by surprise. It wasn't easy. I suppose it came from a heated tank quite a distance away, and for some reason the pipes didn't stay full. When you turned on the hot tap, for some time nothing at all happened. Then there would be a strange rhythmic thumping noise, as if a terrible army just out of sight were banging their spears against their shields (I hadn't seen *Zulu* then, but when I did, the incredible scene where the unseen warriors approach the besieged Rorke's Drift took me instantly back to Florence's bathroom). The water would come closer . . closer . . . then, suddenly and *always* making me jump, no matter how hard I tried, a tremendous great noise like someone going *PAH!* and a rush of steaming, frothing water.

This morning I lost the game, just as on every other morning I've ever spent in Florence's house.

Back in my bedroom, I went without hesitation to the two drawers in the tallboy where my clothes were always put. Underpants and socks in the one below the middle one, shirts and jumpers in the bottom one. And there were all the things I'd brought in my case – Florence must have unpacked for me last night. I dressed, made a token attempt to get the tangles out of my hair with my hairbrush, then ran downstairs to the kitchen.

'Good morning, Henry,' Florence said from the range. 'Did you sleep well?'

'Yes, thank you. Did you?' It was our usual morning exchange. When I was about six, she'd pointed out to me gently that when someone took the trouble to enquire about your night's sleep, the least you could do was to ask them about theirs in return.

'Indeed I did.' She peered at the rashers of bacon on the eye-level grill she'd installed above the range. They looked to me to be almost done. 'I had a fascinating dream about a man in green who kept hamsters in a Gladstone bag.'

'How could they breathe?'

'He left the top open. I hope you're hungry.'

'I am. Is it nearly ready?'

'A few minutes more. Why don't you have a look round while you wait?' She had remembered another of my coming-back rituals: I liked to see if I could spot any changes since I'd last stayed with her.

'All right.'

I went into the drawing room, and straight away spotted a change: the big bay window looking out over the Fens was now empty. Garth was gone.

I ran back to the kitchen. 'Florence, where's Garth?' Immediately I regretted the anxiety in my voice – I was nearly ten, for heaven's sake, far too old to be worrying about a rocking horse! 'I mean, I thought I'd . . .'

'He's out in the stables,' Florence said imperturbably. 'He tended to block the light, in the window, and I thought you wouldn't mind.'

'No, of course not.'

She was busy buttering bread. 'You've just got time to go out to see him, if you're quick.'

Suddenly that was the one thing I wanted to do. I turned and hurried out of the back door, across the yard and under the arch that led to the old stable block.

There were three stalls, and two of them had their doors closed. The middle one had the top half of its door fastened back. There was a white-painted sign on the lower half, and on it neat black letters said, 'GARTH'. I thought to myself, it's nice of her, but isn't it going a bit far for a rocking horse?

Then, probably in response to the sound of my footsteps, a dappled-grey, friendly-looking face popped out over the door, and the pony whickered gently in greeting.

His markings and his expression were so *exactly* like those of the original wooden Garth that for an instant I really believed Florence had brought my rocking horse to life.

Then the absurd thought flipped back to wherever it had come from and I ran forward to greet what I was certain was my pony.

'I've got to go,' I said to him eventually. 'Florence said I had to be quick, and anyway I'm starving. I'll be back soon as I can.'

His hooves clopped briefly on the stone floor of the stall as he moved away from the door. I thought perhaps he was turning his back in disgust at my putting hunger above the important business of getting to know him, but he was probably just returning to his haynet.

I ran in to Florence and without thinking threw my arms round her waist in a quick, hard hug.

She said, 'Do you like him?' and I could tell she was laughing.

'Yes. He's terrific. Where did you get him? How did you . . .' How did you find a pony so like my old mate, I wanted to ask, but something stopped me. Was I really sure I'd welcome the answer?

But she must have known what I was going to say. She said matter-of-factly, 'It was a whim, to see if I could find a pony just like your rocking horse. I asked around, and friends kept a lookout for me. We were lucky.'

'Thank you very much.' Belatedly I remembered my manners. 'It was very . . .'

'Henry,' she interrupted, 'you don't need to go on.' She sounded almost cross, and I looked up at her apprehensively. Her face softened. 'You've already thanked me,' she said gently. 'When you came dashing in and rugby-tackled me.' She smiled, and I grinned back. 'I don't want your tea-party manners, thank you very much.' She turned back to her cooking and I thought she added something else. But I didn't quite hear what it was.

I thought about what she'd said as I went up later to make my bed, so full of breakfast that the stairs were quite an effort. What did she mean by tea-party manners? Out of the misty blue of memory came a scene at Florence's tea-table: she had made Florentines, and my mother had put one on my plate. I remembered thinking, Florence's Florentines. Then I took a bite, and I didn't like it – the combination of the dried fruit in its gooey biscuit base and the rich, dark chocolate was too much for my juvenile stomach. Apart from a bite-shaped segment, I left it.

'You can get down, Henry, if you've finished,' my mother said when she saw I wasn't going to eat any more. 'What do you say to Florence?'

'Thank-you-very-much-that-was-lovely,' I rattled off automatically in Florence's general direction.

She said quietly, 'Henry, come here, please.'

Nervously I did as she said. She put her hand on my shoulder and looked down into my eyes. Then she said, 'It wasn't lovely, was it, because you left it.'

I didn't know what to say. 'Sorry,' I muttered.

She gave me a little shake. 'You need not apologize,' she said kindly. 'I don't mind that you left the Florentine. But I do mind, a little, that you said to me something you didn't mean.'

Her eyes on mine were intent, and I couldn't look away. 'Sorry,' I said again.

To my great relief she smiled. 'No, *I* am sorry. You were only doing what you have been taught.' Her expression changed as she shot a look at my mother. Then she looked back at me. 'You meant well.'

I had escaped, after that. I've no idea what sort of a discussion went on between my mother and my grandmother when I was out of earshot, but, now at least, I can take a pretty good guess.

But, walking slowly up the stairs on the first morning of my new life with Florence, the memory still puzzled me. Tea-party manners. Did that imply saying things you didn't mean, like my mother calling all her friends 'Darling' and telling them how wonderful they looked, only to say when they'd gone, wasn't their hair a mess and *did* you see that dress!

Florence said I'd already thanked her by hugging her, and suddenly I saw. That had been sincere – she'd made me so happy that I just had to let her know. Then, later, when I'd started on my pretty little speech, it had been at a different impulse: the echo of my mother's voice as she nodded towards her mother-in-law and said, 'Henry, what do you say?'

I was relieved to have worked it out. But I wasn't

so pleased about the other thought that had been born in my mind.

That Florence didn't like my mother.

I couldn't wait to get back to Garth, but the demands of an older friendship took precedence. I asked Florence if there was anything she wanted me to do for her – I wouldn't have minded what it was, that morning, in view of what she'd just done for me, although I have to admit that this was not the attitude I normally took. I was neither more nor less willing than the average nearly-ten-year-old to help around the house.

Florence said, 'Thank you, Henry. There is nothing for the moment, but if you like you can resume your job of seeing to the hens, later.'

'Then can I fetch Eric now?'

She stared at me, but her eyes were dreamy and I got the impression she wasn't really seeing me. I was about to ask again when her eyes flashed back into focus and she said, 'Of course. Come outside and I'll show you where to go.'

She pointed down the road. 'To the bridge, then turn left along the path beside the dyke. Straight on for two hundred and fifty paces till you get to the large willow tree, and through the gate into the lane. Turn left, and it's the second house on the right.'

I repeated the instructions. 'Okay.'

'Ask for Thea,' she said. Then she went back inside.

I set off at a trot. I was glad it was across country and not along roads – the Eric I remembered hated having to be on the lead. I had a sudden vivid picture of him, gold coat gleaming, muscles moving smoothly and strongly, shoulders bunching as he raced along. I reminded myself that he'd have changed, that he'd no longer be the eager puppy I'd last seen two years ago, and I couldn't wait to see how he'd grown.

I reached the big willow, and vaulted the gate on to the lane. 'If you must climb a gate,' Florence said in my head, 'do so at the side where the hinges are because that's where it is strongest.' I ran past one house and up to the next. The second house on the right.

It looked a bit shabby, and I wondered briefly what Florence's friend Thea might be like. It quite surprised me that someone in Florence's circle could be so different from her, because the long grass on the front lawn, the tangled, untrimmed hedge, the peeling paint on the windows and the cracked pane in the front door were not things Florence would have tolerated. Perhaps Thea was *arty*. It was a word I'd heard my mother use to describe one of her tatty and disorganized friends, a woman whose watercolours were lovely but whose dress sense, according to my mother, was 'jumble sale with Co-Op trimmings'.

I went up to the front door and knocked. The little brass knocker was in the shape of a figure with wings. I waited, composing my face into a suitable expression for greeting ladies.

The door opened and a girl stood there, clutching the edge of the door in a tight white-knuckled grip as if she were afraid I was going to force my way in. Not that she could have stopped me – although she appeared to be about my age, she was shorter and slighter than me. She had very fair hair, cut short so that it looked sort of feathery, and her eyes were a clear light blue like the summer sky in the early morning.

She didn't say anything, so I thought I'd better. 'Can I see Thea?' She didn't answer. 'I'm Henry, I've come for . . .'

'I know what you've come for.' Her voice matched her expression: she looked and sounded deeply miserable. She turned away, closing the door till the latch caught, and I heard her give a low, sweet whistle. I wondered if Eric were near, if he had sensed my presence. Or perhaps – awful thought! – he was out for a walk with Thea and I'd have to wait with this depressing girl till they came back.

Then there was a scuffle of feet, the door opened again and there he was.

'Eric!' I said joyfully, bending forwards and slapping my hands on my thighs in the way that always used to make him jump up at me.

He was standing at the girl's side, and he didn't move. His bright, intelligent eyes looked into mine, and, stretching towards me, he sniffed at me. He gave a polite wag or two with his long plumed tail, then he turned and looked up at the girl.

'Come on, Eric.' It was humiliating to have to appeal to him twice. I'd acted out this moment so many times, and it had always ended in happy licks and bounding, celebratory leaps. Not a quiet, obedient dog apparently waiting for someone else's permission before coming to me.

'This is Henry, Eric,' the girl said. I noticed that her voice was shaking. 'You're his dog, you've got to go with him now.' Then she took him by the collar, dragged him – rather roughly, I thought – through the door, and slammed it behind him.

I was amazed. Was that it? I waited, but other than the noise of feet racing up the stairs immediately after she'd slammed the door, there was no other sound.

'Right, then, Eric,' I said in an attempt at heartiness, 'let's go home!'

He'd been well trained, and at my command he

fell into step beside me. Over the gate and into the field, and he trotted right at my heels. When we were nearly back at Florence's road, he stopped. He turned and looked back the way we'd come, and gave a low, sad whine.

I looked back too. Sitting on the gate under the willow was a small bright-headed figure.

Hurt, cross, I took hold of his collar, just as she had done. 'Come *on*, Eric!' I said harshly. And together we came back home to Florence's house.

I knew straight away he wasn't happy. He knew his way around, knew where his basket was, where his water bowl stood, always filled. Knew what time to present himself for his dinner. But he was like a polite house guest: if he could have done, he'd have put on a pleasant but nervous and insecure smile every time I caught his eye.

Because his sadness was making me miserable and I didn't know how to cope with it, I pretended it wasn't there. For the next few days – it was half-term, and I wasn't going to have to go to my new school till the following week – I spent most of the daylight hours with Garth, whose exuberant, extrovert and affectionate personality was the perfect antidote to the unsatisfactory Eric.

But I couldn't stay out with Garth all day. There always came the moment when it was time to go in. And there would be Eric, mourning, listless, his presence both a deeply hurtful irritant – why can't you love me! – and also, in some strange way, an accusation.

On the third night, Florence spoke. I suppose I always knew she would. She called me over to sit by her on the settee, then said quietly, 'You've been away two years, Henry. And he wasn't much more

46

than a puppy when you left him. Too young to have fixed you in his heart.' She paused.

I said, desperately trying to keep my voice level, 'You mean he's forgotten me.'

She frowned. I waited tensely for what she would say – somehow I knew that it would be the truth, no matter how it hurt, and I braced myself.

'Think of yourself when you were young. When you were one and a bit, let's say. There were people you liked, I'm quite sure, people you had fun with, and who gave you affection and made you laugh.' I nodded. There must have been, my parents had always had lots of friends. 'Do you remember any of them?'

'Yes! I –' Desperately I tried to think. It was no good. 'No.'

'Well, it's like that for Eric, too. With you.' Hearing his name, he whined gently, and came over to lie down by her, head on her foot.

He didn't so much as look at me.

I understood.

If Eric's affection had been transferred to Florence, I could have borne it better. But to have him pine for a girl no older than me who didn't even live in the same house, that was intolerable.

'I suppose *she's* been looking after him a lot,' I said, emotion making me sound surly and unpleasant.

'She has. And her name is Thea, as I told you.' *That* was Thea? The girl with the light hair? What happened to the artistic woman in a floral smock? I'd assumed the girl was her daughter, or her grand-daughter – how could *she* possibly be Thea? Apart from anything else, she was too young to have a name like that. 'She will miss him, very much, now that you're back,' Florence said gently.

Against my will I felt a stab of pity for Thea: I knew

47

all about *missing*. I fought it. I said, getting up, 'I'm going to say goodnight to Garth. If Eric doesn't want to come with me, he can stay with you.'

I went out, closing the door accidentally-on-purpose behind me so that Eric couldn't have followed even if he'd wanted to.

I couldn't have stood it, just then, if he'd opted not to.

Next day, I was coming in for lunch after a great morning out with Garth when I caught sight of a movement out in the road. I slipped behind one of the big trees in the front garden and looked more closely.

I could see someone crouched down on the other side of the front hedge. The someone was whispering, 'Eric,' over and over. Then from the house there was a streak of gold, and he flashed past me, leapt over the gate and raced down the road to whoever it was who had called him.

I went closer, right up to the gate, and looked out along the road.

Thea was kneeling in a puddle, arms round Eric, and he was licking her face and giving small whines of joy. She had her eyes closed. He loved her and he didn't love me: I hated her.

Then I saw that she was crying. As she pushed him back in through the gate, I could see the shine of tears on her cheeks.

I felt like a spy. It felt wrong to witness the two of them, and, ashamed, I turned and ran away.

That evening I said to Florence, 'I think Eric misses Thea.'

She studied me for some time. Then said, 'I think so, too.'

'Did he – I suppose he often went to her house. I mean, if you were going out, like when you came to meet me, I expect you often left him with her.'

'I did. And, when it became apparent how well they got on, I used to let him go to see her even when I wasn't going out. Most days, in fact.'

She fell silent. I knew she was waiting. Eventually, though it cost me a bit of my heart, I said, 'It doesn't bother me if he still does. Goes to see her, I mean.' Then the reality of what I was saying – and, more, what it would lead to – got through to me and I had to stop.

Florence observed quietly, 'A dog like Eric can only have one master. Or mistress.'

I realized exactly what she was saying. I said angrily, 'I *know*.'

It was very rude, and I half expected her to say so. But instead she reached out and took my hand. 'It's a very generous offer, Henry.' Both of us were quite well aware of what the offer was without spelling it out. 'Why, do you think, are you making it?'

I couldn't say because I saw Thea crying. Anyway, was it that? I'd seen my mother cry heaps of times, and it had never affected me like those silent, painful tears of Thea's. My mother cried when she didn't get her own way, and wasn't that exactly what Thea had been doing?

No. It wasn't. Because, whereas my mother always made sure she had an audience – not a lot of point, otherwise – Thea had thought she and Eric were unobserved.

Eric. Sad Eric, with pain in his eyes, his head going up and his ears pricking every time there was a light footfall in the road outside. And only once had it been the one he was longing for.

'It's because Eric misses her,' I said brusquely. 'He

49

ought to be allowed to choose for himself who he lives with.' And, I could have added, quite clearly he doesn't want to live with me. But I didn't. It sounded too self-pitying. I wanted Florence to think I didn't care.

I think she knew I did. She said, very quietly, 'Well done, Henry.'

Thea must have come very early in the morning, because when I came down to breakfast, Eric had gone.

On the Sunday evening before school started, she came to see me. On her own. I was out in the stable giving Garth a vigorous going-over with the dandy-brush – with school beginning, I wouldn't have so much time for him – and I suddenly became aware someone was watching me.

I turned, and there she was. It was funny, but I almost didn't recognize her. She looked quite different. It was, I suppose, that I hadn't seen her happy before.

She drew in her breath, but nothing happened. I got the impression she was trying to say something and finding it difficult. She had another go.

'I just wanted to say,' she burst out in a rush, 'I know you loved him too and thank you.'

Then she spun round and fled, under the archway and off out of sight, her sandals slapping against the road.

I turned back to Garth. Putting my arms round his sturdy neck, I buried my face in the coarse hairs of his friendly mane till I felt better.

Five

School began, and as the New Bug starting halfway through a term, I was something of a nine days' wonder. There were some comments of the 'reckons he's too good for the likes of us, coming from abroad and all' variety from the more bucolic of my classmates, but after I'd punched one of them and made his nose bleed (he dropped my satchel in the mud and trod on it) they left me alone. I was placed next to a boy called Roger who by good chance also had a pony, and soon the tentative branches of friendship we put out began to grow thick.

The teacher was called Miss Hall, and I realized quite soon that she was different from any of the teachers I'd had in my expatriate schools. She was younger, for one thing; she was unmarried and so didn't have a child or two of her own in the school; she was far more dedicated and a lot more strict.

She asked me to wait behind after morning school on the Friday of my second week.

'How are you settling in?' she asked pleasantly.

'Fine.' There was no need to tell her about the satchel incident or its aftermath.

She perched on the edge of my desk, arms folded,

51

looking at me intently. 'Do you find the work more difficult than in your previous school?'

I wanted to say, yes I bloody well do! I'd been appalled at the amount of stuff we were expected to get through in a lesson, even more appalled when the other children accepted these Herculean tasks without protest, submissively bending their obedient heads and getting down to it. It had soon become apparent that my nonchalant attitude to my work wasn't going to do, here: the days when I could coast along without much effort and still be in the top five or ten of the class were gone for ever.

'Um – there's more of it,' I said meekly. There was something about Miss Hall's brown eyes that made you decide meekness was the best option.

She didn't speak for a moment or two, but I knew quite well she wasn't finished. Eventually she said, in a thoughtful way, 'I don't know you very well yet, Henry, but it seems to me you're the sort of boy who quite likes a challenge.' I felt that was going a bit far – it would all depend on the challenge. 'So this is what I propose,' she went on. She paused, and, looking up, I met her eyes.

I knew in that moment that she'd rumbled me. She knew the whole story of my schooling to date, knew how I'd rushed my lessons and skimped on my homework, relying on a good short-term memory and a winning way with words to get me out of trouble. And it wasn't going to wash with her.

She said quietly, 'You stop leaning back with your arms folded looking bored and start using your very capable brain a bit, and I bet you I'll be giving you an A grade by the end of term.'

I couldn't believe she'd said it. She was *bribing* me, for goodness' sake! No teacher I'd come across before

– and I'd come across quite a few – had ever done anything like that.

I felt stupid. There I'd been, pretending this little village school and everyone in it was beneath my lofty attention, and she hadn't been fooled for a moment. No wonder she'd put on my first piece of written work, underneath the abysmal mark of four out of ten, 'You are not trying, Henry.'

She was apparently waiting for a response. I muttered, 'Okay.'

'What was that?'

I straightened up. 'I said, okay.'

I thought she might tell me off for that, too, since my answer had stopped only just short of rudeness. But she didn't. She got off the desk and said, 'Go outside now and get some fresh air till the bell goes for class.'

I said, 'Yes, Miss Hall,' jumping up and hurrying towards the door.

But she called, 'Henry?', and I had to stop.

'Yes, Miss Hall?' I didn't turn round.

She said, very kindly, 'You've come a long way to join us. I hope you'll be happy here.'

I looked at her. She was smiling. It struck me that I'd just made a pact with her, and in some obscure way that I couldn't work out, I was glad.

I'd wondered if Thea might be in my class, but she wasn't even in the school. It was a bit disappointing – if she had been, I'd have been able to keep a link with Eric. I went past her house a few times in the evenings and at the weekend, but there was never any sign of life. One day, going past with Florence on the way back from a long walk over the Fen to look for butterflies, I said, 'Where does Thea go to school?'

Florence stopped, and stood in the lane looking at the shabby house. The stillness was absolute, and suddenly I knew that nobody lived there any more.

'She has gone to a new school,' Florence said. She glanced at me. 'Just like you, she began at half-term. Quite a coincidence, really, since she's also moved to a new home.' I hadn't expected the stab of dismay that went through me.

'Has she taken Eric with her?' I already knew the answer.

'Of course.' Florence put her hand on my shoulder. 'That was why it was so splendid that you gave him to her. You see, Thea didn't in the least want to go to her new home.' She smiled at me companionably, as if she were saying, unlike you. 'Thea's parents are no longer married,' she went on, 'and Thea's mother decided she wanted to go off and do some travelling. So Thea has gone to live with her father in Gloucestershire, and she goes to a school nearby.'

I imagined living on my own with my father. I asked, 'Does she have an –' An amah, I nearly said. 'I mean, who looks after her when her father's at work?'

'He works at home. He's a writer.'

'What does he write?' Maybe he wrote adventure books! I was making a wonderful picture of Thea's dad being some sort of Anthony Buckeridge or Frank Richards when Florence said, laughing, 'He's a journalist. He writes for newspapers.'

'Oh.'

I still found it hard to imagine a child living just with her father. Who made the beds? Washed the clothes? Cooked and kept the place tidy? My father never did any of those things. But then neither did my mother. On the other hand, by the look of Thea's mother's house with its broken pane (which actually had now been mended, probably in preparation for the house being left empty) and its unkempt garden, possibly Thea wasn't accustomed to having all those things done for her anyway.

Florence started walking again, and I turned away from the depressing sight of the empty house and fell into step beside her.

'She's got Eric,' Florence said, as if she were thinking along the same lines. 'She won't be lonely with Eric.'

Something in her tone made it quite unnecessary for me to ask, as I'd been going to, if she thought Thea was likely to be happy in her father's house.

The weeks raced past, and the long days of summer were filled with interesting things from the moment I got up till the moment I put out my bedside light and went to sleep. I'd fallen into the routine of life with Florence as if I'd never known anything else: it was as wonderful as I'd thought – known – it would be.

I even liked school. When I'd got over being daunted by the oppressive weight of Miss Hall's expectations, I found that she was right and I was wrong; I *could* manage the work, and, although I could never have confessed it, I actually quite enjoyed doing it. Of course I went through the ritual moaning and groaning – '*THREE PAGES* of sums! I'll never get it done!', or, 'An essay on the Romans in the Fens! *YUK!*', but it was for my classmates' benefit.

Florence took an interest in all that I did. It was a novelty for me to have someone at home to discuss my work with, since all my mother had ever said when I told her what we were doing in school was, 'Very nice, Henry.' Or, at the most, 'I hope you're going to get a good part in the Nativity play this year.

You must tell them I'm an actress, surely they know a Thespian gift runs in families.' And she'd adopt a pose, even though there was only me to see it.

Florence, I soon realized, was far, far more clever than my mother. Or my father, probably, although since he had never talked over my school work with me either, I had no way of knowing. But it seemed to me that Florence was probably more clever than anyone. She had books – hundreds, thousands of books, arranged on shelves covering all of one vast wall in her drawing room – and, whatever the question, whatever the topic under discussion, she could provide the answers. Not just to do with homework or lessons, for we talked endlessly, over our meals, when we were out walking, whenever we were together and she wasn't busy thinking about something else. Without noticing, I caught from her a love of learning – finding out, she called it; 'Let's go and find out, Henry' – which has stayed with me all my life.

At the end of term, Miss Hall handed out the envelopes containing our reports. They included the grades she had awarded us. As she gave me my envelope, I tried to read her expression. Her face was sombre.

I've failed, I thought. I was so disappointed that for a dangerous second or two there was a big lump in my throat and a prickling behind my eyelids. I stuffed the envelope in my satchel – I was tempted to ease it open and sneak a look, but I didn't dare – and somehow endured the last half-hour of the day. Then we were dismissed, and Miss Hall's cheerful voice wished us a happy holiday. Possibly she was looking forward to it as much as we were.

I went home dragging my footsteps. Florence, I knew, was doing a special tea to celebrate my breaking up, but I didn't feel like special celebratory teas any more.

I stood in the kitchen and gave her the report. She looked at me for a long moment, then, without speaking, reached in a drawer for a knife and slit open the envelope.

She read down the page of Miss Hall's writing. Her face was expressionless, as sombre as Miss Hall's had been. I was about to burst out in protest – I'm new, I've only been there half a term! I'll do better next year! – when she lowered the report and looked at me.

She began to smile. Then to laugh. And said, 'Miss Hall says you're better at maths than you think you are, but that English is your strong suit, closely followed by history. She says you've applied yourself well and achieved an excellent standard, especially in your written work.'

She held out the report for me to read.

My eyes shot to the column where the grades had been entered. Opposite 'English' there was an A.

Looking back at my first summer holidays with Florence, I have to say that it was one of the happiest times of my life. I suppose most children remember their tenth summer with pleasure – the fortunate ones who are loved and secure and have enough to eat, anyway – since at that age begins freedom, the joy of being answerable to no-one. Florence set times for me to be home – half past twelve for lunch, half past four for tea and half past seven for supper – and she liked me to tell her where I was going. Other than that, I could come and go as I liked. (I suspect that in fact she usually knew exactly where I was, since she was on friendly terms with Roger's mother and with the mothers of the various other schoolmates I spent my time with. But, being Florence, she didn't let on.)

I kept being surprised at all the things that had changed in the three years since I'd last lived in Florence's house. Barn-door latches I hadn't been able to put a hand to had suddenly dropped to within easy reach, trees I'd baulked at climbing now offered accessible and easy footholds, dykes I'd never been able to jump without getting at least one foot wet had shrunk so that now I cleared them in a single bound. And even the house itself, four-square, golden brick and grey slate, white-painted sash windows and friendly glassed-in porch, seemed much more approachable than it used to.

Some mornings over breakfast at the big kitchen table, Florence would say, 'I thought I might go out for a drive today. It's set fair,' – she would glance out of the window – 'and I propose to take a picnic.'

Then she would return to her toast and Oxford marmalade, humming to herself. After a little while I would say, 'Er – where did you think you might go?', and she would reply, 'Cambridge, to take a punt to Grantchester,' or, 'Grime's Graves, to go down the flint mine and then picnic in Thetford Forest,' or even, 'Walberswick, to see if I can spot an avocet.'

Drinking my tea, I would act as nonchalant as she. Then I'd say casually, 'That sounds great. It's ages since I've been there,' or, slightly wistfully, 'I've never been there.' She would then look up at me, eyes wide with surprise, and say, as if it were the most unlikely thing in the world, 'You don't want to come, do you?'

I never managed to say, 'Yes, please' without laughing.

I think that epitomizes Florence's attitude towards me. She was happy to let me do as I wished with my free time, and she was equally happy with her own company – after all, she'd been going off on her jaunts by herself for all the years before I came to join her. Or so I thought then. But if it so happened that she was going somewhere I wanted to go too – and that applied to everywhere she went, in our early months together – then she was always delighted if I joined her.

But there was never any pressure. Never any sense of *ought*.

We went on so many trips in the course of those first holidays. At least two a week. Without being obvious about it, Florence was imprinting East Anglia firmly on my brain, and by the time I went back to school I knew the layout of the three counties, Cambridgeshire, Norfolk and Suffolk, well enough to take over the route planning and the map reading from her.

Wherever we went, our travels were accompanied by a commentary which, for all that it had the sparkle of fresh invention, must have been a repetition of facts and legends she had often related before. Or, if not actually related, then certainly thought about. At first I used to marvel that one head could hold so much, then I began to accept it as just another facet of her. There was a sense of recognition, sometimes, as if I'd already heard what she was telling me, and I realized eventually that this was because I had – she'd imparted the information to me in my bedtime stories.

One day she drove me around the stretch of coast between Felixstowe and Southwold, and standing on the shore, as if it had been suggested to her by where we were, told me the tale of a prince who had no crown and no wealth, and who lived in the forest with the wolves. Although his father was a king, she said, his mother was humble, and, lacking both the means and the intelligence to control her son, had let him run wild until, one day, he didn't come back.

'He didn't want to be found,' she said with a smile when I asked why his mother hadn't fetched him home. 'He preferred to be out there hunting with the wolves, living in the dwelling he'd made for himself deep in the undergrowth.'

For a second I was the lost prince. I could see a hut roofed in branches, all but hidden by the dark overwhelming trees. In my nostrils was a musky, meaty smell which I guessed must be the scent of wolf.

Florence was explaining how eventually the prince's father summoned him and let him live at court. 'But perhaps,' she said sadly, 'he would have been happier left out in the wild.'

'Why?'

She closed her eyes for a moment as if she were seeing the things she was describing, then, opening them, stared at me. 'He left undone the task that was his to do,' she said. 'Something existed – something evil – which it fell to him to destroy. He failed, and in failing, he lost the thing he loved most in all the world.'

I thought she was going to say more, but she didn't. After some time, she turned and led the way back to the car and we went home.

I didn't know why that story stuck in my mind more than all the rest – perhaps it was because I was taken with the idea of living with the wolves, perhaps because I felt a pang of pity for anyone who had lost something he loved. Eric, after all, was still a relatively recent loss, even in the swift-moving timescale of a child. Whatever it was, I couldn't get the sad prince out of my mind, and when I went to bed that night I dreamt of him. He – or was it I? We seemed to be one and the same – was lost, searching in a blinding white mist for something he – I – was desperate to find. And there was pain – my leg hurt, so much that it eventually woke me. Fumbling for the light, throwing back the covers to inspect my throbbing thigh, for a split second a fragment of my dream came back and I thought I was lying in the black oozy mud of the Fens in winter.

Then the pain and the image went away. After some time, I settled back to sleep.

My birthday fell in August. Florence gave me a mug with a lion on it to use for my morning tea and a big, lavishly-illustrated book called *East Anglia from the Stone Age*. It looked a bit daunting at first, and I was going through torments trying to cover up my disappointment – I'd seen from the shape of the parcel it was a book, and hoped it was either something to do with horses or else a new Biggles book.

Then I started to read it, and I didn't have to fake a reaction any longer. This was nothing like the history books we had at school; this was full of pictures and charts and interesting little snippets to catch the imagination: the Romans didn't normally shoe their horses, but when they were travelling up paved roads such as Ermine Street or the Icknield Way, the pack-animals had special temporary shoes called hippo-sandals; when the Vikings launched a boat, it was considered auspicious if virgin blood were spilled; a horribly-screaming woman haunted the flint mines at Aylmerton; when Boudicca's troops chased the Romans down to Londinium, they cut the Roman women's breasts off. And – by now I was sharing the choice bits with Florence – 'Listen to this! St Edmund was the last king in a dynasty called the *Wuffingas!*'

I don't know what Miss Hall would have made of some of that.

I went on reading to Florence while our toast went cold and our tea scummy, then she said gently, 'I take it you're pleased. I'm so glad. I was afraid you might think a history book made a dull present.'

It was exactly what I had thought, of course, and I felt myself go red. 'I –' I began, but tactfully she interrupted.

'Why don't you open your other presents?' she suggested.

There was a football from Roger, which was jolly nice of him but not a surprise since I'd been dropping heavy hints all week. Two of the other boys I played with had sent cards – they'd also come in for some hint-dropping – and my grandparents from my mother's side had sent me a postal order and a card with a yacht on it.

My parents, to my surprise, had sent me a Swiss army knife. It was just what I wanted, and, rather ungratefully, I wondered how they'd known. Perhaps Florence had been dropping hints, too – yes, I decided, that must be it, otherwise I'd be unwrapping something like new pyjamas in a wildly unsuitable colour like black, probably made of silk and decorated with dragons. There was a card – my mother must have written it at the last minute, because she'd signed for both of them: 'From Mummy and Daddy, with lots and lots of love.' He probably went off to work before she'd remembered to ask him to sign for himself.

I held the knife in my palm – it was beautifully heavy, with a promisingly large number of attachments – and stared down at my mother's writing. Mummy and Daddy. Lots and lots of love.

I realized with a strange feeling in my heart that I

didn't miss them at all. That, since the moment I'd seen Florence waiting for me in the VIP lounge, I'd hardly given them a thought. And, in view of the very expensive present they'd sent me – even if Florence had tipped them off, it was still nice of them – the realization made me feel bad.

Lots and lots of love. Did they love me? Did they miss me, wish I were still there, go and sit in my empty bedroom and cuddle my discarded teddy? (I'd never have thought of that for myself, Roger's sister told me in a moment of mischief that it was what his mum had done when he went to stay with his grandparents for a week, and although he thumped her and seemed to be ashamed of having such a soppy parent, I always rather liked Roger's mum afterwards. It was, as ever, a question of the grass being greener: I'd have liked a mum like that.)

No matter how hard I tried, I couldn't convince myself that my parents were pining for me any more than I was for them.

Florence must have read my thoughts. I don't suppose it was very difficult, under the circumstances. She said, 'I expect they're thinking about you today, on your birthday. Perhaps they're remembering your previous birthdays, and wishing you many more.'

It was clever of her, as, although it put my parents in a pleasant light, it was a believable pleasant light. Had Florence said, oh, they'll be missing you badly this morning! How awful for them, having their only child so far away on his birthday!, it would not only have upset me but also made me mistrust Florence's judgement.

As always, she knew exactly how to handle the situation and exactly what to say.

I put my cards on the mantelshelf and picked up my presents to take them upstairs to my room. Except for the penknife, which went in my pocket. By the time I came down again to help Florence pack the car for our birthday trip to Cambridge (I was going to spend my postal order), my parents were once more as far away from me in spirit as they were in body.

Looking back, I often wonder if I have glamorized Florence and the start of my life as a permanent resident in her house at Willowford Fen. I'm sure that, somehow, it was in my mind as I flew home that things might not be as wonderful as I had imagined. Did I conceive the thought myself, or did someone – my mother, my father, speaking their concern out loud unaware that I was listening – put it into my head? I don't know.

I do know this. That, when I got back, I found I hadn't glamorized either Florence or the life into which she admitted me at all. She accepted me as I was, reaching out to me from the very first moment with that special, understated, unobtrusive welcome that was her hallmark, so that I merged into her household truly as if I'd always been there. My nine-and-a-half-year-old self is in my mind with total clarity, for all that it's thirty years and more ago, and with no effort at all I can feel the warmth of Florence's love now just as I felt it then.

No wonder I didn't miss my parents.

Six

Miss Hall and the teachers who succeeded her for my next year in the village primary school did their best with me, and the best was good enough: I passed my eleven-plus and went to grammar school. It was the one Florence's gardener's grandson had gone to, and it wasn't Ely – my mother had been quite right. Florence had indeed once known a French teacher there – my mother was right about that, too – but he retired the year before I arrived.

Roger went on with me, and although our friendship served us well for the first few weeks in a strange, much bigger school, we both made new friends and soon saw less of each other. We no longer rode together, since I had come to the unwelcome conclusion that I was rapidly getting too long in the leg and much too heavy for Garth. Retirement was looming unless, as Florence thought we should, we could find some smaller child in the village willing to exercise the old chap once or twice a week.

Sometimes – quite often, really – I thought about Eric, and that would lead on to thinking about Thea. Florence must have believed I'd forgotten all about them; not knowing she was wrong, she went to unnecessary pains to keep their memory alive. 'I've had a letter from Thea,' she'd say. 'Would you like to read it?' If I answered honestly and said, 'No thank you,' she'd look a bit hurt, so I used to take the pages from her – Thea wrote reams, I wondered how she found the time – and glance through them, going, 'That's nice,' or 'How rotten for her,' as occasion demanded. There was usually a bulletin about Eric, and I always read those bits. According to Thea, he was thriving.

There wouldn't have been much time for either looking after a dog or riding a pony, what with a longer school day, longer journeys to and fro, more homework and rugby twice a week. There wasn't even much time for going off visiting with Florence, and for a year or two I was so preoccupied with school, school friends and school activities that I scarcely noticed. She didn't seem to mind my involvement, in fact she encouraged it, never objecting when I said I was off to stay with friends for the weekend – I think she used to take advantage of my absence to go away herself – and always welcoming the friends back to stay with us in turn.

I used to watch her with my friends, first the boys, then the girls. She was always Florence, but in some way that I couldn't put my finger on, something of her went missing when we had company. No, not exactly missing, for I knew the absent quality was still there. It was just that she chose not to reveal it to anyone else.

My friends, boys and girls, all thought she was terrific, and I don't think it was just because she was so hospitable. A boy called Phil who was a close friend in the year we did our 'O' levels once remarked that she was like a female Merlin, all-knowing and with an aura of power about her (he had a thing about the Arthurian legend). I said that was strange, since she'd been born and bred in the Fens and, gravely proud of her pure East Anglian heritage, would have been insulted by being likened to a Welsh wizard, to which Phil replied, 'You know what I mean!'

I did, actually. She was certainly all-knowing – history had long been my best subject, thanks to Florence – and perhaps she did have a certain indefinable power about her. If she had, she generously used it to my advantage: I passed nine 'O' levels, history and English with Grade One. Phil said, 'Told you so!'

With my seventeenth birthday at the end of my lower sixth year, our travels began anew. I had been driving Florence's car on the quiet for years – there was an old disused airfield near Thetford and she'd been teaching me virtually since I could reach the pedals – and I passed my driving test two weeks after my birthday. She had got rid of the old Ford Popular which I remembered from the very early days before I lived with her, replacing it in 1968 with a Morris Minor Traveller which she bought from one of the ladies in the WI (We'd joked about it having an immaculate pedigree of the 'one careful lady owner' sort, then, once it was ours, Florence had been disgusted to find the back filthy with dog-hairs).

The day after I passed the test, Florence held the car keys out to me.

'You can take over the driving now,' she said in her I'm-brooking-no-argument voice. Not that I'd have argued anyway. 'The young make better drivers than the old.'

I wasn't at all sure she was right. Not in her own case, at least – she had always been an exceptionally good driver and still was. 'I'm quite happy with you at the wheel,' I said. 'And you're not old.'

She smiled at me. 'Yes I am. I'm over seventy.'

A parade of images filtered through my mind: Florence striding out and me having to trot to keep up with her – she could still outwalk me, even then; her weatherbeaten but healthy skin and her clear grey eyes; her thick hair, springy with life; her capable, lively, brilliantly intelligent mind. She was seventy? Not to me. To me she had stayed at exactly the age she was when my mind first reached out to hers and I christened her 'Flonce'.

I couldn't put all that into words. She'd have hated it, and I'd have been furiously embarrassed. So I took the keys from her and said, 'Good Lord. I shall never let you drive again.'

For my first day at the wheel, we went to Bury St Edmunds. To my surprise, for she was not a church-woman, Florence had said she wanted me to see Saint Edmundsbury Cathedral. Until we were inside the cool and almost empty building, I didn't know why.

She had wandered away from me, and I hesitated to follow in case she wanted some time to herself. I gazed around, my eyes drawn upwards from the elegant cream pillars of the nave to the brilliance of the painted ceiling above. Florence had told me that the new east end of the cathedral had only been completed a couple of years ago, and there was a sense of still-wet freshness about everything beyond the nave altar. I walked slowly along the cloisters, idly taking in the different patterns on the stitched blue kneelers neatly propped up on the pews.

I caught up with Florence in the choir. She wasn't doing anything as out of character as praying. Or, at least, she wasn't praying to the Christian god whose house this was.

She was standing before the Bishop's Throne, head back and eyes fixed on one of the winged buttresses, which was surmounted by a carving of a wolf guarding the head of Saint Edmund. Her face wore an anguished expression I'd never seen before. I went to stand beside her. I wanted to take her arm, for the sudden fear was in my heart that she felt ill. But I held back.

Just as well. Aware without turning that it was I who stood by her, she said, 'A beautiful piece of work. Modern, you know, for all that it commemorates a legend over a thousand years old.'

I was about to make some comment, but abruptly she turned from her contemplation, taking my arm and marching me back down the aisle. 'What is it?' I asked quietly. 'Are you all right?'

She glanced at me, her expression slightly impatient. 'Of course I am. There is something more important than Saint Edmundsbury Cathedral that I wish you to see.'

I thought she wasn't going to elucidate, but just as we reached the doors, she turned to me and said, 'He was never buried here, do you see.'

Emerging on to the street, we went a few hundred yards down the road, then turned right through the archway of the Norman Tower and into the ruins of the Abbey of Saint Edmund. Without hesitation, she strode off along paths between flowerbeds and under trees, until we stood together among the ancient grey stones of the old buildings.

I got the impression she had aimed for an exact spot, for she seemed to take up her position with reference to two great pillars that stood in the middle of the ruins, roughly where the tower would have been. Then, after a few moments' silence, she began to speak. And, although I'd often have liked to, I have never been able to forget what she told me.

As I'd grown older, I'd noticed that Florence had ceased to bowdlerize her storytelling. Not that she ever did a lot of that – it was, as I think I've said in another context, her way to tell the strict truth, even if it hurt or distressed. But she had refrained from telling me the gorier tales of East Anglia's past until she considered I was mature enough to hear them.

I was, quite obviously, mature enough now.

'The great building which once stood here commemorated, they say, a man who died rather than deny his faith,' she said. 'We are standing in front of what used to be the altar, under which was his last known resting place.' She stood straight, like a loyal soldier at attention, and her quiet but intense voice seemed to soar right up into the still summer sky. I glanced uneasily over my shoulder, but it seemed we were alone. 'King Edmund,' – I noticed she deliberately called him King and not Saint – 'the last of the Wuffingas of East Anglia.'

It was a sad story, one I'd discovered for myself in the book Florence had given me when I was ten, and which, when I repeated it to her, she'd received with a strange mixture of sorrow and elation. She had puzzled and upset me then, and I'd pushed the unwelcome emotions to the back of my mind, forgetting all about them till this moment.

'Descendant of Wuffa, first of the Anglo-Saxon kings of East Anglia,' I contributed – she seemed to be waiting for me to speak – 'Ruler of his people when the Vikings went on the rampage in the middle of the ninth century. Saint Edmund was taken at the battle of Hoxne, and would have been spared if he had done as the Vikings ordered and turned to their gods. But he . . .'

'King Edmund would not have been spared had he gone on his knees to every Norse god in the pantheon.' Her voice was harsh suddenly. 'He was a king! A figurehead, a rallying point for his people! Would the conquerors have let him live, under any circumstances? Not they!' She had answered her question before I had a chance to – I got the impression she was hardly aware I was there. 'The Vikings were ruthlessly efficient, and allowing overthrown kings to remain alive to cause trouble was not in their rules.' Suddenly she spun round to face me. 'How did Edmund die?'

'They say he was tied to a tree and shot with arrows.' I'd read that when I was a young child, and the picture it had made in my mind was too vivid to make thinking about it easy. A human body, pinned to a tree by the arrows that pierced it. Just to make the image totally real, I'd seen a painting of the Martyrdom of Saint Sebastian when Florence had taken me to the Fitzwilliam in Cambridge: I knew exactly what arrows in the flesh looked like. 'Then the Vikings cut his head off,' – that bit was easier to bear, you'd be past pain once your head was off – 'and threw it in the woods, where Edmund's army later found it, being guarded by a wolf.'

'That is indeed what they say. But they are inaccurate.'

'But they found the tree!' I felt like a gullible fool, but I'd said it now and I might as well go on. 'A tree fell down, near Hoxne, and they found a Viking arrowhead in it!'

'And carved on the arrowhead, "I killed King Edmund"? Do not believe all that you read, Henry. It is possible that he was treated in that way, for the Vikings were sacrificing him to Odin, and such victims were put to death by a combination of hanging on trees and stabbing with spears or arrows. Odin was called the Lord of the Gallows, and he was depicted sitting under a gallows tree. But for the sacrifice of a king, there was something more.'

I wasn't sure I wanted to hear. But how could I not? I waited, feeling the sweat break out on my forehead and across my back.

'For a beaten king, the Vikings reserved the rite of the blood eagle. The body was opened up down the spine and the ribs and lungs removed, the rib bones broken and spread outwards so that they resembled the wings of an eagle. And that, it appears, was what they did to King Edmund.'

I wouldn't have thought it'd have affected me. I'd seen worse things in horror films, read of more brutal tortures in lurid novels. Possibly it was because Florence was speaking of a real man, and I knew it. For a moment I could see black before my eyes, but then from somewhere I gathered some courage. And some pride – if an elderly lady could speak of such things without distress, surely a seventeen-year-old boy could hear them without disgracing himself?

I drew a breath, then another, trying to rid my mind, as my ribs opened and lifted, of the picture of Viking hands at work on a vanquished king's body. After a while, the rushing sounds in my ears ceased and the painful thumping of my heart slowed down.

Beside me, Florence had raised her hand, as if in valediction, towards the place where once an altar had stood over a fallen king. She said something – it sounded like, 'King of the East Angles, last of his dynasty.' But I couldn't be sure.

Then she turned and walked away.

She was withdrawn on the way home, and hardly spoke. Once or twice I heard her muttering, but when I said, 'Sorry? What did you say?' she didn't respond. That in itself wasn't unusual – she often talked to herself, and when I teased her about it, would say spiritedly, 'I'm addressing the most intelligent person present!'

There would be no teasing tonight. I didn't know her in this mood, and it worried me.

When we got home she went ahead of me into the house while I put the car away in the garage. Joining her in the kitchen, I found she'd put the kettle on and was bending to look inside the slow oven to check on the casserole she'd left there earlier. She said, in her normal voice, 'I'm making a pot of tea, but you can have a drink if you'd rather.'

I got myself a can of beer and sat down at the table. When she'd finished with the casserole she poured her tea and came to join me.

Still feeling disoriented by the distant Florence she'd been that afternoon before she decided to come back to the here and now, I didn't know what to say. I was about to begin some silly remark – wasn't it a beautiful sunset? – when she spoke. And it was no surprise at all to find that her thoughts were still with the murdered king.

'The last of the dynasty,' she said thoughtfully. 'God knows what became of the rest of his family. Killed, probably. Enslaved, perhaps.'

I recalled her passionate words about Viking ruthlessness. 'Efficiency', she'd said it was. 'A son or other heir would be as dangerous to the Danes as a king,' I said. 'He'd be an equally good figurehead, wouldn't he? I mean, the Vikings wouldn't have taken any chances.'

'They would not.' She was staring at me. Or perhaps staring through me. I couldn't tell. Her wide eyes had a strange wild look in them, and I had the sudden frightening thought, there is a part of her I do not know.

There was silence in the kitchen except for the deep tock of the clock in the hall. And an incongruous bubbling sound from the range: she'd moved the casserole up to a higher oven.

Then she spoke. In a conversational tone that didn't match the fire in her eyes, she said, 'King Edmund should have learned from the legends of his own people. If he had profited by the example of what happened to his ancestor Siegwald, then perhaps the dynasty of the Wuffingas would have survived.' She looked expectantly at me, but I could not fulfil her expectations: raking through my memory, I found no entry under 'Siegwald'. I shook my head.

'You don't recall? No matter. I am not surprised, for it comes under the category of legend and not fact, if that term is not a misnomer when applied to the Dark Ages.'

I'd thought she was about to tell me the legend. But the silence extended, and I realized she wasn't. Why not? We had sat here, either side of the kitchen table, for evenings without number, and gradually over the years the great volume of stories and fables that she carried in her head had been transferred to mine.

So what was different about this one?

She got up and poured herself another cup of tea. 'I think I shall go upstairs,' she said. 'I am rather tired.'

'What about your supper?'

She smiled. 'You have my share. I'm sure you'll manage it.'

There was no doubt about that – I was ravenous. But also a bit concerned. 'Are you all right?'

Her smile deepened. 'Yes, Henry. I am.'

She went towards the door, carrying her

replenished cup. I was about to say goodnight, when, her hand on the doorknob, she stopped.

She turned to me, and the weariness in her face had been replaced by a different expression. In the instant that her eyes met mine, she looked, surprisingly, *eager*. Then her face straightened and she said off-handedly, 'You might look up the legend of Siegwald, if you've nothing better to do.'

Then the door closed behind her and I heard her footsteps going away down the hall.

I helped myself to a huge plate of casserole and two baked potatoes, and another can of beer to help it down. I was intrigued about Siegwald, certainly, but I was a growing lad, as Florence would say when I had thirds of Sunday lunch, still at an age when the appetite for food is usually stronger than the thirst for knowledge.

When I'd finished, I took a cup of coffee through to the drawing room and prowled up and down the ranks of books. Florence's categorizing system was straight-forward, and I knew from long experience where to find the section on the Anglo-Saxons. The trouble was that this was the area of history in which she was most interested, so that there were far more books in this section than in all the others put together. Where was I going to find the story – no, it wasn't even a story, it was a legend – of a misty, almost-forgotten figure who, I found when I opened the first book, didn't even figure in the genealogical table?

I worked along the top shelf and started on the second. And, in a small book with marbled paper, its tan leather cover cracked and smelling of camphor, I found in the index, 'Siegwald'. There were two entries: 'possible illegitimate son of King Raedwald' and 'legend of the Cunning Man and the infant'.

I'd found him.

The little book had been written in 1884, and the writer had obviously been aware of the publishing strictures of the day. He had a passionate story to tell, it was clear, and it must, I thought, have been intensely frustrating not to have been able to give it its head. He was dealing with raw human emotions, with lust, with sexual desire so strong that it overrode sense and reason, with deception and betrayal of the basest sort, yet he had to content himself with phrases such as, 'The young prince was filled with longing for the beautiful wife of his cousin.'

Yet somehow this unknown writer – his name was P. L. Middleton, and I have never come across him anywhere else – had managed to get the passion across. Reading between the lines, this is the story he told:

Siegwald was a bastard son of Raedwald. His father, however, acknowledged him, for these were violent times and a king couldn't have too many sons (of his legitimate issue, three sons were killed in the space of nineteen years, only one of them in battle). Siegwald lived within the circles of the king's court at Rendlesham; it was there that he met his cousin Egenhere, already an old man by the standards of the day, and his cousin's young wife. She was called Althicca, a name which suggested strongly to P. L. Middleton that she was of native British stock and not one of the Saxon or Scandinavian 'newcomers'.

Siegwald fell deeply in love with her, and it was the sort of attraction that is all-consuming and will not allow the poor miserable sufferer any relief until the object of his desire has been won. But, according to P. L. Middleton, Althicca was a devout woman and a dutiful wife, and she made it clear that she did not reciprocate his feelings. In his desperation, Siegwald sought the help of a 'cunning man'.

I was surprised to find the term used of someone who had lived in the seventh century. But I knew what it meant: cunning men were a sort of male equivalent of wise women, and they still existed within living memory in our part of England. But they had long since been stripped of the greater powers which once had been attributed to them.

Powers, some said, almost approaching wizardry.

Siegwald begged the Cunning Man to give him a night with Althicca. The wizard, reading right the flame in the younger man which would not let him rest, went into a trance to divine whether or not the request should be granted. And what he saw in his trance left him in no doubt: visibly shaken, he told Siegwald he should have what he wished, adding in a strange tone, 'For thy work this night shall future children laud thee.'

Whatever glimpse he had seen of the future, he would not divulge, saying merely to Siegwald, 'Thou shalt have thy way with the woman. But give me thy word that when I ask for payment, thou shalt yield it. Whatever it is that I ask.'

Siegwald can't have been well-up in the ways of wizards. Or perhaps he could bear his hunger no longer. Whichever it was, he agreed without condition to the Cunning Man's terms.

The wizard manufactured a distant emergency requiring the presence of the king and his advisors, one of whom was Egenhere, and when the king's party had departed and night fell, he created an aura to fall around the head of Siegwald so that, in the dim light of a Saxon bedchamber, he might be mistaken by Althicca for her husband.

It was here that P. L. Middleton must have kicked against the obscenity laws of the late nineteenth century most forcefully. What he would have liked to ask, I'm quite sure, was, how the hell could Althicca have been fooled? I was certainly asking it, for here we had a faithful and demure wife, married for several years, believing that the wild, lustful, firm-fleshed and overwhelmingly passionate body that was pounding away at hers that night was none other than her elderly husband's.

What on earth did she think had got into him?

It just wasn't credible. All I could conclude was that the wizard had put a spell on her, too. And that I damned well hoped she'd enjoyed it, that some of the lust which rode Siegwald like a sharp spur had infected her, too.

And that the memory of it had helped in the morning when, his magic aura gone, she discovered who it was that lay beside her.

Mortals should not deal with cunning men. The wizard, his scheme going exactly to plan, fuelled the rage and jealousy in Egenhere's heart so that, on discovering his wife's infidelity, he persuaded the king to banish Siegwald and put Althicca away in a cell deep in the Fens. Siegwald, not knowing where she was, for months threw himself into battle in the desperate hope that it would take his mind off his agony. But it was no state of mind for a fighting man, and he suffered a serious wound to his leg. Making his way back across the Fens towards Rendlesham – for surely the king would overrule Egenhere and allow a wounded hero to come home? – he came across Althicca's prison.

He saw instantly that she was heavily pregnant, and the shock of having him appear in front of her very eyes made her go into premature labour. So Siegwald witnessed the birth of his son, on a bed of rushes in a cold stone cell, brought into the world with the aid of a grumpy old woman.

And a wizard: the Cunning Man materialized in the doorway just as the baby took its first cry, and it was he who cut the cord and who held the child up to the light of the sun.

'I claim my payment,' he said to Siegwald, who, bemused from the various shocks he had received in quick succession, didn't understand. 'Thou gavest me thy word,' the wizard reminded him. 'For a night with the woman, thou wouldst give me whatever I asked. I demand the child.'

Althicca, still dazed with pain and weak from loss of blood, shot up, gave one great cry of protest, and then fell lifeless back to the floor. Perhaps death was preferable to what she had just heard proposed.

Siegwald caught the wizard by the arm, getting in his way as he bundled the baby up in his cloak and prepared to depart. He stumbled outside after him, but, hampered as he was by the wound in his leg, the swift figure of the footsure Cunning Man soon left him far behind. Hurrying as best he could back to the cell for his horse, he plunged once more into the maze of willow-lined tracks that crisscrossed the Fens.

And was never seen again.

P. L. Middleton ended his account of the legend of Siegwald with the following cryptic comment:

'The legitimate line of the House of Wuffa died out with the murder of King Edmund by the Vikings in 869.'

I was tired when I went to bed. It had been a long day, and I'd further lengthened it with the time I'd spent looking for and reading the story of Siegwald. I'd expected to fall asleep quickly. But I didn't.

Something right at the edge of my mind was claiming my attention. Something about Florence, and her

79

choice of our day's destination – 'There is something I wish you to see' – was niggling at me, absorbing more and more of my brain like a puzzle I knew I could solve if only I could bring myself to try. Then when we'd got back she'd pointed me towards Siegwald knowing, as surely she must have done, that I would take her 'You might look up the legend, if you've nothing better to do,' as the direct instruction it was.

Siegwald and the illegitimate child. Taken away by the Cunning Man, so that when mankind thought he had seen the last of the Wuffingas, a hidden bloodline went on perpetuating itself in the loneliness of the Fens. What had happened to the child? Its mother was dead, its father had tried to follow its abductor but failed. Did the Cunning Man know about babies? Did he . . .

Suddenly I saw Siegwald, lying on the black ground, blood on his thigh. And remembered a dream of childhood when I'd identified so strongly with the pain of a wounded warrior that it had woken me up in panic.

I'd had that dream because Florence had told me a story. Now, in a roundabout way, she'd brought the same story to my attention again.

And I didn't know why.

Sleep now seemed as unreachable as Jupiter, so I turned over on my back, linked my hands behind my head and addressed the problem from a different angle. Florence had told me about Siegwald – even though I couldn't remember her referring to him by name, he was without a doubt her 'prince without a crown who lost the thing he most loved' – on a trip to Rendlesham, where the Wuffingas had their court. An illegitimate son with no wealth and no prospects, he'd have been pretty insignificant, of value only as one more fighting man. Until he fell for his cousin's wife, and wove another thread into history's complex tapestry.

Probably as a result of being seventeen, and as horny as the next seventeen-year-old male (at least in the privacy of my own bed), my mind soon forsook grandiose thoughts about history's tapestry and honed in on Siegwald having the hots for Althicca.

It was unsurprising, really, that I dreamed of her. Dreamed, anyway, of a beautiful veiled woman whose forbidden body under the enveloping gown beckoned me irresistibly. I saw myself in bed with her, making love to her. Or maybe it wasn't me – for I didn't know how, then – but someone else whose body I had temporarily invaded. In one of those crystal-clear moments of dream that you don't forget, I gazed down into her eyes and, seeing her love for me, hated myself for my betrayal of her which I knew was to come and she did not. I was loving her, with my body, my heart and my mind, yet I was to bring about her death. And there was no guarantee she'd understand it wasn't my fault.

I woke sweating, the sheets wet.

It was a long time before I slept again.

Seven

In the October of my upper sixth year, my parents came home for a visit. They'd been before, of course, arriving at Florence's house to stay for a week or so just as they used to do when I belonged to their part of the family. Finding that I had very little to say to them and, furthermore, that I felt awkward and tongue-tied in their company, I used to spend as much time as I could out of the house. They must have been as relieved as I was that we didn't have to spend too long together, for they never protested when I got up from the lunch table with a very unsubtle look at my watch and said, 'Goodness! Is that the time? Please excuse me, but I must hurry if I'm not going to be late.'

They never asked what I wasn't going to be late for, and I never told them.

Florence, as always, understood and kept her peace.

This visit, though, was different. For one thing, they were coming for a month; it was going to be impossible to pretend I was rushing off to unspecified appointments every time we met. For another thing, they were at something of a crossroads in their life, and it soon became apparent that Florence and I were required to offer our opinion as to what they should do.

My father was fifty-five, and in the company in which he worked, it was the policy to retire men early if they had served abroad for most of their working life. The decision facing my parents was, simply, whether to come home for their retirement or to stay out in Hong Kong (the company had opened a main office out there shortly after I came home to Florence, and my father had worked there ever since, travels to other places in the Far East now reduced to short business trips or holidays with my mother). My mother, quite clearly, was for staying in Hong Kong. My father, although he loved the life there as much as she did, seemed to have some lingering dream of returning to England and buying a pretty cottage in whose garden he could grow roses and prize marrows, and from whose little wicket gate it would be but a short step down to a friendly pub where there were log fires in winter and lots of jolly locals waiting with bated breath to hear his Far Eastern equivalent of *Tales from the Raj*.

Florence and I exchanged a glance over the dinner table when he had just divulged to us this unlikely ambition. I knew exactly what she was thinking. Confidently, I left it to her to disillusion him.

'What a wonderful idea, Richard,' she said warmly. 'And your decision is timely, for although the trend in England for some years now has been to buy picturesque old places and "do them up", as they call it, there are still many such cottages left on the market. Unfortunately –' she glanced at my mother, who was mutinously stabbing at a roast potato as if she wished it were my father's head '– the houses which are still available tend to be the most primitive. You know, dear,' she patted my mother's hand, 'the ones which are situated miles off the main road down muddy lanes, with cesspit drainage and faulty wiring. But these are minor setbacks, aren't they?' She gave my mother a brilliant smile, as if to say, you're not going to be daunted by cesspit drainage, are you, dear?

My mother said sarcastically, 'We've seen one or two like that. Richard seems to think they're the most desirable ones.'

'Amanda, you're exaggerating.' He sounded as if he was repeating a remark he'd made dozens of times before. I was sure he had. 'There was just that one in Oxfordshire which I particularly liked. I grant you it didn't have . . .'

'It didn't have *anything!*' she exploded. 'Sweet FA in the way of amenities – no gas, no mains drainage, not even a *hint* of heating, central or otherwise, and there were *mice!*' On the last word her voice rose to an extremely mouselike squeak. I wanted to applaud. Perhaps she'd been a mouse in the latest Am Dram production.

'All old houses have mice,' Florence remarked. 'We have them, don't we, Henry?' I nodded.

My mother paled. She was looking round anxiously along the skirting-boards as if expecting to see a battalion of mice in the shadows, waiting only for us to finish our meal before pouncing on our left-overs with scratchy little claws and greedy nibbling mouths. 'What do you do about them?' she asked faintly.

'Nothing.' Florence was still smiling, but I heard the steel enter her voice. 'We ensure that they cannot get at the food nor pollute the kitchen work surfaces, but other than that we leave them to their own devices. Henry and I do not believe in killing things.'

'What about flies?' my mother asked.

'Netting over the pantry windows.'

'Cockroaches?' My mother had a horror of cockroaches, and her screams at finding them in the Hong Kong flat had been known to shatter glass.

'Keep a clean kitchen, and you're not troubled by them.'

My mother looked uncomfortable. As well she might – Ah Yen, I clearly recalled, had been slapdash around the kitchen, never mopping up spills and letting the rubbish bin overflow so that there were always rich pickings for the cockroach fraternity. And I couldn't imagine that my mother's standards were any higher than Ah Yen's since she never voluntarily entered a kitchen, and when she did it was more likely to be to get another cold tonic out of the fridge than to roll up her sleeves and start scrubbing the floor.

'I suppose you're a Buddhist, or something,' my mother said rudely. '*They* go on about life being sacred.' She sounded as if such a view were not only incomprehensible but also slightly risible.

There was a silence. My father looked uncomfortable, and my mother, sensing eventually the frosty blast of Florence's disapproval, gave a foolish laugh. 'I *mean* . . .' she began.

Florence said quietly, 'Life is sacred.' Then she stood up and began to collect our plates. I went to hold the door for her as she swept out.

Even though she was carrying a pile of dirty plates, I didn't think I'd ever seen her look more majestic.

The debate went on in a desultory way for several days. My parents were sent thick wads of property details from estate agents dotted all over the southern half of England – my mother wouldn't even contemplate living north of a line joining Norwich and

Birmingham, and Wales and Scotland might not have existed – and they set off on one or two viewing trips.

But the damage had been done. The rot had set in when Florence mentioned the mice, and now that my mother had been put on the downward path, it was easy to press home the advantage with apparently innocent remarks about burst pipes when one was miles from a plumber, lanes so muddy in winter as to be impassable, rising damp, dry rot, bats in the attic and, of course, the perpetual trump card of the cesspit.

I began to feel quite sorry for my father. Especially the day they came home from a three-day trip to Sussex, where they'd viewed, amongst a dozen other properties, a particularly attractive sixteenth-century cottage with late roses still blooming in its garden and, probably, a few prize marrows in the vegetable patch.

They'd stayed in the jolly pub just down the road.

My father had clearly fallen in love with the place, and from my mother's look of fury tinged with desperation, it seemed likely she'd been trying to talk him out of this wild infatuation all the way home.

'Florence, can't you make him see sense?' she asked in a weary voice as she lay back, eyes closed, on the sofa, a huge gin and tonic in her hand. My father was out of the room – under the influence of his new-found love, he'd bought himself a tweed hat and had gone upstairs to look at himself in the big mirror in the spare room.

Florence said, quite kindly, 'Amanda, I've never been the sort of person who made her children see sense. Not in the way you mean, which I believe equates with making him see the way you want him to.'

My mother had the grace to look slightly ashamed. Only slightly. Then, 'But he'd hate it!' she burst out histrionically. 'It's all very well seeing the place on a sunny day when it's at its best. But what about winter? Being snowed-in? Having to make conversation with those ghastly country people who never go up to town, never go to the West End, never see shows or go to concerts, never even read, for all I know, and whose main interests in life are church fêtes and *walking!*'

It struck me that Florence and I had missed a clincher even more effective than the good old cesspit: we should have emphasized how everyone in the country walked, for it was the one thing my mother would never, under any circumstances, do. To start with, she always wore very high heels (she was short, and all her life had wanted longer legs), attached to shoes so impractical that she crippled herself after ten tottering paces. For another thing, she seemed to think there was something demeaning about moving along on her own two feet rather than under the power of the internal combustion engine, and even for the shortest distance, would have my father get the car out to drive her.

I wondered, silently blessing them, which of the people she'd met in Sussex had let drop the crucial role of walking in the life of everyone who lives in the country.

I thought it was time I made a comment. 'You could get yourself a nice pair of hiking boots,' I suggested.

That day, she was wearing a two-piece in a sort of mauvy angora wool. It looked very nice on her, but was hardly the sort of outfit to be enhanced by a pair of boots. She looked at me witheringly. 'Oh, do shut up, Henry!'

I did. Listening to her grumbling on, I heard the

echo of her cross retort in my head. She had further refined her speech in the years since I'd lived with her, and now my name came out as if it had a lot more vowels in it: Hienerieh.

That night she went to bed before supper with one of her heads. The next day she wouldn't get up at all. My poor father, obviously feeling ashamed of having a fifty-three-year-old wife behaving like a child of eight, made rather feeble apologies for her. He said she had a migraine, and Florence, knowing the truth as well as he did, tiptoed up to the room where my mother was pretending to be asleep and drew the curtains. They were thick velvet, lined with an extra insulating layer, and when drawn, as effective as the blackout. Unless she got up and drew them back, which would undermine the migraine story, my mother wouldn't even be able to while away the hours of her self-imposed solitude by reading.

I took my dad out for a ride in Florence's car. We didn't go anywhere special, just here and there. We stopped for a pub lunch, and later went for a walk around Wicken Fen. He wore his tweed hat all day.

As we went back to the car, he said sadly, 'I'm afraid we won't be living in England, Henry old chap.'

Quite a large part of me felt sorry. We'd had a great day. I knew why they weren't going to stay, but I thought perhaps I shouldn't let on. I said lamely, 'Oh, dear.'

'I can't do it to your mother,' he burst out miserably. 'She's so sensitive, you know, Henry, and the thought of her having these attacks of hers every time there's some sort of rural crisis is – well, it's more than I can stand.'

I quite agreed with him. It would have made me furious, too.

But that can't have been the emotion he meant, because he went on to say pathetically, 'I can't bear to see her in pain, you see.' In pain! I wanted to say, she's not! The only pain she's suffering is possibly in her hands, from the effort of winding you round her little finger.

But I didn't. I didn't speak at all, because he added, very tenderly, 'I love her so much.'

They say, probably quite rightly, never come between man and wife. I suppose it applies even if the man and wife in question are your own parents. It wasn't easy, but I kept my mouth shut.

Later, when I'd calmed down, I thought about it again and I saw that, in her fashion, she loved him too. As long as she got her own way, she was as sweet and affectionate as a starry-eyed teenager. And she was right – he wouldn't have been happy in his lovely Sussex cottage once the novelty had worn off. Like her, he'd been an expatriate too long. He'd have missed the frivolous society, the parties, the drinkie-poos, the long afternoons of poolside barbecues, the luxury existence, even the Am Dram, God help us, quite as much as she would.

And he looked absolutely frightful in his tweed hat.

They took Florence and me out to dinner the night before they flew back to Hong Kong. We went to a restaurant in Trumpington, and, because for our various reasons we were all as happy as sandboys, we were dressed up in our best and feeling very festive.

I watched my parents as, heads together, they pored over a shared menu. They could have had one each, but my father had his arm round my mother's shoulders and she was clutching his wrist, so that they each had only one free hand. He whispered something in her ear, and she giggled, blushed slightly and whispered something back, pressing a tender kiss to his cheek as she did so. It wasn't difficult to conclude that the exchange had had something to do with what they were going to do when we'd all retired to bed that night.

They looked like newlyweds.

Feeling that it was verging on voyeurism to watch them, I turned to Florence and asked her if she fancied meat or fish for her main course.

Over coffee my mother asked me – belatedly, as everything had been decided with the firmness of twelve feet of set concrete – if I was sure I was happy about them returning to the Far East.

'Of course!' Perhaps that was a bit heartless. 'I mean, I shall miss you, Mother, but I can't be as selfish as to let my feelings stand in the way of what's so obviously the best thing for both of you.' I wondered if that was laying it on a bit thick – she gave me quite a strange look. But my father, bless his simple heart, exclaimed, 'Well said, old man. Have another brandy.'

Florence had agreed to make an exception to her no-more-driving rule and chauffeur us home, so I did. We had a couple more after that, too, and we were both more than merry by the time we got back. Florence sensibly said a quick goodnight and left us to it, but my mother was inclined to linger, draping herself round my father and standing on tiptoe to kiss him. It seemed to sober him up remarkably swiftly. I heard him say, 'Give me a few minutes with the boy, darling, then I'll be up,' to which she replied something I didn't catch, which was just as well as it made him give a low-pitched laugh in his throat.

I had made myself scarce and gone into the kitchen for a beer. He came in after me, closing the door behind him.

'I just wanted to say, old man, that we – I –' He stopped. 'What I mean is – Oh, bugger it.' He lurched across the room and, very awkwardly, put his arms round me.

I was amazed. He hadn't hugged me since I was nine. I was moved, and for a moment the finality of him going off to settle for ever more thousands of miles away struck me as forcefully as it was obviously striking him.

After a while I pushed him away – gently – and got a second beer out of the fridge.

'No, not for me, thanks, I – er – I –' He glanced over his shoulder, and I remembered his assignation upstairs.

'Sorry.' I grinned at him, and he grinned back.

'Women!' he said indulgently.

We stood for a few moments longer, neither of us knowing what to do next. Then together we spoke, I to say, 'Well, I mustn't keep you,' he to say, 'We're always there, you know, for anything.'

And, also together, we both said, 'Okay.'

Then he turned and walked quickly out of the room, leaving me to my beer, my thoughts and, I must admit, not a few regrets.

Eight

After Christmas that year, I settled down to the business of 'A' levels. In earnest: in the course of my lower sixth year, my teachers had suggested that, with a really determined effort, I might get into Cambridge. I had been in two minds as to whether Cambridge was worth a determined effort – I knew quite well what they meant by that, and I could see myself with no time to call my own for months on end – when Florence happened to mention that her husband had been a Cambridge man.

I knew very little about my grandfather. His photograph stood in a costly leather frame on Florence's bedside table, but I'd always found it hard to reconcile the young handsome man in army uniform with my elderly grandmother. Perhaps it would have been easier had there been a photograph of the young Florence beside him, but she wasn't the sort of woman to have pictures of herself about the place. Soon after I came to live with her, I had asked about him – I'd been ill with a cold that went to my chest, and on one or two bad nights had been permitted the luxury of crawling into her tall, wide bed with her – and she told me he had been a soldier in the Great War.

Typical of her, she hadn't boasted about just what sort of soldier he had been. I'd discovered that for myself, rooting about in old albums and scrapbooks one rainy afternoon. Lieutenant Henry Woolgar – childishly egotistic, no doubt my interest in him was fuelled by his having the same name as me – had gone out to France in 1915 and survived in the trenches for over eighteen months, gaining promotion to captain in the process. He had been killed in July 1917 on the first day of the third battle of Ypres, commonly known, as it said in the history book, as Passchendaele.

In a little box at the back of the drawer of scrapbooks was a medal on a crimson ribbon. On the medal was his name and the words 'For Valour': my grandfather had been awarded the VC.

I asked Florence how he'd won it, not understanding then that since the VC was only awarded when there had been an overriding danger of death, the action was probably the one which had taken his life. She said, with neither pride nor sorrow discernible in her voice, that he had saved several of his men by destroying a German machine gun. It was years later that I discovered the full story: Florence and her husband were married in the spring of 1916, when he was home on leave, and their only son – my father – was not quite four months old when my grandfather's outstanding bravery had widowed his wife and robbed his son of a father.

When I was in my twenties, I went to Ypres and saw my grandfather's name inscribed among the tens of thousands on the Menen Gate. I wasn't the only grown man with tears on his face when the buglers of the Ypres Fire Brigade stopped the traffic and played, as they do every evening at eight o'clock, the 'Last Post'.

This unknown hero, then, this forefather with my

name, had been a Cambridge man. Clever Florence, to drop the information so casually into our conversation at just the right moment. Throughout the rest of my lower sixth year I worked as I'd never done before, or since, with the happy result that I was invited to my grandfather's old college for an interview and, in the following autumn term, took the Cambridge entrance exam. They must have liked what the interview and my exam performance had told them about me – or perhaps it was the good old Woolgar name – because I was informed that, as long as I gained three reasonable 'A' level passes, a Cambridge place would be mine.

My eighteenth birthday fell in August, but Florence and I decided to postpone our celebrations until we knew one way or the other about 'A' levels and Cambridge. It would only, we reasoned, be a matter of a week or so. I wasn't as confident as Florence, and I didn't think I could cope with the party we were proposing to throw with my future in the balance.

On the day of my birthday, Florence and I went out to dinner in Cambridge. I can't remember what we ate, nor what we talked about over the meal, all such minor matters having been driven irrevocably from my head by what she told me over coffee.

It was a strange place for such a revelation. A pleasant, discreet restaurant, with pleasant, discreet middle-aged-to-elderly couples and parties forming its clientele. Perhaps that was why she chose it, knowing that, brought up in her traditions, I would know better than to react to what she was going to tell me in such a way as to put our fellow diners off their food.

Over the quiet hum of conversation, she said to me

after we had toasted each other with our brandies, 'Do you recall the story of Siegwald? We mentioned him that day we went to Bury St Edmunds.'

'Yes. He fell for his cousin's wife and was unwise enough to get a cunning man to assist him into her –' I'd been going to say, into her underwear, the birthday mood having gone to my head, but stopped myself '– into her bed.'

I smiled at Florence. But for once she didn't respond: her face wore a watchful, anxious expression, like someone straining to catch a distant sound. 'Florence?'

She smiled then, a quick movement as if she were impatient to get back to whatever it was that was preoccupying her. 'Yes, yes. That was he. And you also recall, I am sure, what became of the child born of Siegwald and Althicca's union.'

Althicca. I'd been trying to remember the name. Since it wasn't the most memorable of names, I hadn't been successful. 'The Cunning Man took it,' I said.

'Him. The child was a boy.'

One of those weird silences fell, as if all the people in the room, diners and staff alike, were holding their breath. Then it was gone, filled by the normal sounds of convivial talk and the clatter of cutlery on china.

'Oh.' I tried to observe her without making it obvious that I was doing so. She wasn't herself, and I was wondering why not.

'Did you ever ask yourself why the Cunning Man should want the child?' She was leaning forward, and her eyes seemed to bore into mine.

'Er –' I thought rapidly. 'To punish them?'

She gave a scornful sound. 'Nonsense! He wouldn't have cared a fig for the morals of the matter. Come on, now – think who Siegwald was!'

'The illegitimate son of the king.'

'Yes. And what became of the king's line?'

I remembered King Edmund, last of the Wuffingas. 'It finished with Edmund.' Although it was more than a year ago, I saw again those words in the little leather-bound book: 'The legitimate line of the House of Wuffa died out with the murder of King Edmund by the Vikings in 869.'

The legitimate line. I began to see what she was driving at.

'The Cunning Man knew!' I said. 'He knew what was going to happen in the future!' Suddenly another memory flashed into my mind, of something Florence had said that day we'd stood together over the last known resting place of King Edmund. She'd suggested that had King Edmund followed Siegwald's example, the line wouldn't have died out. 'You said that day that Edmund should have done what Siegwald did. You meant, didn't you, he should have left an illegitimate son that nobody knew about.'

A smile of satisfaction lit her face. 'Yes. But I only said it to get you thinking along the right lines. For one thing, King Edmund was a devout Christian, not the sort of man to conduct illicit affairs. For another –' She paused. Her eyes on me were becoming uncomfortable to bear. 'For another, there was no need for a second secret heir of the blood.'

'Because one already existed. The son of Siegwald.'

'Yes.'

For some moments, the pleasure of solving the riddle she'd posed me filled my thoughts. But then I began to wonder why it mattered. 'I don't see –' I began.

Imperiously she waved her hand for silence. 'Never mind that now. The time will come, but it is not yet.

A more important question for your consideration is, what is your view of the Cunning Man's action?'

I was used to this sort of thing. Often over the homework years we'd talked that way, she stimulating me to think about such things as, what can Cromwell have thought when he saw King Charles's head fall from his body, or, was Lincoln right to award a higher importance to the union of the States than to the emancipation of the slaves? I said, 'If he had foreknowledge that the House of Wuffa was doomed, then yes, of course he was right.'

'And you think that the end justified the means?'

I wasn't sure what she meant. 'What means?'

'Taking a child from his natural parents to be brought up by another.'

It didn't bother me one way or the other. They were dim figures lost long ago in the concealing mists of the past, their emotions no concern of mine. So I just said, 'Yes, I suppose so.'

But she obviously wasn't satisfied. As if she wanted to be absolutely sure, she said carefully, 'And we may perhaps extrapolate from that, may we, that the rights of the child are only of secondary importance?'

'*I* don't know!' It was rapidly getting too heavy for a birthday dinner. Impatiently I frowned at her, on the verge of suggesting we drop it and talk about something else. But her compelling grey eyes held mine, and I found I had no choice but to think up an answer. 'If he was important, if he carried the only chance of his line's survival, then yes, what he wanted had to have less weight.'

She leant back in her seat and for the first time in what seemed like hours, looked away from me. She closed her eyes. Fleetingly she seemed to be overcome, as if a desperate prayer had been answered.

While the spotlight was off me, I took a large slug of brandy.

When, after some time, she spoke again, her voice was low and slightly husky. 'Henry, you will be wondering why on earth I am dragging all this up and what possible relevance it has to your birthday. Believe me, it is of the most imperative relevance.' She reached out and touched my hand, a brief contact of her fingers. They were ice-cold. I looked down at her old hand, brown-spotted, and automatically I covered it with my other hand. But she said, 'Look at me.'

I raised my eyes. Hers were bright, as if she had a fever. And she said, 'I engineered your conception. Like the Cunning Man, I made sure that you would be born. Having done so, the next logical step was, as the Cunning Man's was, to remove from his parents' care the child I had brought about and bring him up myself. So I did that, too.'

My brain seemed to shut down. For a frightening instant I lost the ability to think. Absurdly, I found myself listening to a conversation at the next table: '. . . can't imagine why she'd want to do that, what with him being out playing golf all day. Perhaps we'd better ask Ivy instead.'

Then, painfully, I came back to life. Heart pounding, I said quietly to Florence in a voice that sounded far steadier than it had any right to, 'I think you'd better explain.'

She drained her brandy, then reached for the coffee pot to pour herself another cup. It was indicative of her mental state that she forgot to ask me if I'd like more too. 'You are quite right,' she said humbly. Then she folded her hands in her lap and, eyes cast down, started to say her piece. That was what it sounded like: as if she were performing something she'd rehearsed many, many times.

I sat and listened.

'Your father was not an easy child,' she began. 'Not for me, anyway. I was at fault, I know, for I expected him to be like his father, and it was not fair to be disappointed when he failed to do anything in the least heroic. Perhaps I was too strong a mother. I don't know.' She shook her head, as if dismissing my father and his failings. 'Then he announced he was to marry, and brought home Amanda.' She snorted, and I couldn't tell if it was laughter or disgust. Perhaps it was both. 'He had associated with some unsuitable girls, but Amanda was the worst of all.'

Should I remind her, I mused, that we are speaking of my mother? I decided I shouldn't.

'Amanda was a good-time girl,' she continued, 'flighty, vain, head packed with nonsense, quite unable to produce a genuine emotion from her shallow little heart. I knew straight away what sort of a life she would lead Richard into – poor, indecisive Richard, who never had an idea for himself if someone else would have it for him – and I was almost certain, too, that she would encourage him to go abroad. Her parents had lived abroad throughout her girlhood,' she explained, as if I didn't know it as well as she did, 'and I imagine Amanda developed a taste for being a big fish in a small pond.'

It was uncanny that she spoke of my parents as if they no longer existed.

'But what choice had I?' She lifted her head and her eyes met mine. 'I loved my son, I wanted him to be happy, and, for all that I disliked her, Amanda seemed to make him so. All I could do was watch as it all came about. Marriage, discontent with home, desire for pastures new, departure. And, as I had foreseen from a woman of such monumental self-centredness and frivolity, a firm desire to remain childless.'

I was beginning to dread what she was going to say next.

'They were home on leave one winter,' she said, her voice dropping to a discreet murmur. 'They had come back for Christmas, arriving at the beginning of December so that Amanda would have plenty of time for shopping. Her chief desire was, I recall, to find an emerald green velvet frock with feathers decorating its bodice.' I smiled – I couldn't help it – because to be going so singlemindedly after such a detailed, specific item was typical of my mother, and I knew quite well she'd have gone to every last shop in London until she found exactly what she wanted.

Florence stared at me, eyes anguished. 'She was thirty-five, Henry! Richard was thirty-seven, although that is not as pertinent. But they were more and more set in their ways every time I saw them! What could I do?'

There was no way I could answer her appeal.

'Amanda was not a discreet guest,' she said, mouth twitching slightly. 'She would leave soiled underwear in the bathroom, and certain feminine arrangements were not put away in the drawer as they should have been.' I knew what she meant: I'd been embarrassed myself once or twice when they'd come to stay by my mother's habit of leaving big boxes of Tampax spilling their contents on the bathroom shelf. 'Her diaphragm, too, was often left, after washing, to dry on the edge of the guest room basin.'

I was being embarrassed now. Hugely so. But Florence was oblivious to my discomfort.

'I was aware of the frequency with which they made love,' she stated baldly. 'It would have been difficult not to be.' She smiled wryly. 'I was upstairs one day when they were out. There was a lino tile in the bathroom which had curled at the edge, and I was going to cut off the piece that stood up before someone tripped on it. I had a Stanley knife in my hand.' She hesitated. Some things, apparently, were difficult for even Florence to say. 'The door of their room was open, and Amanda's diaphragm was on the ledge over the basin. I went in and made a tiny slit in it.'

And my mother hadn't noticed, if she'd noticed at all, until it was too late. It was quite something, to sit there in a Cambridge restaurant and be told I was on this earth as a result of a split-second's work with a Stanley knife. I honestly didn't know whether to laugh or cry.

After a while I said, 'I suppose, then, I have to thank you.'

I'd meant it as a joke – I'd decided I was going to laugh, since it was after all my birthday and I was feeling lightheaded – but she didn't take it that way.

'Do you?' she asked earnestly. 'Do you really want to thank me?'

'I wouldn't be here if it weren't for you.'

But she had gone beyond that. 'I took an audacious step.' She looked stricken. 'Didn't I? I interfered most appallingly in the life of two other people – three, counting the life in which my interference resulted – and, not content with that, as soon as it became possible, I brought you home to me.'

I'd been going to argue with that when she'd dropped it in earlier. 'No you didn't. That was my decision. I'd been battling with them for ages before they gave in and said I could come and live with you.'

Her hand crept across the table to hold mine. She didn't feel quite so cold, now.

'I know.' Before I could ask her how she knew, she went on, 'But I can assure you that I wanted it every bit as much as you did. I had suggested it discreetly to your father, once or twice, so when you began your campaign, the idea cannot have been new to him.'

That, now, that was a revelation. I'd fondly imagined all my life that I had achieved what I'd wanted entirely by my own efforts.

She understood. 'I'm sorry,' she said. Funny, that it was the only bit of the whole amazing thing that she apologized for. 'But at least you know now, if you had any doubts, how very much I wanted you.'

I don't think I had ever doubted that.

Suddenly I felt overwhelmingly tired. And there was still the drive home – I'd have to take it slowly. I said, 'Do you mind if we go now?'

Immediately she caught the waiter's eye, reaching for the chequebook in her handbag, my birthday dinner being her treat. She said meekly, 'Of course, Henry. Whatever you say.'

It was the only time in my whole life that I ever knew her meek.

For a few days I found I needed to be on my own a lot. She understood, letting me be, allowing me to sit in silence over our meals and, when the silence became awkward, responding pleasantly to my feeble attempts at conversation.

I thought it all through, many times. I concluded, with startling originality, that what was done, was done. She loved me, I knew that – had always known it – and I loved her. Between us we'd achieved the life together which we'd both wanted, and I for one had no complaints.

The ticklish matter of my conception was something I preferred not to dwell on, although I asked myself repeatedly why she'd done what she'd done. The best answer I could come up with – and it wasn't fully satisfying – was that she'd wanted to ensure the continuity of the Woolgar line. Perhaps, even, wanted to bring into the world a carbon copy of her late husband, the war hero. But supposing the child had been a girl?

In the end, other than accepting the incredible fact that were it not for Florence, the second Henry Richard Woolgar would not exist, I put it out of my mind.

Then relief and happiness replaced introspection; in the space of a day, two letters arrived and my future was decided. I was going up to Cambridge in October.

Now Florence and I could go ahead with planning my party. We made a list of everyone we could think of, and she sat by the phone for hours while I went out on forays for food and drink. A couple of friends and I rigged up some fairy lights in the garden, and Roger's sister's boyfriend brought along his record decks, speakers and a huge stack of records. We arranged rooms for sitting and talking, patios for dancing, long tables in the dining room for the refreshments, and the satisfying tally of acceptances grew.

The evening of the party was fine – someone up there loved us – and as the sunset painted the western sky in neon-orange, the first of the guests began arriving. I felt full of wellbeing and optimism, and I was moved at the warmth and obvious sincerity of people's congratulations, both on reaching eighteen and on my Cambridge place.

I raced through a hundred conversations, pointed throngs of people with empty plates and glasses towards the dining room, danced scores of pretty girls off their feet. Then, when the party was at its exuberant height and the noise must have been audible for miles around – we'd had the foresight to invite all the neighbours – Florence came out to find me on the dancefloor.

'Excuse me,' – she gave the girl I was dancing with a winning smile – 'sorry to butt in, but there's someone at the door.'

I might have asked her why she couldn't go and let them in, but my partner was inclined to drape herself round my neck and I wasn't as keen on the idea as she was. 'Okay.' I ushered the girl to a garden chair on the edge of the patio. 'Have a breather,' I advised her. 'Cool down a bit,' I added under my breath.

The house was relatively quiet after the dancefloor. As I crossed the empty hall, the door-knocker rattled again. It was a tentative sound, as if whoever it was didn't want to disturb us. As if they were unsure of their welcome.

I turned the knob and pulled open the door. 'Better late than never!' I said cheerfully.

In the silence that followed my trite remark, I just stood and stared at her. She had grown, of course. She was slim, and her hair was longer. In the light from the porch lamp, her eyes were still that midsummer-morning blue. And she didn't have a dog with her.

Not understanding, not caring why I was breathing fast, I put my arms round her and drew her to me in a hug. Then I said, 'Hello, Thea. Welcome home.'

PART TWO

Thea

Nine

Before I met Henry Woolgar, I already hated him. He was the boy who was going to take away my dog, and my dog was the only person in the whole world (except Florence) that I loved.

Eric wasn't my dog really. He was on a sort of permanent loan, because Florence said he was happier running wild with me than sitting at her feet waiting for her to entertain him. Although I didn't appreciate it then, that was typical of her – to have detected my need, and found a diplomatic way of filling it so that I ended up thinking I was doing her a favour rather than the other way round. Among all the other things she understood, she knew about children and their pride.

Especially children like me.

My parents split up when I was six, my father going back to live in the Gloucestershire town where he'd been brought up. I stayed with my mum in Cambridgeshire, but she soon found that bringing up a kid on her own was even worse than it had been with my dad around. She wasn't in the least domestic, preferring to study Tarot cards, or bone up on Indian mysticism, or sit sewing patchwork all day, depending on what the current craze was. She had various strange friends, most of them women but a couple of them ragged, hirsute men who wore beads and had smelly feet, and when any of the friends was around, she'd have even less time for me than she usually did. Because of her preoccupations with this, that and the other, she'd often forget to go shopping and she *always* forgot to do the washing. Looking back, sometimes it seems that my early childhood was one long succession of embarrassments. Having to wear a pair of my mum's lace-edged black French knickers to school because I hadn't a clean pair. Going to the village shop to buy something for tea, and discovering that the tiny amount of money in my mum's purse nowhere near covered the cost of a loaf, a pat of butter, a jar of jam and a pack of Bourbon biscuits (the man in the shop was kind, and said not to worry, he'd get the difference off Mum the next time she went in. But I heard his laughter echo in my head for days afterwards).

And the awful day when I brought Jennifer Morris home from school to play with Eric, and my mum was drunk.

I thought then that she was drunk, because it was the only explanation I knew of for her being giggly and red in the face, and draping herself affectionately round the bearded man with the dirty feet as if she needed his support to stand up. Not that he seemed any steadier on his legs than she did. There was a funny smell about them, and their eyes looked strange, the pupils widely dilated. With hindsight, I'm sure they weren't drunk: I think they were stoned. And Jennifer's and my unexpected arrival – not that it should have been unexpected, we'd talked about Jennifer coming to play that very morning and she said it'd be okay – had got them out of bed.

She *should* have remembered. I hardly ever brought anyone home with me, and Jennifer Morris was *important*.

Jennifer Morris took one look at my dishevelled, idiotically smiling mother, turned up her perfect little nose and said, 'I don't think I care to come to tea after all.'

As she stepped daintily away up the path, well-polished black bar shoes making a click-clack sound on the stone slabs of the crazy paving, my mum said blankly, 'Tea? Is someone coming to tea?'

The man flashed me a brief, guilty smile – I don't think he can have been as far gone as she was – and said, 'Sorry, lovie.' He gave my mum a nudge. 'Josie! Come on, girl!' he hissed at her.

But I don't think she heard. Her eyelids were drooping, and the idiotic smile was wavering. The man shook his head and helped her on to the sofa, putting a cushion under her head and tucking her long cotton skirt round her legs. Then, looking up at me, he said, 'Would you like me to make you some toast or something?'

I stared at him, then down at my comatose mother. I thought, damn you! Both of you! Jennifer Morris is tip-tapping her way home full of righteous indignation and a scandalous story which will be all over the school tomorrow! *And she'll never come again!*

I said furiously, 'No!' Then, because I could feel the tears starting and I didn't want him to see, I shouted, 'I hate you!' and, pulling the puzzled Eric with me, ran out of the house.

Jim – that was the man's name – became something of a permanent fixture. In some ways he was the worst person for my mum to introduce into our already haphazard household, because he smoked dope, he didn't appear to do a stroke of work of any kind, he played rock music at all times of the day and night (actually I loved that) and, as far as I could tell, his standards of personal hygiene left almost everything to be desired.

On the other hand, he was one of the gentlest people I've ever met, and, although his presence in my life meant that my mum neglected me even more than she'd done before, his sweet smile and his abstract kindness made up for a lot.

My mum was potty about him. The day he said he was thinking of splitting – that was what he said for leaving – and setting off for India was the most dreadful day of my life. My mum hit the roof. She shouted at him, called him ungrateful, a typical man, take, take, take till a woman had given all she had to give, then disappear and never look back. When she'd finished shouting, she started throwing things at him, then she began to cry. Well, it was wailing, really, uncontrolled sounds like an animal in pain that sent shivers down my spine, her mouth wide open and her poor swollen eyelids dripping great fat tears. When Jim could finally make himself heard, he said, 'Josie, I was going to suggest you came too! You don't think I could leave you, do you?' Then, at long last, she stopped, and I think I was nearly as relieved as she was.

It was only later, lying in my unmade bed in my draughty bedroom, that I began seriously to wonder what the hell she had in mind for me.

I got the answer in the morning. My mum and Jim looked tired, but calm and happy. Mum said offhandedly, 'Sorry about last night, Thea. Jim and I –' she flashed him a loving smile '– had a bit of a misunderstanding. I'm going off to do some travelling,' she hurried on before I could interrupt, 'and you're going to live with your dad for a while.'

'Dad?' I repeated stupidly.

'Yes! Don't say you've forgotten him!'

'In Gloucestershire?'

'Yes, of course. You'll love it!'

I wouldn't. I knew I wouldn't. Because, although I didn't know where Gloucestershire was, I knew where it wasn't. It wasn't just down the road from Eric.

It hurt so much I didn't know what to do. When Mum and Jim weren't looking, I crept out of the back door and did the only thing I could think of: I ran as fast as I could across the fields to Florence.

The very first day I met her, Florence took up her role of chief support in my life. It was soon after my dad left, and I suppose I was feeling a bit lost. I don't think I understood what had happened – I was only six, after all – but I missed him, and I remember being worried by my mother's vagueness over when I'd see him again.

I'd wandered off down the road, and for some time I'd been sitting on the gate under the willow tree. I liked the willow tree, and I used to pretend I could see little green-clad people living in its foliage, using the down-sweeping branches to swing on. Then I jumped down off the gate and walked along by the dyke. At the far end of the path was a bridge, and on the bridge stood an old lady with a young golden-coloured dog on a lead.

The woman was busy with the dog – she was saying, 'Sit!' over and over, very patiently, and when the dog did as she said without her having to push his rump down, she'd give him a pat. When she looked up and saw me, at first she frowned, and I thought she was cross with me for disturbing the lesson.

'Sorry,' I said.

The frown lifted, and she said kindly, 'What for?'

'I thought – I don't suppose I'm meant to be here, am I?'

'You have as much right as anybody,' she said. Then, studying me, she went on, 'But you are rather young to be out alone. That was why I looked angry. It is I who should be saying sorry.'

I couldn't believe it – a grown-up noticing a kid's reaction like that, then *apologizing!* I didn't know what to say.

The lady said, 'You're the child from the cottage over there, aren't you?' She nodded in the direction of my house.

'Yes.'

'Josephine Madingly's daughter.'

'Yes.' It didn't occur to me to wonder how she knew; when you're a child you seem to accept quite readily that adults are all-knowing and all-seeing.

'I'm Florence Woolgar.' She held out her hand and I put mine out to shake it. 'This is Eric,'she patted the golden dog, 'he belongs to my grandson Henry, but Henry has had to return to Hong Kong with his parents, so I'm looking after Eric.'

I patted him as well. His coat was warm, and I could feel the smooth, strong muscles under the skin. He felt as if he were all bunched up and eager to go.

'He's lovely,' I said. 'Where's Hong Kong?' I was hoping it was a long way away so that this Henry wouldn't be back too soon.

Florence laughed, as if she knew quite well what was in my mind. 'Half a world away,' she said. Then her face grew serious. 'It was very sad for Henry, having to leave his dog behind.'

'Did he cry?' I knew I would have done. But I wasn't sure about boys.

'He did.'

I thought briefly, poor Henry. Then Eric reached up and licked my chin, and I laughed in delight. Florence said, 'He seems to like you. Would you like to come for a walk with us?', and I said, 'Oh, *yes!*'

We called at my house and I waited impatiently while Florence went inside to speak to my mum and ask if I could go walking with her. 'We shall be an hour or two,' she said.

My mum wouldn't have cared if we'd been all day. But she smiled in a friendly way and said, yes, sure, that'd be okay.

And we were off.

For two wonderful years, Eric was the centre of my existence. I pretended to myself that he was mine, managing to ignore Florence's frequent references to his real owner, who would some day be coming back to claim his dog. Some day was too vague to worry about.

It didn't matter what was happening in the rest of my life as long as I could rush round to Florence's as soon as I came in from school, because, whatever had gone wrong, Eric would put it right. I'd sit at the table in Florence's warm, cosy kitchen, and she'd put before me a mug of milky tea and a slab of ginger-bread, or flapjack, or chocolate sponge, whatever she'd been baking. With Eric's head resting on my foot, I'd eat and drink my fill – Florence called it 'building up the inner man' – and only after that would she ask me about my day. Then, while the disasters and, rarely, the triumphs, were still fresh in my mind, I'd pour it all out. And Florence would quietly supply more tea, nodding, taking it all in, making it more bearable for me purely because she was concerned enough to listen.

Eric, under the table, would add a whine or two of sympathy. As soon as I'd finished my tea I'd get down on the floor to sit with him, and hugging his beautiful golden body close to me gave me all the warmth and love I needed.

When I was seven, Florence said I was old enough to be responsible, and she left Eric with me while she went away. It was only for a day and a night, but I was so proud it might have been six months. I took him home, groomed him, fed him, walked him, groomed him again, and, using some old blankets I found in the loft, made him the most elaborate bed a dog ever had. I was up at five the next morning to begin all over again, and when I had to take him back to Florence, she said kindly that he seemed to have benefited from his day with me. As if that stay had been a test – which thankfully I passed – she began leaving him with me more frequently, until hardly a week went by without Eric coming home with me at least once.

Then, simultaneously, the two blows fell: the day I raced round to Florence to tell her about having to go and live in Gloucestershire, she told me her grandson was coming home. For good.

I thought – hoped – it was a dreadful dream, and that I'd wake up to find everything was okay after all. But life isn't like that. I slammed round Florence's kitchen, shouting, screaming, and then I threw myself against her and cried till I couldn't catch my breath to cry any more. She stood there, her arms around me, waiting for me to stop. That was just like her – she wasn't particularly demonstrative, but when you really needed her to be, she seemed to know, and then she'd hug you till the cows came home.

Eventually she said gently, 'There. That's enough, now. You know the worst, you've had a good cry, and now it's time to stand up straight and start thinking how we're going to cope with it.'

I had absolutely no idea. I started to sob again, but she didn't let me go on.

'Thea, we have work to do!' Her hands on my shoulders, she pushed me to a chair at the table. Sitting down beside me, she went on, 'We must list the things that are upsetting you so much and attack them head-on. Looked at clearly, the situation may not be as bad as you fear.' I didn't share her optimism. 'Now, what is the worst thing?'

I said, my voice breaking on the word, 'Eric.'

For a moment she looked defeated. Then, rallying, she said, 'Eric belongs to Henry. You've always known that, one day, Henry would come back for him.'

'But I didn't –' I began. Only I couldn't go on, because she was absolutely right.

Leaning towards me, she took my hand. 'Look at me,' she said. I did as she ordered, and her face was very sad. 'I blame myself for letting you become too fond of Eric,' she said. 'It is a pity that you have come to love him, only to lose him. I am sorry, Thea.'

I suddenly thought what the past two years would have been like without Eric. Would I have missed the joy of him, even if it meant I wouldn't now be suffering this pain?

No. Not on your life.

I said, 'I'd rather have had him, even though I won't have him any more.'

Very briefly she smiled, a sad sort of smile. She said, and I didn't know then that someone else had said it first, ' "Better to have loved and lost than never to have loved at all." '

'Will I still be able to come and see him?' I was clutching at straws.

There was a pause. Then she said, very softly, 'Thea, you won't be here, will you?'

The misery welled up and overtook me all over again. No more Eric, no more familiar home and school – even if I didn't like either of them especially, at least they *were* familiar – and a future with a father I hardly remembered in a place I didn't know at all where I'd be a complete outsider. And all because my mum was going away and Florence's bloody grandson was coming home.

Not really knowing what I was saying, I burst out, 'Oh, why can't people stay where they are!'

I saw Florence's mouth twitch. Then she smiled, and then she started to laugh. Impossibly, I found I was laughing, too. Perhaps, being totally drained of tears, it was the only thing left.

Florence made us both a cup of tea. She put quite a lot of sugar in mine. Then, as if she were proposing something I might not like, she said tentatively, 'Of course, I could always come to see you.'

It was as if a tiny light were penetrating the darkness. Not wanting to rejoice till I was quite sure, I said, 'What do you mean?'

'I could come to Gloucestershire. It's not that far. Then we could see each other, and you'd keep in touch with your home.'

It was a funny thing for her to say. If I was going to live with my dad, this wouldn't be my home any more. But it wasn't important, not against what she was saying.

'Will you really drive all the way to Gloucestershire?'

'Of course. I'll stay in a nice hotel and I'll take you out to tea.'

I wasn't going to lose her. She'd still be there, I'd

still be able to share my burdens with her and she'd still help me carry them.

It wouldn't be quite as bad as I'd thought.

She gave me plenty of warning of the arrival of Henry. He was flying by himself all the way from Hong Kong, she said, and she showed me where it was in her atlas. At the same time we looked up Gloucestershire, which seemed no distance at all compared to Hong Kong.

'How old is he?' I asked.

'The same age as you.'

I wasn't sure I'd like to fly all that way by myself.

She asked me if I would look after Eric while she drove to the airport to meet Henry. I said I would. I was determined not to think, this'll be the last time, but I couldn't help it. It occurred to me that I could have said no, but then I thought, why should Eric suffer a day shut up in Florence's house on his own on account of me?

All the same, it was a miserable day.

In the morning Florence telephoned me. She said that Henry had arrived safely, that he was just about to have his breakfast, and that he'd probably be round for Eric later in the morning. Her voice was matter-of-fact, and she gave me no time for tears or protests. I groomed Eric, polished his collar, then, not able to think of anything else to do, sat on the stairs and waited.

He came. No miracle had happened, no typhoon had swept uncharacteristically across East Anglia and removed Henry Woolgar from my life. The door-knocker sounded, I opened the door, and there he was.

'I'm Henry,' he said, with all the aplomb in the world. He was tall – quite a bit taller than me – and stocky, with light brown hair that stuck up at the back and greenish eyes. 'I've come . . .'

There was no need for him to spell it out. I said sharply, 'I know what you've come for.'

Not knowing what I was doing, I shut the door in his face. Perhaps I imagined he'd go away. Then I spotted Eric, ears pricked, sitting tensely at the foot of the stairs. I whistled to him, and he bounded forward to stand at my side. I opened the door again, and the boy said joyfully, 'Eric!'

Eric didn't move. The boy had to call him again, and Eric looked up at me as if saying, is it okay?

Inside me, something shouted with triumph. I thought, *THERE! Eric doesn't want YOU!* I stared at him, about to say something, and saw the misery on his face. For a second, I thought how I'd be feeling if it were me and not him who'd come to reclaim my dog.

I said to Eric, 'This is Henry, Eric.' I gave him a little push, and his eyes met mine in slight reproof. My heart breaking, I hurried on, 'You're *his* dog, you have to go with *him*, now!'

I put my hand through his collar and swept him forward. Then, unable to watch any more, I slammed the door behind him.

I pounded up the stairs to my room and threw myself down on my bed, burying my face in the eiderdown in case the boy should hear me crying. But then I discovered I couldn't bear not to see them go, and I jumped up and ran to the window. They were almost out of sight.

I flew downstairs again, out through the front door and along the lane. I leapt up on to the gate, and watched as the boy and the dog crossed the little bridge over the dyke and walked out of my life.

It was bitterly ironic that my last glimpse of my wonderful, golden dog should be of him standing in exactly the same spot that I'd first set eyes on him.

I tried to keep busy, tried to occupy myself with things that took me in the opposite direction, far away from Florence's house. But I couldn't keep it up. After only a few days, I found myself crouching out in the road, trying to catch sight of Eric through the hedge. And when he heard me calling and dashed out to find me, I realized that being reassured he still loved me made me feel worse than ever.

I honestly didn't know how I was going to cope with it.

The next morning, very early, there was a knock on the door. I waited to see if my mum would go, but there was no sound from the room she shared with Jim so I guessed they hadn't heard. I put on my dressing gown and went down to see who it was.

Florence was standing on the step, and Eric was beside her.

I felt something stir deep within me, as if I'd suddenly been told it was Christmas, and my birthday, and every other wonderful day you could think of. I believe I knew, even before either of us had spoken. I said, 'Are you going out for the day? Do you want me to look after . . .'

She said, 'No, Thea.' And I knew she'd never have done that. Not now. 'Henry thinks Eric would be happier with you. He thinks he misses you.'

I couldn't, daren't, believe it. Henry had every right to his own dog, even if he *was* miserable! I glanced down at Eric, whose eyes were wearing their most pleading expression. I said, 'What do you think I should do?'

She replied, 'I think you should do as Henry did, and decide what is best for Eric.'

'Would he – will he be mine, then? Come to Gloucestershire with me?'

'He will.'

I knew, without a shadow of a doubt, I could make him happy. And as for what he'd do for me . . .

'Then, yes, I'll have him,' I said. Yes! Oh, *yes!*

And Florence nodded in a satisfied fashion and walked away.

Everything seemed to happen very rapidly after that. Arrangements were firmed up for my dad to come to fetch me, Mum and Jim and I made a feeble attempt to put the house in some sort of order, my few belongings were packed, and rucksacks were brought down from the loft and crammed full of dog-eared paperbacks, pipes both for music and for smoking, beads, sandals, and an assortment of Mum's and Jim's most outlandish clothing. They were going to India, then to Kathmandu (I'd have to look that up in my father's atlas, if he had one) and obviously they didn't want to stand out from the crowd.

I endured all the preparations and the panics with amused tolerance. I had Eric, and I was no longer facing the future on my own.

The day before I left, I couldn't stop thinking about Henry. I'd hated him with all my being, and he'd turned out not to be hateable after all. I was ashamed of myself, that I'd felt so strongly about him and been so wrong.

It occurred to me that I might go to him to say thank you. Then my courage failed, and I changed my mind. Then it seemed as if Florence were looking at me, frowning, slightly reproving.

I put Eric in his basket in the scullery, promising

I'd be back soon, then, before I could have another lot of second thoughts, set off for Florence's house. I hadn't thought what I'd say if it were Florence and not Henry who answered the door, but fortunately I caught sight of him as I hurried along the lane. He was going in to the stable where his new pony was kept.

He didn't see me at first. I stood on one foot – my other sandal was full of gravel from when I'd dashed across Florence's drive – and wondered what on earth I was doing there and what on earth I was going to say.

Then he turned round and saw me.

I wanted to get away, as fast as I could, but I had to do what I'd come to do. I opened my mouth to speak, but only an odd, strangled sound came out. I swallowed and tried again, and this time it was better.

'I know you loved him too,' I blurted out, the words tripping over each other and surely incomprehensible, 'and thank you.'

Incomprehensible or not, I couldn't manage any more. I turned and ran for home.

The next morning my dad arrived. He complained bitterly about having to take a dog back with him as well as a daughter – no-one, it seemed, had remembered to tell him about Eric – but he must have realized that the trouble he'd be up against if he said Eric couldn't come would be far worse than the difficulties of squeezing a large retriever into a small flat.

Apart from one brief visit, I didn't go back to East Anglia for almost ten years.

Ten

Living with my dad wasn't as bad as I'd thought it was going to be. In fact, for a kid who was used to being on her own and who had talked herself into a genuine belief that she preferred canine company to human, it wasn't really bad at all.

He lived in a small town on the edge of the Forest of Dean, in a flat in what had been the stable block of a big house. We reached our front door – our only exterior door, come to that – by means of a wooden stair up the side of the building, which Eric found rather alarming the first few times we tried it. Inside was a living room, kitchen and bathroom, my dad's study and one other room which he'd been using to sleep in but which now became my bedroom. He squeezed a single bed into his study and made do with that.

Eric's and my room was the best of all, and once or twice I felt a bit guilty at having turfed Dad out of it. It's stupid how kids take the blame on themselves – looking back, it was hardly my fault that my parents had divorced and that my mum had gone jaunting off to Kathmandu. Anyway, I soon realized that it was much the same to Dad if he slept in a four-poster in a Hollywood boudoir or on a pile of sacks in a cowshed: as long as he had his desk, his electric type-writer and his work, the rest of his life was pretty unimportant.

He earned his living – just about – as a freelance journalist, with regular spots in two or three magazines specializing in the countryside and related matters such as agriculture and leisure activities. He also got into the national dailies quite often, and, together with a fellow journalist called Pam, he was working on a commissioned book for which they'd been paid what he called 'a not inconsiderable advance'. Pam came round in the evenings to work on it with him, and sometimes she'd be there when I came in from school. It was great when that happened because she'd cook us all a meal. She was a smashing cook.

But what Dad really wanted to do was to write fiction. When he didn't have to work on anything more pressing – and sometimes when he did – he'd open the bottom drawer of his desk and get out a massive file of papers bearing the one-word title *GLYNDWR*. He was writing a huge novel, something between fantasy and history, about the legendary Welsh hero Owen Glendower which, even by the time I went to live with him, was already 300,000 words long.

So that was my dad. Preoccupied, deeply involved with his work, and, on his *Glyndwr* days, with his head so far up in the clouds that he couldn't see me at all.

But I was used to fending for myself, and life was easier with Dad because he had more money than Mum. Also there was Pam, who would occasionally blurt out remarks such as, 'Thea's got no decent clothes, Jack! Give me a few quid and I'll take her shopping,' or, 'You can't keep a child cooped up in a hayloft! Give me a couple of bob and I'll take her to the pictures.' Good old Pam. Nowadays, people would instantly assume she and my dad were lovers, but I'm sure they weren't. They got on far too well for there to be any emotional tie between them, and in fact she was actually rather masculine. In retrospect, I can see that my dad was the sort of man who was more at ease with friends than with lovers, and I should think he had very little interest in sex. That was probably why my mum gave him up as a bad job.

I went to the local state primary school, and was neither happy nor unhappy. I didn't make many friends, and there wasn't anyone I liked enough to take home to introduce to Eric. Quite often I thought about Henry Woolgar. If he'd been at my school, would I have been friends with him? I worked hard, dutifully got through my homework, then I'd be off with Eric for what was left of the daylight. Working hard came easily to me – perhaps it was because I lived in an environment where sitting with your head bent over a desk was the norm – and in due course I took and passed my eleven-plus and went on to grammar school.

The letters from Florence started to arrive the day after I moved in with Dad. They went on arriving twice a week without fail, unless the two of us were together, for the next nine years. At first they were short and simple and always ended with a question or two, so that I'd feel compelled to reply. Sometimes she'd mention Henry. Over the months – over the years – we refined our communication into a delicate, subtle instrument that was almost as good as one-to-one conversation. Just as she'd been since the day we met, Florence was the mainstay of my life.

Noticing my regular letter-writing, Dad asked if I

were missing her. After talking at cross-purposes for a while, I realized he thought I was writing to Mum. (I didn't do that – my only communication from her had been a postcard of the Himalayas bearing the message 'F-A-A-A-A-A-R out!!!!!', so I had no idea where she was.) He seemed very relieved when I told him about Florence – I don't think he'd have known what to do with a daughter pining for a mother several thousand miles away. His relief took the form of feigning an interest in the letter I was writing – I'm sure the interest was feigned because it was a *Glyndwr* day and he was itching to get back to the plot, so it was nice of him to spare the time.

'Oh, yes, I remember Florence Woolgar,' he said. 'She invited us to dinner once or twice when we moved into the cottage. I seem to recall she gave us a crib when you were born. Big wooden job, carved headboard of a wolf guarding its young. Antique-looking. I should think it had been in her family for generations.'

I wished I could remember, too. It gave me a warm feeling, to think of Florence providing my crib. To think that she'd been in my life from the beginning. 'She knew who I was,' I said suddenly. 'The day I met her, she said, "You're Josephine Madingly's daughter." '

'Did she?' Dad looked surprised. 'Funny, that she should call your mum by her maiden name. Still, since Josie was a local girl, that's probably how she'd think of her. And Adams isn't nearly as distinguished as Madingly.' He grinned, getting up and ruffling my hair. He wandered back to his study, and I thought that was the last I'd see of him, the summons of *Glyndwr* being so irresistible. But to my surprise, he came back. He was carrying his old manual typewriter and a thick wad of typing paper.

He elbowed my school books and my satchel to one side and with a grunt put the typewriter down on my desk. He said, 'It'd be better if you were taught to type properly. I wish I had been. But still, lots of writers never get beyond two fingers.' He grinned again. 'It's amazing how much more professional work looks when it's typed, although a purist would say you shouldn't type personal letters. Do you think Florence will mind?'

I was sure she wouldn't. And I was delighted. That day, as I struggled for ages to get a clean enough copy to send to Florence, Eric had to make do with a quick run round the garden.

True to her word, she regularly came to visit me, and right from the very first time there was something special about the visits: although it was never mentioned, I felt somehow they were our secret. Of course, Dad and Pam knew, but I had the strong feeling that Henry didn't. Quite why that made it more exciting to have her with me, I didn't pause to work out. Perhaps it was nothing more than a childish love of intrigue.

The first visit was when I'd been with Dad for two months, for all that it seemed longer. She must have decided it'd be best to let me settle in a bit before she came, and it was a good decision – she didn't often make bad ones – because it meant I knew enough of my new home to show her around. I took her to the cake shop where they did lovely éclairs, and she bought me tea. 'Remember?' she said, smiling. 'I promised I'd take you out to tea.'

I remembered.

I showed her my school, and the shop where Dad, Pam and I had bought my new school uniform, and the house where Pam lived. Then, quite sure she'd have had enough of the town, I took her into the forest and we went round all my favourite walks.

On the way back to the flat, she said, 'It's beautiful, your forest. I understand why you love it. But it's very quiet.'

'That's why I like it!'

'Yes, yes, I see that, too,' she said impatiently. 'I mean, there are very few other people. Supposing –' She paused. 'Supposing you slipped and twisted your ankle, and nobody knew where you were. It wouldn't be pleasant, lying there in pain all night.'

'Eric would go for help,' I said stoutly.

'Thea, this isn't a Lassie film. I –' She paused again. I had the feeling she was having trouble finding the right words, and it unsettled me because it was so unlike her. 'I should hate anything to happen to you,' she said eventually. 'I want you to promise me that, when you go walking, you will always tell your father where you are going and how long you expect to be.' Fat lot of good *that* would do! I thought. He probably wouldn't even hear. 'Then,' she was saying, 'if you get into difficulties, he'll know where to look for you.'

I didn't like the idea at all. Apart from the fact that there was no point in it, she was making me feel like a child.

As if she'd read my thoughts, she said gently, 'Thea, you are a child. A very, very precious child.'

I'd never heard her say anything like that before. I'd never heard *anyone* say anything like that. It did, I had to admit, shine a slightly different light on things.

'Okay,' I said grudgingly.

'Promise?'

She put her hand on my chin, turning my head so I was looking up, into her eyes. 'Promise.'

She must have had a word with Dad, too – she

came home with me for supper and stayed on with him for a while after I'd gone to bed before returning to her hotel. After that visit, he took slightly more of an interest in me, certainly as far as my safety went. He enrolled me in the judo club.

Whether it was because of her concern for my safety I don't know, but around that time I began to dream that something was threatening me. I'd be out in the woods – I don't know which woods, they weren't my own familiar forest, being a lot more marshy and with blacker soil – and I'd sense someone behind me. When I turned to look, there was nothing there. Then I'd see a shape moving in the shadows, sometimes man-shaped, sometimes long and low to the ground like a wild animal slinking through the undergrowth. It was always hard to make out – a sort of denser black against the darkness, like a hole in the night sky.

With the strange perception that comes in dreams I knew that it – whatever it was – was following me. And that it had always been there, tracking my footsteps, determined and indefatigable. Once or twice, when I turned in panic, I'd catch a glimpse of its eyes.

They were yellow.

When I was fourteen, Florence invited me to stay with her for the Easter holidays. I was overjoyed – nothing could have given me more pleasure – but I couldn't go if Henry was going to be there. The very thought of him caused me acute embarrassment; I'd been so rude to him at first, when he took Eric and I'd loathed him, and my halting thanks after he'd given him back hadn't included any sort of apology. Even the references to him in Florence's letters made me feel awkward – she'd tell me what he'd been up to (sometimes the things she mentioned were so trivial that I wondered if she was including them just to make sure I didn't forget about him) and I'd feel myself go hot. Did she similarly remind him about me? 'Remember Thea, Henry? The girl who took Eric away?' Poor Henry! He'd hate the very sound of my name.

All my memories and thoughts of him were traumatic, and I was now at an age when it was hard enough being in any boy's company, let alone one who had seen me at my most vulnerable and who probably bore me an outsized grudge.

In my next letter I tried to find out, in a tactful way, if he'd be around. I said something like, 'Will it be all right to bring Eric, or would his presence be a bad reminder?' She knew exactly what I meant. She replied, 'I am sorry, I should have told you that Henry will be away. Please bring Eric.'

My dad took me on the train to London – he said it was a good excuse to get together with some old friends – and he saw me on to the platform at King's Cross for the Cambridge train. We had quite a time with Eric, having to try three taxis before we found a cabbie who would take a large dog. The guard at King's Cross seemed to think he was a guide dog and said to my dad, 'Don't worry, I'll keep an eye on the little lady,' which made us giggle.

'Goodbye, little lady,' Dad said. 'Have a good time.'

'You too.' I hugged him. 'Remember to eat, once in a while.'

For a moment he looked quite sad. 'I'll miss you!' he exclaimed, as if it was a great surprise.

I laughed. 'No, you won't.' He was planning a major assault on *Glyndwr* during my absence. He would be aware of neither time nor place, and a daughter here or there would certainly not pierce his perception.

The whistle blew and the train began to pull away. I watched him wave, then turn and hurry off to the barrier. I wondered if he'd actually bother with the get-together, or if he'd go straight home to his book. I thought probably the latter.

Florence was waiting at Cambridge. In a rare demonstrative moment, she held my hand as we walked out to the car park. I found it quite moving.

'You've got a new car!' I said, glad to have something so mundane to comment on.

'Indeed.' She patted the bottle-nosed bonnet of the Morris Minor Traveller. 'Eric can go in the back,' – she went to open the rear doors and Eric, after a tentative sniff, leapt in – 'which is the perfect place for dogs. It was a pity the last owner of the car didn't think so – when I bought it, we had to spend ages brushing dog hairs off the back seat.'

I didn't want to hear about 'we'. But I knew I was being unreasonable. Since she'd brought him into the conversation, I thought now was a good time to ask where he was. I wanted to be assured, I think, that he wasn't suddenly going to appear.

'Where's your grandson?' I asked.

She was pulling out on to the main road, but spared a moment to shoot me an amused glance. 'Henry has gone away with his school on a rugby tour,' she said. 'Then he's going to stay with a friend and his family up in the Lake District for a fortnight.'

That, I thought, must surely take care of the full length of my visit. It looked as if it was going to be okay.

But she added, almost wistfully, 'I could ask him to come home a day or two early, if you'd like to see him.'

Before I could stop myself I said, 'If he comes back, I'm going.' Realizing how rude it sounded, I tried to back-pedal. 'I mean, it's up to you, of course, but I –'

She said quietly, 'It's all right, Thea.'

And nothing more was said.

It was wonderful to be back. I hadn't realized how much I missed the Fens, how much I had longed to look out on the familiar scenes of my early child-hood. I had a surprisingly strong sense of coming home, and when I said as much to Florence, she looked for a moment almost triumphant. But perhaps I imagined it, for she merely said she was pleased, and that we'd make sure we made the most of my three weeks.

'It will be a chance,' she added, 'for us to visit some of the places which so far we have only spoken of.'

She'd put me in her smallest spare room, which was also the most comfortable one. She'd gone to a lot of trouble, putting fancy soaps on the washbasin, padded hangers with sachets of dried lavender on them in the wardrobe, matching towels on the rail and, best of all, a selection of books on the bedside table. (She had obviously taken them from the main library in her drawing room – I felt uneasy in there because there was a photo of Henry on the table, and every time his eyes caught mine I felt my face go hot.) The books she'd put in my room were all about East Anglia, about its geography, its history, its legends. Diving happily into them on my first night, a deeply reassuring sense of being back with the familiar swept through me: here, in writing, were all the fascinating bits of folklore and legend that Florence had told me when I was too small to read about them for myself. Chords of memory were struck, the images returning with such force that, desperate to see the places where it had all happened, I couldn't wait for our trips to begin.

As if she wanted to begin at the beginning, she took me first to the neolithic flint mines known as Grime's Graves. In a wide, pitted grassy area surrounded by the enclosing darkness of Thetford Forest, we stood on the top of a mound while she told me about the early people who had lived and worked there four thousand years before.

We were watching Eric exhausting himself chasing rabbit smells when she suddenly spoke. 'They came from the south-west, your people,' she said. Before I could interrupt, she amended smoothly, 'The original East Anglians, I mean. Stone Age man crossed the land-bridge from Europe, and spread westwards along the south coast, following the chalk downs.'

'Because of the flints,' I said. I knew, from somewhere, that you found flint in chalk.

'Indeed.' She nodded. 'Over several hundred years, it was discovered that the chalk band turned back on itself, to the north-east, and neolithic men made their way up through the Chilterns and into East Anglia. Here, they found the finest flint of all, and the workings were so extensive that the Anglo-Saxons, coming here two thousand years later, believed the landscape could only have been created by the gods. Hence the name – Grim is another name for Woden, the chief god of the Anglo-Saxons.'

'Why *graves*?' I asked. 'Did they think Woden was buried here?' Even on a sunny spring day, the thought was chilling.

'No. Gods do not die. "Graves" in this context simply means hollows.' She set off down from the mound, walking briskly. 'Come along. I'll just put Eric back in the car,' – she whistled to him and, instantly obedient, he abandoned the chase and ran up to us – 'and then we shall go down underground.'

I wasn't sure I wanted to. Thoughts of buried gods, lying there terribly still and massively vast, were too vivid in my head. But already Florence had gone ahead into a little hut and, when I joined her, was taking a hard hat from the man in attendance and putting it on.

'One at a time on the ladder,' the man said to me. I stood and waited while Florence descended. Then I went after her.

Down, down. Step after careful step, through bands of flint and chalk striped black and white. At the bottom at last, quiet earth all around, pressing in. We were alone down there. It was chilly, dank and totally silent. I was afraid, and my fear was threatening to overcome me. Then the man up on the surface cleared his throat. We weren't alone after all.

Florence, on hands and knees, was peering down the tunnels which led off the main gallery. 'Imagine digging out all this with a pick made from an antler and a spade from an ox's shoulderblade,' she said.

I was looking upwards towards the distant daylight. 'Imagine digging the shaft in the first place.' It seemed an impossible task.

'And the same feat is repeated in shafts and pits all over the site,' she said, straightening up and coming to stand beside me. 'Nearly a thousand of them, some of which were abandoned because the flint was found to be inferior.'

'Think of all that effort for nothing!' It was almost painful, to imagine the frustration. 'They must have hoped like mad they'd find the good stuff.'

'I expect they prayed, don't you?' She had turned away again and her voice was slightly muffled.

'Yes.' To whom? I wondered.

'The Earth Mother.' Again, she'd heard something I hadn't said. 'The Great Mother, the goddess of fertility. Flint is a product of the earth, just as are corn or fruits. A statue was found, you know, in one of the shafts. It was an abandoned mine, with no workable flint. Perhaps they made a little shrine and placed her likeness on it in order to pray for better luck next time.'

She fell silent. The echo of her words died, and now there was no sound. Or was there? I thought I sensed movement, although the two of us stood quite still. Up there in the clear day, the sun must have gone behind a cloud, for suddenly it was much darker and I could no longer see into the corners.

They were there. Very close. So close that I felt their breath on the back of my neck. Neolithic man, distant ancestor, miner and flint-knapper. Kneeling on the hard floor in the light of a rush lamp, a swaying group prayed to a squat and big-breasted figure made of chalk. *Oh, Mother, help us, reward our labour, open to us the rich vein of flint that you hide deep in your body. Listen to your children, help us . . .*

I was sitting on the ground leaning against the ladder, my skin clammy with sweat. Florence had taken off her hat and was fanning me with it. Seeing me open my eyes, the anxious frown cleared from her face. She said, 'I think we had better go back above ground, as soon as you feel up to it.'

They were still there, hiding in the shadows. Lying in the dark tunnels, watching. And the great goddess was waiting for us to leave. Standing up hastily, clutching at the rungs of the ladder because I still felt faint and my knees were wobbly, I said, 'I'm up to it now.'

*　　*　　*

There were other, less disturbing, trips which were nothing more than glorious outings for two people and a happy dog. A day in the Fens, more walking than driving, when she took me to places where peat was first dug four and a half thousand years before, and showed me great dark trunks of ancient bog oaks emerging to the light of day after countless centuries buried in the earth. A trip to the Gog Magog hills, where we walked round the footpaths and up to the Iron Age fort at Wandlebury Camp. A day in Ely, when we climbed the cathedral tower and she made me see the great sweep of the fenland as it had once been: a swampy, secret place hidden by low mists, and rising from it isolated islands of higher ground where unknown lives were lived out.

Our last journey that holiday took us into an area of history which was, she said, positively modern by comparison: we went south-east to the lands around Aldeburgh where the East Anglian kings once held court. We drove through Rendlesham, and she told me that here had stood the royal hall of the dynasty. On to Sutton Hoo, where they found the priceless regalia of Raedwald of the Wuffingas. Where, perhaps, the body of the king himself once lay in the elegant wooden grave ship. And up the lonely, sea-beaten coast to the lost town of Dunwich, where we stood on a narrow strip of shore under the crumbling cliffs and convinced ourselves we could see the shells of houses and the ghosts of people beneath the waves.

'Somewhere out there is a royal palace,' she said dreamily. 'It was built by Sigebert, son of Raedwald, a proud gesture that defied the power of the sea. St Felix crowned him, you know, and that holy crown was buried with two others so that the power that was in them should save Britain from invasion.'

I gazed up and down the wild shore, threatened

now only by the indomitable sea. Three crowns, carrying magic in their substance. I said, 'Are they still there?'

She shrugged. 'Who knows? Legends abound, and it is said that St Felix's crown was lost when Dunwich finally went under the waves. Another is rumoured to have been dug up at Rendlesham at the end of the seventeenth century, but whoever found it put its monetary worth above its historical value, and it was sold and melted down.'

'And the third one?'

'Still to be found.' She looked at me, a half-smile on her face. 'Perhaps, one day, someone will succeed.'

'Do you think –' I began, then stopped. What I'd been going to say would sound silly.

But she said quickly, 'Do I think what?' The smile had gone, and her face was suddenly intent.

'Oh, I don't know what I meant. I was just thinking, would the magic still work?' I laughed, as if to say, aren't we being absurd, believing in fairy tales!

She didn't answer at first. When she did speak, her voice sounded different – almost masculine. 'A powerful man made those crowns,' she said. 'He sacrificed a part of himself, and wrought it into the gold. Where the gold endures, so does his power.' Her eyes fixed mine. 'Such a foe, they fought,' she whispered, 'such a shifting, secret enemy.'

I didn't understand. What did she mean, a secret enemy? 'I thought you said the crowns were to keep invaders away,' I said.

She looked at me, the half-smile returning. And she just said, 'Did you?'

That night I had another of my dreams. Far worse than anything I'd experienced in Gloucestershire, it affected me so badly that I didn't risk going back to sleep but stayed awake with the light on for what remained of the night.

I was in those woods again, the marshy black soil oozing water which froze my feet. I knew the dark shape was searching for me, but I thought I had escaped from it. I was crouched in my hiding place – a hut, it looked like – and I thought I was safe.

Then it came. Like a wolf at first, materializing out of the black ground, narrowed eyes like strips of golden light. Then the shape changed and it was a tall man, dark-cloaked, who put his face right up to mine so that I could smell him. It was a gamey smell, like well-hung meat, and it had an overtone of something like incense, or perfume.

The Dark Man seemed to put out waves of force, and they surrounded me so that I was paralysed. The yellow eyes widened, holding mine so that I fell into their depths.

His voice a low hiss, he said, 'I curse thee. Through the ages I shall follow thee, and there will be no escape, not through all eternity.'

I couldn't move, couldn't speak. And what could I say, when I knew in my bones he was right?

For an instant I saw a flash of brilliant light, as if the sun were shining on a knife, or a spearhead, then it was gone, as suddenly as if a huge dense cloud had exploded across the sky.

All hope was gone. Terror held me, magnified within me so that I sweated and trembled in its grasp.

Then I woke up.

As I lay there, watching the first streaks of light become the dawn of the new day, it was a long time before the fear went away.

When the time came for me to go back, I didn't want to, even if it did mean that the power of my dreams waned from the alarming height I'd just experienced down to the level I was used to. She had made me feel my roots again, and their forceful pull was holding me tightly. I didn't want to leave her, either: I was under the spell of her fascinating personality, and I knew I would miss both the stimulating company and the warm, solid affection.

But I had no choice. Term began the next week, and besides, Henry was coming home.

She took me and Eric to the station, where I was to begin the first leg of my return trip – with any luck, my dad would be waiting at King's Cross, and we'd go on home together. I was looking forward to seeing him again, and I held on to that thought.

She stood on the platform and I leaned out of the window so that we didn't lose our last few moments. She said, 'Thank you for coming.'

'Don't thank me. I've loved every minute of it.' I added, muttering, 'I've loved it much too much.'

She must have heard. Again, fleetingly, I saw that look of triumph on her face, as if something had worked out exactly as she'd planned.

She stared at me. 'This is your home,' she said solemnly. 'Where you belong. Come back, any time. You will always be welcome.'

Before I could respond – if there was anything I could say in reply to her valediction, which seemed unlikely – the train began to move. With a last wave – almost a salute – she turned away.

I found a seat and prepared myself for the long journey back to Gloucestershire.

Eleven

My main memory of the next few years is of hard work. Not only school work, which was okay, but also joining in with Dad and Pam on their next project, which was, as they called it, *Dumbo's Guide to Looking Up Your Own Trunk*. Actually that was only the working title, and was Dad's pun on the fact that the book was a 'How To' thing about geneaology, 'Dumbo' implying it was a beginner's guide and 'trunk' a play on trees, as in family tree.

I had become quite a good typist by then, having taken myself off to evening classes and been taught how to touch-type before it was too late to unlearn the bad habits I'd picked up. At first the only help I gave Dad and Pam was looking things up for them in the reference library and producing beautifully neat final copies of their scrawl, but Pam said making use of me like that wasn't fair. 'The girl writes much more lucidly than you do, Jack,' she told my dad bluntly, 'so I vote we let her draft a chapter on her own.'

As a result, the final version of *Dumbo's Guide* went out accredited to three authors, Jack Adams, Pamela Hughes and T. M. Adams. It was heady stuff, for a girl of sixteen. It was also very generous of them, since the bits I'd drafted had to be fairly extensively reworked. The book sold quite well, and Dad opened a building society account for me for my share of the royalties.

At Christmas in my lower sixth year, we had a surprise: my mum phoned. We'd got back in touch – she and Jim had finally decided they were too old to be hippies and had settled in Australia, from where she'd send me the occasional letter and birthday card. She'd said vaguely once or twice that I ought to go out to see them, but somehow I managed to forget about the suggestion within a day or so of receiving it. It wasn't that I was daunted by the distance – at the back of my mind was the memory of Henry Woolgar flying on his nine-year-old own all the way to England from Hong Kong – it was more a feeling that if I went, pressure might be put on me to stay. And that I couldn't do: Gloucestershire was far enough from East Anglia, Australia was unthinkable. Anyway, it wouldn't have been fair to uproot Eric, and I certainly couldn't have left him behind.

The line was so clear that at first my poor dad thought she was calling from just down the road. He gave a strangled sort of squeak and shouted to Pam, who was in the middle of basting the turkey, 'Jesus Christ, Pam! It's Josie!' He didn't think to put his hand over the mouthpiece, and I wondered what my mum would make of his reaction to hearing her voice after so long.

Pam, always a woman with much presence of mind, strode over and took the receiver from his hand, almost coming a cropper over Eric stationed by the kitchen door, expectant eyes on the oven and its contents. 'Jack's busy being gobsmacked,' she said conversationally, 'he'll be with you in a mo. Do you want to speak to Thea?'

She must have said yes. Half in a daze, I put the receiver to my ear. 'Hello?'

'Hi, there, Thea! Happy Christmas!' She sounded pissed, and I thought, good old Mum, hasn't changed a bit.

'And to you.' I had no idea whatsoever what to say, and I tried to send imploring help-me glances to Dad. Unfortunately he had opened his Christmas bottle of whisky and, eyes closed, was imbibing a large slug straight from the bottle.

My mother said, Strine accent quite noticeable, 'Can't talk long, Thea, this is costing us an arm and a leg. Jim's gone to bed and I'm off to join him, but I just thought I'd wish you all the season's greetings.'

If Jim had gone to bed, they couldn't be in England, unless he was in the habit of going to bed at ten fifteen in the morning. And she'd said the call was costing her a lot. I decided to risk it. 'Where are you, Mum?'

'Home, of course!' She gave a rich, alcoholic laugh. It was nice to hear her so happy. 'Dear old Sydney.'

What a relief. I mouthed to Dad, 'She's in Sydney,' and he mimed a prayer of thanks. I said, 'Happy Christmas to you, too, Mum. And to Jim.' I wondered fleetingly if he was still the king of the great unwashed. And if he still had that look of kindness in his brown eyes, or if being a jobbing builder in New South Wales had forever taken it away. 'I'll get Dad.' I reached out and grabbed him by the sleeve, so forcefully that I heard the material rip.

'No, don't bother,' my mum said, 'just give the old bugger a kiss from me.' There was no rancour in her tone. Then, as if remembering why she'd called, she said, 'Everything okay, Thea? School and things?'

'Fine.' I wondered what had prompted that. 'Why?'

'Oh, you know. Christmas. Thinking about you. Remembering you when you were little.' I heard her sniff. Oh, God.

I almost said that Christmasses were a lot better now than they'd been when I was little, when what *I* remembered most was my parents arguing over who was going to wash up after lunch and whose idea it had been to buy me the drum. But I thought better of it. 'That's nice,' I said lamely.

She seemed to have run out of things to say, and I certainly had. She said, 'Well, cheerio, then,' and I was just about to do the same when she suddenly squawked, 'Who was that who answered the phone?'

I was tempted. Very tempted. After all, what had she ever done for me? But then I thought, it's Christmas. Why make trouble in the season of goodwill?

I said, 'One of my schoolfriends. 'Bye, Mum.'

Sometimes it seems, looking back, that I tried to cast myself into the role of sad, oppressed child in order to dramatize myself. I remember – with shame, I must admit – sitting in front of my dressing-table mirror and perfecting a hang-dog expression of such misery that it even moved *me* to tears. I remember telling an impressionable PE teacher – surely an unlikely combination – that the headache and slight nausea of teenage menstruation was in fact due to 'difficulties at home'. I *wanted* to be a problem child, the girl whose only friend was her dog.

It was grossly unfair of me, and in due course I came to acknowledge it. For all that Mum going off with Jim was an unorthodox way for a mother to behave, it wasn't that unusual, and I was probably better off without her. And her going away meant that I went to live, during what they call the formative years, with my dad, with the pretty permanent company of Pam. Although on the face of it no more the stuff that good parents are made of than was my mum, they did just fine; they treated me like a contemporary (through ignorance of any other way rather than by design), they gave me plenty of freedom, they encouraged me to be independent and they inculcated in me the precious commodity of street-wisdom. And, writers and readers that they were, they gave me a love of the written word which benefited me enormously both in working and leisure time.

Dad and Pam supported me and helped me while I passed ten 'O' levels, and they spent several late nights sitting up with me while the three of us thrashed out what I should go on to do for 'A' level. They were lovely.

In the background, always, was Florence. Our twice-weekly letters had by now grown to the length of essays, although she was understanding when pressure of school work meant that I had to send a less than full reply. Although there was no repeat of my holiday with her, she came to see me several times over the years, each visit largely following the pattern of the first.

Until the last one.

It was in September 1972, and I'd just started my last year at school. During the summer holidays I'd had a job in the local swimming baths, and there I'd met a boy called Steve who, once we'd got talking, took to coming in most lunchtimes. He was a sales rep for a firm in the town selling camping gear. I'd had boyfriends before, but Steve was the first serious one. Serious enough that I wanted to be with him all the time, pined if he didn't turn up for his lunchtime swim and worried myself silly if he didn't phone to say where he'd been. I could only relax if I knew when I'd be seeing him again, and even then I'd live in a state of anxiety in case he called to say he couldn't make it. Or, even worse, stood me up.

It was, simply, young love. He was older than me by four years, and he'd packed in a good four years of experience – I was a virgin, but he certainly wasn't. He kissed like the heroes of my dreams – the difference between his kisses and those of my previous boyfriends, all of whom apparently thought you had to turn your lips outwards and drown your partner in saliva, was as wide as the Great Divide.

I mentioned him in my letters to Florence; I couldn't keep from her something of such importance in my life. But I didn't go into details – if she picked up the wildness of my passion for him and the depths of my quandary over whether or not I should do as he kept suggesting and sleep with him, it can only have been from reading between the lines. Or by long-distance telepathy.

She arrived with no prior warning at her usual time on the Friday evening, and after Dad had made us Bovril toast for tea and excused himself (it was a *Glyndwr* day), she leaned towards me and said, 'And now I should like to talk to you about your young man.'

'Oh! Okay.' Straight away I felt guilty. It was unreasonable – Dad quite liked Steve, and didn't seem to mind if I came home a bit late and looking a bit flustered. Probably he didn't even notice, but if he'd done so, and mentioned it to Pam, she'd have told him in no uncertain terms that I was a woman, not a child, and that he should mind his own business. Pam was a great one for people minding their own business.

Shamefully I regretted briefly that it was Florence and not Pam whom I was dealing with now.

Steve was going to call for me later – we'd planned an evening in the pub before Florence had unexpectedly arrived – and I wondered if he'd mind if we took Florence with us. I looked up at her. 'He's taking me out tonight, to the pub. You could . . .' I trailed off.

Slowly she shook her head. 'I do not think it will be necessary for me to *meet* him,' she said, as if such a meeting were unworthy of her. 'What I have to say is for you to hear, Thea, not for him.'

I was about to protest – something about her tone was angering me, implying as it did that I was being a silly little thing who needed putting straight. Or perhaps that was my guilty conscience talking. I said feebly, 'Go on, then.'

I thought she might be going to warn me of the dangers of relationships with boys, just as, years ago, she'd warned me about going off alone into the forest. Perhaps – and I was squirming at the thought – she was going to tell me about where babies come from and how not to have any.

There was no way that I could have predicted what she did say.

She told me without batting an eyelid that an exact half of her wealth and her property was left to me in her will, provided I was still a virgin when I returned to live in East Anglia. She didn't say it quite like that – not her style, to be so tactless – she said, if I hadn't 'formed any serious and physical attachment'. But I knew damned well what she meant.

At first, the shock-waves bouncing to and fro in my head, I didn't know whether to order her from the house for her presumption or laugh in her face at her cheek.

It didn't occur to me, then, that I might thank her.

She couldn't have expected me to answer. Calmly she got up from the sofa, brushed the crumbs from her tweed skirt and picked up her bag and gloves. 'You must do as you see fit, Thea,' she said. 'I am not offering you a bribe – your moral welfare is, of course, your own concern. I shall stay in my usual hotel tonight and return home tomorrow, after lunch. I shall be in my room in the morning, if you wish to speak to me.'

I watched, speechless, as she let herself out. I heard her footsteps going down the wooden stairs and then fade as she walked off across the yard.

I could hardly believe what I'd just heard. What it amounted to, whatever she'd said about my moral welfare being my own concern, was that she'd just offered me half of all she owned if I didn't sleep with Steve.

Was it Steve she objected to – unlikely, when she hadn't even met him – or the thought of me having a lover at all? *Why?* She was a couple of generations older than me, certainly, and a woman of her age was entitled to be a bit staid about such things. But she wasn't typical of women of her age, she was Florence.

There had to be something else.

I was still sitting in the same spot when Steve arrived an hour later. A million thoughts had raced through my head, and I was still very angry. So much so that I'd made up my mind I was bloody well going to let Steve make love to me that very night, and *damn* Florence for her domineering, interfering ways. *HOW DARE SHE!*

I didn't talk to Steve about her. In fact, chatting to him as we sat in a corner in the pub, it occurred to me that I didn't talk to him about anything that really mattered. Mattered to me, that is. And, watching his face in the dim light, he didn't look quite as handsome as I'd thought.

But his kisses! I reminded myself slightly hysterically. Wait till later, when we're in the car in some quiet gateway and his firm, wonderful mouth is on mine!

I didn't want to wait till closing time, I was too hungry for him. Desperately eager to be gone – before I could change my mind? – I put my hand on his thigh as he drained his third pint and whispered, 'Steve, shall we go?'

He looked at me, mouth open, as if about to protest that there was time for another. Then he must have read something in my expression. Putting his big hand over mine, he squeezed my fingers and whispered, 'You're on!'

We drove out into the forest and down a narrow lane off which there were several clearings and a gateway that didn't get too muddy, even when it was raining. He parked, switched off the lights and the engine, then reclined the two front seats and took me in his arms.

The kissing was as thrilling as it had always been. And this time there was an extra excitement, as if, knowing that I wasn't going to say stop, I was allowing myself really to let go. I put my tongue into his mouth, tracing the outline of his lips, and instantly he reacted, his tongue meeting mine, pushing against mine, and I heard him give a sort of groan. It was a deeply arousing sound.

His hand was under my jumper, his palm cupped around my breast. He reached behind me to undo my bra, then, lifting it and my jersey away from me in one neat and well-practised movement, his head was down on my chest and he was gently taking my nipple in his mouth.

And his hand, freed for more exploration, was creeping up under my skirt, over my thigh and pressing in between my legs.

I didn't know what to do. Was it a sign of too much eagerness for the girl to take off her own tights and pants? But I couldn't wait, he was stroking, touching in a place I'd never been touched before – how did he know it was just there? – and I could no longer sit still.

'Yes, yes, I know,' he murmured against my breast, 'just a little bit longer, let me get you really wet and ready, then it won't hurt you.'

I heard the sound of his zip going down. Then he took hold of my wrist and guided my hand inside his trousers till I could feel him, hard and hot, and I knew that soon, so soon, he would be pushing that frightening, thrilling thing inside me.

I wanted him to. Oh, God, I wanted him to. I'd never experienced feelings like that before, never known how fantastic two bodies together could be.

He was pulling at the top of my tights, urgently, tearing the fabric. Soon, any minute now. It was our moment – my moment, my first time. I'd be like the other girls, know what it was like to go all the way. I'd no longer be a virgin.

Florence's voice sounded loud in my head, but I blotted her out. *NO!* This is nothing to do with you, Florence! This is my life! She spoke again, more distantly.

Then, out of the blue, I saw Henry Woolgar's face before my eyes, the face of the photo in Florence's drawing room. He was smiling, but as I watched the smile faded and he looked unbearably sad. It was the expression he'd worn when I'd gone to say thank you to him for giving me Eric.

Henry?

He was Henry and not Henry. The hair was longer, and the clothes were different. Old-fashioned – a tunic held in with a sword-belt. Florence's voice spoke again, low and commanding, but suddenly both she and Henry were obliterated by a dark shape that was now a wolf, now a man. That deep hissing voice was right in my ear, egging me on, but then abruptly it stopped, and the image of Henry came through even more strongly.

Henry.

Steve had lifted his head and his mouth was searching for mine. My eyes wide open, I tried to focus on his face. Steve, I thought wildly, it's Steve.

Henry's image melted, fading into the face pressed up so close to mine. But it was too late.

Twisting away, taking my hand out of Steve's trousers and pulling his out of my knickers, I said breathlessly, 'No! I can't!'

For a moment he didn't do anything. Except resist. I realized then how much stronger he was than me.

But he was a nice chap. Far too nice for me to have done that to him. Throwing himself back into the driving seat, turning away so that his back was to me, I heard him say quietly but vehemently, 'Shit.'

When my sobbing breath was under control, I said, stupidly, 'I'm sorry.'

I thought he'd tell me what he thought of me. What any man would think of a girl who'd virtually dragged him out there and ordered him to make love to her, only to pull back at the minute before last with the feeble, inadequate words, I can't. At the very least, I thought I'd be walking home.

To my surprise – and gratitude – he just said quietly, 'Me too.' Then, 'Were you afraid I'd hurt you?'

I almost said yes. It would have been a face-saving

excuse for both of us. And almost true – he'd felt enormous in my hand. But somehow I felt that I owed him the truth. He could, with very little effort, have gone ahead and had me, and I'd have been nearly as much to blame if he'd done so. 'Not exactly, ' I hedged. 'It's just that – it's a big step. Doing it the first time, you know. I – I changed my mind.' That was probably the most truthful thing I'd said all evening.

He laughed briefly. Very briefly. 'A woman's privilege,' he said. Then he started the engine. 'Let me know if you change it back again. Otherwise . . .'

He left the sentence unfinished. Under the circumstances, I could hardly blame him.

Later, lying in bed far away from sleep, I wondered how she'd done it.

I went to see her in the morning. I wasn't sure what I was going to say – certainly not to tell her what had happened. What hadn't happened. I think that, despite everything, I didn't want us to part bad friends.

She was sitting in a chair by the window reading the paper. She looked up as I came in, and studied me for some moments in silence. Then she said, 'I am sorry, Thea.'

Before I could stop myself, I said, 'So you should be!'

'What you do with your life is your business,' – her voice was contrite – 'and I had no right to say what I did. You were not to be bought, and I should have known it.'

What was she thinking? It seemed grossly unfair if it was what I feared, that I'd ignored her bribe and gone ahead regardless. 'I didn't!' I cried. 'We – I'm still a virgin!'

Then she smiled. And said, very softly, 'I know.'

More confused than ever, I sank down on to her bed and buried my face in my hands. After a while I felt her hand on my shoulder. 'Come to stay with me again?' she asked. 'Soon?'

I shrugged. Right at that moment it was the last thing I wanted to do.

'Well, give it some thought.' I heard her moving about the room. Then she said, 'I am going down for an early lunch now, before I set off for home. Will you join me?' I shook my head. 'Very well. Goodbye, Thea.'

I listened as she went out of the room, closed the door behind her and walked off along the corridor.

We resumed our correspondence, but not our closeness. I missed it. In June, she sent me a card for my eighteenth birthday and a small registered parcel containing a gold brooch set with garnets and mosaic glass. With it was a note: 'It is time for you to come into your inheritance. Please come to see me.'

Not yet, I thought. I'm not ready yet.

I wrote a polite letter thanking her for the present. Far too polite – it must have hurt her deeply.

Dad, Pam and I celebrated the end of my exams, then, since there was no longer much point in going to school, we went off to Brittany for a week. I sent Florence a card.

When we got back, she was waiting in her car outside the flat. She said she'd only just arrived, but I don't know if that was the truth. After we'd all had tea together, I suggested she came with me to collect Eric from the friend who'd been looking after him while we were away, and on the way back she said, 'I want you to come home, Thea.'

151

I thought of saying, I *am* home. But I couldn't.

I said, thinking even as I did so that it wasn't really me forming the words, 'Very well, Florence. I'll speak to Dad, and if it's okay with him, I'll come at the end of term.'

She let out a sigh of relief. Then said, 'Henry will be there. Since the house will be full of the friends who are coming for his eighteenth birthday party, I shall find you accommodation, at my expense, if you will permit me. And, naturally, we should like you to join in the celebration.'

I nodded.

I felt we had entered a dream realm, where nothing was quite real. What was I saying? What had she made me agree to? Going back to East Anglia? Turning up at Henry's party? Seeing *Henry?* I stopped, staring at her. She was just an old woman, with a kindly face and a touchingly uncertain look in her eyes.

No she wasn't. She was Florence, and I still didn't know what that meant.

She said, 'Come along. Your father will be wondering where we are.'

Term ended. I hung around for a while, telling myself I was still making up my mind. But I wasn't, I'd known long ago what I was going to do.

I told Dad I was thinking of returning to East Anglia and staying, for a while at least, and he seemed to accept it without surprise. He said he and Pam would let me know when they came to London so that we could meet up.

He took me to the station, but this time Eric and I went on alone. Dear old Eric. He was nearly twelve, and it felt right to be taking him home.

Florence was waiting for me at Cambridge. She

took me to a small hotel on the outskirts of Ely, and after ensuring that Eric and I were going to be comfortable, left me to my thoughts. There was no shortage of those.

Next day a letter came. An expensive-looking envelope, containing a stiff piece of black-printed card:

'Florence Woolgar requests the pleasure of your company at a party to celebrate the eighteenth birthday of her grandson Henry Woolgar.'

Henry's birthday. The date of the party was next Saturday and, as she'd promised, I'd been invited. Well, I wasn't going, and that was that. I couldn't – despite Florence, I'd avoided him all my childhood, and I wasn't going to stop now. Anyway, I hated Henry Woolgar, didn't I? He was the boy who'd taken away my dog.

Only he wasn't. He was the boy who'd given me back my dog, the dog he'd loved as much as I did. He'd sacrificed his dog because Eric and I needed each other.

I didn't hate Henry Woolgar at all.

Perhaps the time had come to stop avoiding him.

I had my hair trimmed and bought a new dress. It was pale blue, low-cut and tight over the bust and the hips, with a swirly knee-length skirt. The girl in the shop said it was just right for an eighteenth birthday party, but she'd probably have said that about whatever I'd chosen. It wasn't really to be taken as a good omen.

I had neither seen nor spoken to Florence since she'd dropped me off at the hotel. In the absence of any other offers, I arranged a taxi to take me, but my courage failed at the thought of being the first there. I asked the cab to come at ten o'clock, and by the time we got out to Willowford Fen, it had gone half past.

I watched the taxi's rear lights disappear up the road, cursing myself for having let it go. Now I was out of choices. I walked up to the front door, and the music sounded loudly from within.

I lifted the knocker and let it fall. Nothing happened, so I did it again, slightly more forcefully.

The handle turned, and the door was pulled open. He was smiling, as if certain that, whoever it was, this late guest was going to be someone he'd be pleased to see. His hair was a darker brown than I remembered, and he wore it long, over his collar at the back. His green eyes were now edged with outward-fanning lines, as if he laughed a lot. Straight away, surely before he'd seen who it was, he said happily, 'Better late than never!'

Then, the smile fading from his face, he just stood and stared at me.

I don't know why it was that I wanted to throw myself into his arms. Why I felt, overwhelmingly, that I had indeed returned to where I belonged. I felt myself lean towards him, and I couldn't stop. As if he knew and wanted to make sure I was aware he felt it, too, he opened his arms to me and I fell into his embrace. His strong hands holding me pulled me close – I remembered Florence saying he played rugby – and there was no will in me to resist.

He said, his breath warm and fast against my ear, 'Hello, Thea. Welcome home.'

Twelve

We went hand in hand into the house, and I could see through the drawing room to the terrace beyond, where people were dancing by the light of strings of bulbs in the trees. Slightly to one side – away from the main blast of the speakers – was an area of garden tables and chairs, where older guests were sitting talking. There was an aura of cheerful celebration – Henry's party was going well.

He paused in the hall, still holding my hand. 'Would you like to eat?' he asked. 'The buffet's in the dining room, there's masses left.'

Food was the last thing I wanted. 'No thanks. But I'd like a drink.'

'Of course. What would you like?' He looked into my eyes. 'Champagne is what we should have, but it's for later. There's a cake I've got to cut.'

I knew what he meant about the champagne. I felt exactly the same. 'I'll have a shandy, or something. Anything.'

He went over to where drinks of various sorts were arrayed on the sideboard and made me a lemonade shandy, pouring himself a pint of beer. 'Cheers,' he said, handing me my glass.

'Happy birthday.'

'It's not today, you know. It was in August. The tenth.'

'Leo.'

'Right. What are you?'

'Gemini. Fifteenth of June.'

'You're older than me. I've always wanted an older woman.'

I couldn't speak. The atmosphere between us was suddenly heavy, and I felt a shiver up the nape of my neck. He was staring at me, looking slightly puzzled, narrowing his eyes as if he were having difficulty focusing. It occurred to me that he might be drunk – it was his birthday party, after all, he was entitled to be a bit pissed. I was setting about the mammoth task of revising my first impressions when he said, 'You, as far as I know, are stone cold sober, unless your late arrival is because you stopped off at a pub on the way.'

'I didn't.'

'No. I was joking. And, despite what you might think, I have had three pints and two glasses of wine since five o'clock. Not as sober as you, but not far off.'

I nodded. 'Okay.'

'So what are we to make of this?'

I was almost cross, that he should take this magic and try to rationalize it by talking about it. Then I was overcome with delight, because he'd just admitted categorically that he felt it, too.

'I've no idea,' I whispered.

'Come and dance with me.' He took my glass and put it down with his on the floor. Arm around my waist, he led me out on to the terrace. The music was slow – Nilsson singing 'Without you' – and it seemed we were going to be able to slip in unnoticed amongst the other entwined couples moving infinitesimally round the floor.

We weren't. Just as I was leaning my face against his shoulder, breathing in for the first time the smell of him – a slightly lemony aftershave combined with the scent of his skin and a faint aroma of new cotton shirt – someone right behind me said loudly, 'Henry! This is our dance!'

In my ear he said quite clearly, 'Bugger.'

I turned round. The girl was taller than me and rather plump, her size accentuated by the tight red dress she was wearing. Her dark hair flopped round her face, the curls slightly damp. She was flushed.

'I've had my breather,' she announced, elbowing me out of the way and planting herself firmly in front of him. 'I'm ready again now.'

I wondered what for. Henry said, 'All right, Wendy, but then I must release you so that some of the other men can have a go.'

I wanted to laugh, but Wendy was singlemindedly wrapping herself round him and didn't seem to object to his remark. Hadn't she heard? Now she, I decided, had definitely had more than three pints and a couple of glasses of wine.

Feeling a bit of a prawn standing alone on the dancefloor, I edged back into the house and reclaimed my shandy. From the shadows I looked out into the throng and realized with dismay that there was no-one I knew. No sign of Florence. Not that I was sure I wanted to talk to Florence.

A girl came hurrying in, almost tripping over me. 'Sorry!' she gasped. 'Did I hurt you?'

'No, not at all.'

'I didn't see you. Mike says Henry says we have to change the music and play some fast ones or else Wendy's going to eat him alive. There's some Stones in Roger's car.'

'I'll come and give you a hand.' It'd be better than just standing there.

'Oh, thanks. I'm Laura, I'm Roger's sister.'

'I'm Thea.'

Her brother's car was near to the house, and we each picked up an armful of records.

I said, 'Is that Mike, doing the music?'

'Yes.'

I judged by her smile that Mike was her boyfriend. 'He's doing a good job.'

'Come over and meet him.'

I was introduced to Mike, and Laura found a Stones album which began with 'Jumpin' Jack Flash' and neatly defeated Wendy's tenacious attempts to cling on to Henry any longer.

'I'm the back-up rescue party,' Laura said, and wove her way through to where Henry was putting Wendy's hand into that of a thick-set man in a sports jacket. Turning, he saw Laura, smiled, said something and whirled her into the thick of the dancing.

Beside me someone said, 'I'm Roger. Are you purely decorative or do you move too?'

I smiled – you couldn't not – and we went out to join them.

I hardly saw Henry all evening. We managed half of another dance, but then an elderly man called out from the house that it was time for champagne and cake, and I lost him again. I stood out in the hall for the toast and the brief speeches – the elderly man made one, and Henry said a few words in reply. There was something about him getting into Cambridge.

Florence stood to one side, smiling at him. At one point she looked up and saw me, nodding a friendly acknowledgement. I knew I should have gone up to her and said hello, but somehow I couldn't. Having let so much of the night go by without seeking her out, it would be a bit awkward to speak to her now. But, more than that, I felt uneasy about her.

I was wearing the brooch she'd sent me. I hoped she'd noticed.

After the champagne, most of the older people began to leave. The dancing got going again outside, and I thought that now would be our chance. I went outside and waited. Danced with Roger, and waited. Danced with Mike, then waited some more.

It was awkward, being on the lookout for him and trying not to show it. I was sure people must see me on my own and feel sorry for me, and I hated the thought of their pity. Going to fetch a drink I didn't want, I noticed someone else on their own – a man, standing in the doorway through to the hall, only just visible in the dim light.

I turned my back on him and concentrated on searching through the bottles for lemonade or coke – I was in the mood for either an awful lot of alcohol or none at all, and, all things considered, the latter seemed the more sensible option. I hoped the man would go on standing in the shadows – what was he doing there? Waiting for his girlfriend to emerge from the loo? Getting geared up to leave? – and not come over to talk.

'Are you looking for something special?'

His deep, slightly sibilant voice right by my ear nearly made me jump out of my skin. Florence's dining room was expensively carpeted, but even so, no-one, surely, had any right to move *that* quietly. Perhaps he'd flown.

And, although I knew I'd never met him before, for some strange reason I recognized his voice.

'No, no, I don't really want a drink.' The hasty words echoed in my ears, and I half expected him to say, in that case why are you standing at the drinks table?

He didn't. He didn't say anything, merely stretched past me for the gin bottle. Calmly he poured a large measure into a glass, adding a couple of fingers of tonic.

I wanted to move away. I felt uneasy, with him so close by my side – we should have been merrily chatting, as party guests were meant to, yet the idea of small talk seemed all wrong. I glanced at him. He was dark, both in colouring and complexion, and the strongly-marked lines in his face made him look serious. More than serious – almost threatening.

I pulled my imagination up short. What the hell was threatening about a dark-haired man pouring himself a gin and tonic? Come to think of it, it seemed an excellent idea for him to pour me one too.

I was just about to say I'd changed my mind and would have a drink after all when he looked at me. Straight at me, eyeball to eyeball. And his eyes, reflecting the coloured lights from the terrace, didn't look human.

It was only a fleeting image. He turned his head slightly, and the animal yellow in his irises went away.

I said, 'I think I'll go outside again – I want to talk to . . .'

I couldn't think of anyone's name except Henry's. And Henry had disappeared.

But it didn't matter, because the man was no longer listening. Or I didn't think he was – he certainly wasn't looking at me. I walked off towards the door.

As I went through into the hall, that dark quiet voice said penetratingly, '*Au revoir*, Thea.'

I resumed my wait. I stayed outside – the encounter in the dining room had shaken me a bit, although there was no reason why it should have done. It was probably only my own tension, making the ordinary seem un-ordinary. I thought I'd ask Henry, though, how the man had known my name.

If I ever saw Henry again.

He didn't come back. Hours seemed to have passed – I looked at my watch and it said half past four, but I knew that wasn't right, it couldn't possibly be that late – and I didn't know where he was. The party was dying now, there was no doubt about it, and I was going to have to leave soon.

Where was he?

I decided he must have gone to bed. Perhaps the drink had suddenly overcome him. But he wouldn't, surely he wouldn't disappear while guests were still there?

Why not?

I wondered if I could ask someone. But no, I'd look stupid. If everyone else except me knew he'd called it a day, they'd all laugh at me. There was no alternative, I'd just have to slip quietly away.

I went into the hall, thinking I might phone for a cab. Then I decided against it – if someone came by and heard, they'd know I was alone and without a lift, and might offer to drive me back. I didn't think I could manage polite conversation.

I let myself out of the front door, closing it firmly behind me. I thought, sod you, Henry!

There was a call box up the road, and I set out for it. It was half a mile away, no distance at all in daytime but something else in the dark small hours when you were wearing strappy evening sandals. My feet were already complaining from all the dancing and standing around, and walking was purgatory.

I kept saying, 'Sod you, Henry,' quite loudly. Sod you for being so nice then disappearing. For making me think we'd both felt that magic, then letting me down with such an almighty thump. Sod you for drinking so much that you had to go to bed.

Ouch, my feet. Ouch, my heart.

I told myself it was the pain in my feet that was making me cry. Angry – with myself, with him – I stopped at the side of the road and took off my sandals and my tights, then walked on in the cool grass of the verge.

It was very dark. And very lonely. Out on the Fen a vixen screamed.

Lights shone out, coming from behind. I ducked into the hedge – the last thing I wanted was some party-leaver taking pity on me and pouring well-meant sympathy all over me. I hoped the car would go straight by.

It seemed to be coming very slowly. As if the driver were very drunk. Then a horn sounded. A Morris Minor horn.

Henry said, 'What on earth are you doing?'

I strode on. Sod you, Henry!

He was keeping the car level with me, talking through the wound-down window.

'Thea! Why were you standing in the hedge? And where are your shoes?'

'Here!' I waved them in his face as if I were brandishing some nasty instrument of torture. My tights flapped out and tangled themselves in the radio aerial. I wrenched them free. *Damn*. Forty-five pence down the drain.

'Where are you going?'

'To call for a taxi.'

'Why?'

Was he being deliberately obtuse or was he always like this? I said – shouted – 'Because how the hell else am I going to get home?'

He stopped the car, and I strode off down the road. I heard the car door slam, and he was running after me. He caught me round the waist, and although I struggled, he didn't let go.

'Please,' he said. 'Come and get in the car.'

'I don't –'

'*Please.*'

I went with him. He opened the passenger door, and I noticed that window was down, too. There was a slight smell of vomit, overlaid with Dettol.

He got in beside me. 'It's not very wholesome, but you should have seen it half an hour ago.'

'I'm glad I didn't.'

In the glow of the panel lights I saw him smile briefly. 'I'm really sorry, Thea. I had to take bloody Wendy home, and she was sick. Her parents had gone to bed, and I had to get her mother up to hose her down and see to her, and then I had to clean out the car.'

He sounded so woebegone. I thought, not much of an end to your eighteenth birthday party. I said, 'Oh.'

We sat in silence for a while. The smell was awful. Then he said, 'Where did you think I was?'

'I thought you'd gone to bed.' It seemed stupid, now that I came to think of it.

He sighed. Then said, 'Oh, Thea. You idiot.'

He reached out for my hand, and his was warm and strong.

We sat holding hands for a bit longer, then he spoke again. 'I was thinking,' he said hesitantly, 'all the time I was watching Wendy honk in the car and reflecting what a bloody awful mess she was making and why did it have to be *my* car she was doing it in, that in a while it'll be all right again because I'll be back with Thea.'

'Oh.'

'Then when I'd cleaned up and washed everything with buckets of disinfectant, I came home and there you were gone.'

'I couldn't stay!' I rounded on him. 'How could I go on standing there like a lemon with everyone else in couples and most of them leaving? What else was there to do but go?'

'You could have asked someone where I was.'

'Oh yeah? And supposing they'd said you were taking Wendy home? *They* wouldn't know she was throwing up and not at all kissable!'

'But –' He started to laugh, then conquered it. 'I wouldn't have been kissing her even if she wasn't being sick. Honestly.'

I muttered, 'You might have been. She might have been your girlfriend, for all I knew.'

'She wasn't. She's not.'

'Huh.'

'Thea?'

'Okay.'

'Okay what?'

'Whatever you like.' I tried to pull my hand away – I felt I was being manipulated and I didn't like it – but his grip was too strong. 'All right! Stop grinding my bones against each other, will you? Where *do* you play?'

'Sorry.' He loosened his grip. 'What do you mean, where do I play?'

'What position. In rugby. When I came to stay once, Florence said you'd gone on a rugby tour.'

'Good Lord, I'd forgotten that. *And* that you'd come to stay.' He seemed to find that surprising. 'Come to think of it, I don't think I ever knew.' He paused, as if, like me, he was wondering why Florence hadn't told him. Then he said, 'Easter, it was. My first ever tour. 1969? No, '70. We went to Warwickshire.'

Before he got lost in his reminiscences, I repeated the question.

'Number six,' he said. 'Flanker.'

No wonder he felt solid and had a fist like a clamp.

'You're changing the subject,' he said. 'I want you to assure me it's okay.'

'I just said so, didn't I?'

He sighed again. He had a tendency to treat me as if I were an annoying child. 'Thea, this is important. All hurt feelings aside, I want to know that my knight-errant act hasn't cocked up our first night together.'

Our first *night*. Part of me was demanding how dare he be so presumptuous, while the rest of me was carolling a joyful, fiercely aroused song of victory.

He realized what he'd said as soon as he'd said it. 'I mean, evening,' he amended. And leaned across to kiss my cheek.

I said, sincerely, 'Nothing's spoiled. It really is okay.'

'Sure?'

'Sure.'

'Then if you promise you won't be sick, I'll drive you home.'

He knew where to go. Florence must have told him. In the square outside the hotel, everything was quiet. We sat with the engine muttering quietly and he kissed me again. On the cheek.

'Will you come out with me tomorrow?'

'Yes.'

'When can I pick you up?'

'Whenever.' I didn't want to sound too eager. 'Eleven?'

'Make it twelve.' *Damn!* 'I ought to put in a morning's clearing-up.'

'Perhaps there'll be some more vomit, if you're very lucky,' I said, getting out of the car. It was awful when someone changed the time you'd suggested to a later one, it made it seem they were less keen to see you than you were to see them.

'A man can live in hope,' he replied. 'Goodnight, Thea.'

As I ran up the steps and let myself into the hotel, I heard him drive gently away. Up in my room I threw my arms round the sleepy Eric, who wagged his tail politely in response.

'Tomorrow, Eric,' I told him, 'you're going to meet an old pal.'

I slept deeply for a couple of hours, then woke up just as it was getting light and found I couldn't get off again. I was thinking about Florence.

Why hadn't she come to talk to me? It was her house, and strictly speaking I was her guest since it was she who had issued the invitation. It was hurtful, in the cool light of dawn, that she hadn't paid me any attention at all.

Was she still feeling guilty about what she'd done? It had been unforgivable, sure, but I was prepared to forget it. Maybe she'd been right, too – I seemed to have put Steve right out of my mind, so it couldn't have been love after all. Still, what had love to do with it? We would have had a marvellous time.

She'd said that half of what she had would be mine if I were still a virgin when I came back to East Anglia. How had she known I would? And how was she reckoning to know if I'd done the deed or not? I baulked at that – it was too intimate to think about. Then I remembered that when I'd protested I was still a virgin the morning after I'd let Steve down so badly, she'd said, 'I know.'

How had she known?

The more I tried to puzzle things out, the more questions there seemed to be.

Half her property and her wealth. The other half to Henry, I supposed. Well, that was jolly nice of her at any rate, it was . . .

For the first time I understood fully what she had said. I think I'd been too amazed to start with, then too angry, to take it in properly. Florence was leaving half of everything to me. I was to be given exactly what Henry would have. And he was her grandson.

If she felt like that about me, if I mattered to her as much as he did, then perhaps after all it did give her the right to interfere in my life.

I turned over, thumping my pillow. I knew I had to see her. And soon.

In my dreams I was back at the party, looking for Henry with much greater anxiety than I had done in reality. Now there was far more at stake – I *had* to find him, for only he could carry out some task whose nature I wasn't sure of but about whose importance there was no doubt at all: if he failed, the result would be terrifying.

The moment was fast approaching when he must act. I saw him, and felt an instant's vast relief. But then he was gone, drawn into a moving cloud of dense white mist, and I heard a cry, as if someone were in great pain. I became aware of pain in myself – low down in my stomach, like an acute menstrual cramp, something knotted me up so that I drew myself into a ball to seek relief. I thought I heard the faint kittenlike cry of a newborn baby.

Then that voice came, deep and menacing, and I saw the dark shape of the wolf. Its jaws yawned open and it howled, a noise so frightful that the human sounds were drowned out. There was a flash of yellow as the eyes opened wide, and the Dark Man stood over me. Behind him I thought I saw Henry, trying to reach me, but the Dark Man perceived his presence and, turning, with inhuman strength flung him away.

Once more he stared down at me. The voice spoke those same appalling words: 'I curse thee.'

In my dream I screamed, and then I was no longer asleep but crawling up to wakefulness. Henry was gone, the Dark Man was fading. When he was little more than an outline, he said softly, '*Au revoir*, Thea.'

The shock brought me fully awake.

For a long time I sat hunched up at the end of my bed, and slowly the normal sounds of the morning – a car passing, low voices speaking from somewhere close by, the creaking of a door – reassured me. When I was rational again – or as close as I was going to get – I thought, well, at least there's an explanation, of sorts. Some weirdo at a party spooks me, and my subconscious slots him into a place ready-made for him: he turns into the dark figure of my recurrent nightmares. Very neat!

A neat explanation it might have been. Only I wasn't sure I believed it.

Thirteen

I must have dozed for a while, for when I next looked at my bedside clock it said five to eight. The sign on my door, as well as telling me I wasn't to smoke a pipe, informed me that breakfast was from eight till a quarter past nine, so I had time for a bath.

I took as long as I could over it, and over my breakfast. But all the same it was only five past nine when I got back up to my room.

Three hours to kill.

I changed into old jeans and walking shoes and took Eric off for a long walk.

We made our way out of town and on to a minor road, then a lane, where there was little traffic. I let Eric off the lead – not that he minded being on it nowadays, since he was becoming very sedate – and, walking automatically, without really seeing anything, retired into my thoughts.

It had been crazy to leave the party last night, and I tormented myself for at least a quarter of a mile with pictures of what might have happened had I still been there when Henry got back. Then I thought, it was nice of him to have looked after Wendy. He'd told me he had no interest in her (and I could well believe it, now), so it could only have been his sense of responsibility which made him take her home and make sure her mother saw to her. It was his party, I supposed he would have reasoned, so it was up to him to ensure none of his guests finished the evening wandering about the lanes puking up in ditches.

It came to me in a flash that he'd acted just as Florence would have done. She too was an organizer, the sort of person others would naturally turn to in a crisis. In fact – I was still cross with her – she strayed beyond organizing into downright interference.

But I wasn't going to think about Florence. Not then. I wanted to think about Henry.

Not surprising, was it, that he should be like his grandmother, with whom he'd lived since he was small. Nine, she said he was, when he came back to England. She'd never really said *why* that had been – I'd assumed it was because his parents wanted him to have an English education. But why hadn't he gone out to his parents in the holidays? I'd been at school with girls who did that, boarders whose dads were in the Army or the Foreign Office, or something, and who sometimes left school a day early at the end of term to enable them to catch flights to Sarawak, or Aden, or other romantic-sounding places.

Henry's parents had lived in Hong Kong. He'd done the journey alone when he was nine and a half, so what stopped him doing it again subsequently?

I had no idea.

I would, I hoped, soon have the chance to ask him.

The thought prompted me to turn round, whistle for Eric and head back for the hotel. I'd probably be ready far too soon and have ages to kill, but somehow I didn't want to go any further.

* * *

I changed out of my jeans and put on some make-up. I didn't usually wear much, but he'd seen me in the full slap last night and I thought my as-nature-made-me face might be a bit too much of a let-down. I went over to the window and leaned on the sill; I could see up the road from there, so I'd be able to go down when I saw him arriving. Or would it be better to pretend I hadn't noticed – since that would imply I'd been looking out for him – and wait for Reception to call up and say he was waiting?

Twelve o'clock came and went. He didn't arrive, and I still hadn't made up my mind. I opened the window, craning out to see further up the road. No sign of a Morris Minor.

Then a voice called, 'If you lean out any further you'll overbalance, and I'm not sure I'd be able to catch you.'

I looked down. He was standing on the pavement, arms folded, and he was laughing. It must have been obvious what I was doing. I said, since attack was the best form of defence, 'You're late.'

'Sorry. I found two empty bottles and a used contraceptive behind the shed, so I had to scour the grounds to make sure there weren't any more for Florence to find.'

It wasn't the sort of conversation to be carried out between people two storeys apart, especially on a Sunday. Passers-by were giving us doubtful glances. 'I'll come down,' I said, and hastily shut the window.

I told Eric, 'Henry's downstairs. You'd better give him a warmer greeting than you did last time this happened, or it's no more bones for *you*.'

Funny things, dogs. Who knows what goes on in their heads? Some little door in Eric's memory must have flipped open, because he took one look at Henry and launched himself at him, whining with pleasure and wagging his tail till it raised dust.

Henry looked so pleased I could have cried.

When they'd finished their mutual admiration – it was quite a relief, they were becoming embarrassing – Henry suggested we find a pub and have a drink. He'd parked the car round the corner, and since it was a warm day, we drove out into the country to find a pub with a garden. Eric lay on the grass and we sat down with beer and sandwiches among a small crowd of other Sunday morning drinkers and waited till one of us thought of something to say.

The trouble was, there was too much to say. There *had* been magic between us, last night – there had for me, anyway – and somehow it had pitched us straight into a closeness that usually didn't come till later in a relationship. If it came at all. So, while the usual first-date pleasantries were too time-wastingly trivial, I think that neither of us was prepared to admit to the magic and launch into something *meaningful*.

On the other hand, he might just have been bad at small talk.

We discussed the party a bit. I said I'd liked his friends, and he replied somewhat dryly, 'Apart from Wendy, no doubt.' I wasn't sure how to deal with that, so I rushed into a comment about the gin and tonic man who'd mysteriously known my name.

Henry shook his head. 'Don't think I know him,' he said. 'I don't recognize him from that description, anyway.' He grinned at me. 'He must be a friend of Florence's.'

'Oh.'

We lapsed into silence.

Eventually he said, 'This is silly. There's so much I want to talk to you about, and I don't know where to start.'

'Me too,' I said, almost before he'd finished. 'I feel I know bits of you, because of Florence, but you're still a stranger.'

He looked at me intently. 'You're not.'

He had effectively taken my breath away. I couldn't speak.

'I'll tell you about you,' he said. 'You were a thin little girl with very light hair whose mother ran out on her and who had to be sent all alone to live with her father. Your only friend was a dog, and you had to give him back to some spoiled brat who already had a pony and a nice grandmother. You came to look for the dog one day, and you knelt in the mud with your arms round his neck and cried.'

God, he was making me sound like something out of Dickens. I loathed Dickens. 'It wasn't quite like that. I didn't mind going to Dad, in fact I –'

I don't think he was listening. He was leaning down to pat Eric, fondling the golden ears with his strong hands suddenly gentle. 'You and your dog went everywhere together,' he continued, 'and –' He stopped. Then, as if he'd decided against what he was going to say and was substituting something else, he finished, 'And you still do.'

Follow that, I thought. It wasn't easy. 'Okay,' I said, 'now it's my turn. You were a boy who had a dog and –' But I found I couldn't talk about that. The memory of his face this morning when Eric had recognized him was too fresh. As was the parallel memory, from eight years ago, of how he'd looked when Eric *hadn't* recognized him. '– And who lived with his grandmother because his parents were abroad.' I trailed to a halt. What else was there to say? 'Why did you?' Why not? I thought. I want to know, don't I? So ask him.

'Why did I live with Florence?' He frowned. 'I always wanted to, from when I was very small.' His face lightened. 'If you'd been a child growing up in an expatriate community, you'd know why. Florence and the Fens were far more appealing than Hong Kong and my parents.'

'But didn't you even go out for the holidays?'

He shook his head. 'No. The holidays were when I most wanted to be in the Fens.'

'Didn't your parents get upset?'

He frowned again. Then, after what seemed to be thinking time, said, 'Thea, I don't know about you, but I realized quite early in life that I'd been an unplanned child. Well, I didn't know about planning when I was little, I just knew they didn't want me.'

I couldn't imagine that. However unconventional my parents might have been, I'd never picked up the feeling that either of them hadn't wanted me. 'How horrible!' Already I was prepared to wage war on these awful parents, to take them to task for accidentally having had a child and then being even more careless in letting him know he was an accident. 'They ought to –'

'It wasn't their fault.'

'Of course it was!'

'It wasn't. I –' He broke off. 'I found out something, recently. I'll tell you, but not yet. But, believe me, it wasn't their fault.'

Mystifying. But he'd said, I'll tell you. Implying we were going to see more of each other.

I already knew that, didn't I?

Then he said, 'Thea, do you ever get the feeling you're not in control of your own life?'

I had no idea what he meant. I stared at him, trying to pick up some clue from his expression, but his face was bland. 'No, I don't,' I said firmly. 'I am in control of my life, I sort out what I want to do and then I do it.'

Into my head came an image of Steve. And the memory of how much I'd wanted him. And Florence, stepping in between me and my fiercest desire.

A shiver of deep unease ran through me. What was it that had made Henry think he was being controlled by someone else?

'Sorry.' His hand reached for mine. 'I shouldn't have said that. I didn't mean to worry you.'

'You didn't.'

He smiled. 'Yes, I did. I can tell by your face.'

I looked into his eyes. 'I was thinking of you,' I said honestly.

It was his turn to be lost for words.

After a while I went in and got us another drink, then it was chucking-out time and we had to go. I had no suggestions as to what to do next, and he seemed to be thin on ideas too. We drove into Cambridge, and he showed me where he'd be going in October. We took Eric for a walk along the Backs, then found a café and had a cup of tea.

He said, 'Florence has asked us back for supper.'

I felt resentful. We had done as she wanted last night, Henry hosting his party and I turning up as ordered. Couldn't we be allowed to have today to ourselves?

'Did you say we would?'

'Yes.' He must have perceived that I wasn't best pleased. 'I had to. She gave me a great party yesterday – she paid for the lot – and it would have been ungrateful to say we wanted to go out on our own.'

He was right. But I still felt resentful. She had used her knowledge of him – of his honourable nature –

to get what she wanted. There didn't seem a lot of future in pointing that out, so I simply said, 'Okay, then.'

She had obviously been looking out for us. As we pulled up outside the house, she opened the door and came to greet us. She didn't say much, she just kept looking from one to the other of us, almost as if she were comparing us.

It was weird.

Then she was ushering us inside, into the drawing room where, although the evening was mild, a fire was burning. She had prepared a tray of drinks and there were home-made cheese straws fresh from the oven on a warm plate. She made a ceremony of our drinks: we were all still standing, and she said solemnly, raising her glass to each of us in turn, 'To Henry and to Thea. I welcome you on this the first private occasion that I have you together under my roof.'

I wanted to laugh. Nerves, I expect. Henry was more diplomatic and replied something kind and innocuous about it being a pleasure to be there. Then we sat down and she asked us how we'd spent the day.

'We went to a pub for lunch,' Henry said, 'then into Cambridge. Eric christened every railing post between King's and the Silver Street Bridge.'

'Isn't it nice to have him back?' Florence said. 'It's a long time since I saw him lying on the hearthrug. Did you show Thea your college?'

'It's not mine yet,' he replied modestly. 'But yes, I did.'

I watched him out of the corner of my eye – we were sitting next to each other on the sofa, facing Florence who was in her armchair the other side of the fire – and noticed how the lines round his eyes deepened when he smiled. Florence was looking at him less covertly. When she wasn't looking at me, that was.

Something felt – not *wrong*, exactly, but strange. What was it? Letting their conversation flow round me, I tried to puzzle it out.

Then I knew. Something *was* wrong: she was. She was acting as if Henry and I were an established couple. Looking at us so triumphantly, as if she were saying, see how well they go together! The business with the drinks, toasting us as we stood in front of her. Even the way she phrased her question: how did you two spend your day?

She was taking one hell of a lot for granted.

From somewhere – straight out of hell, for all I know – a devil was in me. I got up and said to Florence, interrupting her reminiscence about how pleasant it was to punt down to Grantchester and why didn't Henry and I try it? 'Florence, please could I use your phone?'

She looked a bit startled. She wasn't used to being interrupted. She said, 'Yes, of course, Thea. You know where it is.'

'Thanks.' I went across and opened the door into the hall. Timing it carefully, before they could resume their conversation, I said with just the right degree of nonchalance, 'I promised Steve I'd ring him this evening.'

You'd think she'd been struck. Her face paled and her mouth dropped open. For an instant before she recovered herself, I saw how she'd look when she was very, very old. Perhaps it was telepathy, perhaps it was that I was beginning to understand how her mind worked; whatever it was, I knew what she was thinking.

I'd kept my side of the bargain and had still been a virgin when I returned to live in East Anglia. That was all she'd asked of me. To keep her side of it, she was now honour-bound to leave me half of everything.

Even if I disappeared tomorrow, met Steve in some quiet out-of-the-way spot and we marked our reunion by screwing like a pair of jack-rabbits all night long.

I enjoyed my sweet revenge. For a minute or so out in the hall, the receiver in my hand while, finger holding down the rests, I dialled Steve's number, I felt like a punished child who has drawn a rude picture of the teacher.

Then, as if I'd been doused in cold water, I remembered Henry.

GOD!

What should I do? If I went back into the drawing room and said Steve wasn't in or I'd changed my mind, Florence would think she had been reprieved. But if I let it be thought that I'd just had a wonderful chat with my boyfriend, what would it do to Henry and the magic?

I was still trying to decide when the drawing room door opened again and they came out. Florence looked at me – into my face, so I don't think she could have noticed I was still holding down the rests – and said frostily, 'We are going in to dinner. Please join us when you have finished.'

She stood back to let Henry precede her into the dining room – he hadn't so much as glanced my way – then followed him in and very pointedly closed the door behind her.

To say the rest of the evening was awkward would be an understatement. I hardly spoke, Florence appeared to be in a state of shock, and it was left to

Henry to make various staccato remarks about things like last night's party and did we know so-and-so's daughter had gone to America. Poor chap, he was down to the bottom of the barrel by the time we were having our coffee and asking if we'd read any good books lately.

I longed to leave. Longed to take his face in my hands and make him look at me while I told him.

At last Florence got to her feet and said that, if we didn't mind, she was going to retire. 'Henry will drive you back to your hotel, Thea,' she said. Then, unexpectedly, 'I think it would be best if you were to leave Eric with us.'

It was like a punch in the ribs. As if she were saying, do what I want you to do and I'll be nice to you. Defy me and I'll withdraw my patronage, starting with the dog.

Then I made myself look her in the eye. And she didn't look vindictive, she just looked sad.

I almost went up to her to give her a kiss. But I was so confused that I could no longer tell if it was right to obey the instinct or not. So I just said, 'Okay. Thank you very much for dinner, Florence. Be seeing you.'

As he slammed the car door Henry said, 'Who's Steve?'

I didn't answer. He said again, 'Thea, who the bleeding hell's Steve?'

I hadn't heard him swear before, not like that. I said, 'Once you've driven us a decent distance away from *her*, stop and I'll tell you.'

'Don't call her *her!*'

I muttered under my breath, '*Her.*' It was childish, but I couldn't help it.

We drove for ten minutes or so, then he stopped at the side of the road and said somewhat caustically, 'Right. I'm all ears.'

I didn't know what to say. Out in the car, alone with him, the magic had come back. And I was regretting with every fibre of my being ever having mentioned bloody Steve.

Eventually I said, 'He was someone I went out with for a while. I wrote to Florence about him, and she came down to see me.' I couldn't tell him what had made her rush from Cambridgeshire to Gloucestershire with such haste. Nor what strange proposal she had made. 'But I decided I didn't want to see him any more. It ended before I came back here.'

I could hear his immediate question racing towards me. 'Then why did you phone him?'

'I didn't. I –' This was the stupid bit. 'I was holding down the rests. I didn't phone anyone.'

He just said, as well he might, 'Why?'

'Because –' Because what? Because I think Florence manipulated me, bribed me to give up Steve so that I came back heart-whole and hymen-whole for you? I couldn't say that. 'I don't know.'

He didn't speak for a while. Then he said, 'Was it to show me that you're not mine for the taking? To make sure I know there are other men after you?'

'*No!*' I didn't want him thinking that – I'd always despised girls who played one man off against another. It seemed such a waste of time. But I couldn't tell him the truth. Not yet. 'I can't explain exactly, but please believe that it wasn't that.'

The silence fell back, but this time I could hear him thinking. And, as I'd imagined he would, he said, the edge of a smile in his voice, 'Then you *are* mine for the taking.'

I leaned towards him and put my hands on his face, my fingers tracing along his jaw. I looked into his eyes – he was smiling more broadly now – and said softly, 'What on earth makes you think that?'

Humour seemed the best way of lightening the mood. Thank God, I thought, for a man who can see the funny side of things. He said, 'Something to do with the way you're leaning against me.'

Instantly I straightened up and sat back in my own seat. 'I'm not, I'm . . .' I began.

He put his hands on my shoulders and pulled me towards him. Then he kissed me.

Fourteen

It wasn't like any kiss I'd had before. It wasn't like like the wet-flannel, inexperienced attempts of the boys back in Gloucestershire, it wasn't like the instant-passion-inducing, experienced Steve. Henry kissed me softly and tentatively, but he held me so close, and the kiss went on for so long, that somehow I knew this was the most important thing that had ever happened to me.

Boys I'd kissed before would have tried to put their hands up my jumper, although – except in the case of Steve – they'd have been beaten off. They'd have got breathless and sweaty, and moaned a bit, and said things like, wasn't I sexy and wouldn't I go a bit further because I'd be sure to like it once we got going.

There was none of that with Henry. There was just being held so close to him that I could feel his heart-beat. And that incredible, gentle kiss that seemed to go on for ever.

When at last we broke apart and, his arms round me, I was leaning against his shoulder, I felt that some sort of bond had been made between us. I hoped he felt the same.

After some time he said, 'I'll drive you home.'

Just that. I was overwhelmingly relieved, because anything more, whether a comment on the day, the evening or the kiss, would have been wrong.

When we reached the hotel he got out to see me up to the door. Briefly he touched my hand. 'I've got something to do in the morning,' he said. 'I promised Mike I'd help him set up his disco – he's doing a silver wedding party. I'll call for you after lunch. Okay?'

I nodded. 'Okay.'

The room seemed lonely without Eric to welcome me. I lay wide awake on my bed, thinking of Florence, thinking of how I'd behaved, and, most of all, thinking of Henry. It was an impossibly long time till tomorrow afternoon.

In the morning, when I'd had breakfast, tidied up a bit, done some washing and was sitting wondering what to do next, Reception called up to tell me I had a visitor. Rushing to the window, I saw the Morris Minor parked right outside. I raced downstairs, not even pausing to lock my door, but it wasn't him. It was Florence.

She was standing with her back to me, staring out across the square. When I'd got over the disappointment, I said, 'Good morning, Florence.'

She turned. 'Thea.' For a few moments she just looked at me. Then she said, 'Will you walk with me?'

There was doubt in her face, as if she thought I might say no. Touched far more than I could admit to myself, I was hit with the memory of what she'd been to me down the years. And I thought of the brooch she'd sent me, for which I'd barely thanked her. Suddenly it didn't matter that she'd been manipulative and interfering, that she'd organized my life so that I was here, where she wanted me to be, rapidly falling for her grandson. Wasn't that what I wanted, too?

She was strong, she was bossy, and it didn't do to cross her. But also she was kind, and wise, and the one person who'd been there for me all my life. I went up to her and wordlessly put my arms round her.

At first she resisted. Then she put her hand up and touched my cheek. She just said, 'Oh, Thea.' It was enough: we both knew it was going to be all right.

We walked into the city centre and found a seat in the sun, on the lawns before the cathedral. There was a lot I wanted to say, but the habits of a lifetime die hard and I waited for her to lead the way in. I didn't have long to wait.

'Henry goes up to Cambridge at the beginning of next month,' she said. 'It would make me very happy if you came to live at Willowford Fen.'

Several thoughts hit me all at once. *Live.* Did that mean for ever? I was to inherit on her death, along with Henry. Was I to move in now and stay there for the rest of my life? And what about Henry? How would he feel if I became a permanent resident? How would the two of us feel, living under the same roof?

The last question was something I backed off from. I couldn't think about it, not now. And I realized with relief that it wouldn't actually be like that, since Henry would be away in his college at Cambridge.

I said – it was the best I could do – 'What will I do all day?'

She shrugged, as if it hardly mattered. 'Whatever you wish. Come and go as you please, read, garden, help around the house if you want to.'

I was reminded of some Victorian miss, living a life of futility until some steady, sensible man came along to turn her into a wife. My pride hurt, I said, remembering at the last moment that, since she'd just offered me a free home, this was not the time to sound surly, 'It's what I'd like to do. But I'll need to find a job. There's no way I can live off you.'

She said again, 'As you wish.'

'I've got good "A" levels!' I said, too loudly. 'I don't want to go to university,' – I'd had enough of life on a shoestring – 'but I'm damned well going to have a career!' I was stung by her attitude. Maybe in her day it had been all right for a young woman to treat marriage and family as her only purpose in life, but this was the seventies, and women thought differently now. I'd show her! I'd get the best bloody job a school-leaver *ever* got!

There was a silence between us, angry on my part, unreadable on hers. But it was a shame to feel angry with her now, when we'd just made such a momentous decision. And it seemed we had – fleetingly I thought of Dad, and I wondered how he'd take the news that my temporary stay in East Anglia had turned into something more permanent. Into, perhaps, for ever.

The thought wasn't disturbing enough to make me hold back from committing myself.

I said quietly, 'When do you want me to move in?'

She turned to look at me, her grey eyes narrowed against the sunshine. 'What about tomorrow?'

And, since there was nothing else to say, I agreed.

Henry didn't arrive till after three – he said he and Mike had had an awful job finding the place for the disco, which was miles further away than Mike had thought – and when I'd finished saying it was okay and no, I didn't mind, I said, 'It's tomorrow.'

'What is?'

He was unlocking the car – we were going into Cambridge to eat and go to the cinema – and I thought perhaps he hadn't heard. 'I'm moving in tomorrow,' I repeated as we slammed the doors.

He shook his head. 'Sorry. Where?'

It wasn't that he hadn't heard. She hadn't told him.

For a silly moment I wondered if it was a secret, and I wasn't supposed to tell him. I pushed the thought away. 'Florence asked me this morning if I would go and live with her. I said yes, and I'm moving in tomorrow.'

He stared at me. He didn't look especially pleased. In fact he didn't look anything. I thought, oh, God, he hates the idea. He's thinking I'll be there all the time, he'll be pushed into being with me and, since it's his home too, there'll be no escape.

'It's all right,' I said huffily, 'you'll be away most of the time, won't you? And anyway I'm going to get a job, so I'll only be there in the evenings and at weekends.'

He started to laugh. 'I'd better tell you what was going through my mind, since you've got it as wrong as you possibly could.' He reached out and took my hand. 'I was thinking, great, she's going to live with us, she'll be right under my nose all the time and I don't know how I shall keep my hands off her. Then I thought, bugger, Mike reminded me this morning that I'd promised to go walking in Yorkshire with him for a week and he's booked up our accommodation.'

A week. That neatly took up practically all the time till he went up. Damn. Oh, *damn*.

Throwing caution to the winds I said, 'Do you have to go?'

It was hopeless and I knew it. This was Henry, Florence's grandson. A man who chivalrously took stray women home from parties. A man who, as a boy, gave away his dog to a worthier cause. He wasn't going to let down a mate, especially when the mate had already fixed up all the arrangements.

'Yes.' He sighed. 'We've planned the itinerary, and Mike's full of it. We're going to have a few beers in the highest pub in England.'

He didn't sound at all excited at the prospect. I felt sorry for him, that something he'd no doubt been looking forward to as much as Mike had suddenly lost its charm. Then I felt a tiny twinge of triumph: didn't it say something about his feelings for me, that he didn't want to go away from me?

I was torn between letting him know how much I'd miss him, which with any luck would make him feel even worse, or being gallant and pretending I'd be fine, and far too busy settling in to have time to pine for him.

'Well, it's probably just as well you'll be out of the way,' I said briskly. 'There'll be a lot for Florence and me to do.'

'Such as what?'

He was concentrating on getting past a tractor pulling a trailer of muck, and I couldn't see his expression. 'Oh, I don't know,' I said vaguely. 'This and that.'

We were past the tractor, and he turned to look at me briefly. 'I wish I weren't going,' he said. 'I'll miss you.'

Then I felt a pig for not having said so first. It wasn't too late – I hoped it wasn't – so, repaying his honesty in like coin, I said fervently, 'I'll miss you too.'

It was a declaration, I suppose. The first time we'd

said something important to each other. Whatever, it had the result that we didn't let go of each other all evening. We walked hand in hand through the Botanic Gardens, then when it was time to go and get something to eat, we sat with our knees pressed together under the table, my foot resting on his. In the cinema, he put his arm round me and we had a discreet kiss or two when the action slowed up.

He parked round the corner from the hotel, and we sat in the car, still holding hands. I didn't think I should ask him in – it was after eleven, and anyway I was sure he'd say no. But I didn't want to leave him, and from the way he was gripping my hand, I was pretty sure he didn't want me to go.

'I'll phone you,' he said.

The thought was instantly brightening. 'Oh, good.'

He leaned across, putting his arms round me and pulling me close. 'Be happy,' he muttered.

A week seemed an age. And when he got back, he'd be leaving again almost immediately. Happy? He didn't know what he was asking.

'Oh, I will,' I said. I'd meant it to sound sarcastic, but it didn't. I was quite glad it didn't. 'I've got masses to do, anyway.'

'So you said this morning.' He sounded as if he were amused. And disbelieving.

'I have! For one thing, I've got to find a job. I can't sponge off Florence, and besides I didn't work my socks off getting my "A" levels just to sit around sewing fine seams and dead-heading roses!'

'Florence takes care of the roses. She's very possessive about them.'

'*Shut up!*'

'Sorry.' He straightened his face. 'What sort of a job are you thinking of?'

It was a good question. My mind was a complete

blank. I thought of saying that I'd have to see what was available when suddenly I thought of Dad and Pam and Dumbo's Guide. 'I'm a published author,' I said grandly. 'I shall make my career in the literary world.'

'Wow.'

'I will, just watch me!' Dad must have contacts, so must Pam. And they'd both do their best for me, wouldn't they?

'Of course you will. I expect you'll be a working girl by the time I get back from Yorkshire.'

He was making fun of me, and I didn't mind. But all the same, something in me was rising to the challenge. I reached in my bag for my purse, and, getting out a pound note, slapped it down on the dashboard. 'A pound says I will.'

He covered my pound with one of his own. 'You're on.' He opened the glove compartment. 'We'll put the stake in here, and the winner can claim it next week.'

Next week. He was going away, in the morning. The moment had come, and there wasn't any point in prolonging it.

'I'm going in,' I said. I had the door open and was out of the car before he had time to reply.

I heard his muttered, 'Oh, bloody hell,' and the slam of his door. Then he had caught me up, his arms round me stopping me in my tracks. Right there in the street he kissed me, and it was neither tentative nor particularly gentle. It set me on fire, and, hardly knowing what I was doing, I was kissing him back, urgently, my tongue seeking and finding his in a moment of such wild sweetness that I felt my knees go weak.

I was sagging against him, my head reeling, almost sick with desire. Pulling his mouth away, he kissed my cheek, my neck, warm lips against my skin, breath hot under my hair. With all my being I wanted him.

Suddenly he straightened up, hands on my shoulders holding me away from him. 'No,' he said, but it sounded as if it were more to himself. 'Not – oh, Thea, don't look at me like that!'

I swayed towards him, wanting to feel his body against mine again. But obviously he'd decided we weren't going to go on. He was, apparently, as strong in mind as in body. At that moment it was something to be regretted.

'See you when you get back,' I said when I could manage speech.

'Yes. Take care.' He was backing away, no longer touching me.

'You too. Don't fall off any mountains.' I took a step along the pavement, towards the hotel doorway. Another step. Three.

'I'm not climbing any.' He had the car keys in his hand.

I couldn't bear it any longer. 'Goodbye!'

I ran the last few yards, up the steps and in through the door. As I closed it behind me, I heard him drive away.

I kept busy. I did have masses to do, just as I'd said, so it was easy to keep every moment full. In the morning I packed, and then straightened my room – staying in a hotel was a novelty, and I just couldn't get used to the idea that there was someone else to fold the towels, wipe the basin and tidy the bed.

Florence came to fetch me around eleven. I wondered if she were on her way back from dropping Henry at the station – he hadn't said that they were going by train but it seemed likely, unless they'd gone in Mike's car. If he had one. But you didn't take cars on walking holidays, did you?

As we approached the house, I tried not to think of the Henry things. Remembering him opening the door to me the night of his party, or standing back to let me go in first the evening we had dinner with Florence, were too painful to contemplate now that he wasn't here. As if she picked up my feelings, Florence said,

'I've put you in the small spare room, where you were before. I thought it would remind you of our happy times together.'

Before you met up with Henry again, she could have added. It was perceptive of her, and kind.

'I'll go and unpack.'

But as I set off up the stairs, she called me back. 'Thea, you haven't very much with you, have you?'

I looked down at my small case. 'No, but I –'

'Yes, I know. You thought you were only coming for a visit. What I mean is, perhaps the time has come for you to send for the rest of – for some more of your things.'

She was right to correct herself. I might have been swept along on her tide this far, but it didn't mean I was going right up on to the shore with her. When – if – it came to saying goodbye for ever to Dad and Gloucestershire, it was going to be my decision. No-one else's.

But I didn't need to say that to her. She knew quite well what was in my mind. 'That's very kind,' I said politely. 'I'll write to my father and ask him to send a few necessities.'

'Or you may telephone him, if you wish.' She was turning away, and her voice was almost disinterested. The moment had passed.

*   *   *

We had lunch together, and took Eric for a walk. Then, with the evening sun pouring in through my bedroom window, I took a long and critical look round my new domain. I decided that if Florence could provide me with a desk of some sort, I could turn the space under the window into a study area. I'd get Dad to send my typewriter, and a selection of my favourite books. Perhaps I'd be allowed to put up some more shelves – my own books plus Florence's ones on East Anglia, still on the bedside table, would easily fill a small shelf unit. Dad could send my print of Symond's Yat, too – it'd look nice on the wall by the bed.

It occurred to me, with a slight shock, that I was viewing my move to Willowford Fen as if it were as much of a permanency as Florence had suggested.

Next day I phoned Dad. When I told him that I wanted both a trunkful of personal effects *and* advice on my future career, he suggested it'd be a good idea to meet up the next day in London.

'I'll bring your stuff,' he said, 'it'll be quicker and safer than sending it unaccompanied. And I'll bring Pam, too,' – I hoped she wasn't in earshot, since she wouldn't have taken kindly to the suggestion that she was going to be brought, like my trunk of belongings – 'she's always full of good ideas, she's the person to talk to about jobs.'

'Well, if she doesn't mind,' I said.

'She won't. She misses you.' He hesitated, then said, 'We both do.'

There was an awkward silence. So much had happened since I returned to East Anglia that I couldn't honestly say I'd missed either of them. 'I – er, I've –' I began.

'Course you haven't missed us,' he said robustly.

'You're not meant to, you're meant to be out there having fun and cramming your life with new experiences.'

I'm doing that all right, I thought. Dear old Dad. 'All right, then, I'm not missing you.'

'That's my girl. See you tomorrow.'

The rest of the day loomed, with nothing pressing to do. Then over lunch Florence asked me out of the blue if I remembered Henry's pony.

Garth. How could I forget Garth? If I closed my eyes I could see nine-and-a-half-year-old Henry looking at me over Garth's dappled-grey neck, his eyes wide with pain and surprise.

Don't think about that.

'I remember,' I said shortly.

'Despite having reached the grand old age of fifteen, there is plenty of life in him,' she said. 'Three of the youngsters from the village exercise him, but not always as regularly as one could wish. You're small, and not very heavy,' – she looked at me critically as if judging my weight to the nearest pound – 'and I wondered if you would care to take Garth out for an hour or so this afternoon?'

'I haven't ridden for years.'

'One doesn't forget,' Florence said, in the kind of voice with which it was better not to argue.

'Supposing I'm heavier than you think and I tire him out?'

'You can't be heavier than Susan Earnshaw. But if you think Garth is exhausted, you will have to walk home leading him.'

Go out on Henry's pony. It was, now that I was getting used to it, a wonderful idea.

'I will,' I said. 'I'd love it.'

When I came down from changing into jeans, she

had put a pair of riding boots by the front door.

'Size five,' she said. 'Any good to you?'

I took four and a half. With thick socks, the boots were perfect.

There wasn't any need to ask who they had belonged to.

I caught the bus into Cambridge next morning and was sitting drinking coffee with Dad and Pam at Liverpool Street station by half past ten. Between them, bless them, they'd lugged Dad's big old boarding school suitcase crammed full of clothes, books, posters, records and, as Pam put it, 'other odds and sods we thought you'd miss if you didn't have them'. I was quite eager to get the case unpacked and see just what they considered came under that category. They'd also brought the typewriter.

They were impatient with my thanks, and clearly had something they wanted to say. As soon as there was a gap in the conversation, they both started to speak at once, then Pam put her hand on Dad's and said affectionately, 'You're her pa. You tell her.'

For one amazing moment I thought they were about to tell me they were going to get married, but my instincts proved right after all and they didn't. But the news was nearly as surprising.

'We've got you a job!' Dad said gleefully. 'Or at least, Pam has. Well, an interview. But we're sure you'll get it! You're just what he wants, you write fluently, you're well-organized, and you're bound to get on with him. And the job's worthy of a girl with your qualifications.'

He rabbited on like that for a good half minute, during which Pam glanced at me and cast her eyes heavenwards. When he paused for breath she said kindly, 'Shut up, Jack, for God's sake. I've changed my mind, *I'll* tell her after all.'

I muttered, 'I bloody well wish one of you would.'

'Sorry,' Pam said penitently. 'It's a friend of mine – of my brother, in fact – who's ex-army and who now amuses himself writing. He's done his memoirs – he got them published in some ex-service society magazine – and he's done his family history. He actually bought our Dumbo book to help him with that, and it was him writing to ask if I was the same Pamela Hughes who was his old mate Sam's sister that put us in touch again. Are you with me?'

I nodded, managing not to comment that she was being nearly as long-winded as Dad.

'He's now starting a new book about the history of his town, and he wants an assistant. He's not short of a bob or two,' – she neatly forestalled the question I was about to ask, which was how could this chap afford an assistant? – 'his parents left him a packet. And this is the great bit – guess where he lives?'

'Durban,' I said flippantly.

'Don't be daft!' She frowned. 'He lives in bloody Thetford!' I don't think she had anything against Thetford, it was just the heat of the moment. 'Isn't that incredible?'

It was. And it was sweet of them to be so eager. I reached out and took hold of their hands. 'You're smashing, both of you,' I said, kissing their cheeks, 'and it's incredibly efficient of you to have come up with something so quickly.'

'Well, we knew about it already,' Pam said, looking briefly at Dad. 'As a matter of fact, when he mentioned he needed professional help, I was thinking of doing it myself. But I'd rather stay with – where I am.'

I was just digesting that when I realized what she'd said. 'I'm not professional help!' I said.

'Yes, you are. You're the co-author of a book,' Dad said.

'And besides,' Pam added, 'he's a sucker for a pretty face.'

They gave me the address and telephone number, and ordered me to phone him when I got back and not to put it off because they'd told him I'd be calling. The idea was that I'd go and see him, ostensibly to discuss the work but really to see if we took to each other. Assuming we did, we'd then arrange a salary. I took Dad's advice on how much to ask for in order to appear neither green nor greedy.

When I could think of nothing more to ask – I thought of another twenty things on the way home, when it was too late – they saw me and the suitcase and the typewriter on to the train and kissed me goodbye.

'Let us know how it goes,' Pam said. 'We'll be rooting for you!'

Dad gave me a hug and twenty pounds. 'To help with the expense of becoming a working girl,' he said when I tried to push it back. He stared down pointedly at my jeans. 'At least buy yourself a skirt!'

I did as I was told and phoned my prospective employer as soon as I got in. So soon, in fact, that I was still panting from having wrestled with the damn suitcase and the bloody typewriter all the way up from the bus stop.

His name was Gordon Willis, and from our first few words I knew we were going to get on. After nearly twenty minutes' conversation – Florence came into the hall from the kitchen halfway through to see what I was laughing at – we had agreed that the interview was now a mere formality and that I should present myself at his house the following morning prepared to stay for the rest of the day.

I put the phone down and turned to face her. I said, 'I've got a job!'

'Where?'

I told her, still so full of it that it was only afterwards I thought it strange that her first question should be where? rather than, doing what, or working for whom?

She was as pleased as I was. So much so that she abandoned her plans to cook supper and said we'd go out to celebrate.

Moving in. Arranging my room. Walking and talking with Florence, riding Garth. Dashing to London to meet Dad and Pam, enjoying all the excitement – and the slight nerves – of getting a job. Oh, yes, I kept busy. I had *masses* to do.

But he was there, all the time. There was a little place in my heart now that had the shape of Henry, and only he could fill it.

Busy or not, I missed him like hell.

Fifteen

In the general spirit of new-job excitement next morning, Florence offered to drive me to Thetford. It was kind of her and I nearly accepted, then I thought I ought to start as I meant to go on, and said thanks but I'd go under my own steam. I'd worked out that if I got the bus into Ely and the train to Thetford, it'd take me just over an hour.

When I mentioned this to Florence, she commented that she'd better see about teaching me to drive.

I'd said I'd be with Gordon Willis around mid-morning, so I had plenty of time to get ready. Bearing in mind Dad's disparaging glance at my jeans, I dressed in a smart skirt, a white blouse and a jacket, and borrowed Florence's Burberry in case it rained. She came out to the bus stop to see me off.

The journey went smoothly, and I found my way to Mr Willis's house without having to ask for directions. He opened the door to my unconfident knock and said, 'Thea Adams, I presume? Or is it Dr Livingstone?', then took me inside and gave me a cup of coffee.

Our 'interview' lasted about five minutes, after which time he said, 'Sorry to keep staring at you, but you look so elegant I'm a little in awe of you. I keep thinking I'm sitting face to face with a solicitor.' So much for the smart skirt.

I said, 'I usually wear jeans, but I thought they might be too casual.'

'Not for me, old girl,' he said feelingly. 'Spent years of my life spitted and polished, don't mind how casual people are now. Off duty, that is.' As if to illustrate his point, he was wearing a khaki sweater with cloth bits on the shoulders – frayed – and a large hole in the front. His twill trousers might once have had some shape – might once even have had a crease – but their elegance was now a dim and distant memory. Yet for all that he was shabbily dressed, his hair was well cut, he'd obviously shaved that morning and he smelt pleasantly of soap.

'Jeans in future, then,' I said. Then realized there mightn't be a future. 'I mean, that is –'

But he said firmly, 'Yes. Jeans in future,' and stood up to shake hands on the deal.

He took me through to his study, where he'd put a second desk beside his own. My desk was obviously inferior – most desks would have been, since his looked like oak and was probably antique and worth thousands – but he'd had the consideration to provide me with a decent chair. The morning flew as he outlined what he was trying to achieve, how he was going about it, and what he'd done so far. We broke for lunch – we walked down the road to his local for beer and sandwiches, for which he paid – then in the afternoon I got down to my first task, which was a history of Thetford Priory.

At five o'clock he announced that work was over for the day – for the week, since it was Friday – and asked me if I'd join him in a drink.

'Oh!' I couldn't believe it was so late. 'No, thanks all the same, I think I'll head back.'

199

'Just as you like.' He was at the sideboard, pouring himself a generous measure of Glenmorangie. I wished after all I'd said yes. 'Now, before you go, how do you want me to pay you? Weekly or monthly, cheque or cash?'

We'd agreed my salary that morning. Since what he was offering came only just below Dad's upper 'greedy' limit, I'd accepted instantly. It seemed a lot of money for doing something I was going to enjoy in the company of someone I already liked.

'I think monthly cheques would be okay, Mr Willis,' I said.

He lifted his glass to me. 'Fine. To our association, then, Thea. And by the way, I'd prefer it if you called me Gordon.'

I went home singing. Sitting on the bus I said softly to my reflection in the steamy glass, 'Henry Woolgar, you owe me a quid.'

A woman of her word, Florence took me to the local Post Office in the morning and bought me a provisional driving licence. Then we bought a set of 'L' plates and booked me in for driving lessons.

'Now we're going to let you have a go,' she said as we drove off into the countryside. 'I'll take you to the place I took Henry and we'll see how you get on.'

At first I didn't get on at all, finding it quite impossible to synchronize clutch and accelerator. The engine would scream up to about a million revs and in a panic I'd take my foot right off the pedal, at the same time letting in the clutch with such a bang that the car shuddered to a relieved stop and I'd have to start all over again. But suddenly I got the hang of it: on our third circuit of the old airfield, I went round without once having to look down at my feet.

Florence said she'd take me there a few more times before my first lesson. 'You'll do very well,' she said as she drove us home. And I thought, as I'd been thinking for years, if Florence says so, then it must be true.

Sunday dragged. I'd taken Garth out, been for a walk with Florence and Eric, practised edging the car forwards and backwards in the drive for a while, and it was still only twenty to twelve. After lunch Florence said,

'I don't want to interfere, Thea, but why don't you make yourself comfortable in the drawing room with a good book? I wouldn't suggest it, only you do seem to be at a loose end.'

'Good idea,' I said. 'I'll have a look through your local history section, there might be some things that Gordon could use.'

She stiffened. 'In what way?'

'Well, for his research,' I said. 'You know, his history of Thetford.'

Then I realized I hadn't told her that bit. When I'd got back from meeting Dad and Pam, I'd just said the man I was phoning was a writer. I hadn't *known* what he wrote, then! And somehow, although I'd told her all about his desk and his clothes and his Glenmorangie, I hadn't mentioned what he was working on.

She was looking at me intently. 'Sorry,' I said, 'I forgot to tell you.'

I don't think she heard. She was shaking her head slowly, a slight smile on her face. She muttered something, and although I didn't quite catch it, I thought she said, 'How very interesting.'

That was reasonable enough. But then she added, 'And how wonderfully apt.'

For the rest of the day I lost myself in Florence's books. I hardly noticed the rain pouring down against the window, nor the gradual darkening of the sky. At some point she came in with a cup of tea and some toast, and she must have put the light on. I hoped I said thank you, but I doubt it: I was in another world.

As I worked slowly along the shelf marked 'East Anglia before the Saxons', it was as if an invisible hand were guiding me, making the volumes fall open at the very page that would evoke the strongest memory. All the right bits of my brain were stimulated, and without effort I remembered everything I'd ever been told about my own part of Britain. I heard my mother, telling me that Madingly was an ancient Norfolk name. I heard Dad, joking about Mum being small and dark like our far ancestors. And of course I heard Florence, talking, teaching, rounding out my knowledge so that, without appreciating it, I had the complete picture.

For I knew that what I was reading wasn't new to me: I wasn't learning it, I was *reminding* myself of it. It was all there in my head, and had only needed a bit of prompting to come surging forwards.

It was very exciting.

Late in the evening, at last I put the books away. I hadn't looked at them all, but my mind was overloaded and I could no longer take anything in. I lay back in my chair, eyes closed, and the images slowly began to unfold all over again.

I saw the small dark-haired people making their settlements. Following the chalk, mining the flint. Saw them in their homes, living off the produce they'd farmed themselves, sewing their clothes of wool and leather with needles made of bone. I saw the Fen people, living their secret lives in the tiny settlements where islands of clay rose out of the misty marshland. I saw them digging peat for their fires, giving themselves a measure of comfort in the sedge-thatched dwellings and driving out the all-pervading damp.

I saw a great East Anglian tribe rise in revolt against the invader from the south. A proud and independent people, they were led by a fierce, fair woman who avenged the atrocities of the interloper with brutal, systematic slaughter. Flogged, made to watch while her daughters were raped by Roman slaves, like a fire-storm Boudicca swept Colchester away and then fell on London, chasing the great governor Suetonius halfway up Watling Street before he checked, prepared his defence and turned on her, annihilating her forces like a strong wind flattening corn.

Somewhere I had read the line, '. . . and it is believed that the sad relics of the Iceni, army and people moving miserably as one, slunk furtively homewards to disappear into the secret heart of the Fens . . .'

The secret heart of the Fens. Was that right, was that where those poor people had gone? Leaderless – for Boudicca had poisoned herself as the Romans slaughtered her people all around her – had that seemed the only thing to do? The Romans hounded them, killing men, women and children alike, even when the tribe knew themselves to be beaten and would have surrendered. What a homecoming for the few that made it, with no animals – they took them with them on the march and none returned – and no crops ripening to harvest, for who was there to cultivate the land when all of the Iceni had risen as one against the Romans?

For a time as I sat there it seemed impossible that these events had happened nineteen hundred years ago. Rights and wrongs aside, I saw only human suffering, identifying so closely with the anguish of those long-dead people that I was close to tears. I was with them, I was one of them. I had seen my man slain, a Roman sword cutting so deeply into his throat that his head was all but severed, and my manic attempts to put him together again had done nothing but deluge my cloak with his warm blood. I had suffered Roman hands on me, stealing my jewels, assaulting my flesh. And I had carried my young son all the long way home, for as well as being all I had left, he was the future.

'"Army and people slunk home to disappear into the secret heart of the Fens,"' I said aloud. 'Where we lived a life of fear, always hiding, never knowing whom to trust.' Hardly aware of what I was saying, I had no idea where the words came from. 'And when their Empire rotted and fell and at last the Romans left us, a new threat came from over the North Sea, and still there was no peace.'

Sacrifice.

The word echoed in my head, and I didn't know if I had spoken it out loud or merely thought it. Sacrifice. What sacrifice? I went back over what I'd been reading. Vikings, launching newly-built ships from the shores of East Anglia. A long shingle beach, men dragging on ropes, the bound and helpless figure of a young woman tied to the wooden rails down which the boat slid to the sea. Virgin blood, to bless the new vessel and give it life.

Sacrifice.

I was aware of time passing – years, maybe – then suddenly I saw another young woman. I felt a fierce stab of empathy with her, more powerful than anything I'd experienced before. She wore a mantle of blue, and her head was veiled. She was unhappy – in despair – for she had been ordered to marry an old man with yellow, sagging skin and charnel-house breath. As if I were her and could see what no-one else perceived, I stared into his hooded eyes and knew him for the sadist he was. I – she – protested, but only to be overruled. Someone in a long fur-trimmed robe – a king? A lord? – was speaking, pronouncing my doom. His words were difficult to understand, but he seemed to be urging a policy of adapt and survive. Marrying our women to the men from across the water was the first step in the integration which would be our salvation – the invaders were too strong for us, and would be a part of our land for ever. Unable to rid ourselves of them, we must learn to live alongside them.

Behind the king a dark figure stood leaning in an archway, barely visible in the shadows. He looked at me, and the light from a flaming torch threw a flash of yellow across his eyes. His face held triumph, as if what was to happen to me was at his instigation. As his gaze held mine I saw images, hideous images of what was to come. A bride, led to her marriage bed and left to the mercy of an old man for whom cruelty was the only effective stimulant.

I was the sacrifice. I was the bride of the foreigner, and he would use me, abuse me, hurt me.

There was a rushing in my head, and blackness in front of my eyes. I felt as if they were very near, those ancient people, that they were in the shadows outside Florence's safe four-square house, that only the solid yellow-grey bricks prevented them from creeping up behind me and clutching me to them to claim me as their own. And I thought I heard the howling of wolves . . .

I'd fallen sideways in my chair, and nature, as she does, had arranged things so that my drooping head received the blood it needed to bring me round. Shakily I stood up – I didn't think I could stay in that chair any longer just then – and, tiptoeing into the hall, closed the door firmly on both the room and my dire thoughts of what had just happened there. The familiar house made malevolent by my fear, I crawled up to bed.

In the morning it seemed like a bad dream, hardly remembered, only the most vivid images retaining their power to terrify. I showered and dressed, listening to the radio in an attempt to rid my mind of the picture of a man with his throat cut, windpipe and neck bones severed like something in a slaughterhouse.

Of the image of a young woman, given like a chattel to a man who could do exactly what he liked with her.

I didn't manage any breakfast.

Florence looked at me intently and asked if I felt all right. I said yes, thanks, and hurried from the house, saying I had to catch my bus. I wasn't ready to talk to Florence.

Public transport proved a good antidote to the horrors in my head: the distracting power of a small boy with a runny nose on the bus, and a fat woman overflowing on to my seat on the train, brought me right back into the twentieth century. By the time I got to Gordon's house, I was feeling quite all right again.

All the same, I was glad I was going to be dealing with Middle Ages master masons and Thetford Priory monks. Whatever they had got up to, it was going to be mild compared to the Britons of the Dark Ages.

Gordon greeted me with the cheering news that the morning's post had brought a letter from a publisher saying they were interested in the book.

'That's great!' I said. 'Congratulations.'

'You've brought me good luck,' he said, thumping me on the back. 'Although I suppose "interested" means just that, and we ought to restrain our enthusiasm till we've got something more definite.'

By the look of him, he was going to find that difficult.

'Oh, let's not restrain anything,' I said. I was going to add that in my admittedly limited experience of the publishing world, it was better to enjoy the highs as and when they turned up, since almost invariably they were followed by lows, such as editors changing their minds and deciding they weren't interested after all. But he was looking so happy that I didn't have the heart.

'To work!' he shouted, forging ahead into the study as if he were leading the charge. Following behind, I settled down at my desk and picked up where I'd left off on Friday. Henry I was just about to lay the foundation stone of the Priory of Our Lady . . .

'Coffee, Thea.' I looked up to see Gordon standing in front of me with a huge steaming mug and a plate of biscuits. 'D'you want me to open a window?' he added. 'You look a bit peaky.'

Damn. I'd thought I'd forgotten about last night, and it was disconcerting to find out that obviously my body hadn't. 'I'm fine,' I said.

I said it too snappily, and he looked quite hurt. 'Sorry, I didn't mean to bite your head off.' He was such a nice man, I really was sorry. 'The thing is, I –' I heard myself speaking. Was I really going to tell him? 'I was reading something, last night. Some books on the ancient inhabitants of East Anglia, and how the Iceni rose against the Romans.' Apparently I was. 'How, much later, the native Britons got invaded by the Vikings and then the Anglo-Saxons. I started thinking about the brutality of it all.'

He perched on the edge of my desk. 'Go on.'

'Well, it was late, the house was quiet, and I suppose I let my imagination run away with me. I – oh, it sounds stupid!'

'You got scared,' he finished for me. 'What's stupid about that?'

'There was nothing to be scared of! I was safe and sound, all those things happened hundreds of years ago! *I* wasn't about to be hacked to death by the Roman army! *I* wasn't going to be sacrificed . . .' I broke off. I didn't want to recall that bit.

He didn't speak for a while. Then he said, 'Thea, isn't that the whole idea of studying history? To obtain an understanding of how our forebears lived? *And* how they died?'

Somehow he was making it seem so normal. I could have hugged him. 'Yes, you're right,' I said. 'Florence says –'

'Sorry. Who's Florence?'

'Oh, she's the woman I live with.' As I said it I realized I'd phrased it wrongly – he'd be thinking I was in some sort of lesbian arrangement if I wasn't careful. 'I mean, she's –' What was she? It was hard to explain without giving him the whole story.

So I did.

'Willowford Fen,' he said when I'd finished. 'I know the house you mean.' He stared at me with a new intensity, and I got the impression he was about to say something important. But after a moment he turned away and said easily, 'Quite an inheritance, eh?'

'Yes.'

'And presumably she's leaving it for you and her grandson to share with the intention that you marry.'

'Oh, no, I don't think so.' Surely not even Florence would have written a will based on something so uncertain. 'She probably imagines that . . . that . . .'

That what?

Suppose he was right? Out of nowhere I heard Henry's voice. *Thea, do you ever get the feeling you're not in control of your life?*

Was that what he believed? Did he *know* about the extraordinary will? If so, what did he make of it? God, perhaps he was being so nice to me purely *because* he knew!

That thought was so ridiculous I almost laughed. It just couldn't be true! Could it?

Even in the confusion, I knew I wasn't going to get anywhere thinking along those lines.

Gordon was walking back to his own desk. 'Oh, well, you know best,' he said. 'Right, a couple more hours' work, then we'll stroll out for a bite of lunch and walk home via the Priory ruins. Okay?'

'Yes.' I dragged my attention back to my work. It took me a while, but eventually I managed to push the whole worrying question of Florence to the back of my mind.

Not that it was going to stay there. When Henry gets back, I vowed, before he goes up to Cambridge and gets preoccupied with that, I've got to talk to him.

Sixteen

Henry wasn't expected back till Tuesday night or possibly Wednesday morning, so when I left Gordon's house and made my way to the station, I thought it must be Florence waiting there in the Morris for me.

'Florence said I should let you have some driving practice,' Henry said, 'but I think we'll wait till we're somewhere quieter than the middle of Thetford at half past five.'

'What are you doing here?' I couldn't see his face; he was looking away from me, concentrating on doing a U-turn which even a fledgling driver like me could see wasn't likely to win smiles of approval from the Law.

'Meeting you.'

'You're supposed to be in Yorkshire.'

'Mike caught a cold and was feeling sorry for himself, so we came back early.'

I forgot everything except how nice it was to have him with me again. I sat there beside him unable to stop smiling.

'Yes, thanks, we had a great time,' he said. 'Yes, the weather was good, and no, we didn't get lost, and yes, the beer in the highest pub in England was worth the climb.'

'You owe me a pound.'

'I know. Florence told me about your Gordon Willis.'

Florence. I said, 'Henry, we've got to talk.'

'Why, has he been putting his hand on your knee?'

'No!' Why on earth should he think that? 'Of course not, he's at least forty! I don't want to talk about him, I want to talk about Florence.'

As if it were a conditioned response, he looked at his watch. 'I said we'd be back by six,' he muttered. 'You were a bit late, there won't be time for your drive after all.'

For a scary moment I almost felt she was there, in the car with us. Unseen, unheard, yet still we were obeying her.

'*Henry!*'

We were at the lights, and my shriek nearly made him jerk into the car in front.

'Don't make me jump like that! What the hell's the matter?'

'Please, Henry,' I said, making my voice very calm and reasonable, 'I need to talk about Florence *now.*'

'But –'

'Can't you phone her? Say we won't be back till later?'

'She'll have dinner ready.'

'Please.'

He glanced at me. 'All right.'

We drove in silence for the mile or so it took to find a call box. He was gone for some time – surely longer than it took to say what he had to say? – and when he got back in the car, he still didn't speak. We turned off the main road on to a lane, and he stopped in a gateway.

'Right. What is it you want to talk about?'

He couldn't have been more daunting if he'd built a granite wall round himself.

There wasn't any point in leading up to it gently, so I said, 'I think she's trying to control us. She wants us to – she wants us for each other. When I told her about Steve, she came rushing to see me and she told me she was going to put me in her will provided I didn't sleep with him. All right, not in those exact words,' – he had begun to protest – 'but sure as hell that's what she meant! And then she arranged it so I came to your party. God, for all I know she probably made sure it was you and no-one else who came to let me in!'

I didn't really think it was likely. But he said, very quietly, 'Funny you should say that.'

'Then that evening we had dinner with her,' I rushed on, 'when she said all that about welcoming us together under her roof! It was as if we'd just announced we were getting engaged!'

His head was turned away, and he was looking out of his window. 'Is that such a dreadful prospect?' he said.

'Don't joke! For Christ's sake, Henry, we've only known each other five minutes! But that's not the point – it's *her*! She's manipulating us, she's making us do what she wants!'

'She didn't make me want to kiss you the other night. I managed to want that quite unaided.'

'Don't, please don't!' To my disgust I was almost crying. 'It isn't that I don't want what she wants, it's just that I want to want it for myself! Oh, I can't make you *see*!'

He turned towards me then, putting his arms round me and pulling me close. 'Shh, shh, it's all right.' His hand stroking my hair was soothing. 'You don't have to make me see, because I already do.' He paused, then, his tone as reluctant as if he were betraying all he held dear, said, 'She's been doing it all along. Since I was born. Since before I was born.' He sighed. 'And the bloody awful thing is, I don't know why.'

I was so relieved that for the moment the why didn't matter. 'You said did I think I wasn't in control of my life. That was what you meant, wasn't it? That I wasn't in control because she was?'

He nodded. 'I'm afraid that's just what I meant.'

'What made you say it? You didn't know then that she'd been interfering with my life.'

'No, I didn't. I was thinking of my own life, of something she's recently told me. We'd been talking about my parents, if you recall, and I said that my unplanned arrival wasn't their fault.'

A deep unease was creeping up the back of my neck. 'You said you'd tell me. Would now be the moment?'

He smiled briefly. 'Probably not, but who cares.' He paused, then said in a rush, 'My parents practised birth control. My mother had one of those cap things, and Florence told me she made a hole in it. Florence did, I mean.'

I couldn't believe it. Of all the incredible, awful things to do! God, I'd thought she'd manipulated *me*, but it was nothing compared with what she'd done to Henry's poor parents!

'How *dreadful* for them!' I imagined his mum, and the ghastly suspicion dawning. Did she discover the sabotage? Put it down to rubber fatigue? Did she ever, ever, suspect the truth? 'Your poor mother, having to carry and bear a baby she didn't want, then having to look after the wretched little bugger! No wonder you got the impression you weren't wanted, you wouldn't have been there at all if it hadn't been for Florence! She must have . . .'

A very strange feeling came over me. I'd been

213

thinking of this unwanted pregnancy as just that, and then suddenly it occurred to me that it – he – was Henry. That the life brought into being by Florence's machinations was him, this man sitting beside me whose arms were still round me.

He was obviously thinking along the same lines. 'The wretched little bugger is quite pleased about it, actually,' he said. 'Although I admit it took me some time to come to terms with the fact that Florence is responsible for my existence.'

I sat and tried to take it in. Tried to guess at whatever could have been in her mind.

And – this was the impossible bit – tried to get it into my head that whatever she was doing now was part of a much greater plan which had begun nineteen years ago.

If not more.

'I'm scared,' I said. 'What are we going to do?'

He sighed again. 'I have absolutely no idea.'

Great, I thought. 'Do we tackle her?' It was easy to think of doing so, alone there with Henry. Somehow I knew it would be different, face to face with her at Willowford Fen.

'With what?'

'Well, for a start we could ask her why she wanted her son's wife to have a baby so much.'

'Could we? I don't think I could.'

'But –'

'Anyway, that's fairly obvious.' I got the impression he was hurrying us away from the subject. 'My grandfather was a war hero, and I think Florence was disappointed in my father, who wasn't – isn't – a hero of any kind. If my father didn't have any children, she'd lose out on a second chance. I mean, –'

'Yes, it's all right. I know what you mean.' He was, as I might have guessed he would be, embarrassed by what he was trying to say. 'She thought to herself, my son's a bit lily-livered, so let's see if the good old Woolgar war-hero genes will turn up in the next generation.'

'Something like that. And, of course, she had to have me come and live with her so that she could see how I turned out.'

'She'd brought you into being,' I said, almost without thinking. 'You were here because she'd made you be here. She probably felt that gave her the right to do with you what she thought best.'

He was utterly still, totally quiet. He was hardly even breathing. I said, beginning to panic, 'What? What is it?'

'Siegwald and Althicca,' he muttered.

'Who?'

'A couple in a legend. A Cunning Man – a wizard – arranged it so they had a child. Then he took the child. He said he had a claim on it, because he'd made it be born.' He put his hand up to his face, rubbing at his head as if it ached. 'She has a similar claim on me.'

Instantly I said, 'She *thinks* she does.' I grabbed his hand, pulling it away from his face and holding on hard. 'She doesn't have to be right about it!'

'She brought me up!' he shouted. 'She helped me, taught me, got me into Cambridge. She made me what I am. I owe her something, don't I?'

'Yes, and so do I!' I shouted back. 'She's been an important, good influence in *my* life too, hasn't she? And I'm grateful, very grateful. But *I'm* not grateful enough to let her push me around without so much as a murmur of protest!'

I thought I'd gone too far. Surely no man would take from a woman the implication that he had no will of his own but tamely did what someone else told him?

But he just said distantly, 'You're probably right.' Then, 'We'd better go back.'

It seemed the discussion was over. I couldn't believe it – were we going to leave it like that, nothing decided, nothing even agreed? I wanted to demand, what are we going to do? What will we say to her?

I began to speak. Then something stopped me: suddenly he wasn't approachable any more.

I don't know how I knew. He looked just the same, but there was a subtle aura about him, as if he'd withdrawn to a place where I couldn't reach him. Florence, it was damned bloody Florence. Without intending to do so, I'd managed to bring him to a point where he was faced with Florence, the past and duty on the one hand and me, the future and rebellion on the other.

Had I thought I'd win?

I hadn't.

We were heading for home. I said desperately, 'What happens now? Where do we go from here?'

'"We?"' He didn't look at me, just kept driving. 'What "we"?'

My mind raced. 'I –' What could I say? I like you? Like you a lot, want to be with you, think I'm falling for you? And wouldn't I just end up looking stupid if he said, that's your misfortune.

'Thea, it makes no difference to me that Florence is keen for us to get together.' He sounded cool, even slightly amused. 'She may have been manipulating us, to use your word, but since she's manipulating me into something I'd be doing anyway I can't see that it's important. But since it obviously matters to you, you'd better tell her so and suggest she leaves you alone.'

He'd gone in one short speech from 'us' to 'I' and 'you'.

What about the magic? What about the sweet joy of kissing him? I knew he'd felt both emotions as strongly as I had.

Or I thought he had.

But then how was I to tell? We had, as I'd just so tactfully reminded him, only known each other five minutes. And maybe I'd been kidding myself about the magic; probably it was just strong sexual attraction by another name.

We were almost back. There wouldn't be a chance to speak to him once we were in Florence's domain. The vitally important talk which had been meant to unite him and me against her had done quite the opposite: it was I who was left on the outside.

'Henry, what are we going to do?' I reached out to touch his knee, and for a split-second his hand moved from the steering wheel as if to cover mine.

But he must have changed his mind.

'I'll be going up in a couple of days,' he said, in the same cool, terrible voice. 'You've got your job. We'll both be busy.'

Too busy to be together?

It was unbearable. But I'd borne worse than that in my time. As the car stopped in the drive I jumped out, banged the door and ran inside, straight up the stairs and into my room.

Let *him* make my excuses to her. I wasn't going to! I threw myself on my bed and said over and over again through the tears, 'Sod you, Henry.'

The next two days were dreadful. Having him so close – we were together at breakfast, dinner and all through the evening – yet knowing how distant he was from me was a constant torment. Florence must have felt the atmosphere, but she put it down to

Henry's imminent departure. She took me aside and said kindly, 'I know it's hard for you both, Thea. But he won't be far away, and you'll be able to visit him, I'm sure.'

If only she'd been right.

In one of my few conversations alone with Henry, I asked him to have a word with her.

'What do you want me to say?'

'Well, could you tell her we – that I –' I couldn't manage it. 'She thinks I'm going to be visiting you,' I hurried on. 'Could you put her straight?'

'I hope you will visit me,' he said. And walked away.

The day he went, I broke down and told Gordon all about him. I told him about Florence, and how she'd pushed us together, although I kept to myself the bit about what she'd done to Henry's hapless parents. Gordon was very sympathetic, and didn't seem at all put out at having his assistant sobbing all over her desk. Perhaps you got people sobbing in the army, and he'd become used to it. He handed me a box of man-sized tissues and made me a cup of strong coffee, then said,

'Poor old Thea. I thought you were looking glum – I'm glad you decided you could confide in me.'

It was a nice thing to say. I didn't tell him it hadn't been a question of *deciding*, more of having no option. I had to tell someone!

'What do I do now?' I sniffed.

'What do you want to do?'

Race into Cambridge, throw myself on Henry and tell him that I'm sorry. That I don't care either what brought us together, as long as we stay that way. That was what I wanted to do, but life had taught me that we don't always get what we want.

'I don't know.'

'Do you want to hear what I think?' He got up and poured us both more coffee.

'Yes, all right.'

He smiled. 'You might sound slightly more enthusiastic! No, it's okay, I'm only joking. I think you should let things ride for a while – you can't make sensible judgements when you're upset. Give yourself time to think about Florence's interference, and Henry's apparent acceptance of it. It seems to me –' He broke off. 'Do you mind if I speak bluntly?' I shook my head. 'It seems to me that what's upset you is having Henry knocked off the pedestal you've put him on. You thought he was perfect, and discovered that since he's too amenable to his grandmother's orders, he's not.'

'I don't –'

'Nobody's perfect, Thea,' he said earnestly. 'When you get older – oh, God, this is when I say, "When you're as old as I am –" you'll know everyone has feet of clay.' He put his hand over mine. 'For now, do nothing. That's my advice.' He grinned at me. 'Now, if the floodgates are shut, let's do a couple of hours' work then I'll take you out to drink strong beer.'

We did just that. I had three halves of a dark and bitter stuff which made my head swim, so much so that I had to have a lie-down on Gordon's sofa when we got back, and even after that could only manage to type a few letters. He was very understanding, and said it was his fault and not to worry.

When the time came to go home, I wished I could have stayed with him.

The Henry-less days passed, and I realized very quickly that life would have been a whole lot more awful if it hadn't been for Gordon. Willowford Fen without Henry was not a place I wanted to be. Florence was preoccupied, as if she too were mourning his absence; she would often disappear for hours with only Eric for company, and I saw very little of her. Perhaps she needed to be alone.

One evening when I was coming home from Gordon's, I saw someone in the lane outside the house. He was standing by the hedge looking over into the garden, and there was something in that watchful stance that was familiar.

He must have heard me. He turned and said softly, 'Good evening, Thea.'

It was the Dark Man from Henry's party.

Flustered, although I didn't know why, I said hastily, 'I'm afraid Henry's not here. He's gone to Cambridge. I mean, gone up. He doesn't live here any more.'

The man smiled, as if he were near to laughter. 'I know. I did not come to see Henry.'

'Florence probably won't be home either. She often goes for a walk at this time. Shall I go and . . .'

I trailed off, already regretting the words: I'd just told him I was alone with him. Why was he disconcerting me so much? Wasn't it the most normal thing to call on a friend?

Why was I so eager to see the back of him?

He was watching me, as if he followed the track of my thoughts. He said eventually, 'I did not come to see Florence, either.'

That left me. Why on earth should he want to see me?

'I'm going straight out again,' I lied. 'I . . .'

He was laughing openly now. 'I expect you are,' he said. 'But you misunderstand. I have not come to ask you out on a date.'

There was something slightly odd about his speech.

As if English were not his mother tongue. For a moment I was distracted by wondering where he might be from, then the bizarre nature of the encounter struck me again and, of all things, I felt afraid.

'I'm sorry but I really must go in,' I said, taking a step to the side so that I could move round him. I felt cold suddenly. 'Florence will be wondering where I am.'

Then I remembered I'd just said Florence was unlikely to be there.

For an instant I felt such despair that I wanted to cry. Oh, God! I can't . . . He's going to . . .

Then he stepped aside to let me pass. Instantly I was flooded with warm relief, as if someone had just told me that a horrifying piece of bad news was nothing but a hoax.

'Thank you,' I said. What the hell was I thanking him for? I hurried through the gate and up the path, towards the sanctuary of Florence's house. 'I'll tell her you called.'

He didn't respond. I thought he was going to leave without another word but then, just as he'd done before, he said quietly, '*Au revoir*, Thea.'

Florence was in the kitchen. She glanced up as I came in.

'You look tired,' she said. 'Would you like a cup of tea?'

I nodded. I sat down at the table, reminded of childhood and coming into this very kitchen at the end of a gruelling day at primary school. I wished with sudden fervour that my worries now were as simple as they'd been then.

'That man from Henry's party was outside,' I said.

She stiffened. 'Which man?' Then, as if making a conscious effort to relax, picked up the pot to pour my tea.

'The tall dark one. Slightly foreign-sounding.'

She stared at me. 'Foreign?'

'Yes. Well-dressed, about . . .' How old was he? When I came to think about it, I had no idea. 'Forty? Fifty? He knew who I was – he called me by my name.'

She went on staring. Deep in her eyes I saw something – a premonition? An awareness of peril? – but then it was gone and she was shaking her head. 'I don't know anyone who fits that description. He must be one of the guests whom Henry invited.'

I felt the same shiver that had run through me out in the lane.

'That's just what Henry said. I mean, that he didn't know him and he must have been one of your friends.'

She shrugged. 'Possibly one of the other guests brought him.'

She got up to fetch the biscuit tin, her interest in the conversation apparently at an end. But I couldn't stop thinking about the Dark Man – he'd disturbed me, and I didn't know why.

It had been funny that he'd looked so familiar out there in the dusk. I'd only seen him once, after all, and in poor light. Yet I'd recognized him instantly, as if . . .

As if I'd known him very well. And, judging from my instinctive recoil from him, hadn't liked him very much.

I could feel a headache coming on. I hoped supper wouldn't be too late, because then I could have an early night.

He came into my dreams. I was standing in front of him pleading for something with such intensity that it hurt. And he was smiling, as if it turned him on to have me abject before him. There was a sort of arch-way above him, and his face with its secret expression was lit by an orange flame. His eyes looked lupine, and, as if my dreaming mind were making the connection, I seemed to hear the long desolate howl of a wolf.

Something woke me. I lay sweating and shaking, hugely relieved to be out of my dream yet with a part of me still held in it.

As I calmed down, I knew why the Dark Man was familiar. I was quite sure, now. I'd seen him on other occasions, as well as at Henry's party.

I'd seen him in my nightmare visions of the Dark Ages. He'd sent a young terrified bride to the bed and the bestiality of a cruel old man.

It was even more of a relief to get to Gordon's house next day. He was used to me looking depressed – poor man, he was incredibly patient – but that morning I must have gone off the bottom of the scale.

'Bad night?' he asked sympathetically.

'Awful.' Hardly stopping to think, I plunged in and told him.

I'd expected him to respond with some bracing remark and, after a restorative cup of coffee, the suggestion that a good morning's work was the best thing. That was what he usually did.

Today was different. He looked – I didn't like to admit it, but he looked anxious.

'Florence didn't know this man?' He was pacing up and down behind his desk, hands in his pockets.

'She said not.'

'And you're sure that Henry didn't either?'

'Yes, quite sure.'

'And anyway he said – implied – it was you he'd come to see?'

'Yes.'

There was a long pause, during which he must have completed several hundred yards of pacing. Then he stopped and, resting both hands on his desk and fixing me with an intense stare, said, 'There's more to this than you realize. The whole thing. Florence, Henry, her manipulation of you, her extraordinary will. I've had my suspicions all along, but now you've . . .'

He stopped. The sight of me gaping at him would have been enough to put anyone off his stroke.

'On the other hand, I might be barking up the wrong tree entirely.' He smiled. 'Sorry.' He came round to the front of his desk and, perching, went on, 'Thea, I've got a suggestion. I was going to wait for a while, but . . . Well, I'll mention it now and you can be thinking it over.'

He reached behind him for an envelope. 'Read that.'

A couple of weeks went by. Miserable, worrying weeks – as well as everything else, I was now facing the biggest decision of my life so far, and I had no idea what I was going to do. Henry came home for a weekend, and we spoke to each other like strangers. Then he phoned one Friday evening, said he was playing rugby the next afternoon and why didn't I go to watch?

My heart leapt. I told myself as I put the phone down that it had nothing to do with the prospect of seeing him – and alone, if you discounted twenty-nine other players, two touch-judges and a referee – it was because there was something I wanted to talk to him about.

He'd told me where to go, and to dress warmly. I set out in the morning; I told Florence there was some shopping I wanted to do first, but it was really because I didn't dare stay in the house any longer in case he called to say the match was off and not to come.

Cambridge on this Saturday morning was heaving with people. It was cold, too, so I found a coffee bar and made two coffees last an hour and a half. Then I went to watch Henry play rugby.

I didn't enjoy the game at all. Not that there was anything wrong with it – I wouldn't have enjoyed anything that afternoon, I was too full of nerves. When it was over, he came sweating and steaming off the pitch, a victory smile on his face.

'Hello,' he said.

I smiled back. 'Hi. Well played – nice try.'

'Thanks.'

He scratched his face, leaving a trail of mud across his cheek. 'Er – I'll have a shower, then we'll go and have tea. Do you mind waiting? I won't be long.'

'Okay.' I couldn't, I thought, get much colder.

He was seven minutes. I timed him. Walking back to his college, he held my hand.

His room overlooked a court, where there were lawns and a statue. Everything looked old – wooden stairs, paintings along the low-ceilinged corridors – and probably was. In retrospect, I wished I'd taken a closer look. But I wasn't in the mood for appreciating beauty that day.

I sat down at his desk and he made tea. He'd bought some biscuits, but neither of us touched them. After an awkward silence, he said,

'I miss you.'

'And I you.'

'What are we going to do about it?'

I looked at him. He'd washed his hair so quickly that he'd left quite a lot of mud. I wanted to reach out and wipe it away. 'I don't know,' I said.

'If you came to see me here,' he said tentatively, 'Florence wouldn't need to know we were together.'

'What difference would that make?'

'Well, I thought then we'd be able to progress at our own pace. Or not, as the case may be. We wouldn't feel she was watching our every move.'

It touched me that he'd thought about it enough to have a solution to suggest.

'When would I come?'

'Not often, I'm afraid.' He waved towards the stacks of books on his desk. 'One of the first aims here seems to be to show you that you had no concept of what constituted hard work until you came up to Cambridge. I don't have a lot of free time, but –'

'Evenings would be out,' I interrupted. 'It's a bugger of a journey, and I'd have to walk the last bit.'

'Saturdays would be okay,' he said. 'Except next Saturday – we're playing away, so we'll have to leave early and God knows when we'll get back.'

'You have to play, do you?'

'Well, I want to. It's –' He was saying something about the physicality being a release, after six days spent cramming information into his head. But I stopped listening.

I'd forgotten the man thing. Stupid of me, when I'd had such fine examples of it as Dad and Jim. There was a quotation I'd come across, which summed it up so perfectly that I'd committed it to memory:

> 'Man's love is of man's life a thing apart,
> 'Tis woman's whole existence.'

Byron said that. Good old rollicking Byron. And he, having had so many women, ought to know.

It wasn't going to be *my* whole existence. I wasn't

going to be like my poor mum, breaking her heart when she thought Jim was taking off for the Himalayas and leaving her behind. Oh, no. I was going to take a leaf out of those men's book and keep love, whatever that was, where it belonged.

'We're not going to manage to see much of each other,' I said. He'd finished his apologia and seemed to be waiting for me to comment.

'No. I'm sorry.'

I stood up, walking over to the window to look out. Not because I wanted to see what was there, more because I couldn't bear to look at him.

'I've got something to tell you.'

'Oh yes?'

'Gordon – Gordon Willis – has been commissioned to write a book on First World War campaigns. He's going off on a prolonged research tour. Northern France and Belgium first, then down to the Dardanelles, wherever they are.'

'Turkey,' he said automatically.

'Right.'

'So you'll be losing your job.'

I turned round. 'No, I won't. He'll need an assistant, and has suggested I go with him.'

There was a silence. Painful, pregnant and prolonged. Then he said, 'Will you go?'

After a time I returned to the view outside and said, 'Yes.'

I didn't go back to Willowford Fen. I trudged the incredibly long way out to the station, then caught a train to Ely. And another to Thetford.

I phoned Gordon from the station.

'I'm ringing to tell you I've decided,' I said.

'And what have you decided?' He sounded as if he were laughing. Oh, God, I wished I were.

'To accept your offer. Go to France and everywhere with you.'

There was a pause. He'd known I was seeing Henry, so he'd understand what my decision implied. Or I hoped he would. He said, 'You're sure?'

'Quite sure.'

'I'm glad.'

There was another pause, during which the pips went and I bunged in some more money. 'Where are you?' he asked.

I told him.

He said kindly, 'Oh, Thea.' Then, almost shyly, added, 'Shall I come and fetch you?'

I said, 'Yes, please.'

In the morning he drove me to Florence's house. She came to the door smiling – I'm sure she thought it was going to be Henry and me, arriving to give her a blow-by-blow account of our first night together. Watching her face fall at the sight of Gordon, I felt a moment's vindictive pleasure.

'Where's Henry?' she demanded.

I shrugged. 'I've no idea. Sitting in his room doing an essay? Cleaning his boots? Out for a jog?'

I pushed past her into the house, aiming for my room and the world record for packing a very large suitcase.

'Thea!' She hurried upstairs after me. 'What are you doing? Who is that man outside?'

'It's Gordon. I'm going to France with him.'

'You're *what*?'

She'd caught me up and had her hand on my shoulder, spinning me round to face her.

'We're going to research a book together.' I wrenched myself free.

'You can't! What about Henry? Does he know?'

'*Bugger* Henry!' I almost said, bugger you too, but managed not to. 'I don't need his permission, Florence! I don't *belong* to him!'

'But you have to be together!' She corrected herself. 'You want to be together, I can sense it! Why, you've been miserable without him! I don't understand.'

'No, you don't, do you?' I'd been cramming things – clothes, towels, spongebag, shoes – into Dad's big case. Now I stopped, turning to face her. 'You can't conceive that people might have minds of their own and refuse to do what you want them to, can you?'

'Thea, what are you saying?' There was anxiety in her face, and one hand was at her throat. 'You can't mean that you and Henry do not – are not –' She didn't seem to want to put it into words.

'No, we're not. We don't love each other, we're not going to make our future together and we've no intention of changing our minds just to please you.' I put my face close to hers. 'Bad luck, Florence. Back to the drawing board.'

I slammed the case shut and, typewriter under my other arm, hefted it to the stairs, bumping it down to the detriment of my packing. Just as well I hadn't bothered to fold anything. Gordon got out of the car to help me get my luggage into the boot. I couldn't imagine what he was making of it all.

As we turned in the drive and prepared to set off again, she appeared in the open doorway. She cried, 'Thea!'

I pretended I hadn't heard.

We nearly made it. If we'd left just a little earlier, we'd have missed Henry. But we didn't. As we reached the gate, he was racing up the lane, driving a small Austin van he must have borrowed from somebody.

A pall of mist crept across the scene. In it was a dark shape, at first loping along close to the ground, then stretching up, tall and commanding. He stood at the end of the drive, turning his hooded head first towards us, then towards Henry. Could Gordon see him? Could Florence, hurrying from the house to catch us up?

I didn't know.

But I could see him, and so could someone else. Eric, roused from his slumbers, was padding up the drive, moving faster than he had done in a long while. In the midst of everything else I felt guilty – I hadn't said goodbye to him.

The shape by the gate was changing, the dark outlines flowing from one form to another. Now it was wolf-like again, and for a freakish moment as Eric ran up to it, the two animals circled each other, ears flat, teeth bared. I realized then how huge the wolf was.

'Eric!' I screamed. '*Eric!*'

The wolf had gone. The Dark Man was now in the lane, beckoning Henry, gesturing as if to say, Hurry! Eric, barking wildly, chased after him, running up the road and hurling himself at the insubstantial shape.

A shape which, together with the mist, must have obscured Eric's view of Henry and Henry's view of him. Still going as fast as the van and the road permitted, perhaps responding as much to his own instincts as to the Dark Man's beckoning, there wasn't a chance in hell that Henry could stop.

I didn't see, I only heard. A screech of tyres, a bump, and a yelp that blended with a howl of triumph until the awful sound of pain faded and only the howl remained.

Gordon said, 'Oh, my God.'

He put his foot down and we shot off up the lane, coming to a halt in front of the Austin. The mist was clearing now, and I could see Henry. He was sitting in the road, and Eric's head was in his lap. There was a lot of blood on his hands.

'I didn't see him,' he was muttering. 'Just didn't see him.'

The wild words tried to burst out of my mouth. Couldn't you have swerved? Did you have to hit him so hard?

But I could see Henry's hand, stroking Eric's shattered head as gently as if he were caressing a sleeping puppy. The hand was trembling.

'It wasn't your fault,' I said. 'Of course you didn't see him. And it's ages since he ran like that, you couldn't possibly have expected him to . . .'

'He's quite dead, you know.' Henry's voice was strangely matter-of-fact. 'Yes, quite dead.'

He bent his head over his dog, and I turned away.

Gordon touched my arm. 'What do you want to do?' he asked.

I looked up into his kind, strong face. I should have said, I've got to stay. They'll need me, Henry and Florence, we'll bury Eric together, make a ceremony of it as befits such a dog.

But I could still see the last tatters of that sudden mist. Out of the corner of my eye I thought I caught a dark shape, eyes glinting yellow under the black hood. He had made it happen, he'd made poor Eric run like that, right under the wheels of Henry's car. He was ruthless and cruel, and he'd destroyed the happy, affectionate creature who had first brought Henry and me together.

An image came into my head of the two of us, split apart by an impenetrable wedge of black.

My knees were shaking so much that I had to hold on to Gordon for support. He noticed, and put an arm round me.

'It's the shock,' he said. 'We'd better go back to the house, see if Florence –'

'*No!*'

Not Florence. She had been pushing us together, but whatever aim she had in mind, it wasn't something which that dark shape liked. Ever since I'd come back – no, long before that – he'd been there, haunting my dreams, counteracting the happiness with darkness and fear.

Well, he'd won. Oh, I wanted to stay – how could I not? – but I wasn't going to. He was evil – he hadn't needed to kill Eric, since Gordon was already removing me from Henry and Willowford Fen. It had been a touch of pure malice, something heartbreakingly awful to underline his victory.

And if I stayed, what would he kill next?

I heard again that howl of triumph.

I couldn't look at Henry, and I didn't want to look back at Florence. I said to Gordon, 'Let's go.'

His face registered surprise, and he seemed about to speak. '*Please!*' I sobbed, and, after a moment, he nodded.

We got in the car and he drove carefully past the Austin.

For the first few miles I was numb. Feeling nothing, I looked out of the window, enjoying the autumn colours in the hedgerows.

But, unfortunately, the numbness didn't last.

PART THREE

Flying Blind

Seventeen

I don't know how I let her go.

From the moment I put my arms round her on the doorstep the night of my party, I knew there was something special about her. Maybe it had always been there, maybe she had got into my system that indelible day I saw her in the lane crying into Eric's golden coat. She'd grown beautiful, that was half the trouble. Not conventionally so, perhaps, but something about the fair hair and the clear blue eyes got right through to me. And there was her mouth, top lip, Bardot-like, fuller than the other. I don't remember noticing that when we were children. Nor do I remember wanting to kiss her so badly that I was almost afraid to hold her.

She was stubborn, pig-headed, independent and totally unable to see things from anyone's point of view but her own. That was obvious on the first night, when she went storming off, cross and upset that I'd disappeared and not stopping to wonder where I might have gone. Christ, did she imagine I *wanted* to take bloody Wendy back? But some things you just have to do. Nobody else was about to volunteer, and letting Wendy weave away by herself in the vague direction of her home just wasn't on.

Beautiful and unreasonable. You'd think the two might have cancelled each other out, with perhaps the beauty just losing out so that I'd have fancied her but not enough to put up with the unreasonableness. Not, anyway, once she'd shown how she felt about Florence. It made me angry, that she refused to understand my relationship with Florence. She damned well ought to have done. And Florence and I were used to each other – she was used to me coming home when I said I was going to, and I was used to considering her and not chucking her carefully-made arrangements out of the window. Thea, on the other hand, I had only known five minutes. As she herself pointed out.

But I kissed her. Once in an exploratory sort of way – in case she didn't want to as much as I did – and once with rather more passion. And that time there was no question of her not wanting to; her mouth opened to mine and she almost sucked me in. She was incredible. If Florence hadn't been friends with the couple who ran the hotel, who knows what might have happened.

Then I had to go with Mike to sodding Yorkshire. An ill-timed holiday if ever there was one, *and* I caught Mike's cold. Maybe if I'd stayed with Thea that week, things would have happened differently. Maybe if she hadn't had all that time to think, her obsession with Florence's manipulation wouldn't have had the chance to grow so wildly out of control. Who knows. But I went, and when I came back, things weren't the same.

To a certain extent, she was absolutely right. Florence did interfere with people's lives, and I was the living proof. She'd obviously gone too far with Thea, too – although it was unlike her to have been so tactless – and had antagonized her to the point where she was determined to do the opposite of what Florence wanted, even if it was also the opposite of what she wanted herself.

Did she want it? Hard to tell, when the 'it' was me.

Then, sitting out there in the car on a dark country lane, she had the nerve to say that I let Florence push me around. She'd gone from a mainly unjustified criticism of Florence to a totally unjustified one of me, and I was so angry I wanted to take hold of her and choke an apology out of her. She'd got it so wrong, and I didn't have the words to put her right. Florence arranged things, sure. She seemed to know what you wanted, and somehow she got it for you. God, I ought to know, she'd been doing it for me most of my life, from the moment she agreed to let me live with her onwards. But that didn't warrant the accusation that I let her push me around! *Nothing* warranted that.

Florence, whom I'd known and loved ever since I could remember, dismissed and slandered by Thea, newly arrived, fiercely arousing, but whom I didn't care for at all.

Or so I told myself.

Once I'd gone up, there was so much to do and to think about that, some days, I almost succeeded in keeping my mind off her. As well as constantly having all the work to get through, there was rugby, rowing, and a whole new way of life to get used to. Living in a seventeenth-century building in one of the most beautiful towns in the world didn't take a lot of getting used to – Florence had, by some private arrangement, managed to get me the room my grandfather had before me, and the view down into the court gave me pleasure each time I looked out of my window.

I made a lot of new friends, especially among the other freshmen. I bought a bike, and cycled out along Huntingdon Road to renew acquaintance with Phil, who'd been a close friend while we were doing 'O' levels. A couple of other boys from my school were also up at Cambridge, but their familiarity didn't outweigh the fact that I had absolutely nothing in common with them, and when one of them suggested we went together to a freshmen's hop, I said no, thanks, I was doing something else.

I was getting on just fine. Wasn't I? Then I made the mistake of going home for the weekend. And being with her again, watching her face, her mouth, her body, undid all my resolve. I almost lasted the week, but on the Friday, no doubt under the resolve-weakening influence of a couple of pints, I called her and invited her to come and watch the rugby.

When I came off the pitch she looked half frozen. Her lips were blue and she was huddled so tightly into her coat that she looked smaller than I remembered. She congratulated me on my try, and I stared down at her hardly taking in what she was saying, just wanting to hold her, hug the warmth back into her. Take her into my bed and make love to her till we both melted from the heat of each other's bodies.

I took her back to my room and made her a cup of tea. I wanted to touch her so badly that I had to sit on my hands. I suggested how we might manage to see something of each other, but, although she'd just admitted she missed me, she was quite unprepared to make any effort to put it right.

Then she told me she was going off with Gordon sodding Willis.

I'd got her all wrong, hadn't I? Just as well I didn't love her.

I don't know what made me go out to Willowford Fen that Sunday. It wasn't because I thought I could make her change her mind – I wasn't even sure I wanted that. If our relationship counted for so little that she was willing to chuck it away and go off with someone else, I had no intention of pleading with her to stay.

It's incredible, but I think I was summoned.

Whatever, the impulse was strong enough to send me haring round till I found someone willing to lend me a car, which I then gunned out to Florence's as fast as it would go.

They were just leaving, Thea and bloody Gordon Willis. They were at the gate, and Florence was hurrying after them looking upset. It had been a nice bright morning in Cambridge, but out there a mist was rolling off the Fen, so that I seemed to see them only intermittently.

And that was how I came to run over Eric.

I find it hard to think about that, even now. Thea said it wasn't my fault, and in the remorse I suffered afterwards, I held on to that.

Thea. You'd think something as awful as Eric being killed would have made her decide to stay. But it didn't – I remember her patting my shoulder, then she and Gordon got back in his car and drove away.

She was heartless, as well as stubborn and independent.

And so I let her go.

Florence and I buried him under the apple trees at the end of the garden. We consoled ourselves by reminding each other that he'd been getting old and stiff, that it was better to go quickly – 'He can't have known anything about it,' we said – than to suffer an increasingly painful old age.

I was surprised at how much it affected Florence. She became strangely edgy, watchful almost. I wondered if she was missing Thea. It seemed likely: I was. What had Thea told her? Had she taken all her stuff and moved out for good, or had she said she was off on a working holiday and would be back in a few weeks? I badly wanted to know, but couldn't bring myself to ask.

It sounds callous, but, what with missing Thea and grieving for Eric, it was a relief to leave that sad household and get back to college.

I kept away for some time. I phoned Florence one morning, just to see how she was and let her know I was okay, and said that I was very busy but that I'd try to get home for the weekend soon. She just said, 'Very well, Henry.' If she'd had news of Thea, she didn't mention it.

It was a torment, wondering where she was. If she was still with him in Thetford, I could go and see her. Tell her –

Tell her what?

Anyway, it wasn't likely she was there. She was probably off in France, or Belgium. Or the bloody Dardanelles. Wherever she was, she was out of my life.

I made up my mind I was going to turn my back on her. What a waste it would be, to pine for someone who'd gone when so much lay waiting for me! Cambridge, I thought, here I come.

I was able to put my new plan of campaign into action almost immediately; I went to a party with Phil and got drunk. For a while I felt great – everything was fine, I was happy, and the woman I was dancing with had a great chest. I took her outside into the cold darkness and kissed her, and was edging my hand inside her dress to feel her remarkable breasts when suddenly everything began to swim.

'Sorry,' I muttered, removing my hand and pulling her clothing together again, 'think this isn't a good idea.' I leaned back against the wall, trying to focus on a lamppost which seemed to be moving round in slow circles.

She looked at me, amusement in her face. 'Didn't you like what you found?' she asked.

'Yes!' I spun my head to stare at her. Bad move. Jesus, I had to get away from her, and fast. 'Got to go,' I said, 'sorry, but –'

'But you're going to be sick,' she finished for me. 'What a shame. I was enjoying you.'

She was smiling. In my drunken state, she seemed wonderful – kind, understanding, attractive, humorous, sexy. I wondered who she was. Not an undergrad – too old.

I said, 'Will you come out with me?'

'Now?' She was laughing openly.

'Tomorrow. Soon. I'm Henry.'

'I know who you are. Yes, okay, Henry.' She took the pen out of my jacket pocket and wrote a number on my hand. 'Give me a call when you sober up.'

I watched her as she walked back inside. Her hips moved with a sort of undulation, wonderful to watch but not a good idea for a man who had had several pints too many and a couple of whiskies into the bargain. Trying vainly not to appear as unsteady as I felt, I made my way home.

The next day was Sunday, and I waited till lunchtime to call her. Before I'd fallen into bed I'd copied her phone number on to a pad, which was just as well as it had rubbed off the back of my hand during the night. If she'd written her name, that had rubbed off too, so I had the embarrassment of phoning an anonymous woman. What I'd do if someone else answered, I had no idea. If it was a man, I'd have to put the phone down.

'Hello.'

It was her. I was quite sure. 'Hello, it's Henry.'

'Henry. So it is.' The amused tone was faithfully relayed along the phone wires. 'How are you feeling this morning?'

'Fine!' The headache would soon clear. 'And you?'

'Likewise. Nice party, wasn't it?'

'Er – yes.' I couldn't even remember who had thrown it. 'What are you doing today?'

'I'm going to have lunch with my mother.'

Bugger.

'Would you like to come out for a drink this evening?' It was a faint hope – she'd probably say she was washing her hair, or doing her ironing, or had to have an early night because it was work tomorrow. Did she work? At what?

'I'd love to.'

'What did you say?'

'I'd love to come out for a drink.'

'Oh!' I rounded up my thoughts and pointed them in the right direction. 'Where shall we go? I'm afraid I haven't got a car, but I do have a bike.'

'I don't enjoy sitting on crossbars.' Something about the way she said it made it the most suggestive thing I'd ever heard. 'I have a car. I'll pick you up. Seven thirty? I'll wait for you on King's Parade. Don't be late or I'll get moved on.'

'I won't be.'

When I'd put the phone down and was standing

grinning stupidly down at it, I realized belatedly I still hadn't asked her name.

Phil came to see me. It had been he who'd invited me to the party, and he reminded me I still owed him for the beer we'd taken.

'Where did you disappear to?' he asked. 'I saw you dancing with that woman, then you'd gone.'

'I came back here. Alone,' I added, since a knowing and quite unjustified grin was spreading over his face.

'Waste of an opportunity,' he remarked. 'Lovely body.'

I didn't think he meant mine. 'You don't know who she was, do you?' It wasn't the easiest of questions to ask.

'You mean you don't?' I didn't blame him for the derisive tone.

'We only had a couple of dances.' I wasn't going to tell him about taking her outside and almost throwing up all over her.

'I don't know her name,' Phil said. 'She's some-one's older brother's friend. Lots of them arrived together, in a group.'

Someone's brother's friend. Great.

I was on King's Parade by twenty past. The idea of being late and having to watch as she was moved on wasn't to be contemplated. As well as having omitted to discover her name, I also had no idea what car she drove, and consequently I spent an anxious ten minutes trying to peer inside every vehicle that slowed to a hover.

Dead on half past, a horn bipped and someone shouted my name. Spinning round – somehow I'd expected her to have come from the Trumpington

Street end rather than Trinity Street – I saw a dark green MGB parked by Market Street.

I ran across the road and got in beside her.

'Hello, Henry,' she said. She was busy getting back into the traffic, which consisted largely of wandering bicycles, and wasn't looking my way. Smacked in the face by the combined impact of her perfume and the way the seatbelt cutting between her breasts made them look even larger than I'd been picturing them, it was a moment before I said feebly, 'Hello.'

'It's Julia,' she supplied.

Julia. And she was as dark and mysterious as my image of how a Julia should be. This evening her long hair was piled on top of her head, and instead of last night's tight-fitting, low-cut dress, she was wearing what looked like a suit over a high-necked blouse.

I said, 'Where are we going?'

She'd turned right into Silver Street and we were now going up Queen's Road. 'Overcote Ferry. There's a pub I know on the river.'

'The Pike and Eel.' I knew it, too. 'It's quite a way.'

'Not that far. Anyway I feel like a drive – I've been cooped up with my mother all day.' She didn't sound as if she'd enjoyed it. 'You don't mind, do you?'

She looked at me briefly. Her lipstick showed up very dark in the dim light. I said, 'No, not at all.'

Once out of town, the traffic was light and she was in a hurry. Or perhaps it was a response to having been shut in with her mother. The car shot up to eighty, and she drove it expertly. Reluctant to break her concentration, I kept quiet.

The pub was on the west side of the river, and we approached it via St Ives and Needingworth. There were quite a lot of cars in the car park. I looked round, hoping to recognize one – she was the sort of woman you'd want to be seen with.

We went into the main bar, and found a table under the window. I asked her what she'd like, and she said gin and tonic. I got myself a pint. Then I went back to sit beside her.

She'd been watching me up at the bar, and her dark eyes stayed on me as I crossed the room. When I'd put down the drinks, she lifted her glass and said, 'Here's to it.'

I didn't know how to respond so I just said, 'Cheers.' Then I got stuck into my beer – if I hurried with that one and had another, perhaps it would stop me feeling so inhibited.

She took hold of my wrist – on the hand holding my glass – and her fingers were long, cool, and tipped with painted nails. She said, very quietly, 'It would be more fun if you weren't drunk, this time.'

Suddenly I didn't feel inhibited any more. Hot, confused, randy, yes. Inhibited, no. Maybe inhibited had been preferable. Grabbing at the first thing that came into my head – I couldn't sit there beside her any longer not talking, not if it meant she was going to fill the gaps with provocative remarks like that – I said, 'And what do you do, Julia?'

She burst out laughing. Letting go of my wrist, she said, 'Are you deliberately changing the subject?'

What the hell did I say? I stared at her. 'I'm not,' I said quietly. 'God, I'm not. But –'

'Okay. I'm a beautician.'

It had to be something like that, although her clever eyes indicated that she must have intellectual as well as practical skills. 'Good Lord,' I said. 'What does that mean, exactly?'

'Face and body hair removal, leg-waxing, facials, massage,' she said nonchalantly.

Massage. I remembered the opening of *From Russia with Love*, where the near-naked masseuse worked herself up to a sweat on the supine body of the enemy agent. Her breasts had all but fallen out of her bikini top each time she strained forwards. I forced the images of Julia similarly engaged right to the back of my mind.

'And there's a lot of call for that sort of thing in Cambridge?'

She was struggling with her amusement – I got the clear impression she knew exactly what I was thinking – and said, 'Oh, yes. Enough for me to run a small salon. And I also do house-calls.'

Christ! What was she telling me? A masseuse who did house-calls. It was like an ad in *Mayfair*. But surely I was maligning her. 'Don't you –' I broke off.

'Don't I what?'

She was looking at me again, eyes fixed to mine, and I couldn't look away. 'Don't you worry that people are going to expect more than you're offering?' It was clumsy, and probably insulting, too, but she didn't seem to mind. She shrugged.

'It's always happening. Men – women, too, but it's mainly men – ask me what I charge for extras. I just tell them I don't do extras.'

She sounded very assertive. Perhaps that was how she convinced the people who asked for extras.

'I like doing sportsmen best,' she went on. 'They understand all about overworked muscles, and they appreciate the benefits of a strong pair of hands getting deep into the tissues. A man fresh off the football pitch doesn't want fingertips stroking his skin, he wants someone working so hard on him they're soon as exhausted as he is.'

We were back to my *From Russia with Love* fantasy. And it wasn't my fault. I said – I couldn't stop myself – 'I play rugby. I often finish Saturday afternoon aching all over.'

She looked at me critically. 'Where do you play?' I heard Thea in my head, asking the same question. But Julia added, 'In the pack?'

'Yes. Flanker.'

'Lower back, gluteus maximus and shoulders.' She flexed her hands, dropping her eyes to study the movements. Then, as if she'd been thinking something over and had come to a decision, she lifted her head again and stared into my eyes. 'I could stop you aching, if you'd like me to.'

I said huskily, 'I would.'

I didn't think I could manage any more of that conversation. I got up and bought her another drink, and tactfully she began to ask about how I was settling in at Cambridge. I was going to get a third round, but she said she'd had enough. I suggested rather half-heartedly that we eat – the idea didn't appeal to me at all – but she said she wasn't hungry.

We were sitting either side of a table bearing only empty glasses, and she didn't want another. Did I suggest we go? Was she leaving it up to me to propose what we did next, or was she going to go on being assertive and tell me?

She glanced at her watch. 'We may as well go. I've got some things to do before I turn in.'

It was enormously anti-climactic to have all the thrilling but vague possibilities that had thrummed in the air between us end in so prosaic a manner. She would drop me back in King's Parade, I'd wish her goodnight – might even shake her hand – and she'd hurry off to iron her overall and shine her shoes. *Christ*.

But it didn't turn out that way. Two-thirds of the way back, she turned off into a side road and stopped the car. After a couple of moments' awkward silence – awkward on my part, anyway, because unless she'd stopped to answer a call of nature, there could only be one other reason and I didn't know who was expected to make the first move – she reached out and put her hand on my thigh.

'Wing forward's legs,' she murmured, her fingers working in the muscle. Then, palm of her hand flat, she went higher. Not high enough, but it was a start. I put my arm round her, pulling her close, my other hand stroking her cheek. She said, 'Last night I seem to remember you kissing me. Do you remember that too?'

'No,' I said. 'I don't remember it at all, so I'm going to have to begin all over again.'

I bent my head and her mouth was full and firm under mine. Her tongue traced round inside my lips, and the excitement which had been gathering ever since I got into her car burst chaotically through me. I moved my hand down to her throat, finding the tiny buttons of her blouse and miraculously managing to undo them, and at last my fingers reached the goal I'd been aiming for the night before. Her breast was round and soft, the nipple as hard as a little pebble. I hoped it was an indication of desire – I'd read about women's nipples aching with desire – but on the other hand it might just have been the cold. She seemed to be liking it, and when I bent down to touch with my lips and tongue what my fingers had been exploring, she gave a deep sigh and pulled my head tighter against her.

I would have been happy to go on doing that all night. Happier still had we progressed further. But after a measureless time she gently pushed me away.

'Don't think I'm not enjoying it,' she said softly, holding my face between her hands and kissing my forehead, 'but I think we'd better stop.'

'Sorry. Of course.' I moved back to my own side

of the car, trying surreptitiously to cope with the agonizing effects of trousers that were now far too restricting.

I was aware that she was watching me. 'Why "of course"?'

'Well, I thought you – that we –'

'It's a postponement, Henry.' I wished I could see her, but it was too dark. 'Just a postponement.'

When she'd finished buttoning herself up, she started the car and drove us back to Cambridge. We drove in silence – I couldn't think of one thing to say – but as I was getting out of the car, she said, 'Are you playing next Saturday?'

'Yes.'

'And will it make you ache all over?'

'Yes.' Similar, I thought, to the way I'm aching now.

'Would you like me to put that right?'

'Yes.'

I heard her laugh. A low, sexy sound, overflowing with promise. 'I'll pick you up. Same time, same place.'

Then she drove away.

Eighteen

It was a strange week. I felt almost that I had become two people, one of whom mourned for what I had lost while the other waited in nervous excitement for what was to come. The thrill of Julia hadn't burned out the pain of Thea – nothing could have done that – but I had talked myself into believing that she was out of my life and, moreover, that I was well rid of her. She had hurt me – I was unwilling to admit how deeply – and she had diminished my self-confidence. Never was a man on the rebound more in need of a Julia.

During the day there was, fortunately for my sanity, more than enough to keep my thoughts on a higher plane than the purely carnal. I was no longer dazzled by how much work I had to get through, and consequently I was beginning to see that it was well within my capabilities. Once or twice, I had even earned a word or two of praise. But work, however absorbing, could not hold centre stage in my thoughts once I'd gone to bed: the dark hours belonged to Julia.

The trouble was that I didn't know what to expect. I'd never been out with a woman significantly older than me before – I was beginning to doubt that I'd been out with a woman at all, since all previous associates were suddenly looking very girlish, compared to Julia.

Except Thea. But I wasn't going to think about Thea.

I thought of myself as reasonably experienced for a man of my age and my class. The sort of girls I met didn't leap into bed with just anyone – they probably didn't leap into bed at all – and I'd never even gone as far as suggesting it. The general view seemed to be that a man needed a nice girl to go out with and a bad girl to have fun with, only – in common, I suspect, with most of my friends – I hadn't yet encountered the bad girl. Until I met Julia.

Was I reading her right? God, surely there couldn't be any doubt! In the face of what seemed overwhelming evidence that I was, I started to worry about what she'd expect of me. I hadn't made love before, no matter what I might have hinted to my friends, and Julia would be sure to discover my innocence in a matter of moments. Would it make a difference? Should I pretend to a track record I didn't have?

Over and above all that was the question of precautions, as in 'taking precautions', that dainty little euphemism that was just fine in the abstract but a different matter when one was suddenly thrown into urgent need. If – when? – we made love, would she expect me to be prepared? Wouldn't she take it as something of an insult if I assumed she was on the Pill and therefore ready for whoever happened along? She wasn't married – was she? God, I didn't even know that – so there was no reason why she should have been any more prepared for intimacy than I was.

I would have to see to it. Whichever way I looked at it, I couldn't escape the conclusion that it was up to me.

*   *   *

Had I been a fatalist, I'd have thought that my liaison with Julia was meant to be. Because, sitting with Phil in his college bar one evening, the answer to my problem turned up. He'd gone up to get us another half-pint each – you could only buy drinks on the chit system, but when it was my round I slipped him the cash – and when he came back with the full glasses, he was laughing.

'Simon's on a promise,' he remarked, sitting down.

'What?'

'Simon. Fair-haired chap over there.' He nodded towards a table across the room. 'He's just signed a bar chit for two brown ales and a bag of crisps!' He laughed again.

I was going to have to show my ignorance and ask what was so funny. 'I don't know what you mean.'

'It's the same price as a packet of three,' he said, voice dropping to a whisper. 'But brown ale and crisps looks better on your bar bill.'

'You mean you can buy them? Here?'

'Yes.' He looked quite proud, as well he might. It was a definite feather in his cap to be at a college where they were so advanced in their thinking. 'Great, isn't it?'

Now he was looking smug. That was going too far. 'How many brown ales have *you* signed for, then?' I asked.

'Well, I –'

'Go on! How many?'

He muttered, 'None.'

I thought rapidly. If I asked him to make a purchase for me, would he remember Julia at the party and put two and two together? Yes, he was bound to, and I wasn't ready to have anyone else knowing. I was going to have to be devious.

'Early days yet,' I said, and he flashed me a smile of gratitude. 'I'm in the same boat.' I sat for a while looking idly round the bar, as if the subject were closed. Then, hoping he'd think the idea had only just occurred to me, I said quietly, 'Do you think we should get some? I mean, if it's okay and no-one's going to know, perhaps we should get into the habit of carrying some around with us. In case –'

There was no need to enlarge on the 'in case'. Phil had got to his feet, reaching in his jacket for his chit-signing pen. 'Good idea,' he said, only blushing very faintly. 'Give us the cash, and I'll do it.'

As I went home, my hand in my pocket closed round a new and unfamiliarly-shaped packet, I amused myself at the thought of how my need – I'd decided to err on the safe and absurdly optimistic side and asked Phil to get me twelve – had had the pleasant side-effect of enhancing his reputation: he'd bought from his barman, who should have had an Oscar for the marvellously straight face he maintained, fifteen condoms.

At lunchtime on Saturday, when I was hunting for a shin-pad and banging last week's mud off my boots, someone tapped on my door to tell me there was a phone call for me. 'Says to tell you it's Florence,' he said, turning away.

Florence, Willowford Fen, Thea. The thought-train ran through my mind too quickly for me to get my defences in place. But perhaps it wasn't too late to avoid total disaster.

'Just a minute,' I called after the messenger.

'Huh?'

'Will you say you couldn't find me, please?'

He shrugged. 'Okay.'

Wondering what she'd wanted would negate the

good I'd achieved by not speaking to her, so I made myself stop. For quite a while I felt ashamed of myself. Then gradually the thought of the evening ahead struggled back into its place of prominence, and by the time I went out, Florence – Thea – was a pale ghost on the fringes of my mind.

We had a hard game against a superior team, and we were lucky to hold them to 17–13. Their tight-head prop was a bastard, and I wrenched my shoulder three times when he got our loose-head down. I'd also acquired a lovely set of stud-marks on my bum. Craning round in the showers to look at them, I wondered what Julia would have up her sleeve for bruises.

I went back to my room to change, hoping Florence wouldn't ring again.

Same time, same place. At twenty past seven, I went out to wait for her.

She was ten minutes late. Ten minutes in which I decided she'd changed her mind and wasn't coming, that it had all been far too good to be true and that I was going to give up women for life.

She said, 'Sorry I'm late. Traffic.'

The smell of her perfume took me straight back to the previous Sunday. Already she was tying me in knots, and I hadn't even touched her yet. She was wearing black trousers and a big, soft, cream sweater. I could hardly breathe.

'We'll go to the salon,' she said, changing gear and lightly tapping my leg in the same movement, 'I can do a much better job on the plinth.'

Plinth. An image of David flashed before my eyes, standing gracefully on top of his stone block stark bollock naked.

'Right.'

'Did you have a good game?'

'Tough.'

'Did you shower afterwards?'

Why did she want to know that? 'Yes.'

'Fine, we won't have to scrape the mud off first.'

We drove on in silence – I didn't blame her for having had enough of my monosyllabic conversation – and soon she was parking in a side street of houses interspersed with a few shops. She led the way to a door between two shops; on it was a modest plaque which said, J. A. MILLER, BEAUTICIAN AND MASSEUSE. She had letters after her name, but I didn't take in what they were.

'Come in – there's no-one here,' she said, ushering me in and locking the door behind her. We went up a flight of stairs, at the top of which there was a small reception area with a desk and a couple of chairs. On two sides of it were cubicles, one of which had its curtains drawn back to show a narrow, waist-high table with a pile of white towels on it.

'Get undressed down to your pants, wrap a towel round you and lie down,' she ordered. 'I'll be with you in a minute.'

I did as she said. I was feeling so incredibly nervous it was a relief that one of us was issuing commands.

Lying down on my stomach, I waited.

I heard her come in, and turned to look at her. She'd taken off the cream sweater and the trousers and was wearing a short-sleeved white overall. Her hair was pulled severely back into a plait which she'd twisted into a bun. She looked totally professional.

'Any particular trouble spots?' she asked.

'Shoulder,' I mumbled. 'Right side.'

'Hm.'

There was a sound of a bottle being shaken, then a pleasant smell which reminded me of greenery. I heard her rubbing her hands together, then she put them on to me.

At first the combined effects of being anxious about what was going to happen, disappointed that it didn't seem to be what I'd been expecting, and sheer bloody fear made me so tense that I was almost fighting her. Then slowly she overcame me: her hands were strong and she didn't give up, stroking, soothing and kneading till at last I seemed to melt under her and go with her. As I relaxed she dug deeper into my muscles, causing a wonderful reaction of pain and pleasure so well mixed that I hardly knew where one ended and the other began.

Shoulders, neck, back, right down to the base of my spine. Down my arms, the length of my legs. Rolling with the tide now, I was no longer aware of her as a person, just a marvellous, ubiquitous pair of hands. When she said quietly, 'Turn over,' I responded as if I were her puppet, moving smoothly, barely noticing the towel falling to the floor.

She worked up my legs and arms, then over my stomach and chest. Far gone in my world of tactile delight, I had my eyes closed so that I received her, too, through senses other than sight. The scent of her perfume blended with the oil she was using – it was a different smell now, less green, more sweet and spicy – and I heard her breathing. Sometimes I thought I felt a stray wisp of her hair brush against my skin.

Her hands were on my pectorals. All but at rest, her fingers were making the smallest of movements. She said, 'If you turn back again, I'll have a look at those bruises.'

I don't know how I came to be naked. I don't remember the getting there, only the being there. It was logical, I suppose – she could hardly attend to stud-marks on my buttocks if I had my underpants on. I was aware of her fetching another bottle, then of her rubbing something cool into my skin. I pictured my bruises – three close together, and two big ones a couple of inches away. Whatever she was using took the pain away, and in my mental picture, the colouring faded to nothing.

When she broke contact, I felt more alone than I'd ever done before.

I went to sit up, to pull her back. But she pushed me down again, covering me with a huge towel. 'It's all right.' She was smiling. 'I'm still here.'

I lay staring up at her. She was watching me, the smile still hovering on her face, but there was something else in her expression as well. 'This is silly,' she said eventually. 'I thought it would –' She shook her head and started again. 'I imagined it would be easy, but it's not. The trouble is, I think, that although I've just had my hands all over you, they were my professional hands. Whereas what I have in mind now – I mean, what I thought we'd do next, is . . .'

What was she trying to say? I understood about the professional hands – God, she'd made me feel fantastic – but what was the difficulty now? That she couldn't move from treating me to caressing me?

I thought suddenly, she's never seduced anyone in her shop before. Then as quickly thought, she *must* have done! But the more I thought about it, the more likely an explanation it seemed. Aware that I was heading for an almighty put-down if I was wrong, I said, 'Is this a first?'

And she nodded.

It changed her subtly. She no longer fitted the stereotyped older, practised, woman-of-the-world mould I'd tried to put her in. If I was heading for a first time, then so, in a sense, was she. We weren't as unequal as I'd thought.

I said, 'I haven't got any clothes on.'

'No. So you haven't.'

'You have.'

Her smile was back, and she looked her assured self. 'Not very many.'

She wiped her hands on my towel and began to unbutton her overall. I had never conceived of a white nylon overall as a sexually stimulating garment, but then I'd never before seen Julia emerging from one. Beneath it she wore a white lace bra and a tiny pair of panties. Her body was a perfect figure-of-eight, and her curves would have fitted, with only millimetres to spare, the shape men sketch in the air to describe the archetypal woman. She wouldn't have looked out of place on a saucy Edwardian postcard; she was absolutely gorgeous.

I reached up and undid the clip holding her plait. She shook her head, and the shining dark hair spilled over me, sweet-smelling and soft. I took hold of it, twisting handfuls in my fingers, and I pulled her face down close to mine. For a moment she looked into my eyes. Then she kissed me.

For the past however long it had been, her hands had roamed all over my body. Now, her mouth was on mine. And, soon, her hands were on me again, only this time, like a tigress playing with her cubs, the strength was held back. Now her fingers seemed to float above my skin, their touch so light that it was scarcely there at all. I reached behind her, finding the catch of her bra, undoing it and pulling it from her so that, leaning over me as she was, her unrestrained breasts fell forward against my chest. Then I wrapped my arms round her and pulled her closer, and her soft flesh crushing between us was such a novel and arousing stimulus that I tightened my hold till she gasped.

'Sorry,' I whispered, slackening off.

'It's all right.' She was running a line of little kisses down my throat, from below my ear to the hollow over my collar bone. I could feel her tongue on my skin. 'But you don't have to –' She broke off, and I felt her go tense.

'What's the matter?'

'Nothing.' She resumed her kissing, her body slowly relaxing. But then there was the sound of a car door banging in the street, and she lifted her head, craning round to look over her shoulder.

'They're not coming here, are they?' I felt suddenly very vulnerable.

'No, oh, no.' She turned back to me, frowning. 'It's just – oh, bloody hell!' She laughed ruefully.

'What?'

She bent down to pick up her discarded clothes, and I knew what she was going to say before she said it. 'It's being here, in my workplace.' She took hold of my hand, turning it palm up and kissing it gently. 'I know it's stupid, but I keep thinking Karen's going to walk in.'

'Karen?'

'My receptionist.' She had her back to me, and I watched as she did up her bra. 'I'm sorry. I thought it was a good idea, but it looks like I was wrong.'

I didn't know what to say. I was still feeling very aroused – although the thought of her receptionist bursting in on us had taken the edge off it – and the last thing I wanted just then was to watch her get dressed again. I also felt slightly aggrieved – this whole thing had been her suggestion, she'd made all the rules, and now she was running out before the final fence. I said, 'Is this another postponement?'

She looked at me, and I saw an answering flash of anger cross her face. Then it was gone. 'No, but I can see how you'd think it was. I'm not doing it deliberately.'

I swathed myself in the towel and stood up. Enough of playing by someone else's book. I went across to her and put my arms round her. 'We'll get dressed and I'll take you out for a meal,' I said masterfully. 'I'm starving, I've only had a pork pie since breakfast and I played a hard game of rugby this afternoon.' I bent to kiss the top of her head. 'We'll have a few drinks and talk to each other. Then, if we both want to, you can take me home with you and we'll see if the postponements are over.'

She didn't answer for a while and I wondered if I'd blown it. But then she removed herself from my arms and said quite calmly, 'Okay. I'll go and get ready.'

It was better, after that. Perhaps we'd both been acting out of character, she trying to adopt a role of seductress which didn't suit her, I to accept her in the driving seat when all my life – or so I told myself – I'd made the decisions. When we left her salon we were easier with each other, and by the time we were settled in the pub, we were talking as freely as if we'd been friends for ages. I ordered a huge meal – she'd said she wasn't hungry, but when it came to it she discovered quite an appetite – and we had a bottle of wine. I offered her a brandy with the coffee – I was having one – but she said she wouldn't as she was driving.

I looked at her across the table. There was a candle burning, and her skin was glowing. She was very desirable. I said, 'Where are we going to be driving to?'

She watched me, a slow smile widening her mouth. 'I thought I might take you home with me.'

Beer, wine and brandy. I'd drunk enough not to care any more. I'd be okay. *We'd* be okay.

I said, 'In that case I'd better get the bill.'

Nineteen

Everyone remembers the first time they made love. It's a shame everyone can't have a Julia, since I can't imagine how any initiation could be better than mine was with her. We never actually got round to discussing how experienced – or otherwise – I was; she seemed to act on the premise that I hadn't slept with a woman before, probably on the assumption that I'd let her know if she was wrong.

The limits of my experience ran out fairly soon. When she was lying naked beside me on her bed, to be exact, and I had moved my hands from her breasts down to the curve of her stomach. I knew where I wanted to go, but the route was unfamiliar. It didn't stay that way for long: she twined her fingers between mine and guided me, riding tandem on my hand until I didn't need any more direction. As I touched her, discovering with increasing pleasure and assurance the secret parts of her woman's body which up to then had been just words, my confidence was augmented by her clear indication that she was enjoying it as much as I was. As if wanting to reciprocate the feelings I was giving her, her hands began to stroke me, inside my thighs, over my buttocks, and, when I was almost exploding with anticipation, down into my groin.

I moved her over on to her back, parting her legs so that I lay between them. This was where it was going to get difficult – I just didn't know how such things were done. I wondered how to phrase it, then, urgency driving finesse out of my head, said, 'Should I use anything?'

This was the seventies, when you didn't examine someone's medical report before making love. When your main worry was that they shouldn't get pregnant. Her hand on me, guiding me inside her, she whispered, 'There's no need. I've taken care of it.'

Fleetingly it crossed my mind to wonder in what way. Whether she'd prepared herself just for me, or if I was benefiting from a previous liaison. But the thought was gone almost before it had happened, for I was entering her, feeling the soft warm pressure of her on me, and she was giving me more pleasure than anyone had a right to.

It didn't last for long, that time. The effects of the massage, the earlier intimacy, the happy evening, the drink and, above all, the exploration of each other we'd just been doing, had combined to take me far out of control. The release came very soon, and I've never forgotten how incredible it was.

Lying on top of her, slowly I descended from the new heights I'd just reached and reverted to an ordinary human being. Becoming aware of her, the old cliché flew into my head: How was it for you? I didn't need to ask – I'd come too soon, as far as she was concerned, and I knew it. But I didn't know what to do about it; all *I* wanted to do was close my eyes and sleep the sleep of the just-after, but that didn't seem fair on her, when I was feeling the wonderful way I did purely because of her.

Rolling off her, I lay on my back and pulled her against me. I stroked her hair, letting my hand move gradually down until I touched her breast. I thought it would be impossible to get aroused again so soon, and my mind wandered off on to the interesting biological phenomenon of how fingering her nipple should have had such an effect on me five minutes ago when now it did nothing.

But then it wasn't doing nothing any more. And suddenly this wasn't just for her, but for me too.

Again, she guided my hand. This time, she held me on to the place she wanted me to be, and I felt her move rhythmically against my finger, her body arching, legs parting, as if the stretching of her muscles and her limbs enhanced her pleasure. She said, surprisingly loudly, 'Don't stop! Oh, God, don't stop!', then suddenly she was gasping and shouting at the same time, reaching for my wrist, grabbing it tightly and pushing hard so that my fingers slid into her.

I felt it happen to her. Felt the fierce muscle contractions as she came. Felt the expulsion, in a cross between a sigh and a sob, of the breath she'd been holding in. Felt the sweat break out on her body as, finally, all the tension went out of her and she slumped against me.

Heard her cry. That lost, wild, unmistakeable cry of a woman in ecstasy.

As I clutched her tightly to me, I felt surprisingly moved. I'd thought my own orgasm was the most wonderful thing I'd ever experienced, but now, immediately after it, here was something else new to me, something which, in a different way, was equally wonderful.

Every man's first lover should be a Julia. Because, as well as making me feel the most intense physical joy I'd ever had, she taught me the more important lesson of how to give it.

We slept for a few hours, then woke up and made love again. This time I managed to take longer about it, but still I was too fast for her. She had no qualms about talking it over afterwards: she said almost as soon as we were breathing normally again, 'That was better, but it could easily be better still.'

I felt slightly aggrieved; bloody hell, I wasn't used to this, and I'd thought I was doing rather well. She must have picked up my response – which wouldn't be surprising as she'd been picking up every other response in me all night – because she leaned over me and gave me a smacking kiss on the cheek.

'Don't be like that,' she said affectionately. 'I'm not criticizing, I'm trying to help. It'll be far easier for you if you get it right from the start.'

The protesting words leapt to my lips. What do you mean, from the start! Then I thought, what's the point?

'Okay,' I said meekly.

'I'm going to get us a drink and something to eat,' – she was jumping out of bed as she spoke – 'then we'll talk.'

We talked. Between mouthfuls of corned beef sandwich and slurps of Guinness – both of which have had an erotic significance for me ever since – she told me all that she thought I needed to know. About a woman's body, about a man's, and it no longer surprised me in the least that she should know much more about my anatomy than I did myself.

Then, of course, I wanted to try it out. Talking about it had excited me so that I was rock-hard – how did therapists manage, I wondered, and men who lectured on such matters? Maybe they got used to it, or maybe the effect wasn't the same if you weren't naked in bed beside someone like Julia – and this time was the best of all.

Spent beside me, she said afterwards, 'I think that'll do for tonight!'

We had a lazy Sunday. I awoke to find she was already up and about – my fifteen minutes' pleasantly sensual reminiscing were interrupted by her arrival in the bedroom carrying a tray. She'd brought me breakfast in bed. She was, I noticed with disappointment, fully dressed.

'We're going for a walk,' she told me as she went out again, leaving me to my tea and cereal, 'then we'll have a pub lunch and I'll drop you off. I've got things to do this afternoon.'

Clearly, those things didn't include making love with me again.

Once I'd finished breakfast, showered and dressed, I didn't feel quite so bad about it.

We didn't walk far. I felt as if I'd recently run a marathon, and she kept yawning. We perked up a bit in the pub, and when we were on the third round, she reached out and took my hand.

'I'm going to dinner with some old friends next Saturday,' she said.

'Oh.' This, I thought, was it. The brush-off. Great night, Henry, but I'm going to be busy for a while. Today, things to do. Next Saturday, people to go out to dinner with.

But then she added, 'D'you want to come? They're nice, lots of fun. You'll like them.'

I said, 'Thanks. I'd love to.'

She gave an abrupt nod. Good, she seemed to say, that's settled. Then, as if she were now free to open up and talk to me, she said, 'I used to see a lot of them when I was married. They were at university with my husband.'

Several thoughts spun in my head. Husband. Part of me was relieved she'd had a husband – in my conventional mind, it made it all right for her to be such a wow in bed if she'd acquired her expertise within the bounds of wedlock. Then it occurred to me that it was unusual, surely, for her still to see friends of her husband when she was no longer married to him? And, finally, I wondered what had happened.

'When you were married,' I repeated. 'I take it you no longer are?'

'No.' She looked away from me, out of the window. 'He was older than me. Quite a lot, actually. Things were great for a while – five years – but then I began to resent him making all the decisions. It wasn't at all fair of me – to start with, I'd been only too pleased to follow where he led. But he gave me the confidence to think for myself, to decide for myself, and . . .'

'He turned you into someone who didn't need him any more,' I finished for her. 'So you left him.' Poor bugger. Bad luck on him.

But, 'Oh, no,' she was saying, her face slightly sad. 'I didn't leave him, he left me. He's now married to a lovely girl who was an even younger bride than I was.'

'Why did he . . .'

'It was a mutual thing,' she said quickly. 'He could see I didn't need him any more, and he preferred to be with someone who did. All very amicable and nobody got hurt.'

She smiled brightly at me. So brightly that I wondered if it had been quite as painless as she was making out.

'Sometimes these things are for the best,' I said feebly.

'Oh, they are!' she agreed fervently. Then, relaxing, she laughed. 'Listen to me! Don't take any notice, I rarely think about him now. It's just that, last night, I was teaching you all the things that he taught me. He was the most wonderful lover I've ever had.'

Her eyes had gone dreamy. She was making me feel about half an inch high.

I reached for her glass, somewhat abruptly, and stood up to go for refills. She grabbed hold of my wrist.

'Henry?'

I didn't answer. Didn't look at her.

'I'm sorry,' she said quietly. 'That was an awful thing to say. I can't un-say it, but please, remember that he was thirty-four when I met him and had already had one wife and more mistresses than he could count on both hands and both feet.'

'Whereas I'm a beginner who can just about keep it up for three minutes with a calm sea and a following wind.'

There was a silence. Then she said seriously, 'I made it three and a half, that last time.'

I turned to see the laughter struggling in her face. For a split-second I wanted to smack it away, then the impulse to hurt was gone.

'Shall we go home and go for a new all-comers' record?' I suggested. I was quite proud of the wording, given that it was on the spur of the moment.

She hesitated. I felt she wanted to say no, but didn't want to put me down again.

Her eyes on mine, she said frankly, 'I was going to have this afternoon on my own, and besides I'm feeling sore. But . . .'

'But what?'

She stared down into her lap. Although it seemed hard to believe, she looked slightly embarrassed. 'You're turning me on,' she said quietly. 'Suddenly my mind's full of you, and I want you.'

She drove us back to her flat as if she was on the final lap at Monza.

I called her in the week to ask what time she'd be picking me up on Saturday. I knew better than to suggest a meeting before that: she'd said quite plainly, 'See you next weekend,' and I wasn't about to let her know how desperate I was for her. On the phone I was friendly but cool. Or, at least, that was the intention.

'I'll see you at seven thirty,' she said, 'usual place. We're due there around eight, and it's a few miles out of town.'

I had the sudden thought, wouldn't it be funny if the friends turned out to live next door to Florence? If they've invited her, too, and have said to her, you'll love Julia, and she's bringing her latest conquest. Runs through them like wildfire, does our Julia! A right little goer!

No. It wouldn't be funny at all.

'Er – where do they live?' I asked nonchalantly. Joe Cool had nothing on me.

'Just this side of Ely.'

Close, I thought. But not that close.

'Great. See you on Saturday, then.'

'Yes. Oh, Henry?'

'Yes?'

'They dress for dinner. Silly, I know, but it's a hangover from top table days.'

'Fine. 'Bye, Julia.'

It wasn't fine at all. As I put down the phone, I

was cursing the friends of Julia's ex-husband for their nostalgic habits, because it meant I'd have to go out to Willowford Fen and collect my DJ. And I could hardly do that without seeing Florence.

I postponed the visit till the last possible moment, and went on the Friday evening. I phoned her in the afternoon, and she asked if I'd like to stay to dinner. When I said no, because travelling back by public transport got more difficult the later the hour, she said I could take her car back with me.

Was it a ploy, to make sure I couldn't refuse her invitation? I didn't know.

She seemed her usual self. We had a couple of drinks before dinner, and our talk, although restricted to small matters such as arranging to have the car serviced and the gutter that needed mending, flowed fairly easily. Perhaps we both knew we'd talk about her, sooner or later, but that the time wasn't right yet.

The right time came over coffee. I wondered how many of my crucial conversations with Florence had been over coffee. As if she'd suddenly got fed up with discussing everything except what was in the forefront of both our minds, Florence said, 'She's gone, you know. Taken her things and gone.'

'Everything?' If she'd even left a few books, or some clothes, then surely it meant she'd be back.

'Everything.'

There was nothing I could say. After quite a long time, Florence said gently, 'I'm sorry, Henry.'

'Me too.' I managed a weak smile.

'No. I meant that I'm sorry for driving her away.'

'Oh, no, you –' I stopped. Why was I denying what I knew to be true? No matter what I thought, Thea had been convinced Florence was trying to control her. Us. Florence hadn't had the diplomacy to ease off, and now Thea had gone.

'I did,' Florence said. 'And, believe me, Henry, no-one regrets it more than I.'

I looked at her. She met my eyes, and her face was drawn and sad. She was no longer the Florence of my youth, who was in control, who always knew what to do, who was wise and strong. I felt a foreboding deep inside me: up till that moment, I suppose I'd thought my omnipotent Florence would somehow, some day bring Thea back.

But if my Florence wasn't omnipotent any more . . .

That wasn't a thought to dwell on.

'I have to go,' I said, getting up.

'Of course.'

She came with me to the front door, picking up the car keys from the hall table and giving them to me. Taking my DJ from the coat rack, I bent to kiss her. She said quietly, 'Will you be all right?'

What could I reply but 'Yes'?

I drank too much at the friends-of-the-husband's dinner party. As well as the pair of them and Julia and me, there were two other couples, and they'd known Julia's old man as well. In fact they made it quite clear that they still did know him, and that they thought him one hell of a good chap. One of the women said to Julia, 'Matt sends his love,' which I thought she handled with grace, merely nodding and giving a slightly wistful smile.

They were all a lot older than me, that was half the trouble – the other half, of course, was that they were all so wild about good old Matt. They were a lot older than Julia, too, but then she was used to it – she'd been married to someone of their vintage for five years. They were lively and intelligent, and in other circumstances I'd probably have enjoyed their company.

But that night I was hurting, despite Julia beside me looking gorgeous in peacock blue velvet that fitted like a second skin. It wasn't Julia I wanted, and my guilt at being with her in body but not in heart made me feel worse. The cruel thought kept banging at my mind that she, too, was old – bless her, she can't have been more than twenty-eight, but that was a decade older than me. Than Thea – and that wild young Henry had to put up with these staid middle-aged people when he wanted to be whooping it up with his own generation.

Peter Pan decided, with stunning maturity, that the only thing to do was to get pissed out of his brain. It was easy, at that elegant dinner-table: we'd started with smoked salmon accompanied by the palest sherry, then gone on to fillet of beef with a Pinot Noir of which the master of the house was justifiably proud. With our dessert a demi-sec Blanc de Blancs was served, and there was a choice of brandy or port with our coffee. Added to the two large gins I'd had when we arrived, by the time we got up from dinner I could hardly stand.

Julia knew. Not that she criticized; watching me weave between two occasional tables as I aimed for a chair, she said kindly, 'Do you want to go?'

I'd just flopped down among the cushions. Getting up again was momentarily beyond me, but I did want to go. I felt terrible. I nodded.

'Okay.' She glanced round for our hosts. 'Look, I'll go and make our excuses, then I'll come back and help you up.'

'Excuses,' I slurred. 'What will you say?'

'I'll say you're out of your tree,' she replied. 'Don't

worry, they won't think any the worse of you. In the good old days with Matt, it wasn't a decent party unless someone threw up.'

Good old Matt. I risked closing my eyes, then opened them again. As if from a distance, I saw her go up to her friends. Say her goodbyes, kiss a few cheeks. Then she was back, strong arms round my shoulders getting me to my feet.

Holding on to her, I felt a bit steadier. Steady enough, anyway, to make a proper exit.

I stopped in the doorway and turned to face them all.

'Thank you for a delightful evening,' I said loudly. 'Please excuse my inebriation,' – a minor triumph, that word – 'but I have matters of grave concern on my mind.'

Someone laughed, someone else – the host, I think, he was a good sort – said, 'We know how it is, old man. Very nice to meet you, and we hope we shall see you again.'

He didn't add, as well he might have done, when you're sober.

I was hardly aware of the journey back. I may have slept. Then too soon the car was slowing down, and I began gearing myself up for the awesome prospect of clambering out of the car and walking back to my room. Then Julia said, 'Wait there, I'll come round and help you out and up the stairs, then I'll come back and put the car away.'

Stupidly I peered around me. We were in the car park beneath her flat.

I said, my voice full of maudlin self-pity, 'I don't deserve this.'

'No, I don't suppose you do,' she replied, 'but I couldn't have gone to bed worrying about whether or not you'd made it home.'

She helped me into bed, thoughtfully putting a bucket beside me. I watched her hang my DJ in the wardrobe, then she disappeared. Soon she was back. At some point she'd changed out of the blue velvet into a towelling bathrobe.

She came to sit beside me, taking my hand. Looking me in the eye, she said, 'What's the matter?'

If she'd been cross, or petulant, or overtly disappointed that I was far too drunk to make love to her – on the other hand, possibly that was the last thing she wanted – it would have been different. Then, I could have shut myself up in an offended silence and kept my misery to myself.

But she was kind. And I was pissed.

Wrapping my arms round her waist, burying my face in the soft sweet-smelling fabric of her robe, I told her.

I was ashamed in the morning. Better to have thrown up, better to have insulted someone – Julia, even – than to have given way like that. Awake before her – I usually woke up early when I'd gone to bed drunk, which was probably nature's way of ensuring I didn't miss one fun-packed moment of the hangover – I lay and imagined what she'd say to me. She'd be tactful, and would try not to hurt me, but I'd be out. Whichever way you looked at it, she'd have no time for a man who'd told her the things I'd told her last night. I'd worked round to thinking I might as well retrieve my DJ and tiptoe out before she stirred, when she woke up.

I watched her as her eyes slowly opened. She smiled at me, then leaned closer to give me a kiss.

'You smell awful,' she remarked. 'Like a dissipated old wino.'

I didn't ask her how she knew what a dissipated

wino smelt like; I felt the kiss was more than I deserved, and I wasn't going to push my luck.

Her hand was on my chest, fingers circling my nipples, one after the other. Then she moved down to my navel, making the same slow, gentle movements as if she were hardly aware of what she was doing.

But she was. After a while she said, 'Go and clean the stale wine out of your mouth.'

I did as she ordered. As I got back into bed she got out, but she only went as far as the bathroom. Then, coming back to lie beside me, she said, 'Let's make love.'

Later, when I knew her better – very much better – I realized that a man who was half – all right, nine-tenths – in love with someone else was just right for Julia. But I didn't know it then. Then, she seemed like a gift from the gods.

And I wasn't going to be ungrateful enough to refuse her.

Twenty

In the first few weeks after I ran out on Henry, it sometimes crossed my mind that if Gordon Willis had known at our first meeting what he was taking on, he'd have emigrated there and then.

I was very glad he didn't, because I don't think I would have survived without him. He let me talk myself to a standstill, patiently listening as I endlessly went through what Henry had said, what I'd said, what Florence had said, trying to make sense of it all, trying always to convince myself that I'd had no choice, that I'd *had* to finish it. Trying, too, to take the horror out of those ghastly moments culminating in Eric's death. As I'd suspected, Gordon had seen nothing more sinister than a patchy mist, which made me question whether the whole thing had been a product of my imagination. I'd scarcely been myself, after all.

Then I'd think, Eric's dead. And the *how* didn't really matter. Gordon let me cry, and even in my distress I was aware that I was lucky to have someone by my side who was so kind. And so good.

I didn't know, then, that he had an ulterior motive.

He knew when the moment was right to say, that's enough, and fix my attention on something else. I'd got the impression we'd be leaving for Flanders almost immediately – wishful thinking, no doubt – but in fact there was quite a lot of preliminary work to do in England before we could kiss East Anglia goodbye. My impatience to be gone definitely worked in Gordon's favour; it took me just under a fortnight to complete the long list of research tasks he set me.

He had obviously decided that hard work was the best thing for me. Our relationship changed subtly – from the chummy sort of partnership of equals it had been during the short time I'd worked with him on the Thetford history, now he was definitely the leader, I the follower. It was fair enough – the battlefields book was his brainchild, and he had too clear a picture of how he wanted the project to develop for me to interfere. Being an ex-army man, I suppose he was used to taking command, and at that time of my life someone telling me what to do was just what I needed. He kept me busy – kept my thoughts occupied – almost every minute of the day. It was the right solution – for ages I was only happy when I was deeply immersed and had no corner of my mind free to grieve.

I did grieve. God, I did. I told myself I was stupid, that Henry wasn't for me and it was much better to have found out sooner rather than later. That even if Henry and I could have got on, life would have been impossible for me under the influence of Florence. Under the shadowy, brooding wings of that dark, nameless threat I couldn't forget.

And anyway, why was I so sad when I'd only known him for five minutes? Once when I said that to myself, an answer came out of nowhere: that's not right. You've known him for ever.

*   *   *

Departure day came at last. We left England on a bright, cold November day, driving Gordon's posh new camper van down to Dover and taking turns at the wheel – another item on my 'keeping busy' list had been more driving lessons and, at the end of them, my test, which to my surprise I passed. We took the ferry over to Calais, en route to Flanders. I'd looked forward to the moment so intensely, and I thought I'd be overjoyed to be leaving. I didn't expect to stand at the stern rail of the ship crying my eyes out.

Gordon patted my hand and promised me a good, if late, lunch when we got to the other side. He drove us sedately to a small French town called Cassel, which, he informed me, stood on the Grand Old Duke of York's hill. As in, 'When they were up, they were up.' We went to a restaurant where they seemed to know him, and by the time we'd finished lunch and I'd had far more to drink than I should have – finishing with a glass of Calvados so smooth and rich that I became addicted there and then – the Duke of York's marching men weren't the only ones who were up.

I can't remember if Gordon drank a lot, that lunchtime. I expect he did, although he drove as carefully on our onward journey into Belgium as he had done when he hadn't touched a drop. This was something about him I'd come to know – that he could match anyone drink for drink and remain at all times reasonable, pleasant and in control.

It was just as well. I went haywire in our first few weeks in Belgium, and I'm sure I was very rarely reasonable and pleasant. There was hardly a time when I was in control.

Gordon said after a month, 'That's enough, Thea. I know you've had a bad experience, and I sympathize.

You've had the running wild phase, now it's time for reining in and getting your bottom firmly in the saddle.' He was a great horseman, Gordon, and tended towards equine imagery at times of stress. He added more kindly, probably because my jaw had dropped in surprise at hearing him speak that way, 'And I need you! It's not nearly so much fun working on my own!'

Fun. God, I thought, I could do with some fun!

You wouldn't think Ypres would be the best place for someone bent on having a good time – too many spectres, too many sad memories. You'd be surprised – I was. I came out of my miserable haze to find myself in a charming little town full of industrious, pleasant people who, having put in a hard day in the fields or the office or the shop, were ready to play in the evening. Gordon and I stayed in a small hotel on the square whose bar was quite a centre of activity, and in no time we were on chatting terms with several of the regulars. They spoke Flemish – unsurprisingly, since this was bang in the middle of Flanders – but, like people everywhere in the world, most of them had a smattering of English. Enough, anyway, for the exchanging of pleasantries in a friendly bar.

During the day we would go off in the camper van and walk the fields and the woods, with tens of thousands of young men all around us. While Gordon worked out who had advanced where and kept up a running commentary on the lines of, 'What was the strategy behind *that*, for goodness' sake!', I went into a dream world where I almost convinced myself I could see them. Faces beneath khaki caps and tin helmets. Smiling faces, full of eagerness and cheerfulness. Then hurt faces, eyes sunken and dark-circled, wide in horrified reaction to what they had seen.

It would have been easy to weep. But people had been weeping ever since the guns ceased firing. We, now, I told myself as I watched Gordon extract his foot from a puddle that was deeper than he'd thought, we can do something more than weeping. We can write a book. Remind people. Tell them, if they need telling, what it was like. Make sure valuable young lives are never again treated as mere numbers, to throw against an impenetrable barbed wire barricade spitting flesh-ripping bullets.

Fired with that sort of enthusiasm – naive, perhaps, but I felt it sincerely – I turned into the best assistant Gordon ever had.

Getting out of England, leaving East Anglia, Henry and Florence far behind, throwing myself into an engrossing task with someone I grew closer to the longer we were together, I expected to erase Willowford Fen from my mind.

But it wasn't like that. I took it with me. We took it with us – I didn't realize it till the spring, months after we'd come away, but Gordon was almost as deeply involved with the mystery of Florence as I was.

We were in Picardy, staying in a small hotel in Arras where the other guests all seemed to be travelling salesmen. We'd had a long day trudging the banks of the Somme – there weren't any roses blooming in Picardy, it was far too cold and any plants foolhardy enough to put out buds would have lost them to the frost. We were sitting in the bar before dinner, cheering ourselves up with lagers and cognac chasers, when out of the blue he said,

'Do you miss him?'

'Yes.'

'And do you regret not being there with him?'

After the briefest hesitation I said, 'No.'

He stared at me as if, unusual in one so fluent, he was finding it hard to put into words what he wanted to say. Cool, controlled Gordon. He didn't look like himself, either, which was disturbing – he was less the man who'd retired from the army as a full colonel and taken with him the habit of command, more the boy caught out in a prank.

More the penitent about to enter the confessional.

I wished he'd get on with it. As if he picked up my unease, he said, 'It was essential for you to get away, you know. Over and above your need to put distance between yourself and Henry, you had to leave Florence. And Willowford Fen.'

I hadn't expected that. I said numbly, 'What?'

'You were in danger.'

Danger! From what? From whom? I remembered the unwelcome thought I'd had when Eric was killed: if I stayed, who would be next?

'I don't understand. I . . .'

'Thea, be quiet and listen. *Please.*'

The commanding officer was back. I nodded. 'Okay.'

'I don't know where to begin.' He looked away from me, frowning. 'I'm still not a hundred per cent sure, but at the same time . . .' He didn't finish the sentence. Then, turning back to me, he said, 'Damn it. Thea, I've had my suspicions all along. Since you told me how Florence was trying to control you – you and Henry – and certainly since you mentioned her will. Then when you arrived that morning after you'd seen . . .' He paused. 'Something made me verify my suspicions. Try to, at any rate, because nothing's provable beyond doubt, it's all so bloody vague. Circumstantial.' He reached down for my hand, gripping it in both of his. Since he'd stopped having to hold me while I wept, he didn't often touch me. 'I came across it when I was researching the history of Thetford Priory. It's not directly relevant, not to the Priory story. It's relevant to you, though. The more you tell me, the more convinced I am.' He came to another halt, releasing one of his hands to pick up and drain his cognac glass.

Just when I couldn't bear the suspense any longer, he turned back to me. Blowing away Picardy, taking me right back to Florence's East Anglia, he said, 'Have you ever heard of the legend of the Third Crown?'

I could see myself, a vague figure standing on a narrow shore under crumbling cliffs. Someone was speaking. 'Somewhere out there is a royal palace . . . Built by Sigebert, a proud gesture that defied the power of the sea. Saint Felix crowned him . . . and that holy crown was buried with two others so that the power in them should save Britain from invasion . . .'

Three crowns, with magic in them. Two accounted for, the third yet to be found.

I was still on the shore, but slowly the scene before me was changing . . . From a vision of the grey and desolate North Sea, now I could see a town . . . Not a nowadays town but one from the Dark Ages, rows of thatched wooden huts half sunk into the earth, the trodden paths between them hectic with people, wagons, animals. In the middle was a larger, important-looking building, its steeply-pitched roof soaring above the huts, its strong hundred-foot-long walls broken only by small windows set high up. A royal hall. Risen from its watery grave, the ancient town of Dunwyc shivered in front of my eyes.

I was no longer by the sea; the scene had changed again, and I was looking down on an inland settlement, thick forest pressing in around the perimeter fence. Another hall, outside it a banner flying, as if to denote the presence of royalty . . . This had to be Rendlesham.

I had entered the hall, and found myself standing in front of a great central fire which sent plumes of smoke up to the already black roof. The smoke must have got into my eyes, because they felt sore. As if I'd been crying for a long time.

Someone was standing behind me, right at my shoulder. I sensed him even before he spoke.

'Marriage is a woman's lot,' he said in that soft, sibilant voice. 'The fortunate become rich men's wives, the unfortunate ally themselves to peasants and die from drudgery before their time. Without a husband, what is there for a woman?'

I couldn't speak. Wouldn't have known what to say even if I could. A wordless protest sounded in my head, but I was afraid of him, and kept my peace.

He came closer, his head bent to my level so that his breath stroked against my ear.

'Your marriage, lady, is important. More is at stake than your own wishes. Your union with Egenhere is a symbol, for you are of native British stock and he is a newcomer.' A touch of iron intruding into the soft tone, he went on, 'Integration is the only hope for your people. You are conquered, subject. You must adapt to survive.'

I was trembling, both from the fear instilled by his proximity and by his words. He was right, and I knew it.

'Egenhere is of noble blood,' he said persuasively, 'and the sons you bear him will be men of power.' At the word 'power' I felt a long shudder go through me. I recognized it as terror. 'With my continued support –' He corrected himself smoothly. 'With the help of wise counsellors, who knows to what heights the sons of Egenhere may ascend? And he is no better and no worse than any other man. I am close to him, and he –'

I turned on him. Whether he was trying to give me some obscure comfort, whether he was implying that I had no more to complain of than any other woman, it didn't matter – this strange alter ego that was me and yet not me could take no more.

'No worse?' The words were a hiss, and I felt my own spittle wet on my lip. 'No *worse*? He is cruel, he stinks, he is old, *old!*'

He drew back a little, and the yellow eyes narrowed. He seemed about to speak, but then, shaking his head slightly, instead motioned that I should follow him. We walked up to the far end of the long hall, and, away from the fire, I stumbled in the inadequate light. The rushes under my feet felt unpleasantly soggy, and the smell got into my throat. The Dark Man led me to an entrance through to the end section of the hall, partitioned off to give privacy.

He caught my arm, pulling me to his side as he leaned against the archway.

'Behold the king,' he breathed.

There was no doubt which man was the monarch; apart from the fact that he sat on a dais and was attended by two tough-looking warriors whose hands rested on the hilts of long swords, he wore a crown. Not ornate, not bejewelled, a simple circle of heavy gold etched with runes.

'The king,' came the soft words again. 'Crown-bearer, protector of his people. After him will come his son, who, like his father, will wear a crown wrought for him alone, imbued with magic to confound the forces that threaten us. But will the magic be strong enough? Will gold crowns serve to keep the evil at bay? And if not, if the line fails, who then might take power?'

This was treason! I stood there in the very presence of the king while a member of his court breathed sedition in my ear! What was he suggesting? That the king's true heirs would be removed and Egenhere's sons – *my* sons – would rule in their place?

With him, with this fearsome Dark Man, their guiding force?

I tried to pull away, but his grip was too tight.

'Make no mistake, lady,' he whispered. Of all things, now he sounded amused. 'The threat is there, have no doubt of it. He is right, that old man,' – he pointed into the corner – 'in what he predicts for us.' Now he was actually laughing, a rasping, deeply cynical laugh. 'He perceives the threat, the fool, and he believes his little crowns will counter it. Ha!'

I had been transfixed by the figure of the king and his swordsmen, and had not noticed the other man. Half hidden, away from the light of the candles in their tall holders that illuminated the king, he sat alone, face concealed.

Once I'd seen him, I couldn't look away. Although his head remained bent, my eyes were drawn to him by a power I couldn't resist. I tried to back off, but my feet were welded to the floor.

Slowly he began to lift his head. The cloth of his hood moved, and I glimpsed a pale cheek. Turning, the action smooth and unstoppable, his face pointed towards me like a searchlight prying into the blackness.

The hood dropped back, and the intelligent grey eyes met mine.

In the first split-second, I thought I knew who he was. Then, the horror overtaking me faster than I could fight it, I realized I was wrong. Had to be wrong, for all that my eyes told me otherwise.

He couldn't be who I thought he was, because that person was a woman.

It was too much. I wanted out – unable to move, unable even to shut my eyes or look away, I opened my mouth and screamed.

'Hush! Hush!' Hands were on me, holding me down, pushing something against my mouth . . . I tried to scream again, and Gordon said urgently, 'Thea, shut up!'

Gordon. Holding out to me a glass of cognac. Automatically I took it from him, downing it in a single swallow. As its warmth crept through me, the shadows receded. The royal hall was gone – I was sitting in a hotel bar in Picardy where, to my huge embarrassment, I'd probably just treated all my fellow guests to an entertaining burst of hysteria. No doubt they were frightful chauvinists, French travelling salesmen, they'd be giving patronizing Gallic shrugs and muttering the equivalent of 'Bloody neurotic woman!'

I pulled away from Gordon's restraining hands and glanced around. Apart from the man at the next table, who was looking at us doubtfully, no-one else was taking the slightest notice.

I whispered to Gordon, 'What happened?'

He laughed shortly. 'You tell me! I asked you if you were familiar with the legend of the Three Crowns, and I lost you – your eyes glazed over, you muttered a few words I couldn't make out, then suddenly you looked quite terrified and you screamed.'

Oh, God. 'Loudly?'

He smiled. 'Not very. I pretended I was tickling you.'

Army training, I thought. Gets a man used to thinking quickly. 'Thanks,' I said.

'For what?'

'For covering up.'

'Ah.' He sounded relieved. 'I thought you might mean "thanks" sarcastically. As if you were thanking me for getting you into whatever it was you got into.' I stared at him blankly. 'It seems I triggered off some sort of a trance,' he said quietly. 'By mentioning the Three Crowns.'

'You did,' I said shortly. Being so recently returned to where – when – I belonged, I didn't want to think about magic crowns.

'Well, tell me, then!'

I shook my head.

'Thea, it's important! Don't you see? It's possible you've just been given proof of what I was saying. About Willowford Fen being dangerous for you, about Florence . . .'

'*Please!*'

I couldn't bear to think of Florence. Not right then, when her image was before my eyes, nightmarish, strange.

He didn't understand. How could he, when I couldn't bring myself to share it with him? 'Couldn't you just . . .' he began.

'*NO!*'

I'd forgotten the bar full of people. They'd probably think that, finished with tickling me, Gordon was now trying to get his hand up my skirt. 'Please, no,' I repeated, no longer shouting.

He sighed. 'All right. We'll leave it for now.' He

frowned at me sternly. 'But the matter is by no means closed.'

I was afraid to go to sleep that night, in case the scenes I'd witnessed came back in my dreams. I hadn't merely witnessed them, I had to admit – I'd been there. Somehow I'd been a participant, or it felt as if I had.

Magic. Was it magic? I didn't believe in magic, though. Did I? Yet someone had mentioned it, quite recently, speaking of it as if it existed as surely as the power of the wind, or the river in flood. The Dark Man, it had been. What had he said? He'd been talking about the crowns, the one worn by the king and the one yet to be, that his son would wear when he became king. 'He will wear a crown wrought for him alone, imbued with magic to confound the forces that threaten us.' Only it wouldn't. The Dark Man said it wouldn't, and he seemed so sure.

Magic crowns. Gordon had asked if I knew the legend of the Three Crowns, and from somewhere deep in my unconscious, my memory had thrown up this fragment. Not magic at all, was it? All I'd done was remember something I already knew. Something that, without a doubt, Florence had told me on one of those timeless days when we roamed East Anglia together and she talked to me of the history of my land.

Florence. The answer lay, as it always seemed to, in Florence.

That was why I'd had the vision. That was why I'd seen her face, concealed by a deep hood.

But why hadn't her face been on her body? Why, instead, had it turned into the face of the king's seer?

My subconscious must have been confused. Florence was a figure of power, I'd always known that. I'd mixed her up with another similar figure from the past, that was all. I smiled to myself at the thought that she'd be pleased, surely, at my mind's involuntary choice – I must obviously see her as a wise woman, if in my vision I'd cast her in the role of the king's Cunning Man.

I thought of her standing on the shore that day at Dunwich, the day she'd told me of the Three Crowns. Feeling calmer now that I was well on the way to rationalizing away the whole worrying business of the trance, I reflected – not for the first time – on how lucky I'd been to have such a teacher. I tried to remember what she'd said about the crowns – two had been found, one was still lost.

Where had the third one come from? Had that been made for a king, too? And what had happened to it? Gordon had spoken of three crowns, did that mean he could supply some answers?

Maybe I should steel myself to talk to him about it, after all.

I was feeling sleepy. No longer afraid, I let my eyes close.

Out of nowhere the voice came again. 'The Third Crown shall be made for the child that is still to be. The child who shall save his people.'

I saw the Dark Man, just for an instant. Then his enigmatic face faded and I saw someone else, someone for whom my body melted with passion, my heart leapt with love. Someone dressed in cross-gartered leggings and a braided tunic, a sword in a scabbard at his side. His hair was long, and he looked weary.

Then he turned into Henry.

In the morning I'd decided. Gordon had some reason for wanting me out of England. Out of Florence's vicinity, anyway. He'd said I was in danger, from some unspecified threat that had prompted him to ask if I knew of an ancient legend.

I did, although I couldn't see what it had to do with the danger – other than the minor inconvenience of forcing vivid recollections of a past I'd been instructed on by Florence, it seemed innocuous enough.

I was aware I might be kidding myself a bit, deliberately pushing the terror I'd felt to the back of my mind. But if I was, I intended to go on doing so: as I'd discovered to my cost last evening, investigating Gordon's danger and Gordon's bloody legend involved bringing Henry right back into the forefront of my mind.

And, even for Gordon, I wasn't going to lose another night crying for him.

Twenty-one

Late in the summer, Gordon began making plans for a trip back to London to see his publisher. After ten months away, we'd amassed a huge volume of work – our August had been spent in the south of France where we'd parked ourselves on a campsite near San Raphael and, between long sessions of sunbathing, swimming and generally behaving like tourists, had managed to transform our notes and photographs into a satisfactory order. Our impedimenta included a portable typewriter, and I spent hours sitting in my bikini under the camper's awning, typing like fury while French voices called out all around me and inquisitive little children stood, mouths open, watching the weird English girl whose only comment for hours was *'Bugger!'* when she typed yet another wrong letter (the sweat and suntan oil made my fingers slip on the keys).

Gordon came back from the supermarket one lunchtime with a day-old copy of *The Times*.

'The silly season's over, judging by the headlines,' he remarked, throwing the paper down on the table. 'London's back at work, it's time I took the manuscript home.'

London. Home. I didn't like the thought of London

– who would, sitting in the sunshine of the Côte d'Azur with nothing more strenuous to do than consume a decently alcoholic lunch and, after a siesta, go for a swim? – and I had mixed feelings about 'home'. I didn't, I reminded myself, really have a home.

'What about me?' My words sounded dangerously close to self-pity. 'I mean, do you need me with you, or shall I stay here?'

He poured us both a pre-prandial vermouth, absently splashing rather a lot into the two glasses.

'No, I don't need you' – he smiled briefly at me to take any sting out of his words – 'although of course it's always nice to have you with me.' I was just reflecting on how he had a knack of saying things that made you feel warm inside, when he went on abruptly, 'I'm intending to stay in Thetford for a while. Check everything's all right about the house, make sure the arrangements are running smoothly.' He'd engaged a local property management agency to keep an eye on the place, and an elderly gardener called Herbert to make sure the lawns and the hedges stayed trim. 'I don't expect you'd want to go to Thetford, would you?'

The memories were running wild before I could control them: Henry betting me I wouldn't get the job. Henry coming to meet me in Florence's Morris Minor. Henry's face when I told him I was accepting Gordon's offer and going off abroad with him. Every one of them hurt.

After a while I said, 'No thanks.'

Gordon looked at me sympathetically. 'I'm sorry, Thea.'

When he was sympathetic it always made me want to cry. 'Anyway, you wouldn't approve, would you?' I said robustly. 'I mean, you're all for keeping me out of Florenceland, aren't you?'

He turned away. 'I wondered if you still thought about that.'

Of course I did. It was just that I didn't want to talk about it.

'I do.' I said it in the sort of tone that's meant to head off further enquiry.

'So, what are we to do with you?' He, too, seemed eager to move away from dangerous ground. 'D'you think you'd be okay here by yourself if I fly home?'

'How long will you be away?'

He shrugged. 'Two weeks?'

I didn't seem to have much choice. I said, 'I'll be fine.'

In the end, we decided to drive up through France and get Gordon a ferry passage to Dover. The plan was that after dropping him at Calais, I'd set off for Normandy, or Brittany, or wherever, phoning him on a pre-arranged date to see when he was coming back.

That was the plan. In fact I didn't see much of Normandy (and nothing at all of Brittany) because when I phoned Dad from Bayeux to tell him what I was up to, Pam answered and said he was just about to go into hospital to have his gall bladder out.

We'd kept in touch all the time I'd been away, I phoning him from time to time, he writing long letters which I'd collect, sometimes weeks after they'd been sent, from Poste Restante. I wondered why he hadn't mentioned feeling ill, then realized guiltily that it had been seven weeks since I'd spoken to him. And, being good old independent Dad, he'd hardly have complained in his letters.

The guilt turned to daughterly love and concern. I

headed back for Calais and got me and the camper van on the first ferry that would take us.

Dad was, predictably, quite sure he was going to die. He'd always hated hospitals and being ill, and even Pam couldn't talk him out of a morbid determination to look on the black side. Pam and I had a glum couple of days immediately after his operation, but once Dad had got used to the surprise of waking up and finding himself still alive, things got better. He actually became a bit sheepish at having allowed me to rush home so dramatically, and Pam and I teased him something rotten. We'd do silly things like pretending we'd got a catalogue of coffin designs, and talk loudly about whether we'd have purple or white silk for the lining. Once we dressed ourselves entirely in black, veils over our heads and flour on our faces, but, although I'm sure the ward sister saw the funny side, she wouldn't let us in to visit him.

Pam had moved in with Dad by then. When I arrived at the flat and found her installed in the little room that used to be mine, she was quite apologetic.

'He got lonely without you, Thea,' she said. 'So did I.' She gave me a rueful grin. 'Seemed silly for us to go on paying out for two households when we spent most of our time together in one or the other. So we opted for here. Hope you don't mind.'

'Why should I mind?' I didn't usually hug Pam – she wasn't a very huggable woman – but just then I made an exception. Putting my arm round her waist, I said, 'I'm really pleased. And I can't think of anyone I'd rather have to inherit my room.'

She gave a grunt and went a bit pink. Then she said, 'I *have* inherited it, you know. Really. I mean, I sleep in there. There's no hanky-panky!' She looked at me quite crossly, as if I'd been suggesting there was.

'No, I'm sure there isn't,' I said. It didn't seem tactful to add that I wouldn't have minded in the least.

Once Dad was out of hospital, I had to let him have his bed back and sleep on the saggy old sofa in the living room. Except that the sofa gave me backache, the arrangement was quite nice – Dad and Pam had a very old dog called Spats, whom they'd got from the animal sanctuary to fill the void left by Eric (they were heartbroken to hear he was dead) and he slept beside me; I could reach down and give him a companionable pat when I heard him stir in the morning. Unfortunately he often did more than stir, since his waking stretch had a tendency to make him fart. Still, it was one way of making sure I got up in time to use the bathroom first.

I'd phoned Gordon as soon as I'd arrived in Gloucestershire, and he'd been predictably concerned, both about Dad's imminent surgery and about me having had to get home by myself. I'd been strangely moved by his anxiety, and covered up by telling him jokily that he needn't worry, the camper and I were both still intact and it was very rare for people to die having their gall bladders out. He laughed dutifully, and asked me to keep him posted so that he'd be able to plan when he could take me away again.

We talked to each other every couple of days. I developed a strange sort of fascination for our calls, as if, unable to be in East Anglia myself, I was addicted to the sensation of speaking to someone who was – a sort of vicarious visit, with Gordon standing proxy for me. I dreamt of the places I knew so well: of Grime's Graves, of the Fens, of the flat grey shoreline. I dreamt of Florence, and Willowford Fen, and of course I dreamt of Henry.

Part of me wanted to say, sod it, to get in the camper and drive across the country till I was there in body as well as in spirit. It was now late September, and he'd be getting ready to go up for his second year at Cambridge. How would he react if I arrived on the doorstep? He'd be pleased. Delighted, even. I knew that in my heart, no matter how hard I tried to persuade myself otherwise. But then what? What would happen after the joy of reunion? Florence would happen, that's what, I told myself, fanning the embers of my resentment. And she'd bugger it up, just like she did before.

The trouble was, I missed her, too.

When Dad was a hundred per cent again, I telephoned Gordon to tell him.

'That's wonderful,' he said. 'Please give him my best wishes. And Pam, of course – it must be a great relief to have it all behind them.'

'Yes,' I said vaguely. 'I'll do that.'

'So, you're ready to roll again?'

I didn't answer.

'Thea?'

'Yes, I heard. Gordon, why don't I come over there and pick you up? We could stay a day or two, make our plans, get the tickets and things, then set off from there together. It'd be . . .'

'No, I don't think that's a good idea.'

I couldn't accept that he'd turned me down flat. 'But I'd really like to . . .'

'It isn't wise, is it? You know as well as I do it's not safe for you here.'

Stung by his tone – it was quite unlike him to be so bossy – I said, 'Rubbish. What harm can come to me in Thetford, for heaven's sake?'

He didn't answer for a while. I regretted the pause; it gave me time to remember all the things I'd thought I'd forgotten about.

Eventually he said, 'Very well. You're old enough to know your own mind, I suppose, although sometimes I wonder. You'll have to drive over by yourself.' He made it sound like a major hurdle, so I reminded him I'd just managed to get back from France without incident.

'I'll set out tomorrow morning, then,' I said. 'No – I'll come today.' If I left it till the morning, he might change his mind overnight.

With a very audible sigh he said, 'All right.'

I felt a mixture of emotions as I approached my home: happiness, because, whatever places I'd lived in or visited in the meantime, East Anglia was where I began and where my roots were; mingled apprehension and eagerness at the thought that I might bump into Henry; and, so deep down that I barely acknowledged it, fear. Because, although I fought them, the memories of the last time I'd been in East Anglia were rising.

Gordon welcomed me – somewhat brusquely – and in the morning we got straight down to planning our next move. He'd already told me how pleased his publishers were with the manuscript – they'd agreed to his suggestion that, having devoted so much space to the Western Front, the book should deal solely with French and Belgian battlefields, the remaining material in his original proposal to be covered in a sequel. Fortunately for us, their satisfaction had taken a tangible form: as well as taking Gordon out to lunch at one of London's best restaurants, they'd parted with a vast sum of money for the finished manuscript and given him an advance for the sequel. I'd never got the impression that Gordon was hard up, and was less likely than ever to get it now.

On this next trip, our eventual destination was Gallipoli, and we considered flying to Turkey. We decided against it in the end, partly because we'd grown used to being vagabonds (if people in expensive camper vans who chickened out and stayed in hotels as soon as it was wet, or cold, or if they felt like a hot bath, could be called vagabonds), and partly because there were a lot of places between Calais and the Dardanelles that Gordon wanted to visit.

Despite his businesslike air, I got the feeling he had something on his mind. In the evening, relaxing over after-dinner coffee, I asked him why he'd been so reluctant to let me join him in Thetford.

He looked surprised at the question, as well he might since I threw it in hard on the heels of an amiable discussion on our route through Belgium.

After quite a long silence, during which I could almost hear the cogs of his brain whirring round, he said, 'This is going to involve forbidden territory, you know. Are you sure you want me to tell you?'

'What do you mean, forbidden territory?' I don't know why I asked – perhaps I was just playing for time. I knew the answer quite well: he'd have to tell me what he'd tried to tell me before, when I'd determinedly shut my ears and refused to hear because . . .

Damn.

Can I let him tell me now? I wondered. Surely, after more than a year, I can cope, even if this obsession of Gordon's does bring Henry's shade back to haunt my dreams. I pulled my thoughts to a halt: I was thinking of Henry as if he were dead, for God's sake! And he wasn't, he . . .

Suddenly I realized that I wouldn't know if he was.

The ache of his absence hit me so violently that it felt like a physical blow.

'Are you okay?' Gordon asked anxiously.

I looked at him, hardly seeing him. I reached out to him – I needed the human contact – and, bless him, he took my hand in his and squeezed hard.

'I'm okay,' I said. 'It just occurred to me that I don't know how he is. If he's happy, if he's . . .'

I couldn't bring myself to say, if he's alive.

'He's fine,' Gordon said gently.

'How do you know?'

He hesitated, then said, 'I saw him. Oh, not to speak to – I drove out to Willowford Fen the other day, and he and Florence were standing in the front garden.'

I wanted to ask, how did he look? Happy? Healthy? As if he were missing me? Then I wanted to demand what the hell Gordon had been doing at Willowford Fen. And why I hadn't been with him.

'You could have told me!' I said angrily.

And unreasonably. Gordon replied, with understandable pique, 'I didn't because you said you never wanted me to refer to Henry Woolgar again, ever.'

It was exactly what I had said.

'Sorry.'

'All right.'

After another silence, I said, 'You'd better tell me.'

'What?'

Go for it, I thought. Henry couldn't have got further into the front of my mind – it was as if he'd elbowed out everyone and everything else. The damage was done – I might as well hear what Gordon wanted to tell me.

I said, 'Everything.'

'Everything' took the best part of the night. Gordon talked as if he were giving a lecture – perhaps that was the only way he could get it all out, by pretending I was an impersonal audience sitting the other side of the lectern.

He began, unexpectedly, by talking about Florence.

'Florence is a historian,' he said, 'a very intuitive and dedicated one. I know of her, although she doesn't know me. She's recognized as an expert on East Anglia,' (tell me about it! I thought) 'and in particular, her own family's place in East Anglian history. This is only conjecture, but I believe she's made the mistake of accepting as gospel truth something that can at best be described as likely.' He paused, frowning. 'It's something many people do, as if their . . .'

I didn't want him to digress on to an apologia for Florence's behaviour. 'Before, you were going to tell me about the three crowns,' I interrupted. 'How about starting there?'

'I was leading up to that,' he said reprovingly.

'Sorry.'

'The legend says that three magic crowns were made, some time around 625 A.D. One was used by Saint Felix to enthrone Sigebert, another was probably made for Sigebert's successor, or possibly his predecessor. The third one, although mentioned in the legend, doesn't appear to have been actually placed on the head of any king. It seems they were inscribed with runes – that's how the magic was put into them – and that these inscriptions were intended to give the king greater power to resist the invading forces.'

'They were buried, weren't they?' I said. 'Florence told me that. The people thought it would save England from invasion if the magic crowns were hidden on the coast. One was found near Rendlesham – I suppose that was nearer the sea, then.'

'Invasion,' Gordon said quietly. 'Who was invading, that the king and his advisors wanted to repulse?'

'Vikings? Anglo-Saxons?'

'The king and his people were Anglo-Saxons. They'd long been a part of East Anglian society. And the Viking raids didn't begin until the 790s.'

'Who, then?'

'I believe – and I imagine Florence does, too – the threat was already there. That the "invasion" wasn't men coming in ships across the sea but something else, something that worked from within. A sort of fifth column, if you like.'

'I don't understand.'

He smiled ruefully. 'I'm not sure I do. But consider this. Until recently, the Norsemen had a bad press – rape and pillage, and all that. Now we're beginning to see their good points – their seamanship, for example, their courage, and their important role as craftsmen and traders. It's not easy to reconcile the virtues with the traditional picture of savage barbarism, yet we know without doubt that side of them also existed.'

'Surely that was the standard of the times? You could be as worthy as you liked, but you didn't survive if you couldn't hack out a place for yourself and defend it.'

'Accepted.' He got up and went to stand behind my chair, as if to put a distance between us. 'Hacking out and defending are different from the sort of customs the Norsemen went in for.'

'I know.' I said it quickly – I didn't want to hear again the bloodthirsty tales of torture that I was well aware he had in mind. 'What's this got to do with invasion? And I thought you said the crowns were made before the Vikings came on the scene?'

'I did. I said Norsemen – which is a variant on Northmen – not Vikings. This is where some of the uncertainties come in – I'm suggesting that the East Anglian kings, who probably came originally from Sweden, had a mythology in common with the Vikings. They were all Norsemen, and, before the Anglo-Saxons adopted Christianity, they would all have worshipped the same gods. The Wuffingas would have claimed a god or two in their genealogy – Woden would have been a good one.'

I didn't know what he was driving at. I waited for him to go on.

'I believe it's possible that the Anglo-Saxons brought with them from the North lands some ancient power,' he said. 'An evil which infiltrated their fellow Norsemen, the Vikings, as well. Something out of the icy wastes, something that possessed men and compelled them to act out the horrors which the power dreamed up. An "invasion" that came from within.'

My first reaction was of total disbelief.

'Whatever grounds have you got for supposing that?'

'One, the mythology. There are plenty of Norse tales involving the gods' intervention in human affairs, and any god worthy of the name would have had no difficulty in getting inside someone's head and making him act out commands. Two,' – he was ticking the rapid-fire points off on his fingers – 'the sacrificial nature of the brutality. As if it were being done to appease some malign force. Three, the runic inscriptions on the crowns, which were an invocation to the light to counter the "dark bane that comes from within".'

He must have known what I'd say to that – before I'd even got the 'But' out, he held up his hand. 'Yes, all right! No, I haven't got one of the crowns, and nor has anyone. There's an ancient piece of text, though, in a tome from the early 1700s which is kept in the vaults of a museum in Norwich. It records the discovery of a crown, and its subsequent fate – it was sold and melted down. But whoever sold it took the trouble first to write a detailed description, including a copy of the runes. Apparently eighteenth-century scholars weren't up to deciphering Norse runes – that particular scholar wasn't, anyway.'

'But you are.'

'I am. So, I should think, is Florence.'

It was a lot to take in. The concept of a careful description of a crown that was over thirteen hundred years old – next best thing to the crown itself – really made you think. Gordon had read the description, perhaps even seen . . .

'Was there a picture?'

'Yes. The crown was quite plain, just a heavy circlet of gold. And the runes were angular, as you'd expect since they were usually carved into wood or stone.'

A heavy circle of gold, etched with runes. I'd seen it, although not in this life. And I'd heard a low, cruel voice in my ear tell me that gold crowns would be no use.

I felt sick. Back here in East Anglia – God, how right Gordon had been to try to keep me away! – the power was strong, and I was very afraid. Before the faintness overcame me, I dropped my head down into my hands.

I was back in the royal hall. Even before my vision cleared, I knew I was by the smoke and the smell. This time it was packed with people, sitting at long tables and devouring food like wolves round a carcass. The noise was incredible.

'Eat, Madam,' said a cracked voice beside me. As he spoke he leaned towards me, and I caught the stench of his breath. He was old, the top of his head quite bald, long dirty hanks of hair hanging either side of his sallow face. The eyes, a faded blue, bored into mine. His hard mouth stretched into a rictus, the revealed teeth wide-spaced and fanglike.

'Eat!' he repeated, stretching his hand out to pull out a chunk of meat from the communal dish. The gravy dripped on to the wooden table and on to my lap, the hot grease sinking into the blue cloth of my kirtle. 'You are too skinny,' – he poked a sharp finger into my ribs – 'do you not know a man likes warm flesh in his bed?'

The piece of meat came closer to my mouth. It was so gamey that it smelt rotten. His fingers, holding it, had long ragged nails which were rimmed with black filth. He pushed it against my closed lips then, as I kept my mouth tight shut, suddenly stuck a finger in the side of my mouth, forcing my jaws apart. The meat was on my tongue, and his hand across my face prevented me from spitting it out.

I felt the vomit rising. I can't be sick here! Not across the high table! I tried to pull my head away, tried to catch someone's eyes to plead for help, but they were all too intent on eating, too drunk. Half way along the table a man sat on a raised section. He wore a crown, but he was not the king I'd seen before. This was a younger man.

And this, I knew with quick insight, was his coronation feast.

I had to get away. Wrenching myself up and out of my chair, I ran, tripping over stools, rushes, legs of people slumped in corners. I could see an open doorway, halfway down the hall's side wall, and I raced for it, my hand pressed to my mouth. Just in time I stumbled out into the evening air, throwing up in great surges which cramped my body from belly to chest.

After a while it was over. Leaning weakly against the wooden planking of the hall, I closed my eyes.

'Sick, lady?'

He was standing right in front of me. Again, I hadn't heard him approach. His yellow eyes stared into mine, holding my gaze.

'It was the meat,' I said hoarsely.

'The meat,' he echoed. Very deliberately, he glanced down at my stomach. 'Aye, the meat.' He put out his hand and pressed it palm downwards against me. 'No new life quickens yet in thy womb.'

I wanted to smack him away, but he scared me. I stood dumbly, waiting for what would happen next.

'A new king,' he said, nodding towards the interior of the hall. 'Will he fare better than his father? Will the crown give him the strength to fight the foe?'

'Yes!' I shouted. Something was wrong – in my mind a warning rang out, but I didn't know what it warned against.

'Nay.' He laughed. 'The Cunning Man may weave into his runes all the magic he possesses, but his pretty golden crowns will avail him naught. This king, too, will fail to overcome the bane from the North Lands. Like his predecessor, he lacks the right – friends.' The eyes narrowed with amusement. 'Whereas a king who did have the right support at his side . . .' He left the sentence unfinished but, with horrible familiarity, underlined his meaning by pressing his fingers hard into my stomach, pushing them down into my groin. 'Fill thy belly with a prince conceived of Egenhere, lady! There would be a man to fight for.'

He laughed again, a sound that seemed to rise into a growl. Dark flecks raced in front of my eyes, as if it were snowing black snow, and from nowhere a wind sprang up that whirled the flakes into a solid whole. In the middle of it stood the man, only he was no longer a man: he stood, huge and grey, yellow eyes mocking me, jaws open in the chilling howl of a wolf baying to the moon.

I was in the bathroom, leaning over the lavatory bowl. Someone held my forehead.

'You can let go,' I said, 'That's the lot.'

I struggled round and sat up on the edge of the bath. Gordon handed me my flannel, wrung out in cold water.

'I think you should go to bed,' he said.

I nodded. He went out into the bedroom and fetched my night things, passing them to me then tactfully closing the door. I cleaned my teeth and undressed, putting my dressing gown on over my nightshirt. I couldn't stop shivering.

Gordon tucked me up. 'Do you want to tell me?' he asked.

I shook my head violently. Then, as he got up to go, said, 'Yes!'

He smiled down at me. 'Shall I just sit with you for a while?'

'Yes, please.'

There was silence for some time. I stopped shivering, and slowly the image of the Dark Man who became a wolf faded a little. Then abruptly I remembered what he'd said. And how it had been, sitting next to Egenhere. My husband, with whom, apparently, I was to have a child.

No! Not *my* husband! Someone else's, some poor woman who was long dead, long past her sorrow and her pain. I, thank God, was only a witness. Only it didn't feel like that.

Gordon was watching me. The relief of at last telling him flooding through me even with the first words, I said, 'I have dreams. Visions, sort of. About all the tales she – Florence – used to tell me when I was a child. It seems I've fixed on one character, a woman who's been made to marry a ghastly old man, and I see it all through her eyes. There's a king – two kings now, a new one's just been crowned – and a Cunning Man who's sort of the king's wizard, and another strange man who –' I broke off. Who turns into a wolf? '– who's like someone I met at Henry's party. And the Cunning Man looks just like Florence, which is really weird because he's a man and she's a woman.'

Gordon said quietly, 'I see,' as calmly as if he were a doctor and I a patient listing the symptoms of some mundane illness. I looked up and saw his expression, which wasn't calm at all.

'They're afraid of something. The crowns *are* for protection. Only . . .'

'Only what?'

From nowhere I felt tears start. I blinked them away. 'It won't do them any good. The Dark Man – the wolf man – isn't what he seems. He's bad. He said all the magic runes in the world wouldn't keep the evil away.'

Gordon stroked my hands, his own warm and strong. 'I'm sorry.'

I smiled weakly. 'What about?'

'Sorry you feel involved. You don't need to, you know.' He grinned.'It's all long gone.'

'Then why – ?' I stopped.

'What?'

'It doesn't matter.' Long gone, I repeated to myself.

'You're right. Whatever the danger was, it's long gone.'

He didn't answer.

'Isn't it?'

He hesitated, then said, 'Yes. I'm sure it is.'

I went to sleep soon after that, but not for long. My unconscious took control again almost as soon as I relaxed my guard, plunging me straight back to the ancient town and the brutishness. My body was sore and bruised, and there was an agonizing pain across my face; when I put my fingers up to soothe it, they came away dripping with blood. A woman tried to help me, but she was clumsy and hurt more than she healed. The old man was laughing at me, but somewhere in my mind I knew that he hadn't vanquished me. Despite the beating, I had the clear sense that I'd won and he hadn't. I didn't understand.

I was in the hall, trying to eat. Without knowing why, I felt compelled to look up.

A man was approaching, his boots rustling the reeds on the floor. He was tall and long-haired, and his greenish eyes were on me as if he'd been willing me to raise my head. His brown tunic was made of rough cloth, and the sword at his side had no ornate decoration. His cloak was fastened with a gold brooch set with garnets and blue glass, and in his hand he held a spear.

From nowhere a voice said, 'Wolfspear.'

He looked bone-weary, as if he'd been struggling with some foe too strong for him. Against my volition, I began to smile, and he smiled back, the expression lightening his face.

Waking, tears running down my cheeks and soaking my pillow, I shouted, '*HENRY!*'

The door burst open and Gordon rushed in. He

must have been listening out for something like this, I thought vaguely as he sat down on the bed and held me in his arms, he couldn't have got here so quickly otherwise.

Then I saw Henry again, and could think of nothing else but how much it hurt.

Gordon went and fetched me some brandy and, when I was something approaching myself again, offered to sit with me. I said I'd be okay.

As he went out, he looked back at me.

'We've got to get away, as fast as we can,' he said. 'The further we go, the happier I'll be.'

I assumed he meant, away from the danger, whatever it was. It was only much later that I realized his words could have another meaning.

Twenty-two

By December we were in Italy, busy with the ins and outs of some battle in the Alps I'd never even heard of. It was perishing, and we had to invest in boots and ski jackets against the snow. Christmas was approaching, and we both seemed to be pretending it wasn't.

We were out one afternoon photographing a precipice down which the Italian Alpine artillery had had to lower its guns. The light had been good, but later clouds built up and it began to snow. I couldn't feel my ankles, never mind my toes.

'"And all mankind that haunted nigh had sought their household fires,"' Gordon said suddenly, his face pinched with cold. 'Bugger it, Thea, let's go home.'

Home?

'I thought you wanted to head south,' I said, shaken. 'Gallipoli, and beyond.'

He recovered quickly. 'I didn't mean *home* home,' he replied. It must have been the cold, making him careless. 'I meant back to the hotel.'

'Oh, good.' I stuck my hands deeper in my pockets and hunched into my collar. 'I thought we were going to stay here till hell was as frozen over as this place.'

As we drove back I wondered whether there was anything at home – *home* home – to attract him. He loved our work and our travels, that was clear, and hadn't seemed to mind that keeping me out of England had the effect of keeping him away, too. Was there anything – *anyone* – he missed? He had no family, his early marriage having broken up under the stresses of army life in Germany. (When I'd asked what he'd found so stressful about it, he replied somewhat ruefully that it had been his wife who'd felt the strain, so much so that she'd gone home to her mother in Harrogate, divorced Gordon and married a gynaecologist. I said I'd have found marriage to a gynaecologist far more stressful than being an army wife, and he gave me a sweet smile and said ah, but I was that sort of woman.) He had a sister in Ipswich, but I didn't imagine he was fired with the idea of hastening home to be with her, since he referred to her as The Snapdragon.

Still, maybe Christmas in England was better than Christmas in a small Italian hotel, even if it had to be spent with The Snapdragon.

'What shall we do for Christmas?' I asked as we climbed out of the camper. We couldn't go on ignoring the festive season, and now was as good a time as any to bring it up. 'Stay here? Whack on with our notes? Bust a gut and get the first section finished by the New Year?' I smiled at him, to show him I was quite happy with the suggestion – he had a disconcerting way of knowing when I was feeling down.

'Love your zeal,' he remarked. 'But, personally, I'd like a few days off. We'll finish what we have to do here, then we'll go down to Rome and spend Christmas in the cosiest hotel in town.'

I didn't answer. I wasn't exactly thrilled with the idea.

As we crossed the lobby (which, no matter what time of day it was, always smelt of fried onions), he said casually, 'As an alternative, why don't we go and see your dad and Pam for Christmas?'

Small objections like, but there's hardly any room in Dad's flat, and, but they'll already have made plans, flew into my mind and straight out again. We'd manage, somehow. The big question – why are you suggesting we go to England when a few weeks ago you were set on getting me as far away as you could? – raised things I didn't want to think about. He's not proposing we go to East Anglia, I thought, we'll be hundreds of miles away. Perfectly safe.

Safe?

I didn't let myself dwell on that. Going home was a wonderful idea, all of a sudden the only thing what I wanted to do. I said, 'Yes. Why don't we?'

It was one of the best Christmasses. Gordon and I were ready for a rest and a bit of pampering, and Dad and Pam made sure we got both. We all must have put on a good half-stone, and as often as not went to bed in a pleasant state of inebriation. Just as well, since, although I was comfortably ensconced on the living-room sofa, Gordon was sleeping on a camp bed in Dad's room, and they were crammed in so tight that Dad had to get into his bed before Gordon could put the camp bed down on the floor.

Dad and Pam didn't ask us any awkward questions: any other couple would, I'm sure, have been curious about my relationship with Gordon. Any father, in particular, could have been forgiven the odd question as to whether or not his intentions were honourable. But it didn't seem to bother dear old Dad and Pam, bless them, at all. I concluded that, a celibate couple themselves who had apparently never even contemplated straying into each other's beds, they had no difficulty accepting that Gordon and I were the same.

In the New Year, we decided to fly out to Turkey. There was heavy snow throughout the mountains of Southern Europe, and if we'd driven, we'd have had to postpone our departure. It meant, though, that we were faced with the problem of what to do with the camper van, the obvious solution being to return it to Thetford and lock it up safely in Gordon's garage.

I wanted to go with him, and he was equally determined I shouldn't, suggesting instead that I stay in some boring family hotel he knew of near Gatwick while he went to Norfolk. It was impossible to argue to a conclusion in front of Dad and Pam, but as soon as they'd waved us off and we were on our way, we returned to the fray.

'*Why* is it dangerous?' I wailed for the umpteenth time.

'You've forgotten already?' he hurled back. 'Forgotten throwing up in my bathroom? Forgotten your tears of grief for someone who lived well over a thousand years ago but who you identify with so strongly that you share her pain and her fear? Forgotten shouting out for –' He broke off.

Shouting out for Henry, he'd been going to say.

'All right,' I said quietly. 'No, of course I haven't forgotten. But none of that's dangerous! There *isn't* any danger!' Putting to the back of my mind the picture of an elderly dog roused to unnatural speed, running under the wheels of a van whose approach was hidden in a sudden mist, I added feebly, 'Is there?'

There was a a pause. Then he said, 'I can't tell you,

because I don't know!' He glanced at me, frustration in his face. 'Don't you think I would if I could? I just have a strong sense of peril. As if whatever lurks in your dreams – in your visions – might take tangible form and threaten you. That's the best I can do.'

The best I'm *going* to do, he should have said. I got the impression, then as at other times, that there were things he suspected but wasn't going to tell me. It wasn't a nice feeling.

Especially when it accorded so accurately with my own fears.

He'd shut his mouth with an air of finality. I felt a surge of pity for him: here he was doing his utmost to prevent me doing something that might get me into trouble, and all I could do was insist I was going to do it anyway.

'I don't believe there's any peril,' I said, trying to sound reasonable. 'Not really.' I think I was trying to convince myself as much as him. 'I've seen a man, who looks like someone I've dreamt about. So what's unusual about that? I also dream of Florence, of Henry,' – I wished instantly I hadn't mentioned him – 'and I'll probably start dreaming of you, too. You'll probably feature as Saint Edmund.'

It was meant to be a joke, but it fell a bit flat. As if to underline its unfunnyness, Gordon said dryly, 'Thanks. Shot full of arrows or merely sitting looking pious?'

'Sorry. Look, can I come home if I promise to hide if I see any dark men?'

'No.'

'If I stay in your house the whole time?'

'No.'

In the end, I resorted to the adult equivalent of holding my breath and said furiously that if he didn't let me go to East Anglia, I was going to think seriously about finding another job. Equally angry – which was scary as I'd never seen him lose his temper before – he shot back, 'All right! All bloody right! But on your own head be it!'

Only after I'd won my Pyrrhic victory did I stop to wonder why I was so determined to get back to East Anglia.

I kept my promise and stayed in his house till the last afternoon of our brief visit. Then Gordon was silly enough to go out and leave me on my own, with the camper van parked outside and the keys on the hall table.

I drove out to Willowford Fen.

He won't be there, I kept saying, term will have started, or if not he'll be out shopping. Walking. Off with some girlfriend. Ouch. Stuck away upstairs studying. Cleaning his rugby boots.

He passed me, driving the other way. The Morris Minor came round a bend and there he was at the wheel, mere feet away from me. He didn't see me, I was sure of that – we were past each other and off on our different ways too quickly, and, unlike me, he hadn't been expecting to see an old friend. An old love. Anyway, he wouldn't have recognized the camper van.

I went slowly on down the lane till I found a gateway, then pulled off into it and cried my eyes out.

Some time later, someone tapped on the window. Henry!

I spun round. The face bending down looking at me wasn't Henry's. The late sun caught a glimmer of yellow in the eyes.

Then, shape-shifting on the other side of the window not six inches from me, the human features melted and the mouth became wide, gaping jaws,

315

blood-red tongue lolling out over jagged teeth. Into my mind came a vision of the Morris Minor, speeding towards a bend in the road and suddenly running into fog. Tyres squealed, leaving long scars of black on the tarmac, but it was no good: the car plunged across the grass and over a narrow ditch and shot head-first into a tree.

Henry's face showed astonishment as the steering wheel snapped and its column transfixed his chest.

I could hear laughter, gradually changing into another, more terrible sound. As the howl lifted into the still air I started the engine, rammed the camper van into gear and shot off, tyres spinning in the soft verge, winter-bare twigs scratching at the paintwork. Looking in the wing mirror, I could see him standing in the middle of the road, long dark coat sweeping to the frosty ground, his breath like plumes of smoke. Glancing again, there seemed to be flakes of black around him, as if a fire were emitting charred fragments that floated away on the wind.

I couldn't look any more. Pushing my foot to the floor, I raced round the gentle bend and put him out of sight.

It was only a vision, I sobbed to myself all the way home. But he made it, the Dark Man. Put it into my head so I'd know, without any doubt, what he'd do if I stayed. If I tried again to contact Henry.

I could better have borne a threat to my own life.

I was nearly hysterical by the time Gordon came in. When he finally managed to extract from me what had happened, he put through a call to Henry's college, where some anonymous undergrad informed him that Henry Woolgar had just gone out to rugby training and did he want to leave a message?

I felt faint with relief. Okay, I said to that black

presence, okay, you win. I'll go, if you promise to leave him alone.

Silly, to think of extracting a promise from something so thoroughly evil. Whatever value would such a promise hold? But I wasn't in the frame of mind to be rational.

The next day Gordon and I flew to Turkey.

A year went by, and slipped into another. I no longer consciously thought of East Anglia, and the dreaming, vision-making part of my mind now dwelt on other things. It was as if that afternoon in the lane – and the vision I'd seen – had finally scared me off.

Gordon re-enforced the new me by taking me on a mini tour of Europe and the Mediterranean, after which we went on to explore farther afield. I think he was pointing out that there were other worlds than East Anglia, other places as fascinating and rewarding to investigate. Most of our travels were for research – having covered every major battle of World War One in our first two books, we'd turned our attention to World War Two, and in two years I'd been to North Africa, Italy, Burma, Singapore, Hong Kong and Normandy; at the age of almost twenty-two, I was gainfully employed, intellectually fulfilled and financially solvent. A future of much the same was mine for the taking, if I wanted it.

We were flying from Paris to Crete, where we planned to sail from Heraklion to Santorini to celebrate my twenty-second birthday. I'd forgotten any other life than that of the traveller, but it was starting to look as if the running was going to stop, one way or the other. For one thing, Gordon and I had written ourselves out of ideas and, although he was sure it was only a temporary hitch, it meant that for the first time we had no 'next one' to plan.

I wasn't as confident about the future as he was. As he *seemed* to be, for it hung in the balance for him, too: the other reason the running had to stop was that Gordon had asked me to marry him, and I couldn't.

I liked him so much. I loved him, really, although as a brother and not as a lover. Whatever, my feelings for him were too strong for me to contemplate the wrong I'd be doing him if I married him. Six miles above the earth, Gordon beside me engrossed in a book about Knossos, I thought back to the beginning.

I'd been eighteen when I went to work for him, and he'd been forty-three. Twenty-five years was enough of a gap to make him seem like my father's generation, an impression enhanced by his being a friend of Pam's brother. However, such gaps have a way of narrowing: working together, sharing the ups and the downs and the everyday middles, travelling over half the world side by side, brought us as close as a long-married couple and probably closer than most.

But, physically, we'd kept our distance. Perhaps the trend was set that night when he picked me up from Thetford station, let me cry my heart out and put me to bed in his spare room. Who knows, things might have been different if the comfort he had given me then had gone beyond holding my hand and giving me cocoa-diluted rum. But he was too decent to take advantage of a girl in distress, especially when she was only eighteen. And also, perhaps, too proud – he would, I think, have been put off by the thought that I was only turning to his bed because I'd been booted out of Henry's.

For four years we'd roamed the world and laid our heads down at night in adjoining rooms. Only once – in Penang, where we'd grabbed a week's sunshine and beach-lounging between Hong Kong and

Singapore – did paucity of accommodation mean we'd had to share, and even then we'd had twin beds. Anyway, nothing could have happened because – fortuitously was it? – I went down with food poisoning.

It wasn't that I found him unattractive. He was in fact a nice-looking chap: fair, not over-tall, with the sort of Edward Fox smile that lifts a middling face into something special. He had the bearing that the army gives a man, not only physically – in a good carriage – but also in manner. Whatever sort of troubles threatened in the course of our travels, from toothache in Rangoon to a misunderstanding with a furious customs officer in Cairo, he could always be relied on to know what to do. (He'd defused the very alarming situation at Cairo airport by asking in a voice worthy of Wellington, 'Does anyone here speak English?')

We worked well together and we were the best of friends. Then, in a Paris restaurant where we were having lunch before catching our flight, Gordon had changed everything.

'Forty-five minutes till we need to be at the airport,' he said, lighting an after-dinner cigarette.

'Plenty of time.' I fanned at the smoke: I was still eating. 'I'm stocking up before we take to the skies – you never know what you're going to get on a charter flight.'

I don't think he heard.

'Thea.' He reached out and took my hand. 'Thea, there's something I want to say.'

He was looking at me, his eyes holding mine. Four years of closeness hadn't been for nothing: suddenly I knew what was coming.

'I'd rather you didn't,' I said quietly.

He didn't question the fact that I knew. He asked, 'Is that your answer?'

319

I hesitated. I was sure it was – had to be – but on the other hand, perhaps I was in a state of shock. It was a shock, to have him turn so abruptly into a prospective husband. A prospective lover, sharer of my bed and my body from this day forth.

Maybe I should think about it for a while.

I said, 'It's a surprise. My instant reaction is to say no,' – we were so used to being frank with each other that it didn't occur to me till later that this wasn't the most tactful way to turn down a proposal – 'but in fairness, I suppose I should give myself time to get used to the idea.'

'I wish you would.' There was a flash of humour in his face.

'Okay.'

We landed in Heraklion, and booked into a pleasant hotel a couple of streets back from the waterfront. Into adjoining rooms. When I'd unpacked I went and tapped on his door.

He was standing by the window, his back to me.

'The locals are just beginning to collect for the evening stroll,' he said. 'It's called the *vólta*, I've discovered. We'll go down, shall we?' He turned, and I saw that although he was smiling, he looked strained.

'Gordon, I've got to . . .'

'My turn to say, please don't.' He gave a short laugh.

'But . . .'

He said quietly, 'Thea, if the answer was going to be yes, I wouldn't be feeling like I am.'

I went up to him and put my arms round him. For some time we stood there pressed together, then he let me go and we went out to join the strollers below.

*   *   *

We had our trip to Santorini, and I celebrated my twenty-second birthday looking down into the deep blue sea where a volcano once blew half an island out of existence. It wasn't a very happy occasion; we both knew I was going.

There was no real reason for leaving him, yet at the same time it was the only thing to do. I'd tried hard to convince myself that I should marry him, that it made total sense, but then I'd come to the point where we'd had the ceremony and the wedding breakfast, seen off the guests and gone away on our own. And, instead of saying goodnight and going to our separate rooms, we would bed down together.

I could imagine kissing him. But when I tried to make our mental images go further into intimacy, it just didn't happen. Just as before, more than four years ago when I'd almost made love to Steve, something stopped me.

Now in my mind Henry looked weary. And unbearably sad.

There was no way I could marry Gordon. Was there?

And so I would have to leave him.

After my birthday dinner he said, 'You won't go back to England, will you?'

The question surprised me: I'd thought – hoped – we were going to stick with just a tacit acceptance of my imminent departure.

'Oh – no.' Wherever else I went, I wasn't going to England. 'I – er . . .' The truth was, I didn't have any ideas. But he was looking worried, as if he still felt responsible for me and didn't like the idea of me wandering off aimlessly into the blue. Especially if the blue happened to be East Anglia. Since he'd made his proposal, it had occurred to me to wonder if part of the reason he'd been so keen to keep me out of England was to get me away from Henry, so as to leave the field free for himself. But it was an unworthy thought; his continuing concern for me – even now, after I'd turned him down – made that quite plain.

I thought quickly and came up with a plan, hoping it wouldn't sound as fresh-minted as it was.

'I shall sail up to Venice,' I said grandly – I'd noticed when we booked the crossing to Santorini that ferries ran regularly up the Adriatic – 'then catch a train. I think I'll stop off in Belgium – we had such a . . .' I'd been going to say, we had such a happy time there. But I stopped.

He nodded. 'That sounds interesting. What will you do in Belgium?'

'Go back to that hotel on the square and ask if they want a waitress,' I said, laughing.

As I travelled north it seemed less of a silly joke and more of a good idea. Not a waitress, perhaps, but a . . . a what? Could I get work at all, or would I need a permit? Well, if I did, I'd acquire one. I had to work.

I arrived back in Ypres late on a Sunday night. At the station I met an American called Scott – he was a travel courier, and on a badge on his lapel it said, 'Hi! I'm Scott!' He was waiting for a party of his compatriots whom he'd put on a train that morning bound for Ghent; they were late, and he was begining to think they'd gone astray.

It was nice talking to him – I hadn't talked to anyone properly since I'd left Gordon – and I sat down beside him to keep him company. He asked where I was staying, and when I said I hadn't a clue, offered me his colleague's room – the colleague was away. I accepted – it was nearly eleven thirty by then, and I wasn't going to get a better offer.

The train eventually came, and I tagged along behind the over-tired, elderly Americans as Scott ushered them, with a firm but gentle hand, on to their minibus and home to their hotel. Then we went on to his digs where, after a final cup of coffee, we went our separate ways to bed. He'd said there was a good chance I could get work with his company – I'd told him about the battlefields book and how I knew all about the Flanders region, and he said that anyway an English voice always went down well with American tourists.

After a month or so I wrote to Gordon, sending the letter to Thetford. He wasn't there, I knew, but in time he would be. And what I had to tell him wasn't urgent – I just said that I'd found work and lodgings in Ypres, and that everything was fine. I told him the address, prompted by some vague feeling that I didn't want to be cast adrift in the world with nobody knowing where I was. But there was something else I didn't tell him: that barely a week after meeting Scott, his colleague came back and I moved into Scott's room. Not into a chaste twin bed, either, but into a firm-sprung, spaceous double. In one glorious night, I put behind me twenty-two years of virginity; I made up, with interest, for four years during which I'd put my physical self on ice.

I wondered, later, why no disturbing image got between me and a potential lover on that occasion. Not that it bothered me at the time – all that mattered that wild night was that I wasn't on ice any more. Not physically, at least. But perhaps my mental self slipped into the cold storage from which I'd just rescued my body; thoughts of the recent past, and Gordon, were firmly shut away behind the airtight door.

Putting away the past was necessary for survival. Because, apart from the sorrow of no longer having Gordon's happy and considerate companionship (a sorrow which continued far longer than I like to admit), behind Gordon was a deeper shadow. I'd gone off with Gordon to blow someone else out of my head, and I'd never really succeeded: if it was dangerous to let myself think about Gordon, it was fatal to think about Henry.

Twenty-three

I don't know when it was that I finally stopped running and allowed England to pull me home. For so long I'd forbidden myself thoughts of the Fens, and I guess I pushed their quiet appeal so far out of my mind that I forgot it'd been there at all. A psychiatrist would say I was blotting it out because the idea of going back was too painful to contemplate.

I managed to live in America for nearly two years without once visiting a psychiatrist. Pretty good, I thought. Especially since Scott was a regular visitor to the old leather couch, but then possibly that was the effect of living with me.

In a way, it was a repeat of Gordon: after quite a long time of both of us being content with the way we were – I was, anyway – he suggested we get married. Now I don't think I was either more or less a wonderful marriage prospect than the next woman – it was just sod's law that the two men with whom I'd had long-term relationships were both fundamentally *nice* men who wanted to make an honest woman of me.

When I said no to Scott, he wasn't as understanding as Gordon. In fact for a while he stopped being nice at all, and accused me of retarded development:

'You've gotten yourself fixated on that boy from your past and you're refusing to accept the adult model!' was what he said (psychiatrist-speak had rubbed off on him).

There wasn't any point in arguing, although I did try. But he greeted my suggestion that we go on as we were with such scorn that I didn't make it again. I'd hurt him, I knew. And it hurt me that I'd done so.

After the hurt came anger. No, the emotion wasn't strong enough to be called anger – irritation is nearer the mark. I was cross because, again, a relationship that had been working well had to end because Scott, like dear old Gordon before him, wanted to change the rules. Scott and I had enjoyed our life together, moving on from Belgium to Paris, then, when he decided he'd had enough of petulant Americans made nervous by being so far away from home, going back to the West Coast, where his family's warm welcome extended to offering both of us jobs in the family real estate business.

A good partner, a stimulating (and very rewarding) job, a beautiful house by the ocean. And it all came to an end because I didn't want to marry him.

I went up to San Francisco – Scott's home was in San Diego – and for a while lived a solitary life. I turned in on myself and tried to get in touch with my inner feelings – tried to understand 'where I lived', as Scott would have said. I don't know if it was a good idea; it was just that in San Francisco, that's what everyone did. I did derive something positive from it, though – I accepted, at last, that the terrors of the past no longer had quite the same power over me.

Maybe it was then that the Fens saw their chance and slipped in. I began to dream: I saw Ely Cathedral, spotlighted in a beam of sunlight escaping from a lowering sky. I saw mist rising from peat-black water, and sensed that someone I loved was searching for me. I saw Florence in a white robe, her features obscured by smoke. I saw a woman dying in a pool of blood and a man staggering away from her, clutching his wounded leg. And, most vivid of all, a dream – or was it a vision? – that seemed to promise hope – for him? For her? – if only they could have a second chance. Then, there was Florence again, dressed like the Cunning Man, grey eyes wide, hypnotizing, as she stood by a sweet-smelling fire . . .

Fenland scenes, Fenland legends. My home called me in soft tones which turned into a clamour: *come back*.

I left America in the spring of 1979. I was nearly twenty-four years old, and as frightened as a nine-and-a-half-year-old Henry Woolgar flying to England from Hong Kong. More frightened, I should think – I couldn't imagine Henry being scared at the prospect of going back to Florence.

And that, of course, was one of the things that was worrying me. Since I'd left England six years before, I'd had no communication with her. I'd never contacted her, and so, even if she'd wanted to she couldn't have written to me. God, she might even be dead!

Somehow I knew she wasn't.

Anyway, she wasn't my chief concern. Whatever emotions I was going to feel on seeing her – *if* I saw her – would be positive ones. I'd grown up in six years, and, judging from the way it had endured, it seemed my love for her was stronger than my anger at what she'd done.

I think I'd come to the realization that I had to see

her. She'd interfered in my life when I was eighteen, and I ran out on her. I'd raced off down new avenues which took me far away from her, first with Gordon, then with Scott. You'd think I'd have put the events of that summer far behind me.

I hadn't. I still thought about it all, and even when my conscious mind was distracted, Florence's East Anglia would pop up in my dreams. There was that other, ancient, East Anglia too, where violence and cruelty ruled and something evil lay hidden in the shadows. And, always, there was Henry.

The combined effect of the three elements was stopping me from getting on with my life. I could have married Gordon, I could have married Scott, and I'm sure I'd have been adequately happy with either of them. But I didn't; I couldn't bring myself to sever my ties with my home. Would I ever manage it? There was no way of knowing unless I went back and confronted what I'd run away from.

The thought was frightening – even after two years, I hadn't forgotten Gordon's warnings. Should I go to him and demand that he tell me exactly what I was to be wary of? No. He'd been unable to explain it coherently before, so why should it be any easier now? Besides, it would open up old wounds, for both of us.

He'd implied all along that Florence knew, too. I'd ask her.

Florence led directly to Henry: if I go to Florence, I reasoned, she'll be bound to have *some* news of him, even if it's only that he's happily married and living on the other side of the world. As my heart cried out in protest at the thought, I countered the pain by telling myself, at least you'll *know!*

But it wasn't any consolation at all.

*　　*　　*

I called Dad from London and told him I was home. He greeted the return of the prodigal with as little surprise as if I'd been away in Blackpool for a long weekend. But he did sound pleased to have me back.

I got myself a hire-car – it was nice to be affluent – and drove up into East Anglia. At first I couldn't believe this was England – there seemed to be about ten times the cars on the roads, and everyone went so fast it made me nervous. After a while I got the hang of it, and by the time I got to Cambridge I was up there with the swiftest of them.

I didn't let myself think about where I was bound, nor whom I would or wouldn't find there; I knew that if I did, my courage would fail and I'd turn and run. Instead I just kept driving, listening to the radio, looking out at the familiar scenes, seeing what had changed and what had stayed the same.

And eventually I arrived in the village. Slowed, but didn't stop. Drove off down Florence's lane. Came to the phone box towards which, long ago, I'd run barefoot to call a cab.

I dialled her number. After two rings the receiver was picked up and her voice said 'Hello?'

I pictured her standing in the hall. Was she stooped now, the grey hair gone white? No! She'd be just the same!

Suddenly I wanted nothing more than to be with her. I said, 'Florence, it's me. Thea. I'm back.'

There was silence. Oh God, I thought, the surprise has been too much for her! *Stupid*, I should have written to her, given her some warning! Why, she might . . .

Then, even more calmly than Dad, she said, 'Thea, my dear! How lovely. Where are you?'

'Half a mile up the road.'

'In that case,' she said, 'you had better come to tea.'

As I got out of the car and walked up to the front door, it opened, and I knew she'd been looking out for me. She was dressed in a well-cut tweed skirt and a long heavy-knit cardigan, and she was as unstooped as she'd always been. Her hair was still iron-grey and abundant, her eyes as bright and all-observing. I'd been right: she hadn't changed a bit.

She was quite still as I approached. Then as I climbed the step to stand before her, she opened her arms and wrapped them round me. Not able to resist even if I'd wanted to, I hugged her back. I was transported straight back to the child crying to her one true friend because her mother was going away and she was to be torn from her dog and all that she knew and sent to live with her father.

After a few moments Florence said – and I could hear the catch in her voice – 'This is meant to be a celebration, Thea.' She laughed shakily. 'I can't imagine why we're crying!'

She'd never permitted tears for long. Now, pulling away from me but keeping hold of my hand, she led me inside. Although I'd prepared myself for his absence, still it gave me a jolt not to see Eric come forward, tail wagging, to greet me. As if she knew my thoughts – perhaps reckoning this was as good a time as any to get it out of the way – she said, 'He's buried in the orchard. Eric, I mean. I'll show you his grave later.'

'Thank you. I'd like that.' My voice was wobbly.

'We planted a lavender bush to mark the spot,' she said softly. 'We thought it was nicer than a headstone.'

'We?' I couldn't help it.

'Henry and I.' Her tone seemed to say, naturally!

Yes. He'd been Henry's dog before he was mine. And anyway I hadn't been there.

Feeling as if I'd betrayed my dog, I said quickly, 'And Garth? What about him?'

'Yes, he's gone too. A long and happy retirement out in my field, and one morning I found him lying dead beside the hedge.'

She was busy pouring tea – she must have made it as soon as she'd put the phone down – and as if to take my mind away from sad thoughts, she passed me a plate of sandwiches and said, 'Now, tell me about you.' She fixed her eyes on me. 'You look splendid. That colour becomes you, and the jacket is an excellent fit.'

I heard, unspoken, her question: how could you afford it?

I told her about Gordon and the books. About Scott, and my brief career as a travel guide, about going to America with him and working in real estate. 'San Diego's booming,' I said – it might have been an unasked question but she was going to get an answer all the same – 'And as long as you're prepared to do a stroke or two, you can't help but make money.'

She took it all in, nodding, occasionally saying, 'I see.' When I'd finished, she said, 'You married neither Gordon nor Scott.'

It was a statement, not a question. Yet I hadn't told her – perhaps she was guessing by the fact that my left hand was bare.

'No.'

'And you have had no children.'

'No!'

She raised her eyebrows. 'Marriage is not the only estate in which one may produce progeny.'

I grinned at her. She wasn't going to rile me, I'd made up my mind. 'Okay, Florence.'

She answered my smile. She was looking at me so affectionately, so kindly, that her next question was totally unexpected. In a changed tone, she asked,

'What made you come home?'

The smile was gone: she was leaning forward, frowning slightly, as if determined to miss neither a syllable of my answer nor the least nuance in my voice.

God!

I took a moment to assemble my thoughts. Then I said calmly, 'I've been away for six years, apart from the occasional brief visit. I got homesick.'

But that wasn't enough. She said, 'Why did you come here?'

My calm was rapidly being eroded. There were reasons, the best reasons in the world. But I could hardly acknowledge them to myself, let alone reveal them to Florence. I cast around wildly, and finally lit on something that I thought would do.

'This was my mother's home,' I said. 'Perhaps I've been feeling the call of my roots!'

I'd intended the last comment as a small joke. But, far from laughing, her face stiffened into lines of the utmost seriousness. And she said, 'If the pull of your home has won, despite everything, then you are doubly welcome.'

And passed me a plate of cakes.

Long after the dregs of tea in the pot had gone cold, we were still sitting on either side of the fireplace, catching up on the years of my absence. She told me of this or that person I remembered from childhood, who had sold up and gone away, who had moved in. I told her about Dad and Pam, although when she asked about Mum I could only say that she and Jim had gone to live in Sydney, and that as far as I knew they were still there. For some reason that made her look sad, but then the distress cleared from her face and she said, 'Ah, well. *You* are here.'

Sooner or later we had to refer to my abrupt departure from Willowford Fen six years ago. And the reason for it. Neither of us seemed to know how to, though; every time a silence fell, one of us would fill it with another reminiscence, or another question along the 'What happened to Mrs Phillips's son?' lines.

The hall clock struck six – incredibly, I'd been there two hours – and she got up. 'A drink, I think,' she said. Without asking me what I'd like, she poured two large scotches. Then, taking her seat again, said, 'You ran away, Thea. I know why, and I accept that to some extent I pushed you into your precipitate action.' To some extent! I opened my mouth to protest, but she held up her hand. 'Please, Thea. I know what you are going to say.' She smiled at me, and I subsided. 'The irony was,' she went on, 'that whilst I was angry with you for going and sad because I knew you would not come back, at the same time I admired you. You did exactly what I should have done had someone tried to organize my life, and you proved to me, if I needed proof, that you were as strong and decisive as I had thought you were.'

The gloves were off, apparently. We were being frank with one another, for the first time. All the strange mysteries that had enmeshed me since I came to this house were buzzing loudly in my head, urgently demanding attention: I might never have as good a chance of getting an answer as I had right now. I said, 'Why did you do it? And why, whenever you were making headway in getting us together, did the dark –' I bit back the words, '– did events conspire to push us apart?'

All expression left her face, and her eyes seemed to focus on something far away. I thought I saw a haze of smoke pass between us, and for a moment I was back in my dream. Then she said, as calmly as if she were merely refusing another drink, 'I don't think I shall tell you at the moment.'

It had been silly to think she would. But I had, briefly – I'd really thought we were going to talk about that time that began when I was eighteen. When *he* was eighteen, and came to the door on the night of his party and then upset me because he disappeared to take Wendy home and she was sick in the car.

Henry.

Here in his house, sitting in his chair, the longing for him was overtaking me far too fast. I tried to fight it – I'd been doing okay for two hours, for God's sake – but the defences were breached. Memories were coming in like the spring tide, and I couldn't stop them any more.

I said, 'Where is he?'

She answered with a question of her own. Very gently, she asked, 'Was that the real reason for coming back?'

'No! It was because of you, because I wanted to . . .' What was the point? 'Yes.' I looked up and met her eyes. 'Of course it was.'

I felt the hot words bubbling up. Like someone in the confessional, I wanted to tell her everything. About how I'd wanted to die, leaving England. About how I'd drunk myself stupid, and only Gordon's kindness and tolerance had saved me. About how I'd thought, standing on the heights above the Dardanelles, this is okay, I'm happy with Gordon and I'm still keeping faithful to *him*. About Scott, and the needs of my own body betraying me at last.

About the constant presence in my heart of Henry, whom I'd loved so deeply at eighteen that I could no more cut out his memory than I could cut off my own head.

I said, as much to myself as to her, 'I didn't want it to be like this. It's too bloody dangerous, depending on someone else for your happiness. I don't want to love anyone.'

'But you do.'

'Yes.'

Did I catch a look of triumph in her eyes? Hard to tell, for as I watched she closed them. Just for a second, it looked as if she were praying.

I finished my drink and went to pour myself another one. Then I wandered round the room, picking up objects, stopping to stare out of the big window overlooking the Fen.

When at last I sat down again, she said, 'He will come home, if you call him.'

Her words were so absurd that it took some time to accept she'd really said them. Then I burst out, 'What do you mean, if I call him! He's not some genie in a bloody bottle who'll pop up if I rub in the right place! Shall I go out there on to the Fen,' – I was on my feet again, waving out into the twilight – 'and call, "Henry! Henry! Time to come home!"'

She waited for the echoes of my anger to die. Then she said, 'You could do that, yes. But I was thinking of using the telephone.'

Oh, God.

'You know where he is, then?'

'I do indeed.'

'Where?'

'Herefordshire.'

Herefordshire? What the hell was he doing in Herefordshire? Part of me, recognizing that it was the next county to Gloucestershire and Dad, was daring to have the thought, perhaps he's looking for me. But most of me was cheering and laughing, because of all the far-flung, exotic places in the world that he might have ended up, he was in Herefordshire.

The questions were all there – What's he doing there? Who's he with? How did he get on at Cambridge? What did he do when he graduated? But I didn't ask any of them. I said, 'Is he all right?'

Her expression softened; she looked at me with love in her eyes. 'Yes, he is all right. He has grown, in six years.' I knew she didn't mean in height.

'Grown out from under your thumb?' It was unkind, but it was out before I could stop it. Old grievances don't die, they just lie doggo.

She said majestically, 'He was never under my thumb.'

Scott had had a wonderful expression for conveying extreme disbelief. But it was too crude for Florence's drawing room, so I just said, 'Oh, yeah?'

'He was brought up to be considerate, and he was used to doing as I asked.' Her face was stern, but I thought I saw the beginnings of a smile in her eyes.

'Your creation,' I said softly. 'You made him. How awful for you, if he'd turned out weak like his father, because you weren't going to get another chance. Were you?'

She seemed unsurprised that I knew. 'There was never any question of his turning out like his father.'

'Because you made sure it was you who brought him up? But you brought up his father.'

'Indeed. Perhaps I knew better, with Henry.'

I got the strong impression that she wasn't giving me the full picture. That there was another, more certain reason why she'd known Henry would turn out differently. I knew, though, that she wasn't going to tell me.

'The good old Woolgar war-hero genes,' I said. I could hear Henry's voice in my head. 'They turned up after all, did they?'

We'd been fencing with each other, and I felt proud of my killer thrust. But I saw the pain as it went home, and too late remembered that the war-hero had been her husband. 'I'm sorry,' I muttered inadequately.

She sighed. 'Why should you be? You obviously have an admirably clear picture of the whole story. I did want a grandson in whom I might be proud. A descendant worthy of . . .' She stopped. It must have hurt, thinking of Henry's grandfather.

'Worthy of the Woolgar line,' I finished for her.

Her eyes shot up to mine. Now the triumph was there, and it was quite unmistakeable. She said, 'Exactly!'

I didn't know where I was. The contrasting emotions had been following each other too quickly, and I couldn't keep up. When in doubt, have another drink. I stood up, reaching for her glass as well.

'One more,' she said, handing it to me, 'then I must prepare supper. Perhaps you would like a hot bath when you've unpacked.'

She had taken it as read that I was staying. I couldn't think of any reason not to.

'That'd be lovely.'

'And then,' she looked at me over her glass, 'we shall decide which of us is to speak to him.'

To speak to him. To talk again to the man I'd left

with the shattering announcement that I was going off with someone else.

I finished off my third scotch. Perhaps the prospect wouldn't be so terrifying if I was pissed.

Twenty-four

My parents came over to help me celebrate the upper second degree which Cambridge graciously awarded me at the end of three years' study. All of us were surprised at how well we got on together – distance might have lent enchantment (and my mother in particular seemed a very exotic creature after all those years in the Far East), but I think it was more that they now looked on me as a contemporary and a friend instead of a young son who was always a bit of a bloody nuisance.

It was four years since I'd seen them – when they'd come home to sound out the idea of returning to England and the joys of a country cottage – and they both looked as if the expatriate life was still suiting them as well as it had ever done. As always on their home leaves, they were intent on seeing as many people as possible; what with that and doing my mother's usual mile-long list of essential shopping, I felt fortunate that they managed to find a few windows for me.

In the course of one of the many parties and dinners with friends, my father said, 'So, Henry old man. No definite plans. No cushy number with ICI or the Diplomatic Corps.'

It was a sort of résumé: I'd already recited to him the long catalogue of things I *didn't* want to do, which he'd accepted without comment, other than the occasional, 'Good Lord! I should think not!'

'No,' I said. 'Could you arrest the port decanter, next time it comes round?'

'Mm. It's a Taylors Late Bottled, if I know my ports.'

He waited until our glasses were full again. Then he said, 'Your mother and I were thinking it might be fun if you came back to Honkers with us.'

It was an affectation of my mother's to refer to it as Honkers. I'd hated it, before, but in the warm glow of my new-found tolerance, I thought it was rather sweet.

'For a holiday, you mean?'

'We can call it a holiday, if you like. Although if you were to find you liked it out there, well . . .'

He left the sentence hanging. But I knew what he meant: as a long-serving member of the expatriate community, he'd know people in all walks of life and it would be an easy step to remark to some man over the pink gins, 'I say, old chap, my boy Henry's out here. Cambridge degree, bit of a loose end. Got anything for him?' Before I knew it, I'd be in a job.

It didn't sound a bad idea. I was sick of living on a grant, even, thanks to my parents, a generous one.

I said, 'May I think it over?'

He looked so pleased that I hadn't said an instant 'no' that I almost agreed to go there and then.

What was there to stay in England for?

I lay awake long into the night, and in whichever direction I sent my thoughts, they always returned to that simple question. Okay, then, I'd tackle it.

Looked at another way, whom would I miss? Who would miss me?

Florence? I smiled. I was living in her house again – I'd been coming back for the vacations throughout my undergrad years, except when I went off on trips, but after I'd come down for the last time I'd moved in permanently. As always, she seemed pleased to see me when I arrived but gave no sign that she'd miss me when I was gone. The traumatic few weeks around my eighteenth birthday might never have happened.

Julia. Lovely Julia. The physical side of our association had run its course pretty quickly – she really did prefer older men, and I was keen to try out elsewhere the expertise she'd taught me – but the friendship lasted. So much so that, when she made up her mind at last to marry a fifty-year-old physics lecturer she'd known for two years or more, she asked me if I'd give her away.

'I'm too young,' I said.

'You're tall,' she said inconsequentially. 'And I'll keep you up all of the night before the wedding and make you look so haggard they'll think you're my grandfather.'

'Anyway, I'm not sure I like the idea of you marrying a physicist. You'll never know what he's been handling.'

'He handles me beautifully. That's why I'm marrying him.'

'I hope it isn't,' I said sternly. If I was going to give her away, I thought I ought to be *in loco parentis* in other ways, too, and give her a fatherly talk.

She threw a cushion at me. 'Don't be daft. Of course it isn't.'

I knew that already. I'd met her physicist, and he was good news. As it turned out, he made her a good husband – I often went to dinner with them, and sometimes joined them on walking and sailing weekends in their cottage in Norfolk. She was happy, it was plain to see, and happiness made her lovelier than ever.

I often looked at her and remembered. I might miss her, but no way would she miss me.

There had been other girls. Not many, but some. Gilly, who had been my partner at a May Ball and worn a dress with a slit so high up the side of her thigh that I'd hardly seen anything of her all night, even though everyone else had. She had wonderful legs. Monique, who'd come on a Norfolk weekend, got out of her tree on Julia's husband's mulled wine and had fallen off the boat. Hilary, who taught me to read palms. Jackie, who took me home to meet her parents.

I'd had a great three years.

My memories petered out. There was someone I hadn't thought about, but then I never thought about her. Not deliberately, anyway. Once I thought I saw her – it had been just after Christmas during my second year at Cambridge and, leaving Willowford Fen in the Morris one afternoon, I passed a VW camper van being driven by Thea's double. Florence had said she was still abroad, and anyway she couldn't drive, so my logic told me it couldn't possibly be her.

Logic obviously isn't connected to the emotions. As I drove on away from the encounter, my heart was racing and my hands on the wheel were slippery with sweat.

I'd miss *her* if I went to Hong Kong. I missed her wherever I was.

In the morning, I told my parents I'd like to accept their invitation.

* * *

I had no sense of coming back when we flew in to Kai Tak. Not that it was surprising – although Hong Kong had been where I'd lived for two years, the longest stay I had anywhere till I went to live with Florence, I hadn't liked it. My young mind had obviously wanted to erase the Far East: driving off in the car sent by my father's company to meet us, it all seemed brand-new.

And exciting – now that I was free and the world lay at my feet (or so I told myself), I was able to look at the Jewel of the Orient with new eyes. Making our way through the traffic in Happy Valley on the way out to Repulse Bay, I was amazed at how fast everyone moved – the cars, the minibuses known as Public Light Buses, the red Datsun taxis, the little lorries wreathed in thick black exhaust smoke. Even the trams, rocketing off down the stretch of road that ran parallel to the finishing straight on the race course. And the pedestrians – I'd forgotten that peculiar gait adopted by the small Chinese carrying a pole across his shoulders, weighed down with something extremely heavy on each end: they moved at a sort of trot, the legs never managing quite to straighten.

As we drove up the hill towards the cricket club the traffic thinned, and we covered the few miles to Repulse Bay in no time. Rounding the corner into the Bay, where the view out over the islands and the South China Sea suddenly opens up to the right, it struck me how pleased I was to be there.

I said as much to my mother, sitting beside me in the back.

She squeezed my hand. 'Oh, that's lovely, darling. We'll have such fun – shall we start tonight? Shall we stop off here,' – we were passing the Repulse Bay Hotel – 'and book a table for dinner?'

'Why not?' I said recklessly. If she wasn't going to be bothered about jet-lag, neither was I.

We passed the block of company flats where I'd lived as a child, and it seemed smaller than I'd remembered – places always do, when you go back as an adult. On out to Shek-O, my father pointing out the golf-course (it went without saying that they were members), and we pulled up outside the house they'd bought when he retired. I was comparing it unfavourably with what they might have had if my mother had been a different sort of woman and they'd gone for the country cottage in Sussex (my anti-Orient feelings weren't very far beneath the surface) when she said touchingly, 'May I show you round, darling?'

She wound her arm in mine, looking lovingly up at me – even in her highest heels, she still only reached my shoulder – and, little steps tap-tapping on the marble floor like an apprentice telegraphist, she led me inside. She loved it, I could tell, and even though it was far from being my cup of tea – I'd never gone for lacquered furniture, and you can have too much embroidered silk – her eagerness affected me, and I found myself earnestly telling her how much I envied her such a lovely home.

My father, calling the houseboy to help him with the luggage, caught my eye. Admitting me to the fraternity of tolerant males who have spent lifetimes affectionately indulging the whims of the Little Woman, he winked.

My mother and I unpacked while my father set out a drinks tray, then we sat out on the verandah with our gins. None of us was hungry – too full of airline food – so we spent the afternoon asleep on our beds and reconvened for dinner.

I assumed that my parents had a constant pool of

friends just waiting to be invited out to dinner, because although it was such short notice – only hours since we'd touched down – they managed to collect a gaggle of people to join in our homecoming evening. Our guests were gregarious and affectionate, and they all drank as if prohibition were being imposed in the morning. Not that I objected – it was all too easy to join in.

In the course of the evening I accepted invitations to parties, to lunch at the Yacht Club to meet someone's daughter, to go swimming at the Football Club, and to go out on a junk trip the next day.

My career as a Hong Kong socialite was well and truly launched.

Playing rugby one afternoon – I played for the Football Club, and it surprised me how many sides there were in the Colony – I met a man who worked for an airline. Over the post-match beers he told me about his job, which he obviously loved. He was on the management team, and it took him all over the Far East; he was constantly on the move, and the prospects for promotion were good. I implied I might be looking for work in the near future, and he gave me his card. He told me whom to contact, and also to mention his name – 'Tell him we met at the rugger club. That'll make them take you seriously!'

'Should I mention my Cambridge degree?' I asked.

He shrugged. 'Can if you like. Wouldn't hurt.'

That, I thought, puts me in my place.

I phoned the man he'd told me about, mentioning my rugby club acquaintance's name. I got a job. Just like that – it seemed so ridiculously easy that I thought I'd made a mistake, and got myself taken on as an office boy, or someone to clean out the lavatories on the aircraft.

I hadn't.

A few weeks into my Far Eastern jaunt, I was in full-time, very remunerative employment as a management trainee, just about to move into a small flat of my own in Stanley.

Hong Kong in the late seventies was an exhilarating place to be. The threat of 1997 was still too far away to bother about, especially in a place where the present was so fast-paced and intense that you hardly concerned yourself with what might happen next month, never mind twenty years away. The long-term expatriate set was quite small – my parents had been there as long or longer than most of their friends – and we enjoyed a constantly changing transient population. People would come out on contracts – three years for a government department, eighteen months for some construction company – and we'd get to know them. Then before you knew it they'd be off again, seen on their way by an almighty booze-up and replaced by a new face the next day.

I wasn't there all the time. The job took me to Australia, New Zealand, Papua New Guinea, Java, Taiwan, Japan and Singapore. Wherever we flew I went, sometimes for a few days, sometimes for a few months. As I learned the business and my seniority grew, I got better at organizing my time, becoming adept at ensuring I was in Japan for the blossom, in Port Moresby when it wasn't going to hammer down with rain all day every day, and home in Hong Kong for Dragon Boat Day and the Hong Kong Sevens. The latter were still held in the Football Club stadium in my time, and I've never forgotten the thrill of a Fiji–New Zealand final under floodlights with the thunder crashing behind the Peak and the fire-engines standing by to pump out in case the pitch flooded again.

Although I saw quite a lot of my parents and enjoyed their company, I was glad not to be under the same roof. They were long-term Hong Kong people, and I knew that I was not: somehow this gave us different attitudes to the life there, and occasionally it grated. There was the Royal Visit that threw my mother in an almighty flap because she couldn't find a hat to match her dress: when I said I wasn't going to give up a day's junk trip just to stand on the pavement with her, my father and several million Chinese just to wave at distant minor Royalty, she hit me, called me unpatriotic and retired to her bed with a headache. Similarly, it embarrassed them when I refused to go along with the general view that the head of my father's former company, a familiar figure on the Hong Kong social scene, was 'A poppet, all the girls love him,' (my mother) and 'A damned fine administrator, knows the Colony like the back of his hand,' (my father). I remarked that the young woman I'd seen him pawing on the dancefloor hadn't appeared to find him at all loveable, judging by the way she'd raced for the Ladies the moment the music stopped, and that his fine administrative brain hadn't prevented him from losing the Company several hundred thousands on a recent deal. My father gave an injured sniff and retired behind his *South China Morning Post*. My mother developed another headache.

In any case, I enjoyed living on my own. My flat overlooked Stanley beach, and was on the first floor of what, for Hong Kong, was quite an old house – it had been built just before the war. Friends all kept asking why I didn't have an amah – some of them went so far as to offer me a share in theirs – but the spectre of Ah Yen lived on in my soul and I said a resolute 'No'. I thought I saw Ah Yen once – behind me on a tram I heard someone do a monumental hawk, and before I could stop myself I'd turned round. It could have been her – she'd have been about the right age, and she certainly looked like Ah Yen. And there was the spitting . . . But they all spat. A Chinese acquaintance explained to me that to the Oriental mind, it was far more disgusting to observe an Occidental blow his nose into a handkerchief which he then carefully wrapped up and put in his pocket. I wasn't convinced.

The social life was incredible. At one point I found that I was out seven nights a week, and reluctantly I gave up playing bridge. The outdoor life beckoned almost all the year round, even in February and March, when it was cool and humid as opposed to hot and humid. (October and November were the best months – then it was hot and not humid.) When it was cool, you could catch a ferry out to Lantau or Lamma and spend the day walking, finishing with a meal and a trip home under the stars. And there was always Macao, over on the other side of the Pearl river estuary – I took a girlfriend to the Bella Vista hotel one unforgettable weekend, and when, much later, I heard they'd renovated the old place and put it out of most people's reach, I felt a strong, nostalgic regret.

As regards girlfriends, in my years in the Far East I took up where I'd left off at Cambridge. It was the same pattern: meet them, enjoy them, begin – sometimes – to think at last, *this* girl might be different. In the end I stopped letting things develop; most of the girls were no more interested in long-term commitment than I was. With one exception: I recognized how much I'd hurt her, because I saw in her what I'd suffered after Thea.

And, in time, it began to go stale. Another party. So what? A trip to KL. Don't want to go, can't we send someone else? Rugby up in the New Territories. It's not worth the trek through the traffic and the queue for the harbour tunnel.

I applied for a transfer to London. I wondered, in retrospect, if the fact of the airline having plans to extend the London end had been a major factor in my decision to apply for the job. Had I thought, somewhere in the back of my mind, I can always go back to England when the time's right?

My departure caused as much of a stir as a stone thrown into a pool. I went through the round of parties, and took a few trips to places I'd especially liked. It seemed to me, standing on a hillside on Cheung Chau, that the glitter had gone: in the beginning, there had still been beauty, still been places to go which the local population hadn't despoiled. Now, standing staring at wild flowers crushed by discarded cola cans, festoons of plastic bags and the charred remains of someone's barbecue, I felt a strong sense of claustrophobia. Too many people, competing for too small a space. I was glad to be going.

My parents behaved as if they'd half expected my departure. They did say they'd miss having me just up the road, but as my father remarked, three years wasn't bad when I'd only come out for a holiday.

They took me to the airport. I said as I stood in the VIP check-in (there were advantages in working for the airline), 'Do you remember my label? When I was an Unaccompanied Juvenile?'

My father looked blank, but my mother nodded. 'I do.' She gave a hesitant smile, quite out of character. 'I felt –' She stopped, and I thought for one dramatic moment that we were about to have some revelation about how it had affected her, seeing her only son

349

depart to live in England. But, 'I felt like a newly-wed,' she said. She had turned to my father, snuggling up to him as he put his arm round her. 'And it wasn't as if you were going to be unhappy, was it, darling? I mean, you made it perfectly obvious you couldn't wait to get back to Florence.'

'Yes, I did.' I bent to kiss her, catching a hint of Chanel No 5. Essence of Mother. 'You gave me a pound, last time. Dad gave me ten bob.'

My father snorted. 'We're not giving you any lolly this time! Although we wouldn't say no if you offered us your loose change, would we, Amanda?'

I shook his hand, and he thumped me on the back. 'Come out and see us,' he said. 'Any time.'

They walked away, arms round each other. They might be thoroughly settled into their retirement now but, watching them, I was quite sure that the thought of the love nest they were returning to together held just as strong an appeal as it had always done.

As soon as I was settled into my new job and had found myself somewhere to live, I decided to go up to see Florence. I'd expected her to be amazed at my return, but when I called her from my London office she greeted me quite calmly. As if she'd known I was there.

I didn't bother to hide my motive for coming home. Well, I may have tarted it up a bit by saying you could have too much of the Orient, and that I'd missed the green spaces and the less frenetic life of England. But then I thought, what's the point?

'I want to find her,' I said over the first of our evening drinks. 'I accept that it's stupid, that I should have forgotten about her years ago.' Especially, I thought, in view of the number of successors she's had. But I didn't say that to Florence.

She nodded, as unsurprised as if it were the most ordinary thing in the world for a man not far short of his twenty-fourth birthday still to be hung up on a girl he'd fancied for a few weeks when he was eighteen. 'I'm afraid I have no idea where she is,' she said. 'Although I feel that . . .'

'What?'

She studied me for some time. Then she shook her head. 'Nothing. You might ask Gordon Willis if he knows.'

'She's not still with him?' It hurt, to think she had stayed with him when she'd abandoned me.

'Oh, good Lord, no. I shouldn't imagine so.' She smiled gently.

She was being enigmatic, and it irritated me. Couldn't she see how imperatively I needed to know? I'd had enough of beating round the bush. 'Didn't they get married?'

'Married? I think she has married no-one.'

'You're in touch with her, then?'

'No. I have not heard a word from, or about, Thea since she left this house that October morning.'

Then, I wanted to demand, how the hell do you know she's not married? 'Look, Florence, I . . .'

'I will give you Gordon Willis's address.' She got up regally and went to her desk. 'Then you may pursue the matter or not, as you wish.'

I phoned Gordon Willis in the morning. When I said what I wanted, there was a silence. Then he repeated very softly, 'Thea.' More silence followed, then he said, 'You'd better come and see me.'

It was an attractive end-of-terrace house on the edge of Thetford, well cared for, obviously expensive. Inside, it was clear the place had enjoyed the attention of an interior designer. On the walls were photographs – my eye went instantly to one of her, standing in front of a stone monument topped by a stork with down-flapping wings.

'Guynemer's memorial,' he said, coming to stand beside me. 'First World War air ace.'

'Oh.'

I looked at the other photographs. They were good, and I was aware I wasn't doing justice either to the photographer's skill or to the solemn poignancy of the subjects. There was another one, by itself on the big desk under the window: he saw that I'd spotted it, and went to turn it so that I couldn't see. But he wasn't quite quick enough.

A close-up of her. On some bridge, a backdrop of water and old buildings. She had an ice-cream in her hand and laughter in her eyes.

He kept her picture on his desk. I wasn't the only one who missed her.

'Do you know where she is?'

He shook his head. 'No. She went back to Flanders, after she . . . when we finished our last book. She sent me her address,' – he handed me a piece of card, and I recognized her writing – 'but I didn't write. I thought it best . . .'

He didn't say what he'd thought best. I had a pretty good idea. I wanted to apologize for dragging it all up, but I hardly knew the man. 'Do you think it's worth following it up?' I asked, studying the address. Ypres. Where the hell was Ypres?

'You could. Someone may remember her.'

'You don't know if she . . .'

'I know nothing,' he said shortly. 'No more than I've already told you.'

He was edging me towards the door, and I took the hint. 'Thank you. I'm sorry to have disturbed you.' *That* was an understatement. 'I'm an old friend.'

At least I could give him something of an explanation. 'From childhood.'

As he opened the front door we stood for an instant eye to eye. He said, 'I know who you are.'

I went to Ypres. The address turned out to be a lodging house for the couriers of an American tour company. A fresh-faced, fair-haired young man told me candidly that I didn't have a chance of tracing anyone who'd lived or worked there longer ago than last season, and when I showed him a photograph of her I'd pinched from Florence's album, he just shrugged. So that was that.

I stayed a few days in Ypres, but no-one had heard of her and no-one recognized the photo. Once I'd admitted to myself it was hopeless there was no longer any point in hanging around, so I didn't. On my last evening, I went up to the Menen Gate to join in the nightly salute to the Fallen. I was a few minutes early, so I wandered around the giant memorial arch reading the names of the dead under the headings of the various regiments.

At the top of some steps I came face to face with my grandfather's regiment. Two columns of other ranks, a thin few lines of officers.

There he was. Woolgar, Capt. H. R.

The sound of the traffic had stopped: I was going to have to hurry if I wasn't to be late. Running down the steps, I took my place at the back of the small crowd just as the policemen at either end of the arch turned to salute. The buglers lifted their instruments, and on to the still cool air fell the notes of the 'Last Post'.

My grandfather, whose name I bore. A soldier, who had died fighting for his country. Suddenly I felt very close to this ancestor I'd never met, and just for a split-second I thought I sensed the press of all the other forebears that had gone before him. Woolgar, H. R., Florence's husband. How many other Woolgars, reaching back into the far past? East Anglians they'd been, devoted sons of their land who'd loved it as if it were a nurturing parent. As I stood there, I had the strange sense that all the far-ranging knowledge and the hinted-at arcane mysteries that Florence had fed into me throughout my childhood had at last come together, and that I was on the brink of understanding. I seemed to see the bloodline, stretching back through the centuries. An *ancient* family, Florence used to say. How ancient? Pre-Conquest? I pictured an Anglo-Saxon, dressed in thick brown wool, a gold torc at his throat. Then, I imagined men of later ages. Under the Normans, the Tudors, the Hanoverians. My own grandfather, marching off to war in khaki.

I would never know him. Never know any of them. For all that they were of my blood, they were as unreachable as the stars.

The traffic was once more pushing through the arch. The buglers had gone, the crowd was dispersing. Feeling foolish for the tears in my eyes, I hurried away.

If I couldn't find her, I could at least find her father. He was still in Gloucestershire, Florence said, and she gave me the address. It wasn't the way I'd wanted to do it – this was between the two of us, and I wasn't ready to involve anyone else, especially not her father. But there was no choice.

I stayed in Ross-on-Wye, in the next-door county of Herefordshire – in case they asked, my story was going to be that I was there for the fishing and was just looking her up for old times' sake. I hoped he wasn't going to turn out to be a fisherman, because if he was, he'd expose my cover in about ten seconds. I knew bugger-all about fishing.

I hadn't known what to expect. I'd seen the sort of establishment her mother had run, but she'd told me nothing about her father. I was pleasantly surprised: he was a friendly man, hospitable and free-talking. He appeared to share his house with a big woman called Pam who wore crimplene trousers and rolled her own cigarettes; she had the most beautiful hazel eyes.

They were friendly and hospitable, sure. But they had no more idea than Gordon Willis did of where she was. They'd had a postcard from her in the spring – 'April, it was, wasn't it, Pam?' her father said. 'Photograph of some damn great waterfall in Yosemite National Park.' He'd offered to scour the flat for it, which I thought might take some time, but since he was quite sure she hadn't provided an address, I thanked him and told him not to bother.

I went back to my hotel room. I phoned Florence to tell her I'd drawn another blank, and I couldn't keep the depression out of my voice.

'Go and have dinner,' Florence advised. 'A strong drink, some good food and an early night will put you right.'

She sounded so serene, as if it didn't matter a toss that I was at the end of the trail, my last avenue explored and discovered to be empty of hopeful leads.

'So what now?' I asked crossly. 'Any more bright ideas, after the dinner and the early night?' Perhaps I'd go bloody fishing after all.

'Be calm, Henry. Something will turn up.'

'Okay, Florence.' I didn't want to hear any more. 'I'll talk to you soon.'

Before I went to sleep – very late – I formulated a vague plan of getting the names of some of her old school friends from her father. But the next morning I abandoned it: was she really the sort of girl who'd subscribe to the old girls' society and send Christmas cards to people from her past? She didn't send them to Florence or to Gordon or to me.

I didn't know where in the world she was.

I had too much to drink at lunchtime, and had to go for a walk later to clear my head. The effect of the drink and the walk combined to make me decide to give up; on my way up to my room to change for dinner, I told Reception I'd be leaving in the morning.

While I was in the shower the telephone rang. It was Florence. For a moment I thought she might have come up with a fresh suggestion, but she started talking about someone from the office who'd called and left a message for me, and I realized she hadn't.

Then, as if as an afterthought before hanging up, she said, 'Oh, Henry. There's someone here who would like a word with you.'

It was, I suppose, indicative of my maudlin state that I didn't even wonder who. I waited as the receiver was handed to whoever it was, thinking of nothing more earth-shattering than would my headache come back if I had a bottle of wine with my supper.

I heard her draw in her breath. Then she said, 'Hello, Henry. I've come home.'

PART FOUR

The Third Crown

Twenty-five

I packed up and left the moment I'd put the phone down.

I didn't tell her I was going to – I said I'd be coming back to Willowford Fen the next day, probably. Or maybe the day after.

Perhaps I really believed it when I said it. But, standing there in my hotel room, in my head the echoes of a voice I hadn't heard for six years, I discovered I was shaking, tight as a wound spring. The plan of calmly dressing and going down to dinner prior to a peaceful night's sleep was no longer on.

The woman in Reception looked affronted when I said I was checking out. 'You said you were going in the morning,' she said. 'I haven't prepared your bill yet.' She glared at me.

'I'm going now,' I repeated.

'You'll have to pay for tonight.' The glare intensified, as if I was deliberately trying to cheat her out of the cost of a night's board and lodging.

I flicked my Access card at her. 'I'll pay for tonight, tomorrow and next week. Just prepare my bill.'

'Tonight will suffice,' she said with a sniff.

As I was signing my name she unbent a bit.

Perhaps she recognized desperation when she saw it. 'I hope there hasn't been an emergency,' she remarked.

I smiled. 'In a way there has.'

I got down on to the M4 and raced east. There was little traffic, and I made excellent time until I turned off at Slough. It seemed to take for ever to get round to Hertford, and on the A10 there was a long hold-up following an accident. It was after midnight by the time I got to Cambridge, and suddenly the idea of banging on Florence's door in the middle of the night didn't seem so brilliant after all.

I drove on to Willowford Fen. I'd see if there were any lights on, I decided, and if not I'd sleep in the car – it was big enough, and I had a thick coat.

I went very slowly up the drive and pulled up outside the house. I thought at first that it was in darkness, but once I'd switched off the headlights I saw there was a faint glow from between the drawing-room curtains.

It'll be Florence, I told myself. She often stays up late.

I got out of the car, went up to the front door and quietly tapped the knocker.

I thought he might come. If I'd been in his position, *I'd* have done. I was tempted to get in my car and set out for Ross-on-Wye, except I didn't know the name of his hotel.

Florence thought he might, too. I'm sure she

did. Not long after supper – I couldn't eat, just drank cup after cup of coffee – she said she was going to bed.

'I think I'll sit up for a while,' I said, stretching casually as if I hadn't any greater thought on my mind. 'There's a film on BBC 2, it looks worth watching.'

'Then I shall see you in the morning.'

She came across to me, and for a moment rested her hand against my cheek. Her expression was unreadable – did she look happy? Pleased? I couldn't tell – and then she turned away.

As she opened the door, I called, 'Sleep well!'

She paused. Then said – and I could *hear* that she was smiling – 'You too.'

I watched the film. Then a programme about acid rain in Scandinavia, then a discussion group for people who found it hard to make friends. There was a late-night news bulletin and a brief prediction of what tomorrow's weather was going to be like, then nothing.

I was getting cold. I was also feeling sheepish – he obviously wasn't coming, and I'd stayed up for nothing. I hoped Florence had gone to sleep long ago, then with any luck she wouldn't hear me creeping to bed and notice how long I'd waited for him.

There were lights outside, and the soft sound of a car approaching very slowly. Coming up the drive.

I wanted to run, I wanted to be sick. I was trembling and sweating, and I could see the little hairs on my arms standing on end.

It was him. It *had* to be – it couldn't be anyone else.

The engine stopped and the lights were switched off. There was a pause, then I heard a car door open and close.

Then he tapped very quietly on the front door.

She was still dressed, so I knew I hadn't got her out of bed: she'd been waiting for me. I wanted to ask her how she'd known I was coming, but the first sight of her was taking away the power of speech. She wore her hair short now and her face showed more character than it had at eighteen, but those were the only changes. For an instant I had the feeling that everything there had ever been between us, all through our lives, was amassing and assaulting me; she was Thea, and it was somehow *right* that we had come back to each other.

Then she said, 'Come in. You're letting all the cold air in,' and the assault abruptly stopped.

I followed her into the drawing room.

She walked – no, strode – over to the fireplace, resting her hand on the mantelshelf, her back to me. I almost strode right after her, so strong was the urge to put my arms round her, turn her to face me, pull her to me and feel again her body against mine.

It was an urge I resisted.

Six years had gone by. She was still Thea, sure. But a lot can happen in six years, and she might no longer be my Thea. If she had ever been. Just then I doubted it.

Yet here she was. She had, as she'd said on the phone, come home.

The sofa cushions were dented from where she'd been lying. I threw myself down, and felt the warmth that her body had left. It seemed that everything was contriving to unsettle me.

I had to say something: the silence was excruciating. She obviously thought so too, because just as I began to say I was bushed, and maybe it hadn't been such a good idea to come home tonight, but I'd been in two minds anyway and her call had decided me (I was feeling a compulsion to explain my presence), she started to say something about wasn't it late? She must have fallen asleep over the midnight movie.

Behind her the television stood mute, its plug lying disconnected from the socket. Unless she'd switched it off and unplugged it as she came to open the door, which didn't seem all that likely, then I knew quite well she'd just told me a lie.

But I'd just told her one, too. That made us even.

The silence fell again. Heavier, now; crushing.

One of us had to do something. She might be the elder, but I was the man. I'd been brought up to believe that men should be chivalrous, and if there were any nettles to be grasped, it should be the man who risked getting stung. Thea, if she was still the child and the young woman I retained in my heart, would have been incensed at my reasoning, but that was too bad.

I got up from the sofa and went to stand behind her.

'Do you think you could turn round?' I asked. 'This might be marginally less difficult if I could look at you.'

She turned. I was standing so close that her shoulder brushed my arm. It felt like a mild electric shock.

I stared down into her face. Her eyes, wide and candid, showed me she was feeling as confused – as disturbed – as I was. Then, after what seemed a very long time, she began to smile.

'I've been waiting for you for hours,' she said softly. 'I knew you'd come. But now that you're here, I'm . . . I mean, I don't . . .'

'You don't know what to make of me?' I suggested. You're wondering, I thought, why I look familiar – very familiar – yet at the same time a stranger. You're wondering what's happened in the six years we've been apart. What I've been doing. Who has been important to me. Who I've loved.

I know you're thinking all of that – I wanted to say it to her, but couldn't – because I'm thinking it about you.

'You're you,' she said, 'but I can't quite find my bearings.'

She reached out her hand, touching her fingers against my face. Again, the mild shock. Studying her, trying to take in all of her at once, I was remembering too vividly what it felt like to kiss her.

Not yet.

'I'm glad you waited up,' I said. I took hold of her hand and kissed the tips of her fingers. 'I hoped you would.'

We stood smiling at each other. I kissed her fingers again, drawing the tip of the little one into my mouth. Watching her, I saw her eyes widen in surprise. Then, as, briefly, another emotion flashed across her face, she pulled her hand away, at the same time stepping back so that she put a yard of distance between us.

'I'm sorry,' I said.

'Don't be!' Her smile looked slightly forced. 'I – oh, God, I don't know how to put this into words!' She pulled at her hair with both hands, as if trying to drag out what she wanted to say. Then she turned to face me, eyes holding mine so that I couldn't look away. 'I just have this incredible feeling that we're right back where we were. I mean, I *know* it's been years and years –'

'Six years,' I reminded her.

'Yes, okay, six years. And I don't know about you, but for me they've been busy years, with some good times. But –' She stopped, the perplexed frown deepening. 'It's as if they've never been,' she whispered. 'You look the same, you feel the same, and I'm –' Her eyes slid away, and I wondered if she was going to baulk at saying what she wanted to say. But she didn't. 'I'm right back to eighteen.' She looked at me again. 'Crazy, isn't it?'

Right back to eighteen. Recalling the highs and the lows of Thea and me at eighteen, it didn't seem too good an idea to ask in which respect she meant.

Perhaps she meant all of them.

It seemed we were standing on the edge of a great gulf, poised for flight. One word from either of us – one movement towards each other – and we'd be off, racing into things we hardly understood and for which, surely, it was too soon. They were too precious to endanger.

'No, it isn't crazy.' I smiled at her, and instantly she responded. 'I'm finding it disconcerting, too. Seeing you again. I thought it'd be –' What had I thought? I hadn't thought anything, I'd just obeyed the impulse to get to her. 'Whatever, I didn't imagine it'd be like this.' That, anyway, was truthful. She began to say something, but I interrupted her. 'I don't think I can talk to you tonight. I don't know what I want to say.' And I'm afraid I'll get it all wrong. 'Shall we go to bed?'

I wished, as soon as the words were out, that I'd said something else. Anything else.

But it was all right. She was pretending she hadn't noticed. Or I thought she was: moving over to the sofa, she was plumping the cushions, picking up her handbag. Just as any woman would when she's off to bed after a long day.

She waited while I walked out into the hall, then she turned off the drawing-room light and closed the door. Together we went upstairs.

Up on the landing, taking me totally unawares, she suddenly turned, threw her arm round my shoulders and, holding my face with her hand, pulled me down towards her. Her mouth closed on mine, and, with a wonderful singlemindedness – and an expertise she hadn't possessed at eighteen – she was kissing me.

As suddenly, she stopped. Broke away from me. From a safe distance, she said, 'You're back in your usual room.' She was watching me, amusement in her face. I knew she hadn't finished, and I was right.

'I don't think I'll join you.' The amusement had grown to a mischievous, slightly mocking smile, although whether she was mocking herself, me or both of us, I didn't know. 'Tempting though your proposition is, I'm not that sort of girl.'

Then her bedroom door opened and closed in a flash, and she was gone.

In the hours it took me to get to sleep, I relived that kiss over and over again. I wished I hadn't done it, then, remembering how his lips had felt against mine, I was glad – so much more than glad – that I had.

When I wasn't thinking about kissing him, I was obsessed with recalling what we'd said to each other. Not that it took long – our whole conversation seemed to have been more an exchange of what we didn't say than what we did. You look great, I'd wanted to tell him. You always looked good, as a boy, as a young man. Now, with a few more years behind you, and no doubt a lot of experience, you look irresistible. Kind, funny, sexy.

Then I'd get bogged down with thinking about that kiss again.

Round and round my thoughts went. Finally – after three, I think – I resorted to counting sheep.

And as day dreams gave way to night dreams, I thought I could see the bloody sheep, pushing one by one through a hole in a hedge. Further down the hedge was a stile, on which sat Henry, affection in his eyes, a warm welcoming smile on his face, saying, 'I can't be with you because I've got to take the sheep home.'

In the morning I felt better. In charge again, able to face the thought of being with him with something like equanimity. I listened carefully before opening my door – I didn't want to bump into him coming out of the bathroom – but there was no sound of movement. I had a very quick bath – I didn't like the thought of him coming along and trying the door while I was in there, either – then hurried back to my room to get dressed.

Then, when I could think of no more reasons for delay, I went down to breakfast.

He and Florence were sitting opposite each other at the table, on the toast and marmalade stage. The excitement and the heart-stopping drama of last night might never have been; he was talking to her about some business colleague who'd phoned asking to borrow his flat while he was away.

As I came in they both looked up and wished me good morning. I sat down, ate a bowl of cereal and half a slice of toast I didn't want and drank a couple of cups of tea. It was all so *ordinary* I wanted to scream.

Then, as Florence left the table to top up the teapot from the kettle on the range, he caught my eye. Just for a moment, but then a moment was all it took.

And I knew it wasn't ordinary at all.

I don't think I slept at all, that night. I seem to remember hearing an awful lot of hours strike – sod's law would have it that my insomnia should coincide with a night still enough for the church clock to be easily audible out at Willowford Fen. I told myself to relax, I tried reading, I lay in the darkness piecing together all the bits of Shakespeare I could remember.

Nothing did any good. Against the thought of her, three doors away, it would have taken a lorryload of mandragora to knock me out.

Maybe it'd have been all right if she hadn't kissed me.

I'd never know, because she had, and every time my insubordinate thoughts returned to that short moment out on the landing – at roughly ten-minute intervals – I was gripped with the desire to race along to her room so that she could do it again.

It wouldn't stop there, my erotic imaginings told

me. She's learned a lot in six years, she's *experienced*, she's got the art of kissing to a T. To a T. Stupid expression, what have Ts to do with kissing, for God's sake?

I spent some time trying to think of a better way to describe Thea's expertise with her lips. That, too, was stupid, but better than the alternative. Better than tormenting myself wondering how, and with whom, she'd learned. And how many more skills she'd learned besides kissing.

What about you? I asked myself as the church clock chimed four. Julia, Gilly, Monique, Hilary, Jackie. And that was before I went to Hong Kong. But it's different for a man, the chauvinistic thought boomed in my head.

I wondered what Thea's reply would have been to *that*.

It was a relief when, soon after six thirty, I heard Florence stirring. I waited till she'd finished in the bathroom, then went along for a shower and a shave. A quarter of a century with her had engraved her habits clearly on my memory: I knew she'd have the kettle boiling and the eggs and bacon done to perfection as the Radio Four news began (it had been the Home Service when I was a child: she used to get irritated with Alvar Liddell for sounding so solemn about everything).

She greeted me warmly, offering me her cheek to kiss while she dished fried bread on to warmed plates.

'I thought you might decide to return last night,' she remarked.

I didn't know what to say.

She glanced at me, then added, 'Less traffic, I imagine, late at night.'

'Quite.'

I poured tea for us both. I waited, but she didn't go on. If, as I thought, she was well aware Thea had waited up for me, she wasn't going to mention it.

We shared her *Times* as we ate. She broke the companionable silence by telling me that my colleague Jon had phoned and left a message – I'd said he could use my flat while I was away.

'Thanks for reminding me,' I said. 'He's probably forgotten where I told him to find the keys. He's going to . . .'

Thea walked in.

She looked wonderful. I felt a moment's resentment that obviously *she* hadn't been thrashing about all night torturing herself with her thoughts while the bloody clock counted its way through the hours. Then the resentment was gone, pushed out by the sheer pleasure of looking at her. Her hair shone – I liked it short, I decided – and her face was made up with the expertise of a girl in a magazine. She was wearing well-cut trousers, a jumper that clung to and outlined the curve of her breasts, and a very smart jacket of a sort of apricot shade that suited her down to the ground.

As well as looking well-rested and glowingly healthy, she also looked as if she wasn't short of the proverbial bob or two.

She'd changed. Oh, yes, she'd changed.

Calmly she sat down and helped herself to muesli, and, when she'd finished that – I could have sworn she was chewing each mouthful twenty times, but perhaps I was just edgy – she went on to toast.

I wanted to shake her. Wanted to catch hold of her shoulders, force her to look at me and shout, 'What about last night? What about all those things we tried to say to each other? *What about kissing me?*'

But, apart from anything else, we were sitting at Florence's breakfast table. One just didn't lose control at Florence's breakfast table.

'More tea?' Florence asked.

'Yes, please,' Thea said. She hardly looked up from her sodding toast.

Florence got up and went to the range. As she stood topping up the teapot, Thea lifted her head and looked at me.

My eyes met hers. She started to smile, a beautiful, irrepressible smile that spread over her face and somehow lifted the outer corners of her eyes, so that she looked as if she were just about to laugh. Inside me I started to sing.

Then Florence came back with the teapot, and Thea went back to her toast.

Twenty-six

I was so overwhelmed with Thea that for some time I didn't pay attention to Florence.

Mistake.

I don't mean I ignored her. I couldn't have done that, nearly thirty years of conditioning would have made it impossible. I treated her as I always did.

That was where I went wrong.

Looking back, I used to ask myself if things would have turned out differently, had I not let my 'Thea' joy blind me to everything else.

I still wonder, now.

Not many of us are given a second chance in life. We leave someone, let them walk away from us, and usually that's it. We may have regrets, but either they fade with time or else we learn to live with them. When most relationships fail it is, I suppose, because for one or other partner there is no longer any satisfaction. Any happiness. Any point in going on.

Thea and I parted at eighteen, ironically, because a third party had been trying too hard to push us together. With hindsight, I don't think that separation was what either of us wanted, and that seemed to be borne out by our revelations to each other when we got our second chance.

I thought, as she ate her toast with such deceptive calm that first morning, that it wasn't going to work. But that was before she looked up and caught my eye.

My memory of the following half hour or so is vague: we must have continued our polite reserve while breakfast was finished and cleared away, and while we discussed with Florence what we should like to do with the day.

I don't recall what Florence did. I only know that, whatever it was, she didn't do it with us. We went out and got into my car, and I drove us away from Willowford Fen – slowly at first, then, as an irresistible feeling of escape overcame me, quickly – until we were shooting off up the A10 as if something malignant were on our tail.

'Where are we going?' she asked after some time.

'I don't know.' A signpost flashed by. 'King's Lynn, apparently.'

'I don't feel like towns. Let's go somewhere wild.'

I glanced across at her. She wasn't dressed for wild.

'We'll stop and buy you some wellies,' I said. 'Then we'll find a long empty beach and walk. Okay?'

She sank into her seat, a smile of pleasure on her face. 'Okay,' she agreed softly.

We found a chandler's shop in Hunstanton, and I bought her boots and a thick pair of socks. She asked with a flash of her old belligerence why I was paying, and when I replied, 'Because I want to,' something in her expression changed. She left the shop, reappearing a few minutes later with a half bottle of brandy.

'What's this for?'

'In case we get exposure and there isn't a Saint

Bernard handy.' She pushed it into my hands, then marched off back to the car.

We followed the coast road out of town, then turned on to a minor road and stopped in the deserted car park of an inn on the shore. Then, the faint sounds of the sea calling us, we set off alongside the dyke that led through the dunes to the beach.

There were a few people about. Families, people out with their dogs, couples. Arm in arm, Thea and I must have looked like a couple, too. Perhaps that was why, with every step, I felt more and more that we were.

We didn't talk about anything much, at first. She mentioned that she'd done well working in property in San Diego, I told her a bit about my expat life in Hong Kong.

When I'd finished she said, 'Full circle.'

'What was that?'

'I said, full circle.' She turned to look at me. 'The first time I ever heard your name, you were coming home from Hong Kong. You went back, now you've come home again.'

I was going to say a polite equivalent of, so what? but she hadn't finished. 'You told me once that you knew your parents hadn't wanted you. I concluded that meant you weren't happy in Hong Kong, and that was why you came home to live with Florence.' She paused, turning away so that I could no longer see her face. Then she said, 'What made you come home this time?'

There were many things I could have said. Career move, disillusion with the colonial life, sudden desire to check up on Florence and make sure advancing years weren't starting to make it hard for her to cope.

I said, 'I came back to find you.'

She let out her breath with a great sigh that had a

sob in it. I hadn't even realized she'd been holding it in.

'I thought you might have done,' she whispered. 'When I got back to Willowford Fen and Florence said you were in Herefordshire, I thought – *hoped* – it might mean you were going to see Dad. But I couldn't be sure. Even when you turned up last night, I couldn't be sure.'

She lifted her head to look at me, and her eyes were full of tears. 'Did you really?' Her voice was so low I could hardly hear her. 'Come home to look for me?'

I put my arms round her, pulling her close to me, my face buried in her short, shining hair. She smelt – I can't describe it. She smelt of Thea. Somewhere I read that there is a particular smell to each of us, known only to our lovers. Thea and I weren't lovers, but I recognized her smell. Chords of memory sang through my mind, the image of her I'd carried through all the empty years combining with the real live woman in my arms into a moment of sublime joy.

'I've missed you ever since you left,' I said. Perhaps I was admitting it to myself as well as to her. 'Yes, I came home for you.'

For some time we didn't speak. We stood, arms around each other, bodies pressed together, her face against my neck and my head resting on hers. It was as if we were melding.

Someone said, 'Excuse me, please!' and we sprang apart, standing back off the path while two men, a woman and a black labrador went by.

I didn't like the sudden cessation of contact with her, so I reached for her hand. Her fingers entwined in mine and, as the little group marched off away from us, she said, 'I did, too. Came home because of you.'

It was sweet of her – and characteristically honest – to admit it outright. But she hadn't needed to. Although I didn't say so to her, in case she took it as presumption, I already knew. Like her, I hadn't been sure. Until very recently, I'd been wondering if some other purpose had brought her back to East Anglia, and she'd looked in on Florence purely for old times' sake.

But when I said I'd come to find her, it had made her cry. She didn't cry easily; she saved it for monumental things such as hugging her lost dog while she knelt in a puddle. Such as discovering someone she'd been unable to forget had been unable to forget her, either.

There wasn't any more to say, just then. All the details of our six wilderness years, when we were apart and merely marking time, could wait. Now it only mattered that I'd found her again.

That, this time, I wasn't going to let her go.

The wind got up as the day advanced. Hugging her close to me as we walked, I could feel her shivering. I offered her my sweater, but she said it'd go neither over nor under her jacket, so instead we decided to abandon the beach and head for a drink. We trudged back to the path that led up to the pub, but, just before we turned away from the sea, we went to stand at the limit of the waves, staring out over the bleak, agitated water.

'No Vikings on the razz today,' I said. 'No high-prowed boats with menacing figureheads looming up over the horizon.' I don't know what put it into my head – the wide flat shore, I suppose, and the history of my own part of England too well embedded in my mind for this place not to be evocative.

It was an indication of our closeness that she was obviously on the same track. 'The crowns are doing the trick,' she remarked. Her tone was light but, glancing at her, I saw she was frowning. 'Perhaps the third one's somewhere out there.' She waved her arm in a wide semicircle.

'Perhaps. Though the others were found a long way from here.'

'Dunwich and Rendlesham.' She turned to look at me. It was revealing that we both had the same knowledge. Taught to us, I knew, by the same woman. For some reason it made me uneasy.

Beside me, Thea gave a more violent shiver. It seemed suddenly to be much colder.

'I don't know about you,' I said, pulling her away from the sea and up the beach, 'but I'm spitting feathers. *And* I'm hungry. And the car's parked right outside a very inviting pub.'

She huddled against me as we hurried away to the warmth and the promise of food and drink. She made some cheerful remark about people who'd eaten four-course breakfasts having no right to be hungry at half past twelve, and I thought she'd put that brief strange moment behind her.

But, as we reached the sheltering dunes which would cut off our view out to sea, she stopped. Looked over her shoulder.

I didn't know what she could see. I didn't want to know: her expression, for a split second, held a sort of horror.

Taking her hand firmly in mine so she couldn't pull away, I almost ran with her up to the dyke path and towards the safety there is in the company of ordinary people.

It was inevitable that sooner or later we'd talk of Florence. It would have been inevitable anyway, even without the very recent memory of standing on the beach with her presence so strongly with us.

But as we sat in the friendly pub, glasses of beer and plates of hot food before us and the hum of voices around us, at first we covered different matters. Where we'd been and what we'd been doing. Who with. I remembered my night thoughts – my jealous night thoughts – but somehow they no longer seemed so important. When she told me about Gordon Willis, how he'd asked her to marry him and she'd said no, I felt no envy, only pity. Poor man. To have spent so long with her, grown so close to her, only to lose her. And he still had her photograph on his desk.

She told me about an American called Scott, and here my philanthropic broadmindedness slipped a bit. She said, diplomatically, that with him she'd had 'a full relationship'. I didn't ask her to elaborate.

As if she sensed my unspoken thoughts, she said, 'What about you? Any engagements? Any live-in lovers?' She looked at me across the table, and it didn't take any great powers of telepathy to know exactly what she was thinking.

Repaying honesty with honesty – with her, I wanted no lurking secrets that might or might not subsequently emerge – I told her about Julia. The full relationship with good old Scott still rankling, I told her quite a lot about Julia. But she took it in with no visible dismay – I'd forgotten (perhaps I didn't know, then) that women tend to have a more realistic attitude to their lovers' past affairs than do men. Not so possessive, and so, less affected by what happened while they weren't on the scene. However, she did ask what happened in the end, and when I told her Julia got married, and was, as far as I knew, very happy, I kidded myself she looked relieved.

I told her briefly about the others, too. Just the highlights.

'What did you think of oriental women?' she asked. 'I've often wondered what a relationship would be like with someone of a totally different culture. I mean, it would seem to be so exotic, but I'm sure there's more to it than that.'

I didn't have much to say on the subject of relationships with oriental women. I could have given her a lurid description of Wanchai on a Saturday night, the topless bars heaving with lusty male bodies looking for adventure, the drunken servicemen finishing their evening's fun by being persuaded into a tattoo parlour for an embellishment they would certainly regret in the morning. I could have told her about the daughter of a Chinese friend of my parents, whom I escorted to a smart cocktail party up on the Peak, but, if I were to pursue faithfully my policy of honesty, that would have meant telling her how the evening had ended. I'd wanted to impress the girl, but I couldn't remember why, since, although she looked good – lovely, in a classical Chinese way, and dressed with such expensive good taste that she must have been walking around with several thousand dollars on her back – we had absolutely nothing in common and our conversation was consequently limited. I'd gone out of my way to be well-mannered, driving her right up the narrow road that led to her flat (a penthouse in a Mid-Levels block – her father, presumably, paid the rent) and then going round to open her door. It was dark, so it wasn't really my fault that I hadn't noticed the dead dog in the gutter. Trying to extract dead dog flesh from the stiletto heel of a Gucci evening sandal wasn't one of my better moments.

I just said, 'I never got close enough to an oriental woman to judge.'

Her lifted eyebrow suggested she didn't believe

me. So I told her about Suki and the dog after all.

We talked about her dad. I repeated to her his remark that the last communication he'd had from her was a postcard from Yosemite National Park. When I told her he'd said he had no idea where she was now, she looked contrite. Taking out her purse, she sorted out some small change and went straight away to telephone him.

'He sends you his regards,' she said when she came back. 'Said he was glad you'd found me, and even more glad you'd nudged me into giving him a call.'

'It was nothing,' I said modestly.

'That's what I told him. He said to ask you how the fishing went, and I told him you'd never fished in your life.'

'Oh.'

'He said he wasn't a bit surprised,' – I got the impression she was enjoying herself – 'because no fisherman on earth would say he was hoping to catch plaice in the Wye.'

'He caught me unawares,' I hedged. 'I was preoccupied with something else.'

The look she gave me told me she knew quite well what that was.

We'd covered our lovers. We'd talked about her dad. We'd finished eating, and we both had replenished glasses in front of us.

The only thing we hadn't done was talk about Florence.

She said, after the longest silence we'd had so far, 'What do we do when we go back this evening?'

'About Florence.' I hadn't needed to say it.

She nodded. She glanced quickly at me then, as if plunging in before she could change her mind, said urgently, 'She cocked it up, last time. Whatever you say, she *did* manipulate us.' (I hadn't been about to argue: six years had given me the leisure to repent.) 'She interfered to a ridiculous degree, and we let her!'

'*I* let her.'

She touched my hand. 'Yes, but I've come to see that you didn't have much choice.' She grinned at me. 'That's not what I want to thrash out, just now.'

I smiled back. 'Okay. Go on.'

'For some reason, she wanted us to get together. Later, when I was abroad with Gordon, he kept hinting that he was aware what she was doing, and I got the impression he thought there was danger for me. In whatever it was she was trying to achieve. And I used to have horrible dreams, about –' She shook her head suddenly, as if she were denying the memory. 'Don't think about it,' she muttered. Then, again addressing me, she said, 'I didn't know what the hell it was all about then, and I'm still in the dark now.'

'Me too. But you're right, she was determined we should pair off, so much so that she went beyond discretion. She's aware of that, you know – she said to me once she was sorry she'd driven you away.'

She looked surprised. 'Did she?' She frowned, then went on, 'Well, that doesn't necessarily mean she's learned from her mistake.' She turned slightly so that she was looking into my eyes, fixing her stare on me so that I couldn't look away. 'And I don't want to take the risk that she hasn't. Because then she might do the same thing again.'

Echoes of the old irritation came back. That she could still cast Florence as the big bad wolf annoyed me then, just as it had done before. I was about to say something to that effect, but then I saw again the magic interlude on the beach. And felt again her kiss.

Hadn't I learned *anything*? Nothing was more important than Thea.

'What do you suggest we do?' I said quietly.

Her eyes were still on mine, and I could see her relief.

'I suggest we play it down,' she said, so quickly that I guessed she'd already thought it out. 'If we go back this evening full of each other, telling her how wonderful it is to be together again, how we were so wrong to have parted, then the pressure and the manipulation will start all over again.'

'Would that matter?' It was out before I could hold the words in.

'Yes! I mean, not because she'd be pressing us into something we don't want,' – that was reassuring – 'but because if – when – we decide to do whatever we decide, it's got to be *us*! Because *we* want it! Not because Florence thinks it'd be a good idea!'

Her vehemence made her voice too loud in the quiet bar, and one or two people turned to look at us. But it didn't matter. She was right. She'd been right when we were eighteen, she was right now.

Perhaps it was time I let her take the lead.

I put my arm round her, lightly kissing the top of her head. 'So tell me, smart arse, how we go home to Florence and, quoting your own words, play it down.'

She'd thought about that, too. 'She's astute, your grandmother. Misleading her won't be easy – we'll have to do it by deed and not by word. But you could say you've decided to get back to London, and I'll say I think I'll stay on with her for a while, if she doesn't mind. We'll give the impression that we've had a pleasant day, and enjoyed catching up on each other's news, but that's all. Sort of, nice seeing you, must do it again some time.'

'Implying the attraction's gone.' I didn't like saying it, even though I knew it wasn't true.

'Yes.' She sounded as if she wasn't any keener.

'Then what?'

'I'll get out and about, say I'm catching up on old friends. Imply one day I'm off to Norwich, another, into Cambridge.'

'Do you know anyone in Cambridge or Norwich?'

'Yes! Well, vaguely. But that's not the point, the point is, I'll be off on the London train coming to see you!' She looked excited and happy. Then, suddenly, anxious. As if someone had just poured cold water on her clever idea. 'I mean, that is, you may be busy, and . . .'

'Thea, shut up.' I shut her up myself. Even she couldn't keep up the barrage with my lips on hers. 'Yes, I'll be terribly busy, and I won't have a moment for you, and even if I had, I'd lie to you and tell you I had a prior engagement.' I kissed her again, and it went on for longer that time. 'Because I don't fancy you at all, and I can't think of anything worse than having you come to visit me in my private, out-of-the-way London flat.'

We were sitting in a corner of the bar, which was just as well. Some of the other people in the pub had children with them.

'Your nice private flat,' she repeated, eventually breaking away. The excitement we were rousing in each other was getting too strong. She looked at me, amusement in her face. 'Which you've just lent to your friend Jon.'

'*Bugger!*'

She'd used up all her change, but I had some. Jon was very understanding – he didn't even question my feeble excuse that I'd forgotten I'd already promised my flat to someone else – and I felt quite guilty when he said he really hoped I'd have a good holiday.

The time it took to make the call gave me the chance to come back down to earth. If Thea and I were to return to Florence later and pretend we'd done no more than stroll about making polite conversation, it didn't seem too sensible to drive her off somewhere quiet and resume the kissing.

No matter how much I wanted to.

I stood over her at our table. 'My home is my own again,' I said lightly. 'Available as and when.' I didn't think I'd go on: following that train of thought didn't seem too sensible, either.

She got up. 'Shall we go?'

'Okay.'

As we went out to the car, I wondered what you did on a May afternoon in north Norfolk when a cold wind was howling and all you really wanted was to make love.

Twenty-seven

It had seemed the perfect solution, when I expounded it to Henry. 'We'll give the impression we've had a pleasant day. But that's all,' I'd said glibly. Ha! It was hardly a solution at all, when we got back to Willowford Fen.

Looking in the mirror behind the sun visor as we neared home, I was amazed at my bright pink face. I tried to tone it down with make-up, but the colour was still far too evident. We'd have to tell her we'd been for a long walk in the sun and the wind. Easy to believe, for a woman who'd lived all her life in East Anglia. Especially the bit about the wind.

I knew why I was flushed, of course. It had very little to do with the elements. Far more to do with Henry. 'We'd better stop this,' he'd said breathlessly in the car park of the pub: we'd just come up for air from a very long and passionate kiss. But the trouble was, neither of us wanted to stop.

We'd driven off round the coast to Wells, then inland to Walsingham. 'We'll go and look at the Shrine of Our Lady,' he said. 'I've never been there.'

I hadn't, either. It was not the sort of place that would have attracted Florence, so I wasn't at all surprised it had been omitted from our itineraries. But I wondered if he was taking us there now more with the intention of getting our feet back on the ground than broadening our education.

We were models of piety as we walked down the narrow village street to the Shrine. Just as well, since a service of some kind was going on inside, although there were a few other non-participants just there for a look around. We tiptoed round the Holy House, trying to move gently and not make all the candle flames flicker. There was the sound of chanting.

We separated to inspect different areas of the shrine. Even with my back to him, able neither to see nor hear him, I found I knew where he was. And when, after some time of solitary wandering, I sensed someone behind me, I said without turning, 'I've seen enough. Let's go,' and reached down for his hand.

Fortunately it *was* him. He whispered back, 'Okay.'

His grip on my hand tightened as we walked to the doors. As we went out, he put his arm round me. As soon as we reached the street, he kissed me.

So much for getting our feet on the ground.

'Do I look okay?'

He turned to give me a brief glance. 'Depends what you mean by okay. If you mean, do you look like someone who's full of zip because she's been kissing on and off most of the day, then, yes, you look fine. If you mean, do you look sober and sensible, like someone who's done nothing more exciting than change her library book, then no, you don't.'

'Damn. You'll have to keep her talking when we get in, and give me a chance to calm down.'

He smiled. 'I'll say you're going up to wash your hands and tidy your face. My mother always says that. When I was little I used to think of her pushing her eyebrows and her nose back into the right places. I hope you're not planning on taking as long about it as she does.'

'Ten minutes.' We were pulling into the drive.

'Make it five.'

'I'll try.'

Florence was in the garden, kneeling by a border. She waved a trowel at us, and got up to come and greet us. I waved back, then dashed inside.

When my face was tidy enough to have satisfied even Henry's mother – without ever having met her, I had a clear picture of her as someone who would approve of nothing but the best – I went back down-stairs to find them. They were still out in the garden, and I could hear them talking. He was telling her about our day.

'. . . should go there yourself,' he said. 'Wonder-ful stained glass. Thea bought a guide book, didn't you?' He turned to me as I went up to them. 'Before that we went walking on the shore near Hunstanton, and had lunch in a pub.'

He sounded almost disinterested. It really was as if he were describing just an ordinary day. Spent in ordinary – even slightly tedious – company.

For an instant I registered Florence's reaction. But then it was blotted out by my own: even though I knew what he was doing, and why he was doing it, it felt awful. And, worse, I knew I had to join in.

'I'm tired, I'm hungry and I'm thirsty, Florence,' I said, tucking my arm through hers and leading her off towards the house, so that we turned our backs on Henry. I glanced back at him, as if implying that my fatigue, my hunger and my thirst were partly his fault. 'And you look as if you've done enough gardening for one day – what about an enormous gin and a natter with our feet up before dinner? What *is* for dinner? Can I do anything?'

'A drink would be lovely,' she agreed. Also turning to him, she said, 'Come along, Henry. No, Thea, dinner is taken care of – it's in the slow oven, ready for us whenever we want to eat.'

She looked back again. A slight frown crossed her face.

I felt even worse.

She rallied as the evening went on. We had convinced her that the spark was gone, I was sure of that. Her initial reaction was surely straight from her heart – straight from her disappointed, desperate heart.

I think we would have convinced anyone, although, come to think of it, we could not have had a more difficult audience than Florence. But, knowing that, we knew we had to be good. We hardly looked at each other, we addressed most of our remarks to her, and once or twice he contradicted me quite sharply. By the time dinner was over, he was giving the impression that he'd had about enough of me for one day.

I gave as good as I got. In the middle of his description of his nice new London flat, I gave an audible yawn.

I went to bed first, leaving them in the drawing room.

It was one of the most horrible evenings I'd ever spent.

I heard a tap on my door. I was in bed, reading. Or trying to read – there was a pile of colour supplements on the bedside table, and I was flicking through them looking at the pictures.

I'd half expected he'd come.

I got up and put on my dressing gown. Hurrying to the door, I opened it.

Florence was standing on the landing. She said, 'May I talk to you?'

Until I found it wasn't him, I didn't appreciate how much I'd wanted it to be. I managed to mutter something, and stood back to let her in. She went to sit on the edge of the bed.

'Henry's going back to London in the morning,' she said. Her eyes were sad.

I wondered what she was expecting me to say. 'Really?'

'Didn't you know?'

'Oh, he said he might.' I couldn't look at her.

'He says he'll come back at the weekend,' she went on. 'You may . . . that is, I hope you will feel free to stay on. We could revisit some old haunts, and then you will still be . . . I mean, possibly you and Henry might enjoy each other's company when he returns.'

It was dreadful, hearing her sound so hesitant. Florence, hesitant! More than anything I wanted to go to her, throw my arms round her in the sort of hug I used to give her when I was little and something bad had happened, and tell her everything was all right. We're having you on! I could have said. It's all pretence, this disinterested act! We're potty about each other, and today has been the best day of my life!

I nearly did. I made the mistake of giving her a brief glance. To see someone you love – yes, I did love her – looking so down, to know that a word from you will take that look away, and to refrain from saying it, takes a lot of doing.

I refrained. For better or worse, I refrained. Because I remembered too well what had happened before.

'I'll say goodnight, then, my dear,' she said

eventually, getting to her feet. 'I hope you will sleep well.'

'Thank you.' I went to kiss her. 'See you in the morning.'

I couldn't sleep. I didn't even try. I sat on my bed in my dressing gown looking at the magazines, my mind too full to concentrate on even the lightest article. It was the first time I'd been alone all day, and the solitude wasn't welcome. Now that he was absent, he no longer took up my full attention – I had room for other thoughts.

Thoughts about danger. Gordon said there was danger, and my own dreams appeared to confirm it. Danger from a dark man glimpsed in the shadows, who, contrary to the laws of nature, seemed to be able to jump from the Dark Ages to the present and back again, haunting me in both this life and some past existence.

It was all so stupid! I'd managed to push it to the back of my mind after I'd left Gordon, so successfully that I hadn't been afraid to return to my home.

To return to Henry.

I refuse to be scared now, I told myself. What happened before was a result of my teenage hysteria. There *was* no Dark Man. Neither Florence nor Henry recalled inviting anyone of his description to Henry's party, I remembered, so he probably wasn't there at all. I'd imagined him, just like I'd imagined the meeting with him in the lane.

And the spectre who'd tapped on the camper window that time, sending me racing for Gordon and an escape flight to Turkey, had been some innocent tramp in a purloined coat that only looked like a wizard's cloak.

I couldn't accept that any of it was real. Because if I did – if I admitted to myself that, back at Willowford

Fen, the fears were only *too* real – it'd mean I'd have to think about whether I ought to go.

There was no point in considering that. No way was I going.

When there was another tap on my door – after midnight – there was only one other person it could be.

'I'm not staying,' he began as I threw myself into his arms.

I broke off from nuzzling into his neck to point out that he hadn't been invited to stay.

'Okay, okay!' He held my face and kissed me. 'I just came to say I'm leaving in the morning.'

'I know.'

'How do you know?'

I told him.

'I see. Well, I wanted to tell you why I'm going.' He broke off to kiss me again, and it went on for some time. 'I don't know about you,' – I thought he'd done well to remember his train of thought – 'but I found this evening excruciating. I almost convinced myself I'd imagined it all – you, I mean – and I felt awful.'

'So did I,' I reassured him. It seemed a good idea to back up the words with a bit of demonstration, and that took some time, too. 'I really hated it when you said I was quite wrong about Fumitory being the country name for rose-bay willow herb.'

'You were quite wrong. They're two different plants. And I hated it when you interrupted me in the middle of talking about my living room.'

'I didn't interrupt you, I yawned.'

'Quite.'

We stood with our arms around each other. His eyes on mine held me still. I knew, if I'd ever doubted it, that the evening had been the lie, not the day.

'I'm going.' He unwrapped himself and held me at arm's length, possibly in case I repeated my throwing-myself-at-him act and tempted him to stay. But he was right – this wasn't the place.

'Goodnight, then.' I turned away and got into bed, pulling the blankets right up to my chin.

He stood watching me. 'Do you always go to bed in your dressing gown?'

'Invariably.'

He crossed to the door, opening it quietly and peering out on to the dark and silent landing. 'Goodnight,' he whispered. 'See you soon.'

The door gently closed as I whispered back, 'Yes.'

I waited till he'd gone before presenting myself downstairs in the morning. It wasn't easy: I wanted very much to rush out and see him off. But I didn't think I could face a repetition of the previous evening. The pretence of not caring for him and, as bad if not worse, doing something that I knew was hurting Florence, were not things I was eager to do again.

I went down determined to make it up to her. In the bright sunshine my night fears had receded, and I was so happy – because of him, of course – that I'd have done anything to make her happy, too. Anything she suggested. Maybe I'd make a suggestion, I thought as I crossed the hall. Wouldn't she like that, if I said, why don't we go back to Walberswick, or Ely, wherever, because you took me there when I was little and I've never forgotten?

She was sitting in her usual place, cup of tea in front of her, jar of Oxford marmalade and toast rack beside her plate. She looked up as I came in, and last night's sorrow was no longer evident. It crossed my mind, briefly, to wonder if Henry had hinted at the truth. But then I was ashamed of the thought – he wouldn't have done that. He wouldn't have gone back on our agreement, no matter how sorry he felt for her. I knew he wouldn't.

I sat down and reached out for her hand. Her skin felt dry, and sort of thin. She's getting old, I thought. I said, speaking the words just as they came into my head without stopping to consider, 'Let's go to Grime's Graves today. You said last night we might look up some old haunts. Let's go there.'

I listened to the echo of my words. I didn't know why I'd suggested Grime's Graves. It hadn't been one of my favourite places. Still, it was done now, and to retract might have implied a lack of enthusiasm.

She was looking at me intently. She said – or I think she said, 'Are you sure you want to?'

I thought she meant, was I sure I wanted to go out, not was I sure about going to Grime's Graves. I said quickly, 'Yes! Yes, please.'

Then she looked relieved. And, smiling, replied, 'In that case I shall pack up a picnic.'

It was a great day for an outing. We went in my hire car, and it was strange for me to be driving her, instead of the other way round. I wondered if she still had the old Morris Minor – not that it mattered, since even if she had, I'd have opted for the Capri, which, I'd discovered, went like a bomb.

We got to Brandon in no time. The road on out to Grime's Graves was quiet – we only saw one other vehicle. And when we reached the site, ours was the only car in the car park.

Florence said as we stood in the silence, 'Listen. You can hear the earth breathing.'

I listened. The air was still, yet there seemed to be the faint sound of a breeze. Perhaps it was just the stirring of the trees of Thetford Forest, a dark and quiet guardian ring all around us.

But they were some distance away. Perhaps she was right, and it really was the earth breathing.

We walked all around the perimeter of the site. The coarse grass and the bracken were growing up green and sappy in the mild spring sunshine, and we kept to the tracks. The bumps and mounds of the old workings rose up in their hundreds, the infilled shafts looking like the surface of some alien planet hit by God knows what catastrophe.

Off guard, I let my mind wander. Back to an earlier age, when this place was humming with life. When neolithic people lived and died here, their short lives expended on the hard labour of digging deep holes in the chalk and prising out the flint with their antler picks. When their comforts, such as they were, consisted of an open fire in a simple hut which probably let in the cold and the damp.

When someone, some unknown ancestor, had made a chalk goddess and left her, all alone, deep in the earth.

I could see her. See that chalk figurine, as if an invisible hand were holding her up before my eyes. She was quite real; three-dimensional, the darker, golden colour in the deep folds of her body as clear to my eyes as my hand in front of me. The small face, with its stylized features, seemed to wear a knowing look. For a moment, I had the fancy she was communicating with me.

Yes. I saw her as if she were real.

And that was odd, since the only time I'd really seen her was in a small and blurred photograph in one of Florence's books.

Florence said, as I'd known she would, 'We will go down into the ground. Where we went before.'

I felt as if I were moving to someone else's instructions. I heard myself say, 'Okay,' and I was aware of my feet pacing in step with hers. Left, right, left. Along the track between the mounds, towards the little hut which concealed that open wound in the earth.

Someone gave me a hard hat, and I felt Florence's hand push it down on to my head. She said, 'You go first,' and I put my foot on the ladder.

Down. Down. The air smelt cold, slightly damp. The sunshine and the green grass were left behind. Nobody knew about sunshine and grass, down here in the earth.

I was at the bottom of the ladder. I stepped off, the soles of my feet feeling the bumps in the uneven surface. Here, a man had levered out the biggest, finest flint he'd ever found. Top quality, the reward for ignoring the inferior stone higher up and going for the best-grade floorstone.

There, on that shelf, they'd made an altar. A figure had stood there, the goddess of my vision, in front of her a pair of antler picks, the niche illuminated by the light from a chalk cup filled with fat in which a wick burned.

I could hear them all around me. There was a muttering, as if they were talking under their breath. It was reassuring to discover they were as awed by this place as I was. I could smell them: the air was heavy with sweat and the stink of recently cured leather. I could feel them: once or twice someone brushed against me.

But I couldn't see them.

I knew I was in a crowd. I wasn't afraid – whatever we were doing down there, it wasn't something that frightened us. I felt apprehensive, and excited, as if something good were going to happen which at the same time would be impressive in its power.

Earth power. Listen. You can hear the earth breathing.

It was very quiet. We waited.

There was a great crack, and a fissure opened up. I felt the rush of mass movement as we all sank to our knees, then bowed forwards so that our foreheads touched the ground. We were thankful, to the depths of our being, because the fissure was black and glossy. A seam of perfect flint.

The goddess had rewarded us. She had smiled on her children, and we would prosper for a little longer.

A chant was beginning, a hymn of praise. I didn't know the words, but still I joined in, my mouth and tongue forming syllables which had no meaning to me. Except I knew I was saying, thank you. Oh, thank you.

I was becoming tired. More than tired – exhausted. I curled up on the cold hard earth and closed my eyes. How wearisome it had all been, the digging, the breathless effort in the chilly ground, the tension, the excitement, the vigil in front of the altar, the fulfilment. How good it would be to go to sleep . . .

Someone was shaking my shoulder. A voice – a man's voice – said, 'She must have tripped. Good thing we came to check. I can't think how it could have happened, the ladder's designed for safety, and . . .'

'She is perfectly all right.' Florence's voice, slightly impatient. 'Help me get her in a sitting position – there! Thea! Thea!'

She was patting my wrist. I said, 'Hello, Florence.'

For a long moment we stared into each other's eyes. Hers held knowledge, deep, ancient knowledge. I was fascinated, wanting to go on, to know more, while at the same time afraid of what I might find.

Then the attendant said, 'You've got your colour back now, young lady! Feel up to climbing the ladder?' and the spell was broken.

As I put my foot on to the bottom rung, I looked over my shoulder into the corner where the fissure had opened up. It was no longer a promising black crack but a deep, wide gully. All the flint had been dug out, thousands of years ago.

With Florence ahead of me and the man behind me, we returned to the surface. He wouldn't stop talking, and I had to strain to hear them bid me farewell.

Twenty-eight

We didn't stay at Grime's Graves for our picnic, but drove off into Thetford Forest, making our way up a narrow track and finding a sheltered clearing where it was warm enough to spread the rug and eat out of doors.

I wasn't hungry, which was a shame as Florence had made us smoked salmon sandwiches. I managed one, then went on to coffee. Strong and hot – Florence was one of the only women I knew whose picnic coffee tasted as good as the freshly filtered variety.

She noticed, of course. I knew from the way she stopped offering me food that she understood. 'I'm sorry,' I said. 'It's ungrateful, when you've gone to so much trouble,' – there were home-made cheese straws and biscuits, a plastic bowl of salad and chocolate mousses in individual dishes – 'but I just don't feel like anything.'

She nodded in acknowledgement. What do we do now? I wondered. Florence wasn't exactly doing justice to the food either, so there wasn't a lot of point in staying. But, just as I was about to suggest we pack up and go, she reached out and put her hand on my arm. As if to detain me.

'You were privileged, you know.' She glanced at

me. 'Back there in the flint mine.' She paused, and I thought she'd finished. But then she went on, 'I took you there before. I gather you remember?' I nodded. 'Yes. I dare say you remember, too, that something happened? You felt their presence, even then. But perhaps you were too young, because I sensed you were afraid.'

'I was fourteen.' I remembered it, better than she could know. I'd been so scared I could hardly get up the wretched ladder.

'But this time was different.'

How could she be so sure? For a moment I was almost angry, that she should have *known* what had happened. Known beforehand, apparently, what was going to happen. She was manipulating me again.

Suddenly I'd had enough. I said, 'Why did you do it, Florence?' I paused. Then, for if I didn't ask now, maybe I never would, I added quietly, 'Why are you doing *all* of this?'

It couldn't have been an unexpected question. She'd been controlling my life on and off, to a greater or lesser degree, for the best part of twenty years. Surely she must have known I'd ask why, one day.

The day was now.

For a long while she didn't speak. Not that it worried me – I could almost hear her thinking. She'll answer, I thought, when she's good and ready.

And, in time, she did.

'I knew your mother,' she began. 'I'd known of her whole family, for years. The Madinglys were renowned in this area. I don't suppose you know why?'

'No.' It wasn't the most obviously logical of starting points, but no doubt she had her reasons. 'Why?'

'Because they had the longest unbroken run of boy children anyone had ever heard of. Generation after generation, all boys. The eldest would always be Joseph – it was a rigid family tradition. Handsome boys, short but compact and strong, most of them dark but the occasional fair or ginger one. Blue eyes, invariably.' She paused, looking at me. 'Like the Celts. And, before them, like the earliest inhabitants of this land.'

'How can you possibly know that?'

'It is common knowledge.' She dismissed my question with a wave of her hand. For a moment I wanted to challenge her again, but then, as if I'd just been given irrefutable proof, I knew she was right. In the blink of an eye I *saw* those spellbound people deep underground in the mine. And they were small, compact but strong, and dark. Eyes turning nervously up towards the light were blue as the summer sky.

'Then something unexpected happened.' She paused, watching me closely, as if she knew my mind had been elsewhere and was waiting for me to come back.

'My mother came along,' I said. I'm listening, Florence. I'm paying attention.

'Your mother came along,' she agreed. 'First-born child, of a mother not in the best of health and unlikely to conceive again. Hence they gave her the special name reserved for the eldest son. In its feminine form. Joseph became Josephine.'

It was so long since I'd seen my mother. Or heard from her, for that matter – Dad sometimes got a call, and once she sent him a long rambling letter. Josie, she was to us. I didn't think anyone had ever called her Josephine.

Except Florence. That long-ago day, when I'd first

met her, she said, 'You're Josephine Madingly's daughter.'

The thought went as abruptly as it had come.

'She was the only child,' I said. 'I've no uncles nor aunts.'

'I know.'

She was quiet for a very long time. But I knew there was more to come. Eventually, turning to me from whatever distant object she'd been contemplating while her thoughts receded into the past, she said, 'She was a wild one, your mother. Bright, but untameable. She got a grammar school place, but she wouldn't use her intelligence. It was a waste.'

I was angered by her judicial tone. What gave her the right to comment so disparagingly on my mum? Okay, so she'd been a bit of a rebel. Left school with a couple of dismal 'O' levels instead of the satchelful of qualifications she might have had. So what?

'I don't think –' I began.

But Florence cut across me. 'She went down to London, and I lost touch with her for many years. I tried to maintain contact – I wrote to her, but she moved about. Eventually my letters began to be returned to me marked, "Unknown at this address". By then, of course, it was really too late because Richard had already . . .'

She stopped. Cut herself off in mid-sentence as abruptly as a radio in a powercut. Then, smoothly, she continued, 'She met your father in London. I believe he came into the café where she was working and she took pity on him and bought him a meal.'

'Yes!' I smiled, because this was a well-told bit of family history. The poor starving student and the pretty coffee-bar waitress. How he'd fallen for her long glossy hair and her lively manner, how she'd sneaked an extra fried egg on to his plate and been ticked off by the manager. How she'd taken off her apron and chucked it at him, telling him he had no heart and could stuff his rotten job up his backside.

They'd married within three months, because my mum got pregnant.

'When she came home, she was a married woman,' Florence was saying. 'With a husband who had curtailed his studies in order to get a job. There was a baby on the way, and the pair of them were barely out of their teens.'

She made it sound desperate. But surely it hadn't been so awful? In that early time before Dad went, I could remember happy times as well as rows. And they'd had a roof over their heads – the cottage could have been a lovely home, if Mum hadn't been such a lousy housewife.

Something occurred to me. In childhood I had taken it for granted, but now I realized just how lovely the cottage was. Or must have been, before my mum was let loose on it. How on earth had two penurious nineteen-year-olds afforded it?

'If they were that poor,' I said, 'how did they . . .'

'It was mine.' She glanced at me, but I couldn't read her expression. 'I let it to them.'

She didn't have to add, at a peppercorn rent. I wondered how she'd arrived at a figure that would have been just high enough not to look like charity. Or would my parents have cared if it did?

'But –'

Again she interrupted me. 'They were a spirited couple,' she said. 'I liked them.'

Out of the blue I recalled Dad saying he and Mum had gone to dinner with her a few times. Telling me that when I was born she'd given them a beautiful antique crib, its headboard decorated with a carving of a wolf guarding her young. Because she'd taken a fancy to them? Because they were 'a spirited couple'?

Part of me was protesting, arguing that there had to be more to it, that well-off old ladies didn't start handing out largesse to inept young couples just because they were 'spirited'. After all, Florence had had her own family to consider – what would her own son, Henry's dad, have made of her giving away family heirlooms to strangers?

Perhaps she'd given up on Henry's dad and his wife having children. Henry had told me all about that. Perhaps she'd known she'd have no use for the crib and so had given it away to people who did.

Then I remembered that Henry was only a couple of months younger than me. When she gave my parents the crib, she'd have already known he was on the way.

I couldn't fathom it. So I asked her. 'You gave them a crib,' I said. 'My dad told me about it. Why did you do that?'

She said, smiling, very nearly laughing – she knew exactly what I was thinking, as her words proved – 'When in two months' time I should have a grandchild of my own to put in it?'

Then she laughed aloud. 'Henry was born in Singapore. He didn't return to England until he was eighteen months old. By then he was far too large to sleep in a crib.'

And suddenly it wasn't sinister after all.

I found I was laughing, too, the pair of us sitting there in the sunshine as if we hadn't a care in the world. I felt happy, even slightly high, although I'd had nothing to drink but coffee. And I felt a resurgence of my love for Florence, no longer able to recall what it was I'd been worrying about. It seemed so simple – she was kind, she'd been lonely, probably, without enough people of her own on whom to lavish affection. Her son went away, and in any case he'd married a woman Florence didn't get on with. In his absence, what was more natural than for her to find a substitute family? And, heaven knows, no family could have had more need of her than mine.

I couldn't clearly remember any of my real grandparents. My mum's mother had indeed been frail, as Florence had said, and she'd died before I was born. Mum had never got on with her father, and I could only remember a couple of occasions when I'd met him. He'd been a sort of presence in the corner, a big pale face with tiny boot-button eyes, and apparently I'd been scared of him and had nervously bitten into a silver teaspoon, leaving the indelible mark of my baby teeth as a souvenir of my visit. Dad's parents had lived all their lives in Gloucestershire, but by the time I went to live with Dad his father was dead and his mother was in an old people's home.

Florence, for all that she was not of my flesh and blood, was the only grandparent I'd ever known.

Some things, if we've accepted them all our lives, become almost beyond questioning. Earlier on in that sunny lunchtime session in Thetford Forest I'd asked her why. Why did she do what she'd done that morning, why had she been doing all of it? I wanted an answer, needed an answer.

And it was only later – much later – that I realized she hadn't given me one.

We finished our picnic, both of us finding our appetites and eating the lot. Afterwards I went to sleep, which was unexpected in view of the two further cups of coffee I'd drunk. I vaguely remember a dream – those small dark people again, and among them a fair woman in a robe who seemed to be teaching them, or perhaps rather interpreting for them something they had already observed but did not understand. When I woke up I tried to think what you called the person in a primitive society who went off to commune with the spirits and then told the rest of the tribe what they'd discovered. Witch doctor? No. Sorcerer? No.

'Come on!' Florence was packing up the plates and cups. 'You'll get cold if you lie there any longer – it's not so warm now that the sun has gone in.'

She was right – I was shivering. I also had a slight headache. 'How long was I asleep?'

She said very quickly, 'Not long.'

I was about to look at my watch but she thrust the picnic hamper into my arms. 'Put that in the car, please,' she ordered, 'and I will fold up the rug.'

Yawning, I did as she said. I kept the window open as we drove home, and gradually the dream and the headache faded.

She said when we got back, 'Go and have a hot bath. I think you did become chilled, when you fell asleep in the forest.'

I said something about helping her with dinner, but she brushed me aside. 'I can manage,' she said firmly. 'Besides, there's no hurry. Have a long soak, then come down and join me for a drink.'

'But –'

'And don't argue!'

It was nice to be looked after. I trailed upstairs and ran a deep bath, then lay in the heat and the steam for a good half hour. There was always plenty of hot water in Florence's house, and you never felt you were robbing someone else if you kept topping up.

I was about to get dressed in jeans and a shirt when I suddenly thought how much more comfortable I'd be in my dressing gown. It was long and loose, and I wore it a lot when I was on my own. I didn't think Florence would mind. She'd been encouraging me to relax, hadn't she?

I went down to join her in the drawing room, and she offered me a drink. I had a gin and tonic. We sat for a while, and I noticed she was holding a piece of flint, the rich black framed by cream limestone in a pleasing pattern of dark and light. Seeing my eyes on it, she handed it to me. For an instant I was back in the mine, but then the moment was gone.

I said idly, 'What did they do – the Grime's Graves people, I mean – when there was no more need for flint? Did they go away?'

'Oh, no.' She looked at me, grey eyes unreadable. She added something else, but it was half under her breath and I didn't quite catch it. I thought she said, 'They are still here.'

Then she was getting to her feet, picking up our glasses, and I let it go. She suggested we might as well get on with dinner, then I could have an early night.

I suppressed a yawn. 'Thanks, I'd like that. Sorry, I seem to be worn out!'

'That's what comes of a long day in the fresh air,' she observed. 'Come along.' She tucked my arm through hers and we went through into the dining room. I'd wondered if she'd have set the table in the kitchen, there just being the two of us, but perhaps she considered that to be slovenly.

I sat down, and she went out to fetch the food. We had a roast, and as usual a lot of fresh vegetables.

For dessert she'd made a lemon pudding, light and golden, with a wonderfully sharp tang of citrus.

'This is lovely,' I said, passing up my plate in response to her offer of seconds. 'So – sharp!'

'I put grated peel in as well as juice,' she said smoothly. 'Not too bitter for you?'

'No. Just right.'

When we had finished and cleared away, she suggested coffee, but I asked if I could have cocoa instead. We took our drinks back into the drawing room, and I made myself comfortable on the sofa.

It was incredibly bad-mannered of me, but I felt myself falling asleep. I wanted to say, Sorry!, or drag myself off to bed, but all the power seemed to have left my limbs. I looked at her, feeling my eyelids droop, but she didn't look as if it was bothering her. In fact she was smiling down on me with love in her face.

'It's all right,' she said, smoothing the hair from my forehead with her hand. 'Rest. Put your head back. I shall be here.'

She sat down at the end of the sofa, taking my hand in hers.

'Rest,' she said again.

My mind was wandering. I wasn't asleep – or I didn't think I was – yet already I seemed to be dreaming. That robed figure again, talking urgently to the small dark people. From nowhere I remembered that the word I'd been trying to think of earlier was shaman. Then everyone seemed to be hurrying, away from the mines and off into the forest. Travelling fast, children and possessions bundled up and carried in weary arms, exhausted old folk making valiant efforts to keep up.

Safety. The walls of a dwelling around me, and a fire warming my toes. Babies crying, being soothed. Laughter.

Then a new threat. Legions of marching men, banners of imperial purple. Cruelty and oppression, and an uprising under the fierce fair woman who led her tribe to destruction and near-annihilation.

I had been here before.

I cried out, curling up and covering my head with my arms.

A voice – Florence's voice – said, 'Do not be afraid. You are safe here.'

We were in the Fens. Somewhere very familiar, but I couldn't place it. Mist was rising from the still black water, and figures were hiding in the reeds. All was silent. Yes, we were safe here, for nobody but us knew the secret ways. Nobody but us came here, and for us there was nowhere else to go.

Men came from out of the east, over the seas. We were afraid, once more threatened, for we had ventured from our hidden backwaters and were again risking the world. We cannot survive in opposition, we had been told, the only way is assimilation. A stern voice ordering, 'She shall marry him!'

An old man, stinking, cords in his neck standing out as he strained for the release he was determined to have. It was my duty, I knew. I had to obey, had to endure the endless time while he rocked and heaved on me.

Devout and dutiful wife, that was what they called me. Little did they know! And when *he* came to live at court, he was the answer to all that I had prayed for. Devotion? Duty? Ha! What were they against the ferocity of my love for him?

One night. One night, to live on for ever.

Then a cold cell, where I was kept in chains. Banished, forgotten by the world, cared for – if you could call it care – by an old woman who only stayed because she knew her hands would be cut off if she deserted me before my time.

I had given him up for dead. Were he still on the earth, somehow he would have found me.

He did. One joyful day, he did. And then all was confusion, for the baby came and was taken, and he ran off into the Fens in pursuit.

Faintly came that sibilant whisper: 'I curse thee.'

I fell into blackness.

And he had gone.

I was warm. And the pain had stopped – thank God. I shot up – where was he? Was there a chance I could follow him? But I would have to remove the chain from my wrist . . .

The sofa was soft beneath me. There was no chain – around my wrist was Florence's hand, holding me in a gentle grip.

I sank back against the cushions. My head was reeling, and I thought I was going to be sick.

'Lie still,' Florence said quietly. 'I will fetch you a glass of water.'

I closed my eyes. I was aware of her getting up, moving away. I heard her go into the kitchen and run water into a glass. Everyday sounds, dragging me back to *here* and anchoring me down.

It had been a dream. Just a dream, like those I used to have before. But I mustn't start having them again! I thought wildly, because if I do, it'll mean there really is . . .

Don't think about that.

I opened my eyes again, since the room was begining to spin. She came back and gave me the water, arm behind my shoulders supporting me as I drank.

He was gone. Henry was gone, too.

Would he come back?

Of course!

I wanted to cry, but I didn't know why. I wanted to sleep, too, but I was afraid.

'I will help you to bed,' Florence said. 'You need to sleep.'

'Will I dream again?' Even in my own ears my voice sounded wimpish, but it seemed to be beyond me to put any iron in it.

She hugged me as we went up the stairs. 'No, you will not,' she said kindly. 'No more dreaming, tonight.'

She turned back the bedclothes and helped me into bed, tucking my long robe round my legs. Then she covered me up and bent to kiss my forehead.

She stood looking down at me. 'Sleep well, Thea.'

I watched her walk out and close the door. Then my eyes drooped shut.

Twenty-nine

I woke with the knowledge that something was wrong.

I hadn't dreamed again – Florence's comforting prediction had been right – but still I was uneasy. The one dream had been enough, for God's sake, reviving all the fear and the mystery of those nights I'd screamed in my sleep in whatever altered state I'd got into, and Gordon had brought me back, made some sort of sense of it.

Only he hadn't. Perhaps there was no sense to make.

I was right back at the heart of all that had terrified me. And, because of Henry, I couldn't run away. Not this time.

I lay still, scarcely breathing. Moving just my eyes, I looked across at the bedside table: the clock said 9:50.

Was that what was wrong? I'd merely overslept?
No.

The house was totally silent. It was always quiet – Florence moved gracefully and with an admirable economy of movement – but now there were not even the faint sounds which nobody can help but make as they go about their day's work. No distant strain of classical music from the kitchen radio. No gurgle of water in the pipes. No soft noise of someone gently closing a door.

Where was she?

I leapt up, pulling on my dressing gown, and ran downstairs. The kitchen was just as we'd left it after supper, and the kettle on the worktop was cold.

She wasn't in the drawing room or the dining room.

Outside? I hurried to look at both front and back doors. The bolts were still drawn across – unless she'd climbed out of a window, she was somewhere in the house.

Frightened, with a sick chill in my stomach, I went back upstairs, and along the landing to Florence's room. I knocked on the door and called, 'Florence? Are you all right?'

What stupid things we say. Of *course* she wasn't all right, or she'd be where she usually was at ten in the morning, in the kitchen with the majority of her chores done, sitting down with a cup of coffee.

I waited for her to answer. When she didn't, I opened the door and went in.

I'd never been into Florence's bedroom before. I'd peeped in from the landing – when I was little I'd been overawed by the dark wood furniture, which all seemed far too large, as if it had been made for giants – but I hadn't dared go in. I crossed the room in the dim light – the curtains were drawn across all but the middle panel of the window, and outside the day was dull – and went to stand by the bed.

She was lying on her back, propped up by several pillows. Her thick hair was sticking up at the back. She looked different, without her usual neatly-brushed bob.

Her eyes were closed.

For an unspeakable moment I thought she wasn't breathing. Then I saw that the white pin-tucked cotton nightdress was moving up and down. I found myself whispering, 'Thank you, thank you,' a tiny prayer of desperate gratitude addressed to I didn't know whom, then I was leaning over her, touching the hand that lay outside the bedclothes, saying her name over and over again.

She opened her eyes. A faint smile quirked her mouth, then her eyelids dropped again. She said on a quiet breath, 'Thea.'

'What is it? Oh, Florence, what's wrong?' I was feeling her forehead to see if she had a temperature, trying to find a pulse in her thin wrist, frantically wondering how near the doctor was and how soon he could come. Oh, God, he'd be in the middle of morning surgery, bound to be, he'd . . .

'I am rather tired,' Florence said. 'And my feet are cold. Would you fetch me a hot water bottle please?'

Tired. Cold extremities. In all the melodramas I'd seen, those were the symptoms people complained of when they were dying. Oh, no!

'Florence, I must call the doctor!'

'Don't.'

There was such sudden strength in her voice that I was reassured – no-one with those dictatorial tones at their disposal could be dying! Could they?

'A hot water bottle, Thea,' she repeated. Her eyes were open and she was staring at me. 'If you would be so kind.'

I raced into the bathroom and grabbed a fleecy-covered hot water bottle from the hook behind the door, running the water in the basin till it scalded my hands and then filling the bottle. Hardly pausing to

413

wipe the outside, I stuffed it into its jacket and ran back to her.

I wondered if she wanted me to put it in her bed. It seemed a disrespectful thing to do – I was quite sure she'd rather do it herself.

She reached out her hand and took it from me.

'What is it?' I wailed. 'Are you ill? What shall I do?'

Her eyes were once more closed. 'I do not feel quite myself,' she said. I stared closely at her – she looked awfully pale and there were dark rings round her eyes.

'Can I get you anything? Tea? Something to eat? Oh, won't you let me call the doctor?'

'No. And there is nothing I want, thank you.'

I thought that was the end of it. Thought we'd go on like that, she lying with her eyes shut, I bending over her in growing anxiety, till the last trump sounded. But then she added, 'You might call Henry, however.'

Henry? She wanted me to call Henry?

I said stupidly, 'What for?'

She flashed an irritated glance at me, as well she might. She said somewhat icily, 'I should like him to come home.'

Oh, no. She wouldn't send for him, surely, unless she feared the worst? What did she mean?

'Florence, please, won't you . . .'

'Thea, will you do as I ask or shall I go and do it myself?'

'No! You stay there!' I couldn't have her crawling down to the phone. 'I'll be right back, I promise!'

I took the stairs three at a time and landed in the hall with a crash. Phone, phone – there it was, on the hall stand where it always was. I'd pretended to call a boyfriend from that very phone, years ago. Steve, that was it. Great kisser.

Stop it!

Henry. Call Henry.

I didn't know his number. In the careful planning of our subterfuge – for which we were now being punished by Florence falling horrendously ill? – he'd forgotten to give me his address and his phone number, and I'd forgotten to ask. I suppose I'd assumed he'd call me.

Where would it be? In an address book? Note pad?

When I calmed down and stopped acting like a headless chicken, I saw there was a large piece of white card in a slot behind the telephone. It listed the numbers of her bank, stockbroker, solicitor, wine merchant, dentist. And all the other numbers she used regularly. My father's number was there, which surprised me. And there at the bottom was Henry's. I knew it must be the current one – it had been inked in above another which was crossed through.

I picked up the receiver and dialled.

Until he answered, I hadn't realized that I'd no idea what I was going to say. So I just blurted out, 'It's Thea. You've got to come home, Florence is ill.'

He said, the shock audible in his voice, 'What's the matter with her? It's not serious, is it?'

'I don't know, she won't say!' To my shame I found I was sobbing. 'But she wouldn't want you to come back unless it was. Would she?'

'I don't know. I'll set out straight away.' I sniffed, and he said with stunning perspicacity, 'You're crying!'

'No, I'm not.'

'It'll be all right, Thea. Really – she's strong as a horse. You know that as well as I do!' His attempt to brace me had a tinge of desperation.

'But no-one lasts for ever!'

'Yes they do, heaps of people do.'

I giggled. 'That's better,' he said, 'now go and tell her I'm on my way, then make yourself a strong cup of coffee and have a cigarette.'

'I don't smoke.'

'No, I know. I was just being silly.'

'Thank you.'

'You're welcome. All right?'

I knew what he meant. 'Yes, all right now.'

'See you soon, my darling.'

I put the phone back. It was the first time he'd ever called me darling.

It seemed to put her mind at rest when I told her he was setting out at once. She relaxed into her pillows, and I saw her smile briefly. She still said she didn't want anything, but thought she might sleep for a little while.

I took the hint and left her alone. I went into the kitchen and made myself a coffee, then wondered what on earth I could do to fill in the time of waiting for him that stretched ahead.

It was nearly midday. I'd made soup out of the remains of yesterday's chicken – wasn't chicken soup the sovereign fare for invalids? – and got a loaf out of the freezer. Then I'd spent some time in the garden picking flowers, but when I'd arranged them in a pretty vase to put in her room, I decided after all that she might be asleep and I shouldn't risk waking her.

He'll be here soon, I thought. I went outside and stared up the drive to the road. Soon.

As I turned to go back into the kitchen I heard the car. He came slowly in through the gate and parked by the front door, and I ran round to meet him. He had an overnight bag in his hand which he dropped

416

as I raced up to him – he dropped it on my toe, in fact – then I was in his arms.

He didn't say anything, and I didn't either. I just stood in his embrace, drawing vitality from him, telling him without words that it had been awful but it was okay – better, anyway – now that he was here.

I don't know if he heard. Probably.

In time he said, 'How is she?'

'Sleeping. Or I think so. I left her alone – that seemed to be what she wanted.'

'Let's go and see.'

We went inside together, and up the stairs hand in hand. I'd forgotten all about our pretence of disinterest, but he hadn't – as we got to her door and he knocked softly, he let go of me so that, in answer to her, 'Come in!', we entered the room apart.

'Florence,' he said. Just that.

She held out her arms to him, and he went to sit on the edge of her bed, taking her hands in his. 'It is good of you to have come so quickly,' she said. Her voice was stronger than it had been earlier – I began to think she might be feeling better.

'What else would I do?' He bent over to kiss her cheek. I could see her face, and in that unguarded moment I saw how much she loved him. 'What's the matter?'

'I don't really know.' She frowned. He began to say something, but she wouldn't let him. 'And don't you go ordering me to call the doctor – I've already told Thea, I don't want to see any doctor.'

'But . . .'

'I have no faith in doctors,' she said grandly. 'When death comes for me, it comes.' I gasped – I couldn't help it – which made her smile. 'It's all right, Thea, it hasn't come yet.' She stretched out her legs and then raised herself to a sitting position. 'In fact, I believe I may owe you both an apology, because I am feeling perfectly all right. And if that is chicken soup I smell, Thea, would you kindly bring me a bowl?'

I realized I'd been standing with my mouth open, and closed it. For a moment I just stared at her, not quite believing, but she was still smiling, more whole-heartedly now, and at last she looked like herself.

I went across and elbowed Henry out of the way so that I could hug her. 'I'll bring you all the soup you can eat,' I said. 'But don't you dare do this to me again!'

Then, because once more I could feel the ridiculous tears threatening, I hurried away and left them.

'What do you think it was?' he asked later when, with Florence resting after a lunch that was, by sickroom standards, indecently large, we were sitting down in the kitchen to our own meal.

'No idea,' I said through a mouthful of soup and warm bread. 'She's old. I suppose old people get funny turns sometimes.'

'I wish she'd let us send for the doctor.'

'So do I. But she won't. Even if we got him here she'd refuse to see him. Wouldn't she?'

'Yes, I expect so. Perhaps she'd throw her soup at him.'

'She's eaten it all. I could make her a blancmange, or a dish of junket. She could throw that.'

'What *is* junket?'

'I don't know, I've only come across it in books.'

He had finished his soup, and now was holding my hand so that I could no longer eat mine. 'What?' I asked.

'I want to say something.'

'Then say it.' I reclaimed my spoon hand.

'It's difficult, when you're stuffing your face.'

'Well, let me finish, then I'm all yours.'

He must have been thinking about that while I cleared my plate, then stood up and put all the dirty things in the sink. When I came back to hear whatever it was, he'd apparently moved on. He didn't say anything, just put his arms round me and started to kiss me.

Later we crept up to look in on Florence, who, contrary to our expectations – to mine, anyway – wasn't lying prostrate and pale but was sitting up reading a copy of *Country Life* and, in her usual way, snorting at the house prices. We said we thought we'd go for a walk, if she didn't mind, and she virtually shooed us out of her bedroom.

We went along the path by the dyke, through the gate and along the lane to the cottage where I used to live. It was much smarter than it had been in our day, and someone had lavished love and attention on the garden.

'Does it still belong to Florence?' I asked him.

'To Florence? It never did, did it?'

I told him what she'd revealed the previous day, adding my own surmise about the peppercorn rent.

'Good Lord,' he said. 'Wonder why she did that? She's always struck me as too astute a businesswoman to make less than a decent profit out of a capital asset. Still . . .' He looked down at me.

'Still what?'

He shook his head, smiling. 'Nothing.' Before I could press him, he said, pointing at the front door with its smart yellow paint and twin bay trees in tubs, 'That was where I saw you for the first time. When I came to get poor old Eric,' he added, as if I might need reminding. How, I thought, could I possibly forget? 'You only opened the door a crack. You were so miserable that I didn't want to hang around.' He hugged me. 'Selfish little bugger, wasn't I?'

He'd brought it all back, so vividly that I felt a stab of the despair I'd felt on that dreadful day. 'I hated you,' I said, 'because you took him away.' As if a play were being acted out again in my mind, I saw a later scene, in the stable where the young Henry was grooming his pony. 'But then you gave him back, and I didn't hate you any more.'

We were standing facing each other, his hands resting on my shoulders. He was frowning, as if he, too, were trying to bring the past into focus. 'I think . . . oh, I don't know!' He smiled ruefully.

'What?'

'I can't explain. It's just that I feel sometimes that we . . . that you and I . . .' He paused, clearly hunting for the right words. 'It was so traumatic, that business with Eric. It certainly was for me, and it must have been for you, too, just as much if not more.'

'I ended up with him, don't forget.' If he was going to beat his breast, it seemed only fair to point that out.

'Yes, I know.' He put his arm round my waist, guiding me back towards the footpath and our way home. 'But your need was greater.'

'Did you miss him an awful lot?'

He laughed briefly. 'I wish I could say, yes, like hell. But if I'm honest, I don't think I did. If I'm even more honest, I have to admit I got a kick out of having given him to you.' He glanced at me, and from his expression I gathered he thought I might think poorly of him for his admission.

'I'm not surprised,' I said stoutly. 'You were only a kid, you had to get *something* out of giving your dog away. I –'

For an instant the bright day wavered behind a sudden mist, and again I watched Eric die. The dark shape was there, growing, reaching out . . . *No!* I screamed inside my head. *Not now!* I screwed up my eyes, turning my full concentration on to shutting out the terrible sights. And sounds.

It worked. The sunshine was restored, and Henry was still beside me, waiting for me to go on.

'What were you going to say?' My voice sounded quite normal. 'About it being traumatic.'

'Oh.' He didn't sound too eager. 'I thought I'd distracted you from that. I wish I hadn't started on it.'

'Well, you did. So what were you trying so inarticulately to say?'

We'd reached the gate under the willow tree. To my surprise, he grabbed me round the waist and sat me up on the top bar.

'You sat there, just like that, when I took him away from you,' he said quietly. 'The sun was shining on your fair hair, and you looked so small.' Abruptly he stopped. He turned away, his hands in his pockets, and after a moment went on, 'I carried that picture for years. Still do, now. That's what I'm trying to say.' He paused again, but I didn't interrupt. Couldn't, when it seemed to be so important to him – and so difficult – to get out what he wanted to tell me. 'They say we remember best the things that impress us most deeply. The things that make us very happy, or very sad, or that move us a lot. Well, I think that's what happened with us.'

I thought he'd finished. *I* was moved, incredibly, by what he'd said. He was right, I was quite sure, but I didn't dare say so because the words would have come out wobbly. I, too, could remember it all. Every detail. And, further, I remembered how ashamed I'd felt of hating him when he turned out not to be hateful at all.

'I . . .' I began.

But he stopped me. I'd been wrong; he hadn't finished. He turned to face me again, coming to stand in front of me, arms going round my waist and face lifting to mine.

'You got under my skin then, when we were nine, and there you've stayed,' he said. 'I didn't think about it, you were just there.'

It sounded nice. It also sounded exactly how I felt about him.

'It's . . .' I started to say.

Again he interrupted. 'God, I wish you'd shut up for a minute!' His eyes were on mine, shining, happy. 'I'm trying to tell you that I love you.'

Then it was so easy. It always is, isn't it, when you at last put the puzzle together? I wanted to go on looking at him, but, even more, I wanted to touch him. I leant my cheek against his, no longer caring that the tears on my face were even more a dead give-away than a wobbly voice would have been.

I'd run away from him, been all over the place, lived with – loved? – two other men. I'd had fun, achieved a lot. Made money, enjoyed a variety of interesting jobs. Yet nothing had worked. Without him, it had all been just marking time.

Why hadn't I realized? Perhaps I had, for I'd come home. With a bit of maturity, I'd stopped running away and turned to face – and accept – what had been there all along.

Against the warm skin of his face, my fingers twisting in his hair so that I held him there and he couldn't move away, I whispered, 'I love you, too.'

Thirty

I often wondered if it had been her decision or mine to set off on that particular walk. I don't remember having suggested it, but on the other hand, I don't recall that she did, either. If I'd ever asked her, she'd probably have said we both decided it instinctively. She always was a great one for acting instinctively: some of her instincts were quite acceptable.

I hadn't expected the power of the past to affect me as much as it did. To begin with it had merely been interesting to go and look at the old cottage again. To notice how much better it looked with proper care, and to stand there with her admiring the wallflowers.

I suppose it looked so different that, at first, the memories hadn't been triggered. But then I noticed the doorknocker: a little brass figure, with wings. I went back sixteen years without even noticing it, and once again I could feel that brass figure in my hand.

That did it. Before I could impose any control I was seeing it all. Thea at the door, her face strained and hostile. Eric, so reluctant to leave her. My disappointment, turning to anger as I dragged him away and stormed off homewards along the dyke.

And I could see her, sitting on that bloody gate.

Then I did a bit of acting instinctively, too. Not at all the sort of thing I normally did, to lift women on to gates and tell them I loved them.

But I never regretted it.

When we got back, Florence was in the kitchen stirring something in a saucepan – there was the sharp tang of lemons in the air. She was dressed in her usual tweeds and cardigan, and her colour had returned. Standing there over the stove, one hand on hip in her usual cooking pose, it was difficult to reconcile her with the pale bed-bound figure of this morning.

Thea rushed over to her, and, touching her hand as if she couldn't quite believe she was real, asked anxiously how she was feeling. 'Should you be up?' she added. 'I could quite easily do supper and bring you something in your room, there's no need for you to . . .'

'Half a day in bed is more than enough,' Florence said firmly. 'I am perfectly all right!' She clearly thought she'd been too abrupt – she had, Thea was looking quite hurt – and went on more gently, 'I appreciate your concern, my dear. I am sorry if I worried you this morning, and thank you for looking after me.'

She turned back to her saucepan with an air of finality – the subject was obviously closed.

I had the clear impression that she would rather forget the whole thing. She seemed slightly ashamed, which wasn't like her at all. Was it merely that she resented this reminder that she was human, like the rest of us, and as she grew older must expect the odd frailty to develop?

I didn't know. And I had more pressing things to think about. Resisting the temptation to make some

424

consoling remark to Thea, who still seemed upset, instead I said jovially to Florence, 'What are you making? It smells delicious.'

'There is some of yesterday's lemon pudding for tonight,' she replied, stirring steadily. 'I'm making some fresh sauce. And I've put a casserole in the oven.'

I hadn't got as far as thinking what Thea and I might do that evening. Just as well, since the decision had been taken for us: we were staying in and eating with the newly-recovered invalid. The momentary irritation I felt – inspired by disappointment – went as soon as it had come. It wouldn't have been on, in any case, for us to do anything else.

I decided to have a bath before dinner. It should have been a cold shower, but I chickened out. The heat and the steam were relaxing, and I spent a long time in sensuous daydreams. The prospect of the sterile evening ahead, during which I should have to pretend that she was no more to me than an old friend, wasn't attractive. I was beginning to wonder if it was even possible, when the very thought of her was having such an effect.

I finished off with the cold shower, but it didn't do much other than make me feel bits of me were about to drop off.

When I went down, they were in the drawing room. Thea had a gin, Florence a sherry. There was a dish of home-made savoury biscuits on the table. I poured myself a gin and took a handful of biscuits; they tasted strongly of cheese, and had a slightly herby smell.

'Dinner will be ready in half an hour,' Florence said. 'Now come and tell us how you are settling in London. I imagine the life is very different from that which you lived in Hong Kong.'

I talked for a while about the flat, and remarked that it was convenient to have an office close to the West End. Florence made a comment about the traffic.

Thea, I noticed, didn't say anything. She had finished her gin and poured herself another one, and was sitting back on the sofa nibbling biscuits. She looked slightly dazed. She clearly didn't find my conversation very riveting.

She was quiet during the meal, too. Not as quiet as before – she contributed to our discussion about the changes in Willowford Fen over the years since she and I had lived there.

Over coffee, I took advantage of Florence's momentary absence (she'd gone to fetch more milk) and asked her if she was all right. She turned to me, and her expression was vague.

'I'm fine,' she said. 'A bit tired.'

'It's a strain, isn't it?' I said quietly.

She looked uncomprehending. 'What?'

'Keeping up the act. The old pals act.'

Slowly she nodded. 'Yes. Oh, yes.'

Florence pushed open the door, and in the shaft of brighter light shining in from the hall, I could clearly see Thea's eyes.

The pupils were so widely distended that the irises were little more than blue rims.

I found it difficult to concentrate on what Florence was saying. I found it almost impossible not to grab hold of Thea and ask her what was wrong. Was she really just tired? God knows, she had reason to be, the worry about Florence must have been awful, and she'd coped with it on her own till I got there. Probably she needed a good night's sleep.

I poured myself some more coffee. I was feeling slightly drunk – Florence had opened a bottle of wine, and I'd had most of it – and now wasn't the time to go letting my guard slip. Draining the cup, I refilled it again. It mightn't sober me up, but at least it'd keep me alert.

'Let's go through into the drawing room,' Florence said, getting up. 'I've lit the fire.'

Thea made a half-hearted attempt to start clearing the table, but Florence stopped her. Possibly she feared for her china – Thea was being unusually clumsy.

We went and sat by the fire, Thea and I on the sofa, Florence opposite us in her armchair. It was warm and cosy, with the curtains drawn and only a well-shaded table lamp giving soft light. There was a nice smell – Florence must have found some apple wood. No, it wasn't apple – what was it? I frowned, trying to bring the memory into focus, but I couldn't.

A cup of coffee stood on the table beside the sofa. Had I brought it in with me? I couldn't remember. I drank it – I was feeling sleepy now, and it wouldn't do to nod off in Florence's drawing room.

It was very quiet. I could hear rain on the window, quite heavy rain. Sometimes a drop blew down the chimney, landing on the red-hot logs with a sizzle, followed by a plume of steam. The smell was stronger now – it was very pleasant, sort of spicy, and I knew I'd smelt it before, if I could only remember . . .

The fire was burning more strongly. It seemed to be bigger, a roaring conflagration set in a pit in the middle of the room. No, not a room, a hall, a huge hall, the lofty ceiling invisible up there beyond the smoke, the rafters blackened by long years of fires such as this one.

I knew what the smell was. It wasn't apple,

although there were apple trees then – the Romans brought them. It wasn't wood at all, it was the special resin they put on the fire when the harp music played and the bard told his tales, its aroma blending with the smoky air we breathed until the word-pictures painted by that hypnotic voice became visions.

The light was dim, for the magic happened only when the shadows were allowed to creep in from the corners of the great hall. Sometimes a leaping flame would catch an answering glint of fire from the gold shields and swords on the walls, and men would look up, fearful, and remember the dangers. Then we would huddle closer to the hearth, for here inside was the only safety – out there in the vast silent forests, wolves howled. We could hear them. What other nameless horrors lurked deeper in the lost darkness? Dragons? Trolls? Terrible Frost Giants from the Yawning Void? Better not to ask, better just to give thanks to the gods that my father had acknowledged me and permitted his bastard son to live here in the safety of his hall.

The alternative was unthinkable.

I knew: I had lived out there. They treated me with awe, for they believed I could only have survived had I been under supernatural protection. They thought I was brave. They called me Wolfspear, the man who hunted with the wolves. They hadn't seen me crouching in a thorn thicket, howling my terror as loudly as the wolves howled to the moon.

But that was behind me. I had petitioned my father, and he had taken me in. He needed me – that was why I came back. Kings have need of sons, even illegitimate ones, when warlike and dangerous times rob them of too many of their heirs. Even though he was now dead and another king ruled, his newly-wrought crown glistening in the firelight, I was not turned away.

The bards sang, and for a time we saw only good visions. We thrived. And I was content.

Then she came.

Until my cousin brought his young wife to the king's court, I believed that nothing on earth could have made me go back to the perils of the wilderness. Once I had seen Althicca, once I had begun to suffer the agony of my feelings for her, I was no longer sure.

My cousin Egenhere was an old man, the son of my father's eldest brother who had departed to his long rest years since. He was mean-spirited and quick-tempered: once I saw him beat his horse until its flanks dripped blood for the minor crime of brushing him against a thorn bush. He was selfish and cruel, but, although he was universally hated by those who had the misfortune to be subservient to him, no-one ever dared stand up to him. For one thing, he would inherit the throne if my half-brother, the new king, died without issue. For another, he had a strange air of power about him which did not seem to come from within himself: rather it was as if it were cast round him by some outside force. Whether this force was divine or diabolical, no-one liked to question. Perhaps, as I'd heard whispered, he had indeed sold his soul to the Dark.

I do not know what sort of a life Althicca led. It was common knowledge that the purpose of Egenhere's late marriage was to beget a son, so I could imagine what her nights were like. She was so beautiful – so pure, so innocent, so *clean* – that the thought of that filthy old man drooling and slobbering over her made me retch.

Even before I knew I was in love with her.

I wanted her from the moment I set eyes on her, and I'm sure I wasn't the only man who felt that way. But she was demure, and gave no sign that she even knew I existed. Devout, they said she was, a devout and dutiful wife. I knew what they meant by dutiful – her duty was to give Egenhere a son. I didn't – couldn't – think about that. And devout? She was a religious woman, yes, praying to the gods of her own people, those totems and heads and strange figures we couldn't begin to understand. It was quite common for my countrymen to scoff, to mock the Britons for their ancient beliefs. But who were we to say we were right and they were wrong? Althicca's people had lived in this secretive, desolate place for centuries without count, and they had survived. They had withstood greater dangers than we had ever known, and they were still here. Someone must be looking after them.

One morning she came into the hall with her veil drawn across her face. She was alone; Egenhere was in council with the king and the elders. Some women and children sat at the lower end of the meal table, and a group of unmarried girls were flirting and laughing with the young men.

I picked up my jug of small beer and went to sit beside her.

She was trying to hold her veil in place as she ate a tiny piece of bread.

'What ails thee?' I asked. It was the first time I had ever spoken to her.

She turned to look at me. Her eyes were a clear light blue, like the sky on midsummer morning. For some moments she gazed at me, and I put all my love and solicitude into my face.

Then, silently, she lowered her veil. We were too far away from the others for anyone else to see, but none of the savage details were lost to me. He had hit her with something thin and hard – the whip with which he'd beaten his horse? – and across her jaw was a thick scarlet weal. He had laid the flesh open to the bone, and it must have been a mess – the soft white skin of her neck was still dulled by a brown smear of dried blood. I felt sick, but the nausea was driven out by a cold fury.

She said softly, 'I fear it may scar.'

My heart contracted with pity; she couldn't have seen what he'd done to her, or she'd have had no doubt. 'It will,' I whispered. I put up my hand and, touching her jaw very gently with my fingertips, held her face still while I studied her. 'But no scar could detract from thy beauty.'

The words came from my deepest soul, and I said them with all the conviction I could muster. I felt it was vitally important that she believe me – it seemed to me her very survival was at stake. If she let him defeat her now, if she bowed her lovely head in sub-mission, she might never rise again.

The translucent lids had dropped down over her eyes as I held her face. Now, as I let her go, she looked up at me. I drowned in her eyes, my love and desire for her surging through me like a wild storm as I gazed at her. Did she feel it too? Oh, yes, she did – I saw the answering flash, as if we both flinched before the lightning and the crack of the thunder.

And, out of place on that poor beaten face, a smile began. He hadn't conquered her spirit, that devil hus-band of hers: she said softly, 'I thank thee, Siegwald.' She knew my name! 'But, all the same, I shall not risk incurring his wrath again.'

She sat beside me, no longer even pretending to eat, just staring into my eyes. Then – for surely our stillness must soon become noticeable – she put her veil in place once more and got up. She moved awkwardly, as if in pain: unbidden and unwelcome came the thought, what other damage did he do to her that I cannot see?

Then she turned from the table and walked away.

Living so close yet being unable to touch, unable even to speak to each other, was a torment. We were bound by the law: the king's rule over his court was as firm as over the rest of the land; he was no brigand-lord presiding over a wild bunch of outlaws. And, for a woman, the penalty for adultery was cruel.

I watched her fade, and could do nothing to aid her. She recovered from her beating – it was not that which ate away at her. I knew what it was, and it grieved me that I had added to the sorrows she already had to bear.

I wanted her, *needed* her. She was on my mind every minute of the day and night. No matter how hard I laboured during the hours of daylight, no matter how exhausted I lay down on my bed, I could get no rest. Sense and reason were gradually driven out of my head, so that when the chance was presented to me, I had no logic with which to fight the headstrong inner voice ordering me to take it.

The Cunning Man came. I heard them whispering, the youths and the girls wanting love spells, the barren married women whose prayers to Frig were still unanswered. The powerful warriors of the king's retinue, half ashamed of their adherence to his old magic yet queuing to consult him nevertheless.

I waited until the night. All day I tried to summon the strength to go away, anywhere, so that I put myself out of the danger of his power. What I was going to ask for was wrong. And, worse than that, it was potentially lethal.

There was a feast that night, my father's people in celebratory mood, the poet by the hearth surpassing himself, the Cunning Man nodding and smiling his blessing on us all.

She sat at the high table, her fine wool kirtle and tunic as blue as her eyes. On her shoulder she wore a brooch of garnet and gold. Egenhere's attention was on the poet; I stared at her, taking my fill of her beauty. A woman beside her spoke to her now and again, and she would nod and smile briefly in reply. On her other side sat the dark figure of the king's steward, a strange, sinister man whom people feared – it was quite common to see grown men and women make behind his back the ancient sign that averts evil. I had noticed before how he seemed to haunt her, and now he stared at her, a cynical smile on his dark face, as if something about her secretly amused him.

The scar where Egenhere had whipped her had healed into a deep, thin line across her jaw. What was she thinking? Had she any idea what I was planning to do? Would she approve? Would she – for she was a vital part of it – agree?

I drank all the ale and mead that I was offered. They laughed at me, not unkindly, saying someone had substituted Thor's bottomless horn for my jug. And with every draught, reason fled further and further away and I became more determined.

In time, the feasting was over. The king retired to his own quarters, his steward at his side speaking earnestly into his ear. The vats of liquor were at last empty, the bard put away his harp and the poet rolled up in his furs beside the hearth. I feigned sleep, like my colleagues dropping where I sat. Out of one half-opened eye, I watched the Cunning Man.

And my chance came. In the dead of the night, in those darkest hours before the new dawn when the dying take their leave of the world of men, I saw the Cunning Man rise quietly to his feet and glide to the door. With the stealth of desperation, I followed him, running, once I was safe out of doors, to catch him.

As I reached out to touch his sleeve, he turned. It was too dark to see his face, but the glint of his eyes sent a shiver through me. Before my courage failed, I opened my mouth to beg him for his help. But,

'I know thy request, Siegwald,' he said.

'I . . .'

'I have seen into thy heart,' he continued smoothly, 'and also into thy lady's. Thy cousin's lady,' he amended.

Was he issuing a reproof? Gods, he had every right to. I fell on to my knees. 'Wilt thou aid me?' I muttered.

There was a long silence. When I nerved myself to look up at him, he was standing with his head thrown back, staring up into the black sky at the patterns of the stars.

Eventually he sighed. And said, 'Aye. I will.'

Had he seen the answer in the heavens? I didn't know how to ask, but he read my thought.

'The answer is written, Siegwald, but not in the stars. Because I divined thy purpose, and because, against all sense, my instinct was to assent, I have sought counsel.' I drew in my breath in superstitious terror – to be standing right next to one who had recently been in a trance, who had talked with the spirits! I covered my face with my hands.

The Cunning Man sighed again. 'For thy work this night shall future generations laud thee,' he said softly.

I did not understand. But then it no longer mattered – he had said he would help me. I was to have what I wanted. My heart began to sing, so that I scarcely heard his next words. Something about payment – he was demanding that, whatever he asked of me, I should yield it.

'I will, I give thee my word!' I said.

'Whatever it be?'

'Yes! Anything!'

He nodded, then walked away into the blackness.

Not knowing what else to do, I went back into the hall.

Some time later – not long, for my feet were still icy from the outside air – there was a commotion. Shouting voices, the sound of the great doors being flung open, the clash of metal as swords and shields were raised. The king's warriors, racing the length of the hall and out to the stables.

The king, majestic in his fur-trimmed mantle, his personal guard following him and his steward issuing orders. Beside him Egenhere, face crumpled from sleep, a sour smell on him.

I ran to them, demanding to know what was happening.

'We are attacked,' the king said grimly. 'Word has come that our northern borders are under assault by a raiding party. We ride at once.' His hand was on the pommel of his sword.

'I will attend thee,' I said. I could not do otherwise.

But he caught hold of my sleeve as I turned from him to collect my gear.

'Stay,' he ordered. No explanation was given.

As he strode away, Egenhere gave me a vicious glance. 'This,' he said icily, 'is a matter for men.'

I went to the doors and watched them gallop away.

The silence that fell when they had gone was absolute. No-one lamented their departure nor the threat that was its cause. No stable lad or retainer stood scratching his head in confusion. No woman cried her anxiety, no dog howled for a master gone off in the night.

Not a thing stirred.

I knew the stillness was magic. That my moment was now.

I ran back through the hall and made my way to her bedchamber.

Thirty-one

When Egenhere led me from the hall I was ready to leave, even though it meant being alone with him, for the king's steward had sat by me at table and his silent presence unnerved me. If I am to be honest, his effect on me was far, far deeper: he terrified me.

It was the shouting that awakened me. For once I was deeply asleep, for Egenhere had supped well of the golden mead and was drunk beyond the stage at which he would not let me rest until he had tried everything. And had me try everything.

He was muttering to himself as he rummaged among the furs for his shirt, and bent, gasping with effort, to pick up his cloak. He glanced at me, and instantly I shut my eyes – let him think I was asleep.

The shouting continued – an alarm must have been given. I was not afraid, merely glad that the rest of the night was mine to enjoy alone.

I listened as the sounds rose to a climax and, as the king and his warriors rode off, faded away.

Then I turned over, clutched the furs more closely to me, and prepared for sleep.

I thought I was dreaming. The woollen hanging across the doorway twitched aside, and there he stood. He was here, the answer to my prayers! I sat up, the furs falling from my breasts, opening my arms to him.

It was a beautiful dream. I rubbed my eyes, trying to blink myself awake. I looked at the doorway again.

And he was still there. He was moving into the chamber, letting the hanging fall back into place behind him. He was coming towards me, throwing off his clothes. He was at the bedside, he was lying down beside me, taking me in his arms, clutching me to his strong, smooth body with a power that made my bones creak.

It was no dream. Magic, perhaps, wild incomprehensible magic, but he was here. His hand on my jaw, fingers gentle as they had been that day when he gave me sympathy for my wound and took away my heart, he held my face, staring at me. Then he bent his head and kissed me.

He took me to another world. His strength was tempered with tenderness, and I bore the pain with joy, for it was swiftly followed by ecstasy. It was over too soon, the first time: we lay panting together, and, as the sweat on our naked bodies cooled, he sat up to rearrange the furs over us.

Suddenly he stopped. He was staring at the linen on which I was lying.

'There is blood,' he said quietly. 'Did I hurt thee?' His eyes on mine were stricken.

'No.' I reached out to touch him. 'Only for an instant.'

'Then . . . should I not have loved thee? Thy courses – is it that . . . ?'

I could not let him suffer any longer. 'I was a virgin,' I whispered. 'Thou wast my first man.'

He looked stricken anew, and I knew what he was

thinking: had he known, he would have been less impatient. I did not want him to feel any remorse. I was about to reassure him when he said, 'But thy husband! Does he not . . .'

'He is impotent.' I took a savage delight in telling him, in betraying Egenhere's shame. 'He tries, until both he and I are exhausted. But he has never taken me. Not once!'

'And now he shall not.' His hands were on my upper arms, clutching as if he would convince me by his force. His power woke an answering hunger in me and I thrust myself against him, my breasts pushing into his muscular chest, my legs opening to encircle his thighs, his loins.

On a moan of renewed desire he said, 'Thou art mine. For ever.'

For ever lasted for the rest of the night.

When the sounds of the community's first stirrings began, he left me. We could give each other no promises, no reassurances. All we had to offer were the three most precious words in the world: I love thee.

For some time I was in a daze. I would see him, labouring in the yard, tending and schooling the horses. I would watch him at mealtimes. Often, as if aware of my eyes on him, he would look up. Then, although we did not speak, I understood what he was thinking and feeling: his thoughts and his sufferings exactly mirrored my own.

The king and his party returned, having found no trace of the reported incursion. They were in high spirits – they had convinced themselves that whoever had dared to trespass across the borders had been frightened off by the rumour of the king's might. However, not one to take chances, the king dispatched a troop to patrol the northern lands; one of the horsemen he sent was Siegwald.

Egenhere seemed to have been rejuvenated by the jaunt, and his endeavours to consummate our marriage became more strenuous: I suffered him, night after night. Week after week.

Without even the regular respite of my courses.

I realized, with a mixture of joy and horror, that I was with child.

The situation was grave, but not yet desperate – if I could only arouse him just once, surely then I could pass off Siegwald's child as his? Siegwald's child. I did not allow myself to dwell on that thought.

I tried. Oh, I tried. All the tricks he had taught me, that he made me perform upon him, I did as if my life depended on it. Ignoring the nausea, biting my lip to prevent the cry of pain as he pummelled my tender breasts, I was the most enthusiastic bed-partner he can ever have had. We met with success, of a sort – he managed to penetrate me, but, too soon, sank back exhausted.

Even that small achievement was sufficient to make him crow with pride – his rough hand thrusting into my tender parts, he said, 'Now thou hast a taste of me! A wife in truth now, woman!'

He withdrew his hand and inspected the fingers. Then he looked at me. I knew then that whatever I said, whatever excuses I offered about once having ridden astride, about exercising too strenuously when I was a young girl, would carry no weight. His wife was no virgin, and he would not rest until he knew why.

I watched the fury rise in his face. His colour, always high, was darkening to crimson. Rising from the bed, he put on his clothes. Then he said in a voice of ice, 'We shall hear what the king has to say on this matter.'

I begged him to wait, to listen, to consider his words and refrain from telling the king until the morning. From telling the king at all – I tried to imply that it would surely shame a man, to confess to his king that his wife had a lover and, furthermore, to give the humiliating answer he would have to provide when the king asked how he knew.

My wife is pregnant, he would have to say. And the child cannot be mine, for I am impotent.

My pleadings were to no avail, for his rage took him far beyond shame.

He was gone for some time. When he returned, he stood inside the doorway and stared at me. Then he reached for his horse-whip.

He hurled his full strength into his right arm. So great was his passion that he threw off all discretion, and I felt the flesh of my back open under the onslaught. In a huge final effort, he struck me across the shoulder, and as the blackness started to cloud my vision, I saw his face grow purple. In a daze, I watched blood spurt from his nose, vomit from his mouth. With a frightful gagging cry, he fell to the floor.

When I came to myself, they told me he was dead.

My fate was decided in my absence – adulterous wives were not permitted to speak in their own defence. Had Egenhere lived, my punishment would have been worse – as a cuckolded husband, what wealth and property I possessed would have been his. Had he chosen to, he could also have ordered that my nose and ears be cut off, a right which he undoubtedly would have claimed.

But he was dead, and I was spared.

Instead of mutilation, banishment. They sent me to a hovel deep in the Fens, where in the care of a crone who I was convinced was mad, I lay in chains to await the birth of Siegwald's child.

She was no midwife, that crone. Ignorant as I was, I knew more about childbirth than she did, and it was I who told her that my time was near. She did little for me, just as she had done little for me during the previous months. The pains grew, and sometimes I slipped into a grey world where nothing was quite real.

I called for him, endlessly. I saw him in my dreams, and, as on the night he came to me, dream became reality.

He was wounded. He dragged his leg, and around his thigh was a stained and tattered bandage. He held my hands. I knew not where he had been, what he had done; he must have been fighting, but, isolated as I was, no word had reached me of any battle.

Siegwald delivered my child. *Our* child. He was tender and he knew what to do. I recalled his reputation for having a way with animals – Wolfspear, they called him, for had he not survived in the wild, living and fighting alongside the wolves? – and possibly the same skills are required to help any female through the agony of birth.

He gave me something hot and herb-scented to drink, and I went further into my grey world. Then in a piercing spell of clarity our son was born, and I watched as Siegwald cradled him in his arms.

The greyness came back. Grew to black, so that I no longer made sense of the world. I thought I saw the Cunning Man, but I must have been dreaming again. I thought I heard Siegwald arguing, pleading. Then a husky voice said, 'I claim my payment. Thou gavest me thy word: for a night with the woman, thou wouldst give me whatever I asked. I demand the child.'

I seemed to see as if down a long dark tunnel. I had fallen back into the straw, and I could not raise myself. The dream figure of the Cunning Man had the baby in his arms, and he was moving off across the track through the willow-lined dykes as if his feet had wings.

Suddenly another figure materialized, someone whose dark presence made me quake with fear. He crouched over me, yellow eyes narrowed, and in the mist that floated in front of my eyes his shape seemed to change, from man to wolf and back again. I thought I heard him speak, softly-hissed words that emerged through clenched teeth.

'The next king!' he said, the words bitterly caustic. 'Thou thought to fool thy husband, lady, but didst thou not know there was no fooling me?' He threw his head back, emitting a cry that became a howl. 'Egenhere's child! Thou shouldst have borne Egenhere's child! As winter to spring was Egenhere to thee, and the fruit of thy union would have kept alive the dark force, as the seed from the dying year swells to life in the new.' Suddenly the long face was pressed to my cheek, the eyes burning into mine. 'Thou hast borne Siegwald's child, and in its feeble body is nothing of Egenhere, nothing of the dark.'

Saliva drooled from the jaws, scalding me where it fell on to my skin. I tried to shrink away, but the nightmare face came with me.

'I curse thee,' hissed the soft voice. 'Through the ages I shall follow thee, and – '

The mists swirled suddenly thicker, and with my fading vision I saw two scenes at once. In one the wolf became man once more and, with a movement

443

of his hand over my body that made my heart contract with terror, ran off into the shadows.

In the other, something different happened. It seemed that I heard a voice – Siegwald's voice, for all that the words were strange – saying, 'I'm trying to tell you that I love you.'

He was standing there, behind the terrible dark figure which was sliding once more into wolf shape. He was leaning on his spear, and he seemed to need its support. I whispered, 'Siegwald! Do not desert me!' and, with an obvious effort, he straightened.

It was hard to see him; the mist rolled between us, and my eyes would not focus. Yet, just for an instant, it seemed that another Siegwald stood beside him. He was dressed in strange clothes, but Siegwald it was. Of that I was sure.

The two Siegwalds merged and became one. And the one was a strong warrior, armed with a long, wickedly-pointed spear.

Before the wolf could turn round, before he could even have perceived the threat and turned into man-shape to defend himself, the warrior raised his arm and plunged his spear deep into the grey fur of the creature's throat. There was a gurgling sound, a great gush of warm blood, and an unearthly shriek.

Then nothing. No wolf, no man, no blood. Nothing.

Siegwald, poor wounded Siegwald, slumped and weary once more, looked at me. He muttered, 'The child!' and, peering out into the gloom along the path the Cunning Man had taken, turned and tried to run after him. But as I watched he stumbled. Got up, staggered a few paces, then fell again.

And this time lay still.

*   *   *

I cannot let thee lie there alone.

Summoning strength I do not know I have, I crawl to him. He lies with his eyes shut, and his face is pale in the evening light. Blood from the wound on his thigh seeps into the black earth: it must have opened up again as he stumbled and fell. I sink to the ground at his side. Looking down at our two bodies together, I see my own blood mingle with his.

He senses my presence. I watch his face, and see a smile. Then he opens his eyes, sees me, and wraps his arms around me, drawing my head down upon his chest. I hear the thump, thump of his heartbeat, but it is faint. I remember how it sounded that night, when we made love again and again and created the child that the Cunning Man has taken away.

Did Siegwald kill the wolf? Or did the wolf resume human form and live to enforce his curse?

I do not know. Perhaps it was all a part of the dream.

I had a baby, I do know that.

A baby that the Cunning Man stole away.

'Why has he done it?' I whisper. 'Siegwald, what does he want with our son?'

He sighs, his gentle fingers stroking my neck and my cheek. 'I do not know. Forgive me. I have failed thee.'

For some moments I try to fathom what he can mean. Forgive him? What is there to forgive? He has given me the only joy I have ever known, a joy so rare and precious that few experience it. He has loved me. He was sent away, but somehow he found me. Came to me when I called, and lies now beside me with his strong arms and his warm body protecting me from the cold of the night and the perils of the Fens.

'How didst thou fail me?' I ask, turning my face so that I can kiss the smooth skin of his throat.

'I let thy child be taken.'

'Thy child, too,' I say. Does he know? Of course he does – no man ever held up a newborn boy with such wonder in his eyes unless it was his own son.

'Aye.' He sighs again. Then, the puzzlement audible, he asks again, 'Why?'

I try to think. But I am tired, so tired, and my mind cannot seem to concentrate on the question. Instead I see flashes of my life, scene after scene re-enacted before my eyes.

It ceases to be important. In time, I cannot even recall what it is I am worrying about.

'Siegwald?'

Time must have passed, for it is now quite dark and I can no longer see him. He does not answer. *'Siegwald!'*

'I am here. What is it, sweet?'

His arms close round me, but his grip is no longer so strong. His body feels chill, and does not warm me any more.

'Siegwald, is this death?'

At first he is silent, speaking to me only with his hands, which caress me with that special tenderness which first made me love him. And with his thoughts, for I feel his love bathing me like the warmth of the fire. Then, the words coming out with an effort, he says, 'Aye. Art thou afraid?'

Afraid? I have known fear for much of my life. Fear of the dark, fear of hunger, fear of sudden beatings, fear of the threatening outside world. Fear of marriage to a cruel stranger, fear of his uncertain temper.

Fear of going to my death not knowing what it is to love and be loved in return.

That fear, at least, was unfounded.

I am with him, with the one person in the whole world whom I love, who loves me. What is there to fear?

I kiss him again, finding it more of an effort to lift my head so that my lips may touch his skin. I answer him with total honesty, 'Nay, I am not afraid.'

We lie there, and it becomes colder. I cannot feel my feet, and gradually my legs and my body succumb to the creeping numbness. There is no pain: the prospect of sleep becomes more and more seductive.

'Althicca?'

'Aye?'

'It is time to bid thee goodnight.'

This is death.

'Is this the end, thinkst thou?' I wish for his assurance that it is not, but I fear he will tell me it is.

He speaks hesitantly, but he is determined to say what is on his mind. 'Althicca, it is the end for us here.' He pauses for a long time. 'But –' Another pause. 'But I know there is something more.'

'Dost thou speak of the afterlife?'

'I know not.' His kiss on my brow is soft, barely perceptible. 'I shall be with thee again. I tell thee this, and I know it is the truth.' His lips against my hair, he speaks the words so softly I can scarcely hear. 'Thou and I, Althicca, shall be reunited. Before the world ends, we shall be together once more.'

His breathing is shallow. I time my breaths to coincide with his. Slowly, gradually, we fade.

The darkness is absolute. I can no longer see.

His lips to my forehead.

'It is not the end.'

Darkness. Sleep.

Dark.

* * *

It was so dark.

But I was no longer cold. I could feel heat, on the backs of my legs. On the soles of my bare feet.

Feel?

But we were dying! No longer able to feel anything!

What has happened? Have we been saved? Taken into the warmth, our hurts tended? Yes, yes, I'm not in pain!

Why is it so dark? Why can't I see?

Where is he?

I can feel a body against mine. Warm, breathing in time with my breaths. *ALIVE!* Oh, God, alive!

I opened my eyes, and he was lying beside me. I started to say his name. 'Siegw . . .'

No. Not Siegwald.

We weren't lying on a black Fen track, our life's blood seeping away as hypothermia slowly beckoned us into the last sleep. We were in a dim room, lying on a soft carpet, and we were bathed with the glowing light of a dying fire.

There was still that strange smell.

He was stirring, turning his head from side to side. He muttered something, but I couldn't decipher it. Suddenly his arms tightened round me so that I couldn't breathe – I swear I could feel my ribs creak.

'It's all right,' I whispered, my lips finding his throat so that I felt the beat of his pulse, 'We're back.'

I didn't know what I was saying. Back? Where had we been?

He opened his eyes and stared into mine. He said something about midsummer skies, and his fingers went to my jaw, feeling round under my chin. Then he looked where he was touching. 'It's gone!' he said in surprise.

I waited while he made the transition. I knew what he was going through – I'd just been there.

After some time he said, 'Thea?' It sounded like a question.

I repeated, 'Thea. Yes, Henry.'

Several expressions crossed his face: pain, sorrow, compassion. Love, I think. And, driving all of them out except perhaps the love, relief.

He put his hands up to either side of my face. Holding me still, he lifted his head so that his lips touched mine.

I don't know what happened then to him. I know what happened to me, and I guess it was the same for him. I felt a surge of joy and delight race through me, and suddenly I was panting, and hot, and pressing myself so hard against him that I seemed to be melting into him. I knew, *knew*, what it was like to make love with him.

The sensation lasted only a few seconds. Then, as if it had abated for him, too, he pulled away slightly and stared at me.

'Thea,' he said again. It wasn't a question any more.

I fell against him, my face pressed to his chest, and his arms closed around me. Something had happened to us, something I couldn't begin to understand. I wasn't sure I wanted to understand just yet; it seemed preferable to hide my head and hope it – whatever it was – had gone away and wouldn't come back.

I felt sleepy. It was so nice, lying there in front of the fire with him. Safe. Warm.

As I felt myself drift off, it occurred to me that in the morning I'd no longer be able to say we'd never slept together.

Thirty-two

I woke to the sound of the fire being tended.

She lay with her head on my chest, her arms round my neck. She was still deeply asleep.

Someone was crouched by the fire, a black silhouette in a long robe. Through the fog of disorientation I tried to work out who it was. And where we were.

The figure turned, and the orange light of the rekindled fire fell across the face. In that first surprised moment, I believed it was *two* people: it was Florence, but it was also the Cunning Man. Male and female versions of the same face.

I tried to say something, but it came out as a strangled sound without meaning. The figure instantly moved to my side, finger to lips in the silencing gesture. 'Hush! Do not wake her. She has endured much – more even than you know. Let her sleep.'

The whispering voice was slightly hoarse. It could have been a man or a woman. I looked around me, trying to make sense of it, searching for some clue. But it was too dark.

Above me the figure's narrowed eyes glittered. I gazed into them, feeling their power, and for an instant it seemed I hovered once again on the edge of dream. Or nightmare.

NO!

Frantically gathering together what I could find of my own soul, I forced myself to hold on. It didn't matter which one of them it was, either would do.

I had the same quarrel with them both.

I said, the words coming out with more force than I'd expected, 'I want to talk to you!'

The gaunt face broke into a smile. The figure said, 'I thought so. But come and sit by the fire – she should sleep on.'

Gently I disengaged myself, laying her head down on the floor. I found it hurt to leave her: I touched my fingers to her forehead, then down across her cheek to her jaw. The skin was smooth and unmarked.

Visions swam in front of me. I moved away and joined the figure by the fire.

I couldn't find the words to begin.

We sat for some time. I wondered how much of the night was left, and realized with a shock how much I was longing for daybreak. I turned my head, looking for some hint of light through the crack of a door or window.

I thought at first it was an illusion, brought about by my own desperation. I looked away, then back to the same place. This time there was no mistake: against the blackness, a strip of pale light was showing.

Across the bay window where once, long ago, my rocking horse had stood, Florence had left a little gap between the curtains.

I turned to her. Now that I knew – or thought I knew – the trepidation had gone. I wasn't dealing with a Dark Age wizard – God, had I really thought I was? – I was confronting my own grandmother.

Getting angry with my grandmother wasn't likely to be quite so dangerous.

I said, 'What the hell have you done?'

Her lip curled slightly: she really was very like him. She looked at me for a long moment, then said, 'Now is not the time to tell you. You won't remember, tomorrow.'

'Try me.'

She shrugged. 'Very well. But you are still under the influence of the drug.'

'Drug,' I repeated. It came as no surprise. 'What did you give us? And how?'

'It is a complex formula. Our forebears used it, and I have refined the recipe. It works in a twofold manner, containing both hallucinogens which release the vision-making part of the brain, and also agents which render the subject susceptible to suggestion. It was in the lemon sauce and the coffee. They both have a strong taste of their own, do you see, so that the drug was masked. Oh, and I put a little in the cheese biscuits.'

I had a sudden clear picture of Thea, hungry after the assorted traumas of the day, eating her way through a whole plate of biscuits. The picture hurt.

'You, of course, touched neither the biscuits, the sauce or the coffee,' I said coldly. It was a statement; I had no need to ask. 'You sent us on a trip then hypnotized us so that we ended up in the right place.'

It sounded absurd. My logic rose up against the unlikelihood of her being able to do what I'd just accused her of. Only I'd been there. She'd done it.

'That is what we may call the official explanation,' she was saying. 'Do not underestimate the power nor the subtlety of drugs. In the hands of a master, they are a potent tool. What we disparagingly refer to as primitive peoples have always known that, and still do. Seers, prophets, oracles, wise men, shamans, witch doctors. By a variety of methods, they all achieved what we consider to be the unthinkable.'

She stopped speaking, as if that were explanation enough. It wasn't. 'What did they achieve?'

'They went into another consciousness!' She sounded slightly irritated. 'Mankind has always needed guidance. Nowadays some people pray in half-empty churches, the rest get by, ignoring the demands of their spiritual side. Our ancestors were not so foolish. They knew that our everyday experience only scratches the surface, and they listened to those of their number who could go beyond and return with counsel.'

'That's different!' I wasn't going to be knocked off beam by her mini-lecture. I said furiously, '*They* weren't drugged and put into another world!'

Angry in her turn, she flashed back, 'Of course they were! That was the whole purpose of altering their mental state, so that they could enter the other reality!'

I shook my head violently, as if the action would agitate the jumble of weird and illogical things in my mind and make them settle again in a more recognizable pattern. I was totally hostile to what she was telling me, yet, at the same time, a part of me felt she was right. I'd heard all this before – probably from her – and it had seemed to make sense then. Then.

'If I accept what you say – your official explanation – that begs another question,' I said, trying to sound calm. 'What was the purpose of doing it to us?'

She stared at me. 'Think,' she said quietly. 'Think back.'

My anger flared again. She'd been doing that to

me ever since I was a child. 'Think, Henry. Work it out for yourself.' It had always . . .

When I was a child. Something stirred in the seething stew of my thoughts. When I was a child, she'd wanted me with her. I'd thought it was I who had brought about my return to East Anglia, but she'd said it was her doing. She told me that on my eighteenth birthday. The same night she told me how I'd come to be conceived.

'Do you recall the story of Siegwald?' she'd asked me. Siegwald. The prince without a crown, who lost the thing he most loved. I'd thought then she was using it to illustrate that what she'd done wasn't so extraordinary. That others had done it before.

But if that were all, why had she sent us – Thea and me – back to that very time?

There was more. What was it?

'You were close to the answer on the night of your birthday,' she said softly. She had obviously decided I needed some prompting. 'You said, "The Cunning Man knew what was going to happen in the future." You were right. He foresaw troubled times for the Wuffingas, troubles which he tried to counter with the magic crowns. He knew the dynasty would die out with King Edmund – he saw that when he took counsel over whether or not to grant Siegwald's request. That was why he gave him what he wanted – he also saw the other line of the House of the Wolf, the forgotten line. Stretching on, century after century, when the legitimate line was nothing but a dim memory.'

I felt very cold. She was going to tell me the truth, I knew. Already I half guessed; I almost thought that was enough.

'What did they call Siegwald?'

I couldn't see the relevance. 'Wolfspear.'

She smiled in satisfaction. 'Well, then.'

But I wasn't with her. 'So?'

'Henry, remember your Anglo-Saxon!'

I didn't know any. Once, she'd taught me the odd word or two, but I'd forgotten. 'Sorry. It's all gone.'

She sighed. 'The Anglo-Saxon for Wolf Spear is Wulfgar. With usage, it became Wulgar, then Wolgar. Now, it is Woolgar.'

At first I couldn't take it in. Was that what this was all about? She believed our name marked us as the descendants of Siegwald? The tail-end of the forgotten, illegitimate line? And that was why she'd engineered my birth and guided my life?

Something struck me. 'Why should it matter to you? It's not *your* name. You only became Woolgar when you married my grandfather.' It was a cruel thing to say, and I didn't say it kindly. I didn't feel kind.

But she didn't look perturbed. Tranquilly she said, 'It was my name before that. Your grandfather and I came from different branches of the same family.'

I stared at her. 'And that was why you married him.'

'I married him because I loved him, as he did me.' The reproof was clear in her tone.

'Did he share your obsession?'

'Oh, yes.' She said it as if it were the most natural thing in the world. 'He was overjoyed when your father was born. He wrote to me from the Front saying that his life was no longer important, now that the next generation was secure.' Suddenly her face crumpled into sorrow. 'He was still important to me.'

Cutting across my anger and indignation came compassion. I saw her life: married to a man she loved, a kindred spirit whose priorities exactly matched hers. Bearing his son, only to lose her mate. Bringing up that son alone, trying to make him a worthy successor to his courageous and distinguished father. Living with the disappointment of having the child turn out differently.

Then the second bite at the cherry, as the much-desired grandson at last was born. Schooling him in his own history, arousing his interest and curiosity. Oh, yes, she'd done that all right. And she'd . . .

Thea.

I was brought up short, as if I'd just run into a wall. Thea.

Florence had brought us together in childhood, in such a way that it made a deep impression on us. I heard my own words of yesterday – Was it only yesterday? – when I was trying haltingly to explain to Thea what I was thinking. 'We remember best the things that make us very happy, or very sad, or that move us a lot.' That early encounter with her had done all three. No wonder I'd never been able to forget her.

Clever Florence.

She'd brought us together again at eighteen. Even fixed it so that it was I who went to the door on the night of my party to let Thea in. Back into the house, back into my heart, only she'd never left it. Florence had overplayed her hand, then, and frightened Thea off. 'I'm sorry for driving her away,' she'd said. She'd been given another chance, though. Here we were, back under her roof – her control – again. We'd admitted our love, but she didn't know that. We were playing it cool, pretending to be no more than friends.

And friendship wasn't enough. She wanted us to be lovers.

Was that why she'd been driven to a last desperate

step, why she'd feigned illness to bring me home and then, before either of us could disappear again, had plunged us so ruthlessly and efficiently back into the past? Because she thought this was her last chance, and it had to work?

God, *why?*

Florence was sitting hunched on the other side of the fire. She looked smaller, somehow. I heard again her soft sad words: 'He was still important to me.'

Through all the years without Thea I'd felt bad enough, and as far as I'd known she was still alive. What would it have felt like if someone had sent me a telegram saying she was dead?

I put out my hand to touch Florence's. For a moment she didn't move, then slowly her fingers clasped around mine. Gently I said, 'Why did it have to be Thea?'

She raised her head. There was the shine of tears in her eyes; she blinked them away. 'Thea,' she repeated. Then, as if coming back from a long way away, more strongly. 'Thea. She is also of an ancient family, the same line that produced Althicca. Their people were the earliest inhabitants of East Anglia. I had suspected it – your grandfather researched the line thoroughly, surmising what happened before the written record, right back beyond Roman times – and that was his conclusion. It was confirmed when I took Thea to Grime's Graves. They recognized her. They touched her.'

She said it as matter-of-factly as if she'd gone visiting with Thea to an old great-aunt who'd remarked on a family likeness.

'You wanted Thea and me to re-enact the love of our own ancestors,' I said slowly. 'Siegwald and Althicca united the ancient Britons with the new inhabitants, with the strong Anglo-Saxons. They founded a line of their own, which, so you say, is represented by me.'

'And only by you.' Her face was grave. 'The Great War took more than one member of the family. The child I bore was the sole Woolgar representative of his generation.' Her hand was still in mine, and she squeezed my fingers. 'That was why I had to do it. Do you see? If the family was thriving, if all the sons and the cousins had come home, it wouldn't have mattered so much.'

'What would you have done if I'd married someone else? If Thea had?'

She shrugged, and a faint smile crossed her face. 'You didn't.'

We lapsed into silence. But now it was a more peaceful silence. After a while I thought of something else. 'You said that was the official explanation,' I said. With the growing daylight, even that was appearing more and more absurd. I hurried on: what I was about to ask might elicit an answer that was even more absurd. 'Is there another one?'

She looked at me. 'There is.'

'Hit me with it.'

She leaned towards the fire, putting on some more logs. I thought I could smell the resin scent again.

'You should sleep,' she said. 'Why not go up to bed?'

'Not just yet.'

It seemed to grow dark again. I felt lightheaded. Florence, right in front of me, was speaking, and her voice was quiet and hypnotic.

'Life is a cycle,' she said. 'We are born, we die, and our spirit's energy is reabsorbed into the pool. It waits for a time, and then it comes again in another guise.

It is possible, sometimes, to re-encounter those we have met before.'

She looked across at Thea, then back at me.

'It is likely, I believe, that evil may pursue us from one life to another.' Her voice had dropped a tone, as if she feared being overheard. 'In a past existence, the woman who is now Thea was –' She broke off. 'No. I must speak first to Thea of that.' She closed her eyes for a moment, then, opening them, picked up her theme. 'We may also meet again those we have loved before.'

She was watching me closely. I forced my eyes to stay open. 'Love does not die,' she said. 'He knew that. *You* knew that. ''Before the world ends, we shall be together once more.'' ' Silently she pointed at Thea. 'You were right.'

She was getting to her feet, helping me up. 'Now go to bed,' she whispered. 'Sleep.'

I stopped above the unconscious figure of Thea. 'Not without her.'

'Very well.'

I bent down and lifted her so that she flopped across my shoulder. Then, with an effort, I straightened up. Florence went to open the door, and I made my way to the foot of the stairs.

'Henry.'

I turned my head, awkwardly, for Thea's body restricted my movement.

'Yes?'

She was standing in the doorway, the firelight making her once more a dark silhouette. She had something in her hands, and as I watched she held it up above her head. A leaping flame from the hearth caught an answering yellow glint: it was a plain gold circlet, like an ancient crown, and around it ran the wandering pathways of some script I didn't understand.

The sudden flame died, and the hall was once again dim.

Not really knowing if I was awake or asleep, I carried Thea upstairs to bed.

The sleep that followed was so profound that, when I woke, I could not distinguish what I had dreamt from what had really happened. But at least some of it had been real, for I was in my own bed and Thea was in my arms.

I stroked her face, and soon she stirred.

Blinking her eyes, she was obviously confused. She looked like a child waking from a bad dream.

'I'm in your bed,' she said at last.

'You are.'

'How did I get here?'

'I carried you. I didn't think we should spend all night on the drawing-room carpet.'

She smiled. 'What would Florence have said?' Then, as the logical development of that thought struck her, 'God! What'll she say if she finds out I'm in here?'

Before she could go into panic mode and take herself off, I said, 'She already knows.'

'But . . .'

'Thea, the time's gone for pretending. Don't you remember?'

She frowned. 'I don't know what I remember. A dream, I think, but it was more than that. Worse than I've ever had before.' She shuddered. 'I wasn't in control, and it scared me.' She laughed shortly. '*Terrified* me.'

It had scared me, too. 'It wasn't exactly a dream.' I hugged her closer, then told her what had happened when we'd been allowed to come back from our dream to our own time.

460

She said scathingly, 'I don't believe you. Okay, I knew Florence was up to something, but that's totally incredible.'

'All right. But just listen while I tell you what *I* dreamed, and see if it's familiar.'

She stopped me before I'd got much further than a quarter of the way. There were tears in her eyes. 'Please, don't,' she whispered.

'You're convinced?' It was hard to force her admission, and I wouldn't have done it if it hadn't been important.

She nodded. 'I – let's not talk about it. Not now. It's all too – oh, I don't know.'

'We don't have to talk about it ever. Not if you don't want to.'

'I think I shall. But not yet.'

She put her head down on my chest. It felt as if she'd been doing it for ever. Then she said quietly, 'Last night, when I – after I'd – when the dream ended, I felt I knew you. You know, *knew*.'

I did. There was no need for her to elaborate. 'Yes.'

'I feel like that now.'

'So do I.'

I turned her face up to mine and lightly kissed her. She was Thea, whom I'd kissed at length a couple of days ago. She was Althicca, whom I'd made love to with a greater passion than I'd ever known. As we kissed, the passion came back.

We were still dressed – it had been beyond me last night to get my own clothes off, let alone hers. It was a different matter now.

Her body was as beautiful as I'd known it would be. Silently I gazed at her, running my hands over the smooth skin, feeling her respond to me, the excitement quickening in her just as it did in me. She wasn't like a new lover; there was no need to find out by cautious experiment what pleased her, what drove her to delight – I already knew.

As did she: eager to give me the joy I was obviously giving her, she brought me rapidly to the brink of climax.

I waited for her, for I knew it would not be long. Then, the remembered change in her movements and her breathing telling me that it was time, I thrust deeper inside her. Together now, as long ago we had been together, our arms around each other tightened. Together our minds and our bodies soared into the flight of ecstasy.

Immediately afterwards, when I was still up on some plain high above this world, it occurred to me that I'd loved her and lost her, but, through the doings of someone to whom I owed the deepest gratitude, she'd been given back to me. We had another chance.

Holding her to me, my lips pressed to her cheek, I knew that nothing could make me let her go.

Thirty-three

Lying beside him, I was pretty sure he'd fallen asleep, despite the fact that he was still holding my hand. Henry, I thought, this is a fine time to go to sleep. But I didn't blame him – he'd apparently been awake for most of the night, and he'd just used up what was left of his energy making love to me.

I'd never known such joy. It wasn't just the physical pleasure, although that had been intense. It was the – I couldn't find a word for it. Unity? Something like that. As if, at last, we'd taken the final step that wove us into one.

Heady stuff. That was why I wished he was awake – I wanted to ask if he felt the same. Then I thought, of course he does, and it didn't matter any more.

My mind wandered back over what he'd told me. It had shaken me to my depths when he'd started to relate my own dream to me, and I couldn't let him go on – I wasn't ready to live through the fear and the sorrow again. I still wasn't, but I didn't seem to be able to think about anything else.

I'd had all those earlier dreams, too, and also visions, where something – what? – had triggered those strange moments of seeing where, for a few heartbeats, it was as if I wasn't looking out through my own eyes but through those of one of my ancestors. Such things as eye colour and stature are passed down in the genes, I told myself, trying to bring my thoughts down to a sensible, scientific level, no-one argues with that. Why not memories? Just the other day, standing with Henry on the shore near Hunstanton, I'd briefly – frighteningly – imagined I'd taken on the identity of some unknown predecessor fleeing in terror from a Viking ship launch. Where they ensured the gods' protection for the vessel by a sacrifice of virgin blood.

The land remembers, too. Sees, records and stores the violence of man through the long ages of his tenancy of the earth. Replays what it has stored to the eyes and the ears of those who are tuned to pick it up. History is alive and well. And won't go away.

I knew suddenly that Florence was right. It made total sense: she and Henry's grandfather had researched my family history right back into the darkness of the early days, and were convinced they'd found the truth. They had. What happened at Grime's Graves proved that. And what was so awesome about it, anyway? My ancestors had lived here for four thousand years? So what? Probably heaps of people could say the same about their own forebears, if they only knew. We all had ancestors, and they had to live somewhere.

I'd done a nice job of convincing myself that it was all perfectly normal and ordinary. Then out of nowhere came a picture of Siegwald stumbling after the man who was stealing away with my baby. No! Althicca's baby! And then it wasn't ordinary after all.

Siegwald and the Cunning Man. It was uncanny that Henry had told me the same legend that had haunted me so long, even more surprising that it featured in a little book that sat on a shelf downstairs in this very house. He'd given me the official version, if such a term was appropriate.

He hadn't mentioned the Dark Man. The king's steward, who had yellow eyes and howled like a wolf.

Before I could prevent myself I was back in the nightmare, the Dark Man's hand making its occult gestures over me as he laid on his curse. *Through the ages I shall follow thee.*

And I'd seen him. At Henry's party. Outside the house. In the lane, when he tapped on the camper van window and I fled from him.

He killed Eric. Made me believe he'd kill Henry, if I didn't leave him alone.

Gordon had known. He'd warned me of the danger that waited for me in my homeland. Did that mean he knew the rest of the story? And why, if he was right and Florence knew it too, had she been so determined to send Henry and me into the danger from which Gordon had kept me away?

I looked at the bedside clock. A quarter to seven. Once, a long time ago, I'd phoned him late at night and he'd turned out and rescued me. Would he rescue me now, if I asked him to?

I slid out of Henry's bed, careful not to disturb him, then tiptoed out of the room, closing the door behind me.

It took me less than ten minutes to wash and dress. I felt a sense of urgency, as if I was being forced to go ahead quickly before I could change my mind. Outside in the drive, Henry's car was blocking mine; trusting soul that he was, his keys were on the hall table. I took them, got into his car and drove away.

* * *

It was too early for much traffic, and on the cross-country roads I made it to Thetford in a bit over half an hour. It crossed my mind to think how much easier my journeys to and from work at Gordon's house would have been had I had a car then. And a driving licence.

I didn't let myself think about the possibility that he mightn't be at home. It didn't matter, as it turned out, because he was.

He was having his breakfast – he answered the door with a piece of toast in his hand. For a moment or two he just stared at me, then he said, 'I had a feeling you'd turn up.'

He looked just the same. Into my mind flew all the questions you want to ask when you meet again someone who's been very important to you; as he led the way into the kitchen, I said, 'How are you? Been back long? And how's the –'

He was pouring me a cup of coffee, and had his back to me. 'I appreciate this isn't a social call,' he interrupted me, 'so we won't bother with the small talk.'

I wanted to know how he could be so sure I'd come for a purpose, but that could wait. Going to stand beside him, I put my hand over his. 'You're right, I *have* come because I need your help. But please don't dismiss me asking about you as small talk, because it isn't.'

He turned to look at me, and after a moment began to smile. 'Sorry,' he said. And, abandoning the coffee, put his arms round me.

We went through to the study – my desk still stood in the same place, the stacks of paper and the uncovered typewriter suggesting he might have got himself a new assistant. He indicated a manuscript which he appeared to be halfway through proof-reading: 'Alanbrooke. I've gone on to biography.'

'Oh.'

Seeing him again was affecting me, and I didn't know how to get on to what I wanted to ask. Fortunately, he had no such uncertainty.

'Henry came to see me,' he said baldly as we sat down. 'Looking for you. Obviously he found you.'

'Why is that obvious?'

'Because I've never seen you look – Never mind. It just is.'

I had, I realized, been making love with Henry only a few hours ago. Perhaps it showed. 'He came back to Florence's,' I said. 'We're both there with her.'

'And something has happened.' He wasn't asking, he was stating.

'Yes.'

'Well, go on.'

It scared me, even in the reassuring morning light with Gordon sitting in front of me; the shadows were still there. He waited, and finally I found some guts and told him.

When I'd finished, he sat back in his chair and closed his eyes. Then he said, 'It's what I was afraid of. I thought Florence would have the ability to do something like that, which was why I wanted to get you away.'

'But I came home.'

He opened his eyes and grinned at me. 'Inevitable, wouldn't you say?'

'Because of Henry, you mean.'

'I do. She knew, I imagine, that it was only a matter of time. She'd succeeded in implanting you in each other's consciousness as children, and although the plan came off the rails when you were teenagers, there was always going to be another chance.'

'That's what I don't accept!' I leaned towards him. 'She didn't ask me to come home, I came of my own free will! So how can you say she *knew* I'd return?'

'Why did you come?'

'To find Henry.'

'Yes, yes, I know that. I mean, what was the stimulus that made you go to a travel agent in whatever distant place you happened to be –'

'San Francisco.'

'– And purchase your ticket?'

I thought for a while. 'I dreamed of the Fens. And Florence, in a robe.'

He gave me a triumphant look. 'QED. No doubt if you ask Henry the same question, he'll have a similar answer.'

'He came home to look for me! He told me so!'

'Exactly. And, once she had you both under her roof, I bet she didn't waste a moment – she had to act fast, before either of you ran out on her again.'

He was right. Somehow she'd summoned us home – tricking Henry into hurrying back when he'd returned to London – and she'd plunged us back into the past at the first opportunity. 'If what she told Henry was the truth,' I said, 'her purpose was to let us relive our past so that, with Siegwald and Althicca's love alive in us, we would at last unite and ensure the perpetuation of our line. The secret bloodline, descended from the child that the Cunning Man stole away.'

'Yes. But that's not all.'

I had a feeling he was going to say that. 'Go on. Let me hear the worst.'

'What do you mean?'

'There's one bit of the puzzle we haven't touched on. The really scary bit – the bit that made you warn me against coming back.'

'Did I need to warn you?' His voice was kind. 'Weren't your visions enough?'

'No. But then I always was pig-headed. He was the king's steward, Gordon. The Dark Man. I've met him in both lives – he said he would follow me through the ages, and he's doing just that.'

'He *did* just that.'

'That's what I said.'

'No, you said he was *doing* just that.'

I wondered why he was being so pedantic. 'Okay, different tense. But –'

'You said you saw a sort of split-screen image at one point, one half of which showed the Dark Man resuming human form and running off.' He paused, as if waiting for me to take up the tale.

'Yes. In the other half of the picture, Siegwald – well, it was Siegwald *and* Henry, really, they sort of merged,' (it was hard to explain), 'killed him in his wolf form, and he disappeared.'

There was utter silence.

After quite a long time, Gordon said softly, 'Siegwald killed him.'

My hectic night must have taken its toll. Or perhaps I was naturally slow. In the end, though, the penny dropped.

'That was why she sent us back.' I could hardly get the words out. 'Because Siegwald had to kill the Dark Man.'

'Yes. The evil that the Northmen unwittingly brought – the "bane that comes from within" – was centred in the Dark Man. He was a shape-shifter, appearing as the king's steward in his mortal form and as a wolf when he showed himself as the evil deity he really was. Egenhere was his human agent, which was why Althicca had to bear him a child, thus perpetuating the evil. Extend it even to the throne, if the Dark Man's plans had gone right. When she fell

469

pregnant by Siegwald instead, he was demented with rage. Enough to curse her for ever.'

I shivered. 'And Siegwald was meant to kill him.'

'That was his destiny. Hence his name, Wolf Spear. He failed the first time – he was wounded, don't forget, and perhaps just not strong enough – and his mistake permitted the Dark Man to live on and carry out his curse.' He hesitated, then said gently, 'You *did* see him. At Henry's party and outside the house. He had found you again, and he wasn't going to leave you alone. He certainly wasn't going to let you get together with Henry – it seems likely he knew full well what *that* might lead to.'

I didn't want to ask the question, but I had to know. 'Will I see him any more?'

Very firmly, Gordon said, 'No.'

Like a suffocating fog dispersed by the strengthening sun, the shadows lifted. Fragmented, and evaporated.

I felt as if I'd just been set free.

'She knew, didn't she?' I said.

'I'm sure she did. If you and Henry were to fulfil what she believes to be your destiny, you had to be free of the ancient curse. So, apart from the deep emotional bond it created between you and Henry to live for a time in your past lives, it also achieved a practical purpose.'

And Florence, I thought, has never been anything if not practical.

'What now?' I asked.

He didn't answer for some seconds. Then, getting to his feet and picking up our empty cups, he said, 'You go back to Willowford Fen and take up the life you were meant to lead.'

It seemed mean to press him on a point he was obviously reluctant to discuss, but I said, 'Do you believe that? About me – us – being *meant* to do it?'

He looked down at me, and for a moment I saw a weariness in his eyes. Then it was gone, and he said quietly, 'It doesn't matter what I believe. Does it?'

And I had to say, 'No.'

I got back to Willowford Fen just after nine – it seemed extraordinary that so much could have happened and the day still be so young. As I'd driven out of Thetford I felt very sad – I had left Gordon before and thought it was for good, but this time I knew it was. He said he was in the process of selling up and moving abroad, but even if he'd stayed, I knew we would never have seen each other again.

As I drew closer to home and to Henry, though, the happiness grew until I could hardly contain it. Full of eagerness to tell him what I'd found out, I let myself into the house and dashed upstairs to his room.

He was still asleep, lying on his back with one arm flung across my half of the bed. Kneeling down beside him, I brushed the hair away from his forehead and kissed him.

'Henry?'

He stirred, then muttered something. 'Mm? Is that you, Thea?'

I resisted the urge to ask who else he thought it might be. 'Of course. You couldn't wake up, could you?'

'I wasn't asleep.'

'Yes you were.'

He opened his eyes and pulled me closer. 'What's the matter?'

'Nothing.' What a stupid thing to say! I'd been drugged, hypnotised, flung back to relive the harrowing experiences of a Dark Age ancestor, carried up to bed to consummate the love of my life then, on waking, had driven hell for leather to Thetford and found out something so amazing that I couldn't keep it to myself. That was nothing?

'Oh, well, I think I'll go back to sleep then.'

He was teasing, I could tell by the way he was smiling. 'Don't you dare!'

'No, I won't. Perhaps we should get up.'

'What's this "we"? I've been up for hours.'

'Oh, yes. You're dressed.' I thought he looked vaguely disappointed. 'What have you been doing? What's the time?'

Before I could answer his first question, he looked at his watch and said, 'After nine. I wonder what Florence is doing – is she downstairs?'

'I didn't see her, no.'

He was quiet for a moment, listening. 'I can't hear her. She's probably still asleep. She must have been up most of the night.'

An icy finger was stroking up my spine, and I could feel the chill of goosebumps on the back of my neck. No. Oh, please, no.

I pulled myself away from him, crawling around the floor for his discarded clothes and throwing them at him.

He watched me in amazement. 'What are you doing?'

'Florence,' I said. 'This is just like that other morning. Oh, don't you see?' I leant across the bed towards him, willing him to pick up my fear. 'Supposing she really is ill this time?'

It worked. He was up, dressing as if a fire alarm had just gone off. He didn't bother with a shirt. Distractedly I thought, what a lovely physique he's got. Broad shoulders, well-muscled chest. Wonder if he still plays rugby?

Then he was grabbing my hand and we were running along the landing to her room, and there was no space for anything but our terrible apprehension.

As soon as he opened the door and I looked in, I knew this time was different. I don't know how, for she'd been this pale, this still, that other morning. Another of her concoctions, I dare say, had brought about those realistic symptoms. But now, oh, now, it was for real – something was missing in the room, and as I stood there I realized it was her vitality. She couldn't switch that off, even with drugs, and it had been there when she was only feigning illness.

Now it wasn't. The room felt empty.

I ran to the bed, stopping short a pace away. He came to stand beside me, and together we looked down on her.

Neither of us moved.

Then she opened her eyes. 'Too much,' she muttered. 'Drained too much of my strength. Can't . . .'

She was well over eighty. Spry and energetic she might be, but she was still over eighty. And what had it cost her, that tremendous effort to present Henry and me with our own past? I fell to my knees, leaning across the bed and taking her cold hand in mine. 'Please!' I said. I didn't know what I was pleading for.

Henry put his arm round me, reaching out his other hand to her. He said in a remarkably level voice, 'What do you want us to do?'

She smiled, closing her eyes again. 'Good boy,' she said. 'My decision. No doctor nonsense.'

'No,' he agreed.

I had the sudden clear conviction that it was too late for doctors.

With an effort she raised herself, and he helped her to rearrange her pillows. Her eyes were bright, incongruously so in her deathly pale face. She looked intently at us, one after the other. Then she smiled in satisfaction.

'I knew,' she said softly. 'Knew it would happen.'

Was it that obvious? I glanced at him, bare chest, tousled hair, vague look about the eyes. Yes, it was perfectly obvious, and must be in me, too, even if I hadn't just emerged from bed. I met her eyes, and she said, 'And Wolfspear has achieved his purpose. Yes?'

I nodded. I knew what she meant, and she received my assent with obvious relief. 'Knew his presence would make all the difference.' She glanced at Henry. 'Well done,' she whispered.

Did he know? I hadn't told him, and he hadn't mentioned that his exploits in his Siegwald incarnation had included killing a huge wolf. I turned to him to ask, but at that moment he said to Florence, 'Did you go through torments, when we split up at eighteen?' and it became clear that my small exchange with her had gone right over his head.

Perhaps it was just as well.

In answer to his question she shrugged, a tiny movement of her thin shoulders. 'A little. But it was my own fault. Had been too unsubtle. Hadn't allowed for her stubborn nature.' She nodded at me.

'I've never liked having my life directed for me,' I said feebly. I felt I had to give some excuse. Maybe she wouldn't be lying here like this if I hadn't done a runner. Maybe Henry and I would now be happily settled with a brood of young Woolgars to carry on the line, with Florence living in some sort of dowager annexe to her own house, a loved and loving great-grandmother.

It was a nice picture. But inaccurate: the reality was different, and less cosy. Not cosy at all, because it hadn't only been reaction against Florence that had driven a wedge between us.

She was still staring at us, the beginnings of a question in her face. I understood, or thought I did – it might be obvious that he and I were lovers, but did that signify what she hoped it did?

I looked at him. This was something for him to tell her. I whispered, 'She should know.'

'Yes. I'm thinking how to say it.' He grinned at me briefly. Then, leaning down to her so that his face was close to hers, he told her. In words too precious to forget, he said that he loved me and that I loved him. He had always loved me, and wasn't going to be careless enough to let me get away again.

There were tears in her eyes, and I felt the same in mine.

'For ever?' she said quietly.

'For ever.' He turned to me. 'We'll grow old together, here in your house. Fill it with children.'

'Your house, now,' she whispered.

I'd forgotten. All those years ago, she'd made a bargain with me. I'd kept it, and I knew she would have done too.

None of us spoke for quite a long time. It was significant that neither he nor I came out with any comforting remarks on the lines of 'you'll soon feel better'. He knew, just as I did. And as she did.

But still it wasn't easy, to kneel at her side and do nothing for her. I said, breaking the calm silence, 'Isn't there anything you want?'

She looked up at me, her eyes full of love. 'I have all I want,' she said. 'I am comfortable and in no pain. I am very tired, but, because I know there is nothing more now that I must do, I am free to rest.' She sighed, but it was a contented sound, as if she were highly satisfied at the way she had resolved a sticky problem. 'I have you both with me,' she glanced at him, then back at me, 'the two people I love, and you have given me all the assurance I need.' Her eyes on me, she said, 'Safe, now,' and I understood. She paused, waiting to catch her breath. Then, shaking our hands gently, she said, 'I was right. Wasn't I?'

Together we said, 'Yes.'

A little later she spoke again, to tell Henry that her will was lodged with her solicitor. That everything was straightforward, as we would see, and that she'd left clear directions for us. It seemed extraordinary, to converse with a dying woman about what would happen after she was gone, but then Florence obviously intended to die with the good sense and the practicality with which she'd lived.

All the same, it was hard to bear. She must have seen my struggle, and, typically, knew what to do about it. Knew how to give comfort to a grown woman crying at her imminent death, just as she'd known how to comfort a child whose world had just been blown apart.

'Henry, take Thea downstairs. Make her some coffee, and take her out into the sunshine.' Still she could summon those old dictatorial tones that I'd known most of my life.

He stood up, looking at her with a slight frown. 'Will you be all right?' Their faces broke into the same rueful smile at his choice of words: I realized for the first time that they were alike. Living with him, I'd have a reminder of her. It was a comforting thought.

'Yes,' she said. 'Pass me the photograph, will you?'

He knew what she wanted. He went round to the little bedside table on the other side of the bed, picking up a leather frame. I could see a photo of a handsome man in the army uniform of the Great War. He handed it to her, and she looked at it for a long moment before clutching it to her chest. Then she closed her eyes.

Henry took my hand and led me away.

We had our coffee, and our walk outside. It did me good, to be out there amongst growing things. I expect she'd known it would. We seemed to be marking time: I couldn't think of anything we should be doing, and neither, I think, could he. Perhaps we both knew we were waiting.

We made an attempt at lunch. He went up to look in on her, and reported that she was lying there with her photograph, half awake and half asleep, and wanted nothing. Henry and I had ham sandwiches and shared a bottle of beer. It felt strange to be eating on such a day.

After we'd cleared up he announced he was going to walk down the road to phone the doctor. He didn't want to use the phone in the house in case she heard the ping of the bell and realized what he was doing.

'What will you say?' I asked. I'd gone as far as the gate with him.

'I'll just say she's feeling weak and having the day in bed,' he said. 'I know, what's the point?' He kicked at a clump of dandelion in the verge. 'But I can't do *nothing*. And maybe it's as well to alert the doctor, in case she – in case we have to call him out later.'

We both knew the circumstances under which we'd do that.

I put my arms round him and hugged him. 'Don't be long,' I said against his chest.

'I won't.'

He set off up the road at a trot. Half a mile to the call box, half a mile back, and a conversation with the doctor. Twenty-five minutes? I turned and went back into the house.

I went through into the drawing room. The ashes

of last night's fire were still in the grate, and for want of anything else to do, I swept them out and laid a fresh fire. Henry and I might be glad of that, later. Then I sat on the sofa and allowed the happenings of last night to wash over me again. In here, in this comfortable, familiar drawing room, she'd given us the final proof that we belonged together. It was a proof we couldn't have denied, no matter how indifferent we thought we were to each other.

It was ironic that she'd used up the last of her strength convincing us of something we already knew. But had she not sent us back to our past life, the Dark Man would not have been dispatched and our present existence, too, would have been cursed. She had given Henry – Siegwald – the second chance he needed and, this time, he hadn't let me down. We had good reason to thank Florence – she'd given us our future.

When he came back I was crying: it was a sweet relief to tell him why. I wasn't used to leaning on others, but I could see already why people did it. How heartening it was.

'What did the doctor say?' I asked when I'd stopped sniffing.

'He said it was a matter of time,' he replied. 'She's been to see him, apparently, although he said it was with obvious reluctance.' He smiled. 'She told him she had no truck with doctors, but that she wanted his opinion as to how long she had left.'

'Nothing like being blunt,' I remarked. 'What did he tell her?'

'That she might go on for several more years if she adopted a less strenuous life style, but that any major stress could be dangerous. Her heart, he said it was.'

I thought of the major stress she'd subjected herself to last night. Then, because that threatened to upset me again, I said, 'What did he say we should do?'

'Nothing. He said just to be with her, and call him if we were worried.'

'But we *are* worried. And she won't see him.'

'Then we'll just sit with her.'

'But –'

'Thea, she has the right to die as she sees fit. It isn't up to us to impose on her the company of an outsider she doesn't want during the last hours of her life. Is it?'

I shook my head. He was quite right.

'Okay.' He hesitated. 'I'd like to be with her.' He looked at me, a question in his eyes.

'Yes. Me too. I'll be fine.'

I wasn't at all sure I would be, but I didn't think he'd go to her unless I went too. Going up the stairs, I sent up a request to anyone who happened to be listening for a bit of courage.

She hadn't moved. Her breathing was so slight that it hardly lifted her chest. We sat down at the side of the bed, and for some time she didn't seem to register our presence. Then, briefly, her eyes flicked open and she smiled.

'Glad you're here,' she whispered. 'Together.'

She was silent for a long time. Then, as it began to get dark, she said, quite strongly, 'You two have been my greatest task. You have given me considerable anxiety, yet also more happiness than you can know.' She paused. Then, very quietly, murmured, 'Look after each other.' There was something else, but her voice was so soft I barely caught it – it sounded as if, like someone reassuring a child scared of the dark, she'd said, 'I'll be here.'

It was her valediction. We both leaned forwards to kiss her, and, with her as a witness, he kissed me. It made her smile.

She slipped into sleep. As time went by and she didn't stir, it seemed sleep had become a deepening coma.

Just as the first stars were appearing, she gave a soft sigh, and her quiet breathing stopped. Henry put his hand on her wrist.

After what seemed an age he said, 'I think she's dead.'

I sat on by her side while he went down to summon the doctor.

Thirty-four

Willowford Fen, Spring 1992

Neither Thea nor I have ever forgotten the day Florence died. We haven't tried: we speak of it quite often, remembering the details clearly even though she's been gone thirteen years this month. Gone, in fact, isn't the right word. It's not accurate, when so much of her spirit remains with us.

The doctor came straight away in answer to my call. He was a nice chap – still is, come to that, he's been our GP ever since. I can picture him that night, looking down at her with a mixture of respect and sadness in his face.

'She was a great woman,' he said. 'Although she hadn't much time for me. I wish there were more like her.'

Thea asked if there was anything he could have done for her. 'To make her more comfortable,' was what she said, but I knew – probably he did, too – what she was really asking. Could you have saved her had you been called earlier?

He appeared to grope for the right words. Then he said, 'It's possible I *could* have given her something to get her over this attack, but it's not very likely. And even then, it would only have kept her going till the next one. I certainly could have alleviated any pain, but you both say she wasn't in pain.' We nodded like a pair of puppets. 'Well, then, I have to say, no. There was nothing I could have done.' He smiled at Thea. 'I imagine this is exactly the way she would have wanted to go.'

She was happier after that.

We sat with Florence until late in the night, but by midnight Thea was almost asleep where she sat, so I suggested she went to bed. I'd intended to sit in vigil all night, but I got very lonely in the small hours and went to find her. We made love very tenderly and slowly, and I don't think it occurred to either of us that this was disrespectful to Florence: wasn't it exactly what she wanted us to do?

We became swept up, as everyone does, in the post-death formalities. We called her solicitor, who arranged for us to see the will straight away because there were, he said, instructions relating to her funeral.

We went from his office into a pub, where we had a brandy apiece. Florence had had no more truck with organized religion than she'd had with conventional medicine, and she'd requested a straightforward cremation – 'With no insincere words spoken over my coffin by some anonymous cleric I have never met and to whom I am nothing but a name,' (she must have instructed the use of italics for emphasis in that part) – and she ordered that the urn containing her ashes be returned to Thea and me.

We were instructed to dispose of her remains in whatever spot we considered most suitable.

That was the bit we needed to talk about. After

proposing and failing to agree on about thirty different places, we thought we'd let the problem rest for a while. We hoped an answer – preferably the same answer – might occur to us if we slept on it for a few nights.

The house was ours. We'd already known that. In addition, she'd left us a considerable sum of money and a sound clutch of investments. There was also a trust fund set up 'for my great-grandchildren'. She always was an optimist.

I telephoned my parents. My father got rather emotional and said he wanted to attend the funeral. I said there wasn't going to be one, not as such, merely the briefest of cremation services. I related to him her comment about anonymous clerics.

'No hymns and things?' he said. 'I love hymns.'

'Yes, I dare say you do, but it's her funeral and she didn't.'

I heard him mutter something to my mother. Then he said, 'Your mother says you're becoming very bossy.'

'Sorry.' My mother was right. 'Well, come if you want. There's plenty of room here, and Thea and I . . .' Damn. I hadn't meant to mention her.

Predictably he asked, 'Who's Thea?'

She was right beside me, and I couldn't very well play down her importance and say she was just a friend. 'Someone Florence introduced me to when I was a kid,' I said.

'Oh, and she's there for the funeral?'

Again I said there wasn't going to be a funeral. He hummed and hawed for a while, and exchanged some remarks with my mother – I wished he'd hurry up, calls to Hong Kong were unbelievably expensive, even at off-peak rate – then said that if there was going to be no service and no party, then they thought they wouldn't bother. Then he said rather touchingly, 'You don't think she'd mind, do you?'

'I'm sure she'd think it highly inadvisable for you and Mother to fly halfway round the world and back just for the sake of form,' I said.

'Oh!'

I'd been too abrupt. 'I'll tell you what,' I said, without pausing to think about anything more than saying something consoling, 'why don't you come for a visit in the summer, when we're properly settled in?'

Thea kicked my ankle, but it was too late. My father was laughing heartily.

'Is that the royal "we"?' he asked. 'Don't answer that, old man! All right – we'll see you in the summer.'

We went to the crematorium at the appointed time the following week. There were only the two of us: she hadn't wanted anyone else. The vicar was quite understanding, as if he had to cope with putting pantheists to rest every other day. Perhaps he did. Listening to him speaking the old prayers, I didn't think Florence would have been affronted.

In time the small pot of ashes was delivered to us. Not yet having come up with the ideal place, we put it away in the cupboard in the hall.

We fell back into an almost normal routine. I returned to work and stayed in my London flat during the week – she came with me sometimes – and we drove up to Willowford Fen at weekends. A month went by. Six weeks. Then one day Thea said she thought was pregnant.

I was shocked at first – like most men, I said, 'Are you sure?', almost hoping she'd say, no, it was just a joke, I'm not really. Then I began to find the idea quite exciting. We got one of those kits from the chemist, and she did the test a couple of times. The result was the same: she was pregnant.

Lying on the sofa with her that night, I said she'd have to make an appointment to see the doctor. 'And don't go giving me smart answers about not having any time for doctors,' I ordered, 'this is different.'

'I know,' she said serenely. Then, 'Henry?'

'Still right here.'

'I've had an idea.'

'Go on.'

'I know where we should scatter Florence's ashes.'

'You do?'

'Yes. At Rendlesham.'

I smiled and said, 'We could go south a bit and build her a ship at Sutton Hoo.'

'We don't need a ship. But Sutton Hoo would do as well. What do you think?'

'It's perfect. We'll go tomorrow.'

Rendlesham, where the Wuffingas had their royal hall. What better than to let her rest where they had lived? Something was hovering on the edge of my mind, something to do with Rendlesham, something that made me think of the night before her death. But I couldn't bring it into focus.

We went to Rendlesham the next day. There was nothing much to see – a pretty flint-covered church (we kept away from that) and a main road through a village. Thea looked disappointed.

'What now?'

I had an idea. 'Let's go to the coast,' I suggested. 'To Dunwich.'

We made our way through the narrow lanes to the shore, and stood overlooking the place where a whole town, including a king's palace, once fell into the sea. It was wild and lonely, and we thought Florence would approve. I opened the casket and we tipped her ashes on to the beach, where the wind lifted them and blew them out over the sea.

'This is where they lost Saint Felix's crown,' Thea said dreamily. 'The one he used for Sigebert's coronation.'

Crown. That was it.

But now wasn't the time. Now was our goodbye to Florence.

We stood for a long time, then, prompted at the same moment, turned and walked away.

Thea said as we drove off, 'If the baby's a girl, we'll call her Florence.'

We waited till my parents' visit to get married, inviting Thea's father and Pam to come over too. Like Florence's funeral, our wedding was a simple affair, and we didn't have any hymns. But that didn't stop my mother buying herself a vast and elaborate new hat.

They all stayed with us for a couple of weeks, and we got on surprisingly well. My father took to Thea instantly, and she to him. My mother was her usual self: noticing Thea's bump (she was slim and it was hard to miss, even in the early stages of her pregnancy), she was inclined to come out with unfortunate reminiscences about the pain, and insisted that, once the baby was born, it was important to get good help – had Thea anyone in mind? Some robust village girl? At first I hovered about and tried to deflect her, but I soon stopped; I should have realized Thea could take care of herself. When my mother said for the fifth time what a frightful ordeal it had been to give birth to me, Thea gave her a kind look – perhaps, remembering the circumstances of my conception, she was thinking that it hadn't been my mother's choice to have a baby – and said firmly, 'It's sweet of you to be concerned for me, but things are different nowadays. And I think, if you don't mind, we won't talk about it any more.'

Unexpectedly, my mother found a pal in Thea's dad's friend Pam, although it'd be hard to think of two women less likely to find anything in common. They made an incongruous picture sitting on the window-seat together, my mother in a cream pleated skirt, cream kid stilettoes, a chiffon blouse and an emerald-green scarf pinned with a diamond brooch; Pam in men's trousers and a Guernsey, her brown eyes boring into my mother as, rolling a cigarette with one hand (which seemed to fascinate my mother – she asked Pam to show her how to do it) she pounded the other against her sturdy thigh to emphasize how much she disapproved of media intrusion into the private lives of the Royal Family. I'd somehow never imagined Pam to be a closet Royalist.

Thea's dad asked me if I'd been doing much fishing lately.

No matter how well we got on, it was a relief when they all left. I wanted to be with Thea – alone with her – all the time. I sold the London flat and began commuting. It wasn't much fun, but it was what I wanted. I watched her grow larger, and sometimes I dreamt of Althicca.

Our first child was born early the following spring, and we called her Florence.

We shall have to extend Willowford Fen if we have any more children. Florence now has two younger brothers and a sister, and Thea is once again giving me that particular look. Five children? I'm not sure I can cope with the idea of five children.

She is a wonderful mother. It was at her insistence that we started going in for animals – she bought Florence a pony, and Tim and Sammy share a puppy and a kitten. Clare, the youngest, is too small to be responsible for a pet yet, according to her mother, but she will be given a guinea pig, or a gerbil, or some other furry creature, as soon as she is. I think Thea is ensuring that her own children are never as lonely as she was.

I love her more with every year that passes. It's corny, I know, but I still see in her that bright-haired child sitting on the gate. Tim's puppy is a golden retriever, and watching Thea running with him across the fields brings back the past as vividly as a replayed video.

Florence – the original Florence – would, I think, be pleased with us. Four little Woolgars to carry on the line, and possibly – probably – another one too. But, more than that, she would be pleased with Thea and me for making each other so happy, for fulfilling the future which she foresaw for us. I often speak to her and tell her, you were quite right, bless you. At the same time, I thank her.

In the course of thirteen years we've made alterations in the old house and have had the whole place redecorated. We've turned out the cupboards and the attic and cleared a bit more space in the outbuildings. Short of ripping up the floorboards, there isn't a corner we haven't looked into.

But I've never found the crown.

The Prince Without a Crown. My favourite bedtime story – my own children love it, too. I now know his identity, but I don't think the third crown was destined for him. According to Thea, it was meant for 'the child that was still to be; the child who shall save his people'. When questioned as to the source of her information, she said somewhat irritably, '*I* don't know! It's just sort of there. In my head.'

Thea has never gone a bundle on the empirical method.

I've concluded, after a lot of thought, that the third crown was for the child of Siegwald and Althicca. It doesn't seem likely that he was ever crowned with it, but it's nice to imagine it might be somewhere in the house, watching over his descendants.

I think, though, that I must have imagined that moment when Florence stood in the doorway and the firelight shone on the gold circlet in her uplifted hands. If it's here, it's too well-hidden for me to find. Perhaps I'm not meant to – perhaps she intended it to stay out of sight. Perhaps its protective powers only work if it's undisturbed.

But I think it was part of the dream. I expect I was seeing a scene from *then* and not from now. She was the Cunning Man again, holding out the Wuffinga crown to the illegitimate son through whom the line would go on.

Wolfspear, who lived and hunted with the wolves. No wolves here now, just a big golden dog. And a pony, and soon a gerbil or two. But that's fine, that's how she'd have wanted it.

On days when the domestic scene takes over so that there's no room for fancy or for dreams – and, with four children under thirteen that's most days – I forget all about what happened. I'm sure Thea does, too – she's even more in the front line than I am. At least I have an office to retreat to. But sometimes, when we've got the children to bed and we're sitting together in front of the fire, I hold her in my arms and it all comes back.

I love those times.

Was it true, Florence's belief that she and I were Siegwald's descendants? Was it as crucial as she thought, that I should meet and fall in love with a woman of Althicca's line and with her perpetuate the House of Wuffa?

I don't know. I've thought about it, Thea and I have talked about it, but still I don't know. Was it true, or was it just the obsession of an intelligent, wide-minded and imaginative old woman with not quite enough to do?

I don't know.

And, as I look down on my wife and hear the faint noises of my children upstairs as they turn in their sleep, I don't care.